Chasing the Darkness

CHASING THE DARKNESS

A NOVEL

CASSIE SANCHEZ

NEW YORK

LONDON • NASHVILLE • MELBOURNE • VANCOUVER

CHASING THE DARKNESS

A Novel

Published in New York, New York, by Morgan James Publishing. Morgan James is a trademark of Morgan James, LLC. www.MorganJamesPublishing.com

Publisher's Note: This novel is a work of fiction. Names, characters, places, and incidents are either products of the author's imagination or used fictitiously. All characters are fictional, and any similarity to people living or dead is purely coincidental.

Proudly distributed by Ingram Publisher Services.

Morgan James BOGO™

A **FREE** ebook edition is available for you or a friend with the purchase of this print book.

CLEARLY SIGN YOUR NAME ABOVE

Instructions to claim your free ebook edition:
1. Visit MorganJamesBOGO.com
2. Sign your name CLEARLY in the space above
3. Complete the form and submit a photo of this entire page
4. You or your friend can download the ebook to your preferred device

ISBN 9781631956096 paperback
ISBN 9781631956102 ebook
Library of Congress Control Number: 2021936952

Cover Design by:
Karen Dimmick
ArcaneCovers.com

Interior Design by:
Chris Treccani
www.3dogcreative.net

Morgan James PUBLISHING **Builds** with... **Habitat for Humanity** Peninsula and Greater Williamsburg

Morgan James is a proud partner of Habitat for Humanity Peninsula and Greater Williamsburg. Partners in building since 2006.

Get involved today! Visit MorganJamesPublishing.com/giving-back

To the three men in my life who inspired, encouraged, and supported me through every step of this journey.
You bring magic and love to my life.

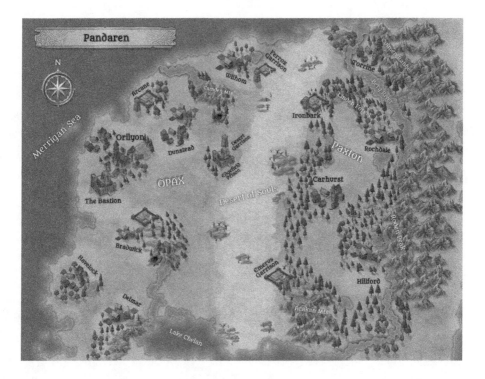

Pronunciation Guide

Characters

    Azrael | Az-ree-el

    Drexus Zoldac | Drex-us Zole-dack

    Jasce Farone | Jace Fa-rone

    Amycus | Am-i-cus

    Maleous | Mal-ee-us

    Emile | Em-i-lee

    Maera | Mair-uh

Places

    Pandaren | Pan-dare-in

    Orilyon | Or-il-ee-un

    Bastion | Bast-ee-un

    Eremus | Air-i-mus

Other

    Spectral | Speck-trull

    Psyche | Sike

PROLOGUE

Orilyon Palace, Pandaren

Torches flickered and the thump of boots echoed through the hallway as Commander Drexus Zoldac of the Watch Guard strode down the corridor toward the war room, followed by his soldiers. Castle guards and servants flattened themselves against the wall, their expressions a mixture of fear and grief. Hours before, the people of Pandaren had celebrated their victory in the war against the Vastanes. Cheers of celebration, though, became wails of sorrow as the palace and the city of Orilyon crumbled into chaos.

"How did he get in?" Drexus asked.

"We're still working on that, Commander Zoldac."

Drexus stopped and slowly turned toward the guard, who glanced up at him and winced. "Work faster," he warned.

The guard swallowed, nodding.

Drexus continued down the corridor, clenching his jaw, trying to rein in his anger. Two soldiers saluted as he pushed open the heavy wooden doors into a room buzzing with activity. Council members argued near the fireplace and his generals surrounded a large oval table studying a map of Pandaren. They stood to attention, saluting as Drexus approached. Kenneth Brenet, head advisor to the king, sat in a corner holding his head.

One of the council members hurried over. "Is it true? Is King Valeri dead?"

"It's true," Drexus said. He ignored the questions yelled at him and walked across the room to put a hand on Kenneth's bony shoulder. "They need you, now more than ever."

Kenneth nodded, set his shoulders, and approached the center of the room. Drexus stood at his side, arms crossed.

"Attention, please," Kenneth said, silencing the room. "As many of you suspect, the king is dead, murdered in his study this evening."

Murmurs filled the room.

"How?" someone called out.

Kenneth looked up at Drexus, who inhaled, resting his sizable hands on the table as he regarded each council member, noble, and general. "An Air Spectral killed King Valeri."

Gasps and shouts of anger reverberated off the stone walls.

"I thought the Spectrals were on our side," one of the council members said.

Drexus fisted his hands. "So did we."

"What do we know about the Spectrals?" Kenneth asked.

General Charlys stepped forward, her eyes darting to Drexus. "There are two main types of magic, physical and mental. A Spectral with physical magic can either control an element or is an Amp."

"What are Amps?" one of the nobles asked, nearing the table.

"Amps, or Amplifiers, have unnatural speed and strength," the general said. "The Mentals are a little trickier, but we've determined there are five types: Shields, Healers, Vaulters, Trackers, and Psyches."

"Psyches?" Kenneth looked from the general to Drexus.

"They can move objects with their minds," Drexus said.

"How do you have this information?"

"When the Spectrals joined forces with the Watch Guard, I assigned General Charlys to obtain as much information about them as possible, just in case."

"With that kind of power?" a councilman said. "How are we going to defend ourselves? Naturals can't fight against magic."

Drexus's eye twitched at the whine in the man's voice. "I'm currently working on something that will neutralize their power. But first, we need strong leadership. I think Kenneth Brenet should rule as steward until the council deems it unnecessary."

The murmurings grew, and a few council members' faces turned red.

"What about Queen Valeri?" one of them asked.

Drexus refrained from rolling his eyes. "She's grieving the loss of her husband, and with her diminished health, we cannot expect her to take the throne." He sensed a shift in the room as men and women nodded their heads—a shift in his favor. "Who supports Kenneth Brenet becoming steward of Pandaren?"

Hands raised, and Drexus smiled.

Kenneth stared at the men and women surrounding the war table. "This is an honor. I can never measure up to our great king, but I will do my best. And my first act as steward is to put into law that all Spectrals will identify themselves and their powers. We have to know who they are and what they can do."

The room bristled with fear.

"All in favor?" Drexus said.

The motion passed unanimously.

Kenneth turned to Drexus. "Whatever you're working on, get it completed as soon as possible. In the meantime, our priority is to defend the kingdom."

Drexus led Kenneth away from the table. "Do I have your support to do whatever is necessary?" he asked.

The thin man stared up at him with wary eyes and nodded.

Drexus kept his expression blank. "I'd like permission to create an elite group of soldiers specifically trained to fight the Spectrals."

"What do you propose?"

"Hunters." Drexus glanced over his shoulder, savoring the warmth of victory radiating through him. "Lethal assassins who will ensure the Spectrals comply with our new laws."

The steward held Drexus's gaze. "Fortify our army, Drexus. And train your assassins. Create a force that will breed fear by the very mention of their name."

CHAPTER 1

Bastion Compound, Orilyon, Seventeen Years Later

For the second time in Azrael's life, he wished for death. But instead of receiving it, he became it. He didn't fear death; he even welcomed it, which was fitting since his name meant Angel of Death. But this time, he had no one to blame but himself.

Pain like Azrael had never known rushed through his body, Drexus's serum transforming him from a lethal assassin to something worse—something everyone would fear. He bit down on a leather strap as another wave of pain crashed through him, his muscles contracting beneath the restraints. Azrael inhaled, focusing on his anger, clinging to the image of the Spectral and his magical black fire. Lust for revenge and power fueled Azrael as agony ripped through him.

Pain is inescapable; suffering is a choice.

Azrael repeated this mantra with his eyes closed, breathing through the torment and ignoring the tubes embedded in him. He'd chosen this path, had known the risks. With the Amplifier serum flowing through his veins, he'd have the strength and speed to battle any Spectral he faced.

If the transfusion didn't kill him.

Large hands pressed down on Azrael's shoulders as his back arched; the taste of leather and blood permeated his mouth.

"Hold on, Azrael," Drexus said, staring down at him. His dark eyes, etched with worry, darted to someone behind the table, out of sight. "This is the last vial. If he dies, you die."

Black spots floated in Azrael's vision; the stone ceiling blurred. His nails dug into his palms and blood dripped from his hands.

Pain is inescapable; suffering is a choice.

1

After what felt like hours, the pain dissipated. Azrael opened his eyes and drew in a deep breath. A hum pulsed through his muscles, making his skin tingle. Drexus removed the straps and Azrael sat up, peering through a dark curtain of sweat-dampened hair.

"How do you feel?" Drexus asked.

Azrael swung his long legs off the table, closing his eyes to block out the spinning room. He focused on his breathing and the magic purring inside him. He flexed his hands and looked up, cracking his neck. The corner of his mouth lifted. "Powerful."

Drexus's gaze narrowed as if he could see the Amplifier magic flowing through Azrael's body. He smiled. "Finally. After so many failed experiments, my most lethal Hunter now has Spectral magic." Drexus rested his hand on his assistant's shoulder, who cowered by the equipment, smiling nervously. Drexus turned back to Azrael, raising his chin. "Your new power will aid our cause and end this war."

Azrael winced, gripping the edge of the table as he staggered to his feet. Drexus reached out to help him, but Azrael pulled away. "I'm curious, Commander, why you didn't get the serum first."

Drexus held his gaze. "I needed to make sure it worked."

Azrael frowned, tying his hair back. "Why me?"

"You're the strongest of my Hunters. I knew you'd survive the procedure." Drexus stared at the tattoos covering Azrael's right arm. "I need you and the other Hunters to find more Amps to replicate the serum."

Azrael nodded, following Drexus's gaze. The largest tattoo—given by his mother when he was ten—depicted a dagger intersecting two triangles at their points. He remembered fighting tears while the needle carved into his skin, his mother insisting the tattoo would protect him. From what, he didn't know; he never had the chance to ask her. The second tattoo was the Watch Guard symbol, the words *loyalty*, *honor*, and *obedience* stark against his tan skin. The third represented his first victim—the day he became a Hunter. Tattoos of every Spectral he'd killed decorated his left arm, but the design would remain incomplete until he had his revenge. Until he found the Spectral with black fire.

❦❦ ❦❦ ❦❦

Azrael strode toward the stables from the Bastion Garrison, buckling his new chest plate, the interlocking armor like a second skin. The garrison in the royal city of Orilyon was the largest in Opax, with unparalleled training and medical facilities. Steward Brenet had spared no expense when he and Drexus added on to the compound after the war with the Vastanes. It was functional and effective, like those who trained within its stone walls.

The courtyard buzzed with recruits and Watch Guard soldiers training. Azrael stopped near a group of second-years and adjusted a trainee's grip on her sword.

"Remember, your weapon is part of you. Keep a steady hand, like this," Azrael said, demonstrating the correct form. The young girl nodded, her eyes wide.

Azrael's team of Hunters waited, strapping on swords or saddling their horses. At twenty-five, he was the youngest assassin to ever lead such lethal warriors. The title of second in command was an honor, one Azrael had paid for—physically and emotionally.

Azrael scanned the Hunters and located Bronn, his first lieutenant, leaning his tall frame against the wall and talking with Sabine.

"Are we ready?" Azrael asked.

Bronn nodded, examining Azrael. "You don't look any different."

Sabine tilted her head, staring up at him. "Oh, I don't know. His eyes look bluer," she said, winking.

"Did the serum work, then?" Elliot asked.

Azrael grabbed Elliot by the throat and lifted him into the air. The Hunter swore and gripped Azrael's wrist, his eyes bulging. Azrael, six-two and two hundred pounds of solid muscle, marveled at the fact that his arm didn't so much as quiver as he held the Hunter above him.

"You tell me," Azrael sneered, lowering the man to the ground.

Elliot rubbed his neck while the other Hunters laughed. "A simple yes or no would've sufficed," he mumbled.

Azrael addressed his assassins—twelve of the deadliest warriors in the land—and a small squadron of Watch Guard soldiers. "Our orders are to find Amps and transport them to Edgefield Prison alive."

"Why the prison?" asked Caston.

"Why alive?" Bronn added, crossing his arms.

"I didn't ask." Ignoring Bronn's scowl, Azrael turned, grabbed the reins of his horse, and swung himself into the saddle.

The three-hour ride to Havelock took his team south through grassy hillsides and sparse forests. The midday sun glimmered on the Merrigan Sea, which bordered Opax, the larger of two Pandaren countries. Paxton, the smaller province, had the Desert of Souls to the east and mountain ranges in the west.

Azrael breathed in the salty air and shuddered as adrenaline and magic coursed through his veins. He lived for the battle, relishing the clash of iron and the smell of blood. With every kill, he felt more powerful, more alive. And now, with the serum, he'd be unstoppable.

He pulled up his mask, revealing the grinning skull intended to invoke fear in those who had the misfortune of coming face-to-face with it. Only Hunters received the skull mask, and only after completing a final task during their initiation. Currently, thirteen Watch Guard soldiers had achieved the honor.

Azrael had just turned eighteen when Drexus had deemed him ready.

"It's time," Drexus had said, crossing his arms over his broad chest. Azrael had been shocked to learn that his last test was to kill the man who'd sold him to the Watch Guard when he was twelve. The shock turned to hunger, then satisfaction as Azrael embraced the fear and recognition in Barnet Farone's eyes.

"For your wife," Azrael had said, slashing his knife. "For your daughter." The dagger cut through flesh and bone. Blood splattered onto his face and the empty whiskey bottles covering the floor. The man screamed, holding up his bloody hands.

"And for your son." The blade cleaved the air with a final blow. Azrael had gazed upon his father's lifeless body, doubting anyone would mourn his death. His father's betrayal had led the Fire Spectral to their village, to their cottage. Because of his father, Azrael's mother and sister were dead.

When he had returned to the compound, his need for revenge somewhat satiated, Drexus changed his birth name to Azrael and he became the Angel of Death, the most feared Hunter in all of Pandaren.

The sound of warning bells pulled Azrael from the past and he leaned forward in his saddle, urging his horse to run faster. The Havelock raid would be his first since receiving the serum, and he yearned to test his new power. Their orders were to take the Spectrals alive, unless they resisted. He hoped they did.

The Hunters and Watch Guard soldiers arrived at the village and split off down the dirt paths between cottages. Azrael strode along the outskirts of town, catching movement out of the corner of his eye. He removed his dagger from the sheath on his leg and rounded the last building.

A man stood at the end of the alley wearing metal contraptions on his wrist. He clicked them together and a spark of blue flame ignited. Azrael pressed his lips into a thin line. Of all the Element Spectrals, he loathed Fires the most.

"Surrender or die, you choose," Azrael said, his voice cold behind his mask.

The man's eyes widened, the dancing flames trembling in his palm. "Why can't you leave us alone? We've done nothing!"

Azrael stepped forward. "You and your kind are traitors to the crown."

The Spectral's eyes hardened, and he transferred the fire to both hands.

Azrael smiled. "Death it is."

His Amplifier magic pulsed and time slowed as a blue wave of fire exploded down the alley. Tapping into his speed, Azrael used the wall as leverage, twisting in midair and dodging the flames. In seconds, his dagger was pressed against the man's neck.

"How did you move so fast?" The man's voice trembled and his fire sputtered out.

"Magic," Azrael whispered.

The Spectral's fear seized Azrael. A sudden dizziness made him stagger, and he nearly dropped the knife before slitting the man's throat. Azrael was halfway down the alley when the body hit the ground.

He squeezed his eyes shut and rested his hand against the wall, waiting for the unexpected emotion to fade.

What the blazes was that?

He hadn't felt that level of fear since he was a child. He pushed off the wall and swallowed, choking back the haunting screams, his failure to protect his family. Never again. He wouldn't allow weakness to have a stranglehold on him.

He shook his head and made his way to the center of town, where the villagers knelt. A soldier handed him a ledger with names of Spectrals and their magic, and Azrael paced in front of the cowering people. "You are harboring unregistered Spectrals and are guilty of treason."

A laugh echoed off the surrounding cottages. "The Watch Guard is guilty," an older man said, standing with his hands clenched. Rocks and dirt lifted into the air, circling the villagers, shielding them from the Hunters and soldiers. The swish of swords sliding from sheaths sounded behind Azrael as the Hunters drew their weapons.

"Do you wish to die?" Azrael asked, using his speed to dart through the revolving rocks. He approached the man, drawing the twin swords that pressed against his back. He stopped mid-stride and frowned. Despair warred with Azrael's lust for blood. The Spectral raised his hands and the ground trembled, creating a fissure separating Azrael from his prey.

Azrael honed in on his anger, extinguishing the unwanted emotion, and charged. He avoided the barrage of flying debris, his body, magic, and steel creating a lethal combination of protection and ferocity. His swords sliced through the air and the Spectral's head thumped on the cobblestones. The sorrow disappeared and the ground stilled.

"Any other heroes?" Azrael scanned the villagers, muffled sobs sounding through the town square. He strode past a woman with tears streaming down her face and flinched; the grief resonating from her made Azrael clutch his chest and stumble out of the square.

The emotion vanished as quickly as it appeared.

"What was that about?" Bronn said, his eyebrows raised.

"Not sure." Azrael crossed his arms to hide his trembling hands, ignoring the concerned looks in a few of the Hunters' eyes.

"Bring in the Tracker," Bronn said to a nearby guard, giving Azrael a wary look.

A soldier led an older woman through the waiting guards, the shackles on her ankles clinking on the cobblestones. Scraggly gray hair hung to her waist. Her milky-white eyes scanned Azrael, sniffing the air.

"Find the Spectrals," Azrael said, avoiding her sightless gaze.

"Already found one," the woman said, chuckling, her vacant eyes boring into Azrael. "Now you're his slave, just like me."

He gritted his teeth. Her disturbing eyes seemed to peer into his soul. "Just do your job," he growled.

The Tracker meandered around the square, sniffing and pointing out the Spectrals without silver collars around their necks, telling a nearby guard what type of magic they had.

"She gives me the creeps," Bronn said, his lip curling.

"She's a necessary evil," Azrael said, even though he agreed with the Hunter. Drexus had kept this Tracker prisoner for as long as Azrael could remember; her unique talents made it possible for the Watch Guard to find those with magic. The soldiers hoisted the unregistered Spectrals to their feet and placed the bands around their necks, then chained them together. The remaining villagers kept their eyes down.

"How do those collars work?" Bronn asked.

Azrael suppressed a shiver, remembering when Drexus had tested it on him. "The commander uses the Brymagus plant, melting it into a liquid and forging it into the collars. I guess that's the reason for all those trips to the Desert of Souls."

"Funny how an insignificant plant can suppress such power."

Azrael rubbed his neck and watched Sabine approach, her brown eyes peeking over her mask. She ran her fingers through her short mahogany hair as she wiped sweat off her forehead.

"Two unregistered, the rest accounted for," she said, staring at the retreating Spectrals.

"Any Amps?"

"One."

"Will that be enough to recreate the serum?" Bronn asked, fiddling with a loose buckle on his armguard.

"Eager, are we?" Azrael said.

Bronn looked up, the muscles in his jaw pulsing.

Sabine edged closer to Azrael, her gaze traveling down his body. "That was impressive. I've never seen someone move so fast."

Azrael brushed dirt off his chest piece and ignored Sabine's advances, having journeyed down that road before. He mounted his horse as the Watch Guard soldiers loaded the captives into a wagon for transport to Edgefield Prison, on the outskirts of the Desert of Souls.

On the ride back to Orilyon, Azrael thought through the raid, remembering the unpleasant emotions he experienced. They must be a side effect of the serum, though he hesitated at the thought of telling Drexus.

The Watch Guard's training purged the emotions that made a soldier weak. Anger and rage were acceptable, but not fear, regret, or sorrow. Those were not an option, especially for a Hunter. An assassin with a conscience was a liability.

He thought about the training and the pain he'd endured for the past thirteen years, the scars he bore from Drexus's discipline. Azrael would not sacrifice all he'd worked for because of a few unsettling emotions.

His knuckles whitened on the reins, not wanting to contemplate what Drexus would do if he knew his Angel of Death could feel.

CHAPTER 2

The rhythm and cadence of training had infiltrated Azrael's life at the age of twelve; that was when he learned to fight, ignore the pain, and shut down needless emotions.

But two hours of sparring the morning after the raid hadn't settled Azrael's thoughts or lessened his irritation. Experiencing those emotions during the raid had unnerved him, and drilling with Bronn was proving ineffective.

"You're in a mood," Bronn said, lunging forward, swinging his sword. Azrael blocked the strike, his arm vibrating.

Sweat dripped down Azrael's face and slid under the power-suppressing collar. He flinched every time he had to wear it, but it was necessary for sparring since he didn't want to kill his lieutenant or drain his own magic. Drexus had warned him that depleting the magic would leave him weak, something he couldn't afford, especially surrounded by assassins.

Azrael grunted and swept his blade at Bronn's head.

Bronn dodged and laughed. "Definitely in a mood."

Azrael snarled and increased the intensity of his attack, allowing the anger to energize him as he advanced, forcing Bronn to block his strikes while pushing him out of the training ring. Bronn's eyes narrowed. He twirled his sword and charged toward Azrael, baring his teeth. Azrael squeezed the hilt of his sword, feinted to one side, and smacked Bronn with the flat edge of the blade—a move he knew infuriated his first lieutenant.

Bronn turned, his face red, and attacked again. Azrael used his momentum, lodging his sword into the hilt of Bronn's, and with a flick of his wrist the weapon hurled through the air. The clatter of metal on cobblestone echoed through the courtyard.

Bronn rushed Azrael, driving him into the ground, and landed a shot to his face and ribs. Azrael bucked his hips and twisted, swinging his leg around Bronn's neck. Bronn's face turned even more red as Azrael completed the chokehold.

"Surrender," Azrael said, squeezing his legs tighter. Bronn held his stare, then nodded. Azrael released him and stood, running a hand through his sweaty hair and breathing in the smell of dust, leather, and sweat. He focused on the Watch Guard soldiers training in the practice area, where swords clashed against shields and cheers rang out as an audience egged on two soldiers wrestling in the dirt. A group of third-years implemented the attack moves he had taught the week before, while across the courtyard near the obstacle course Sabine and Distria practiced with their crossbows alongside the other Hunters. Azrael's gaze landed on Sabine, who smiled. Distria rolled her eyes, her arrow piercing the training dummy between the legs. Azrael raised a brow.

Bronn rested his hands on his knees, his eyes darting between Azrael and Sabine. He stood, dusting himself off. "What the blazes was that?"

"Can't handle the competition?"

They stood eye to eye, opposite in appearance with Bronn's blond hair to Azrael's deep brown. Light versus dark, but only on the outside. Bronn was just as ruthless as Azrael.

Bronn fisted his hands, then took a deep breath. "What's going on with you?"

Azrael stared at his friend—if one could have an assassin for a friend. Hunters valued the Watch Guard code—loyalty, honor, obedience. But the code pertained to Drexus and the mission only, not each other. Every Hunter coveted the role of second in command, especially Bronn; now that Azrael had received the serum, he'd have to watch his back. He couldn't trust his first lieutenant, even though a part of him wanted to.

"It's nothing," Azrael said, returning the practice sword to the weapons rack.

"You sure?"

Azrael turned slowly, frowning.

Bronn held up his hands. "You seem a little off."

Azrael crossed his arms, keeping his face blank. "Just acclimating to the serum."

Bronn held his stare for a moment, then shrugged. "Hopefully we'll capture some more Amps tomorrow. Then we can acclimate together." He walked to the other side of the yard, joining the Hunters and taking the crossbow from Distria. He let a bolt fly. The sound of the arrow hitting its target reverberated through the courtyard, the shaft vibrating dead center.

Azrael shook his head and used a key to remove his collar, sighing as the magic awakened. He'd deal with Bronn later. Right now, he had recruits to train and another raid to plan.

When he finished with the recruits, Azrael went to the Bastion's forge, his shoulders relaxing as steam enveloped him and breathed in the scent of hot metal. Nigel, the blacksmith, pounded a rod of glowing steel which sent sparks into the air. A cloud of mist formed when he dunked the weapon into a barrel of water, obscuring tables littered with various tools. A sizable hearth inhabited the corner of the forge, its soot-stained bricks embracing flames flickering in a mesmerizing dance.

Nigel looked up from the sword he was mending and gave Azrael a quick nod. His short gray hair stuck up at odd angles and grime was embedded in the wrinkles around his hazel eyes.

Azrael ran his fingers down an unfinished dagger, the rough edges calling out to him. He had found solace in the forge at a young age, the place a cathartic retreat for transforming steel into weapons.

"What's on your mind, Angel of Death?" Nigel asked, smirking.

Azrael gave a half-smile as he stared at the stocky man. "What are you working on?"

Nigel dipped the glowing sword back into the bucket of water, the muscles in his arms flexing. The steel hissed and a curtain of steam hung in the air. "Fixing weapons, as usual."

A pile of discarded swords lay on the table. "Want some help?"

Nigel shrugged his broad shoulders. "Sure."

Azrael grabbed a leather apron by a table littered with arrowheads and a container filled with silver liquid; a faint sweetness drifted from the bowl. He looked at Nigel, brows raised.

"The commander's new project," Nigel said, thrusting the sword into the fire.

Azrael frowned, wondering if this was another of Drexus's experiments. He picked up a chisel, his eyes flicking from the liquid to the arrowheads.

What was Drexus up to? Azrael made a mental note to ask his commander when he returned to the garrison.

"Have you tried out your new armor?" Nigel rested on a stool and wiped the sweat off his forehead with a dirty rag.

Azrael had come to Nigel months ago with the designs for his current chest piece. "Yes, it worked well. The interlocking plates kept it light but strong. I'd like to make arm and leg guards."

"Where did you say you learned the trade?"

"I didn't."

Nigel inclined his head.

Azrael continued shaping the blade, then sighed. "In Delmar. Our blacksmith, Braxium, let me tag along." He didn't enjoy talking about his past. What was the point? He couldn't go back in time to protect those he loved.

Nigel nodded and then added, "You have talent, for a Hunter."

Azrael turned away, placing the sharpened dagger on the workbench and pulled off his tunic to wipe his face. He'd lost track of time while training the recruits and hadn't wanted to waste minutes going to his barracks to retrieve a lighter shirt. Azrael's shoulders stiffened when Nigel gasped.

"Who did that to your back?"

Azrael sat on a stool opposite the older man and took a drink of water. He slid his shirt back on, grimacing at the sweat and grime. "Recruit training can be brutal."

"You whip children?"

Azrael's knuckles whitened on the cup. "I don't. But not all the instructors feel that way."

"Did Drexus do that?"

Azrael tapped his finger on the table, staring at Nigel, then looked away. "Why do you stay here?"

Azrael laughed bitterly. "Where would I go?"

⚙ ⚙ ⚙

The next day, hooves thumped in time with the rhythm of Azrael's heart as he rode toward Dunstead. The sun was beginning its descent. The Hunters had ridden inland, where the day was hotter than usual and the heat brought Azrael's frustrations to the surface. He had pondered what Nigel had said the night before. He'd honestly never considered leaving the Guard—it was all he knew. Plus, Drexus would kill a Hunter before letting them go. The idea of a different life was like grasping smoke.

"It's a fine evening for a reaping," Bronn said, pulling his horse alongside Azrael's, jolting him from his thoughts. The other Hunters and soldiers rode behind in standard formation. Drexus's desire to acquire more Amps for the serum had them on another raid, though Azrael couldn't imagine there were that many unregistered Spectrals left in Opax—most had already been taken to Edgefield Prison, or killed.

"Indeed," Azrael said, keeping his eyes fixed on the horizon and the village beyond. Warning bells rang from the chapel. He let loose the reins on his pent-up anger and kicked his horse, dust flying in his wake. He slid on his mask, becoming the Angel of Death to the welcoming screams of fleeing villagers.

Azrael traveled down the main road, the acrid smell of burnt wood making his nose twitch. One of his team must have found a Fire Spectral, and the results of their conflict now consumed a cottage. He pulled his horse to a stop as a rush of heat emanated from the smoldering home, and he shivered as a bead of sweat dripped down his back, his horse pawing the ground and snorting at the encroaching flames. He rode deeper into town, his body rigid, and tried to block out the memories—screams silenced, vacant gray eyes, black fire devouring his home.

Azrael's breath rattled behind the skull mask.

He had never understood why the men—dressed in black robes, faces hidden—had killed his mother and sister. Why had the Fire Spectral left him alive? Azrael shook his head. Ever since the Amp serum, his memory of that horrific night had sharpened like a blade against a whetstone.

"Focus on the mission," Azrael told himself, dismounting from his horse.

Defeated Spectrals and Naturals lined the village square. Sabine hunched, holding her side, pain flashing through her eyes while Bronn pointed his sword at a man's chest. Azrael approached the kneeling man and a wave of fear and anger washed over him. His breath hitched. Metal glinted as Bronn swung his sword, and before Azrael's mind caught up to his body, he blocked the killing strike.

"What the blazes are you doing?" Bronn asked, his eyes wide with fury.

Azrael's sword pressed against Bronn's. "Stand down."

"He injured Sabine. Or don't you care?"

Sabine winced, blood oozing through her fingers and pooling at her feet.

Azrael's anger contended with the Spectral's fear. "I said stand down."

"You care more about this traitor's life than one of your own?" Bronn shoved Azrael, swinging his sword. Azrael blocked it, stepping back.

"Last chance, Bronn. Stand down."

Bronn roared and their swords clashed as he charged. Azrael drew upon his magic, feinted to the side, and spun on one knee. His sword careened for Bronn's stomach, but Sabine screamed, halting Azrael's hand.

"Stop it! Both of you!"

Azrael gritted his teeth and lowered his sword. Bronn pushed him aside, helping Sabine sit on the fountain wall.

What was wrong with him?

Azrael glanced at Bronn and then at the kneeling man. Had the Spectral's fear made him stop Bronn?

He stiffened as a gnarled hand rested on his shoulder. The Tracker smiled, her milky-white eyes staring into the distance.

She sniffed the air, tilting her head. "You feel them, don't you?"

"What are you talking about?"

Her rough laugh grated down Azrael's spine. "You know." She sniffed again, her smile revealing stained teeth. "But there's something different about you. You're not like us."

Azrael shrugged off the Tracker's hand and stepped forward, not wanting to think about her deranged words. He felt the eyes of his Hunters boring into his back like hungry animals sensing weakness. He needed to take command of this situation. "Any unregistered Spectrals surrender now, or those you love will die."

Distria aimed her crossbow at a young man, her eyes hard above her mask, the muscles in her arms tight. The remaining Hunters circled the square, weapons ready.

"Wait!" a voice called out from behind a stall.

"Meredith, no!" The young man tried to stand, but Azrael shoved him down. A woman rushed to his side, throwing her arms around him, and Azrael winced as her sorrow seeped into him. He tried to smother the emotion, grasping for the anger that fueled him.

"Their powers?" he said, stepping away from the woman, glancing over his shoulder into white eyes.

The Tracker shuffled forward, chains clinking, and inhaled. "He's a Water, she's an Amp."

"Distria, take her to Drexus."

Distria lowered her crossbow and yanked the woman to her feet to attach a silver collar around her neck. The kneeling man reached out, tears streaming down his face as water erupted out of the nearby fountain, causing Sabine and Bronn to recoil. Despair like Azrael hadn't felt since he was twelve overwhelmed him, almost bringing him to his knees.

The woman bared her teeth, trying to pull free from Distria. "You're a monster!"

Days of restrained anger spewed to the surface, and the familiar rage Azrael searched for exploded, combining with the woman's fury and the Water Spectral's grief.

"I'll show you a monster!" His sword blurred through the air, and the man's head rolled to Azrael's feet, shock frozen on his face. The Amp screamed. Distria dragged her away, the woman's wails echoing through the town.

Azrael's hands shook as he sheathed his sword, eyes avoiding the blood carving through the cobblestones. "Finish this," he ordered the soldiers, striding away from the smell of blood and the sound of despair.

He stomped down a vacant alley and punched the wall with a yell, leaving a fist-sized hole. He hit it again and again, pounding out the fear and grief until only anger remained. He'd completely lost control in the village square and almost killed one of his own. A Hunter's life always came before a Spectral's.

Loyalty, honor, obedience.

With one final swing, his fist collided with the wall. Chunks of rock skittered onto the ground and a muffled cry came from behind a stack of wooden crates. Azrael panted, blood dripping from both knuckles as he turned. He scanned the alleyway, reaching for his dagger.

"Might as well come out," he said, peering behind a stack of boxes. An older boy held his hand over a girl's mouth, their wide eyes staring into his grinning skull mask. A swirl of dirt billowed around the girl's feet, revealing her Earth magic. His eyes narrowed. He sensed fear laced with determination.

The girl stood and glared, pushing the boy away. "You the Angel of Death?" she said, jutting out her chin.

"I am."

"I thought angels helped people."

"Emile, shut up," the teenager said, trying to pull her back.

"You thought wrong." Azrael eyes darted from her set jaw to the flowers trembling in her small hand. An image of another girl flashed in his mind—holding freshly picked wildflowers, barefoot and wearing a brown dress, dirt speckling her beautiful face.

Azrael ripped off his mask. He bent over as a cool breeze dried the sweat along his forehead.

He told himself to breathe, trying to force the images of his sister out of his mind.

He slowly stood, squeezing the hilt of his dagger. His orders were explicit—capture Spectrals, kill any who resisted.

The boy stepped in front of his sister, a muscle ticking in his jaw.

He just needed to do it. His dagger trembled at his side. He stared into the young girl's eyes, feeling a sudden need to protect her.

"Run," he whispered.

Both their mouths dropped open. The boy tried to drag his sister away.

"Run!"

His shout unfroze their feet and they sprinted down the alley. Azrael stared at the broken flowers until he felt a presence behind him.

Bronn glared, his Hunter's mask smiling as if mocking the Angel of Death. Then he shook his head and walked away.

Azrael glanced to the once-burning cottage. It was now rubble and ash, and dread smoldered in his gut. Bronn wouldn't let this go.

"What have I done?"

CHAPTER 3

Azrael and his team rode back into Orilyon under nightfall, the full moon glinting off the cobblestones. He rode past the harbor on the outskirts of town and breathed in the salty air of the sea. The palace towered in the distance, torches making the stone glow. A member of the Watch Guard strolled along the top of the wall, nodding as the Hunters passed. A light flickered in the west-facing tower, in the rooms belonging to Queen Valeri.

Azrael had only met the queen when he assisted Drexus during meetings with the steward and council, Drexus having brought him to apply silent pressure to any who disagreed with Drexus's plans—the Angel of Death stoked fear in noblemen as well as Spectrals. Rumors about the queen's health varied from being on death's door to healed. Azrael always thought she looked healthy, but she seemed sad and resigned to continue letting the steward rule.

Azrael stifled a yawn, the stables coming into view. His head pounded and all he wanted was to collapse on his bed. He slid off his horse and handed the reins to the stable boy.

"Distria, help Sabine to the medical wing," Azrael said as the other Hunters dismounted. The bleeding was under control, but Sabine needed stitches for the gash in her side.

Azrael trudged toward the Bastion, sighing as Bronn jogged up next to him. He'd given Azrael wary looks the entire ride back to the compound.

"When are you giving your report?" Bronn asked.

They walked up the stairs and through the main doors. Bronn's tone made Azrael's hair rise on the back of his neck. "When I normally do." He stopped in the hallway, the torchlight flickering across Bronn's narrowed eyes. "What?"

"Are you going to tell Drexus?"

"About?"

"About whatever is the matter with you." Bronn crossed his arms. "You lost it back there, and I saw you let that Spectral go. It's the serum, isn't it?"

Azrael stared down the hall, his jaw tightening, and gave a shallow nod.

"Drexus needs to know."

"He would see it as a weakness. You know how he punishes weaknesses."

"Your lack of control jeopardizes the team and our mission. I won't allow it."

Azrael stepped closer to Bronn. "You won't allow it?"

"You know the mission comes first."

A voice from down the hall sliced through the tension. "Hey, you two." It was Geleon, standing with two other Hunters in the shadows of the hallway. "We're going to get a drink, want to join?"

"Sounds like a good idea," Bronn said, his eyes fixed on Azrael.

"Another time." Azrael walked down the hall, following the light from the torches reflecting off the stone walls, forcing his hands to relax. Bronn's stare weighed heavily on his back.

Bronn was right. He needed to figure out how to undo this connection with the Spectrals. Experiencing their emotions was disconcerting enough, but when those feelings dictated his actions?

The Angel of Death could not afford such a dangerous shortcoming.

He knew the mission came first, but a sliver of doubt crept through his thoughts, making him question his purpose after experiencing the Spectral's emotions. The Watch Guard wasn't protecting the Naturals from Spectrals anymore. He couldn't remember the last time an uprising occurred, and most of the Spectrals were registered or in prison. All they were guilty of was defending themselves and their loved ones. Was that a crime?

ᛟ ᛟ ᛟ

The faces of those Azrael killed haunted his dreams—screams echoing through the caverns of his mind, broken wildflowers drenched in blood. He tossed and turned all night before finally succumbing to exhaustion.

Having slept later than he wanted, he dragged himself from bed, still unsure if he would tell Drexus about the serum's side effects. He searched the council room to give his report but found it empty so he headed for the courtyard, where he found Drexus towering over a group of teenage boys and girls, fear etched on their faces.

Azrael stood next to one of his Hunters. "What's going on?"

"Not sure," Geleon said, his face expressionless.

Drexus sneered when he saw him. "Azrael, join us."

Azrael frowned, marching toward the group. Bronn leaned against a pillar, arms crossed and eyes hard. Distria stood by his side.

Azrael stepped into the circle of recruits where a boy was kneeling, his eye black and lip swollen, blood dripping down his chin. Azrael looked from the boy into the cold eyes of his commander and felt a simmering rage rise to the surface.

"This recruit stole food from the kitchens. His punishment is twenty lashes," Drexus said.

"Twenty?" Azrael's stomach dropped. "That seems excessive." Twenty lashes could kill the boy. And for what, stealing some food?

"I'd like you to carry out his sentence." Drexus's voice was like stone as he held out the whip. For a moment, Azrael imagined grabbing his sword and removing Drexus's head.

Drexus's bloodied knuckles whitened, the whip resembling a coiled snake ready to strike. Silence filled the courtyard, all eyes on Azrael and their commander.

Azrael shook his head, trying to shove down the fury. "I'll punish him another way."

"I've given you leeway as my second in command, but that changes now." Drexus stepped forward, his sour breath tickling Azrael's face. "Take the whip."

"No."

The boy's mouth dropped, his eyes wide. Mutters rumbled through the courtyard.

Drexus tilted his head, his eyes flicking to Bronn. "So, it is true," he said, his lip curling with disgust. "For disobeying my orders, you will take his twenty lashes. Add ten more for your lack of judgment, plus another ten for questioning me in front of my recruits." Drexus nodded, and muscular hands grabbed Azrael's arms; a metal collar clicked, and his strength and speed disappeared.

Azrael bared his teeth and threw one guard over his shoulder, turning to punch the other when a yelp sounded behind him. Drexus held a knife to the boy's throat. A line of blood dripped down his neck.

"Do not make this any worse for you, or him."

Azrael lowered his hands, allowing the guard to lead him up the steps to the whipping post. The platform was spattered with dried blood.

Drexus walked over slowly and looked Azrael in the eye. "Your rage is better than that pathetic weakness I saw before." Drexus dropped his voice to a whisper. "My Angel of Death cannot have a conscience."

Drexus nodded again, and the whip cracked through the air, ripping through Azrael's back. He grunted against the pain but wouldn't cry out, not giving Drexus the satisfaction.

Pain is inevitable; suffering is a choice. Azrael repeated the mantra with each strike of the whip.

Blood poured down his legs. His vision blurred. Someone retched behind him. Another lash struck his ravaged back, cutting through muscle, hitting bone.

Azrael couldn't help the cry that finally escaped his lips.

"That's enough," Drexus said.

෧╋෧   ෧╋෧   ෧╋෧

Azrael slowly opened his eyes, a rough sheet tickling his cheek. His magic thrummed inside him, so at least someone had the decency to remove the collar. He hissed against the pain, trying to get his arms under him.

A delicate hand restrained him. "It's best you lie still."

Azrael rotated his head. Sabine sat next to him, her side bandaged.

"How long have I been out?" he asked, his throat dry.

"About eight hours. The doctor gave you something to help you sleep." Sabine removed her hand from his shoulder and sat back in the chair, staring at him. "What were you thinking?"

"Obviously I wasn't," Azrael said, closing his eyes to the pity on her face. Chamomile mixed with a pungent disinfectant burned his nose. Someone groaned from a nearby bed.

"I don't know if what you did was brave or stupid," Sabine said, brushing the hair off his forehead. "When you're ready to talk about what's going on with you, I'm here."

Azrael shied away from her touch, wincing—his back felt like it was on fire.

"I'll let the doctor know you're awake."

Azrael watched her leave, replaying the confrontation with Drexus in his head. Drexus had intentionally called him over to whip that recruit. *So, it's true.* Bronn had told him about what happened in Dunstead. *My Angel of Death cannot have a conscience.* To Azrael's surprise, he had gone and gained just that.

The doctor walked over to him and studied his back. "I'm going to put some healing ointment on this mess—it should speed up the process. I need you to return in a day to change the bandages." He spread the ointment onto Azrael's skin, and a warming sensation flowed down his body. "I wouldn't be doing anything on your back for a few days." The doctor chuckled at his joke as he carefully bandaged the wounds. "You can leave whenever you feel ready."

Some time later, Azrael limped out of the infirmary and stopped, clenching his fists. Bronn leaned against the entrance to the medical building, using a knife to clean his nails. When he saw Azrael, he walked over to him.

"How are you feeling?"

Azrael ground his teeth, the muscles in his jaw popping.

"Look, I'm sorry. I didn't realize Drexus would go to such extremes." Bronn's expression went from apologetic to defensive in a matter of seconds. "He needed to know about the serum's effect on you."

"Loyalty, honor, and obedience above all, right?" Azrael said, scowling at the Watch Guard tattoo on Bronn's arm, the same one on Azrael's. Azrael once wore the brand with pride. Now, he wasn't so sure. What honor was there in whipping a child because he was hungry? Or in blindly obeying orders?

Bronn furrowed his brow. Azrael shook his head and trudged toward the kitchens, his stomach grumbling. He couldn't remember the last time he'd eaten.

"Drexus wants to see you in his study."

Azrael stopped, his hand on the door, keeping his back to the Hunter.

Bronn placed his hand on Azrael's shoulder, but Azrael pulled back from his touch. "I am sorry," Bronn said.

Azrael turned, searching Bronn's face. He nodded and walked into the dining hall.

⚶ ⚶ ⚶

Azrael waited while the scratching of Drexus's quill filled the silence. A large bookcase stood along one wall and maps of Pandaren on the other, showing the Desert of Souls carving through Opax and Paxton. The Brymagus plant, which rendered a Spectral's power useless, only grew in that desert. When the steward declared war on the Spectrals, most fled to Paxton, so Drexus had built garrisons that lined the edge of the desert to protect Opax and the palace in Orilyon. The situation in Paxton had been quiet for many years. Each town had a lord with a small regiment of guards to keep the peace, and they reported to Steward Brenet. The Watch Guard didn't have the resources to conduct raids in Paxton—yet. But it was only a matter of time.

Azrael blinked, noticing the silence, and turned from the map. Drexus was staring, his face void of emotion.

"How are you feeling?" he asked.

Azrael bit down on a sarcastic remark. "Fine," he said, standing rigid beside the closed door.

Drexus studied him. "Good," he said, standing to lean against the desk and crossed his muscular arms. "Why didn't you tell me about the serum?"

"Because I was dealing with it."

"Doesn't sound like it. Explain what's happening."

Azrael bit down on the anger and disappointment and stared at a spot over Drexus's shoulder. "Whenever I'm near a Spectral, I feel their emotions. Fear, grief, and sorrow."

Drexus's eyes widened. He turned his back on Azrael and paced the length of the room, twisting his ring around his index finger. "I wonder if the serum will have the same effect on the others."

"Why wouldn't it?"

Drexus frowned at Azrael and resumed his pacing. "I'll need to test it on some soldiers. I don't want my Hunters developing empathy for their victims."

"Bronn won't like the delay. He's quite eager to receive the Amplifier magic."

Drexus waved as if swatting an annoying bug. "Besides the emotions, how is the serum working?"

"Good, unless there's a collar around my neck and I'm whipped to within an inch of my life."

"One, you weren't that close to dying. I know how hard to push."

"And two?"

Drexus walked to his chair, indicating for Azrael to sit. He slowly lowered, trying not to wince.

"Two," Drexus continued. "Do you understand the power you have? How deadly a warrior you've become? You need to stay focused on our mission. You can't afford to go soft, letting Spectrals escape."

"She was just a child."

"A child who will grow up one day with incredible powers. A child who can now tell others the Angel of Death is actually an angel of mercy." Drexus's face reddened. He stood and walked to a table with a decanter full of amber liquid. He poured himself a glass and offered one to Azrael, who shook his head. Drexus peered into the glass as if searching for answers.

"I was there when disaster struck," Drexus began. "We were celebrating the victory over the Vastanes . . . we thought the Spectrals had saved us until they murdered the king." Drexus went back to his desk and stared at Azrael, his gaze unwavering. "Spectrals have too much power, and we can't allow even one of them to go free."

Azrael tapped his finger on the arm of the chair, trying to restrain his anger. He had been eight when the Vastanes invaded Pandaren, and he had fond memories of playing in the forest, pretending he was a powerful Spectral protecting his sister, the beautiful queen.

"Think about what the Spectrals did to your village. To your mother and sister—"

Azrael's head shot up and he glared at Drexus. "I know what they did. I don't need a history lesson."

Drexus stared over the rim of his glass. "For my plan to work, I need the Angel of Death. Fear of you and the Hunters will keep the people in line. We are fighting for the greater good and will never be at the mercy of anyone again."

"The Angel of Death instills fear in every village we raid. You don't need to worry about that."

Drexus nodded and stood in front of the large map. "I will rule this kingdom with you by my side, if you so desire."

Azrael tilted his head. Drexus had never mentioned ruling Pandaren. "Steward Brenet might have something to say about that. The queen too."

"I'm not worried about the queen." Drexus smiled into his glass. "And Brenet will no longer be a problem. Take three Hunters, ride to Bradwick, and kill him."

Azrael raised his brows. "You want me to assassinate Steward Brenet?"

"Are you questioning my orders again?"

"No, sir. It's just that I want to continue my search for the Fire Spectral."

"The Watch Guard comes before your revenge, Azrael. But"—he raised his hand as Azrael opened his mouth—"after you complete this job, you are free to search for him. How do you know he's still alive? It's been, what, thirteen years?"

"He has to be," Azrael said, not wanting to consider the alternative. Revenge on the Fire Spectral was his life, his mission, his purpose.

Drexus stared at him, the muscle in his jaw clenching. He sat at his desk and continued writing, dismissing Azrael. If all went according to Drexus's plans, Azrael wouldn't be second in command of the Watch Guard, but all of Pandaren. The Angel of Death would strike fear not just in Opax, but throughout Paxton and beyond.

For the first time in days, Azrael smiled.

CHAPTER 4

The sun crested over the hills, turning the sky a fiery gold. An owl hooted in the distance as Azrael breathed in the crisp air—a new day, a new beginning. He appreciated every sunrise—its beauty and purity—something he and his mother had in common. They would sit in the early morning, watching the sky lighten, and she would wrap her arm around him, saying, *Here it comes; the light chasing away the darkness.* What would she think about her son becoming darkness in his quest for justice? Or was it revenge? He had walked a fine line between the two until the night he killed his father. The night he surrendered to the darkness.

He'd never known why Barnet betrayed them. Had his father watched the Fire Spectral murder his wife or seen the others drag his daughter behind their burning cottage? Had he listened as her screams were silenced? Was there any remorse? Azrael wished he'd asked his father those questions before killing him, but the desire for revenge had prevailed over rational thought. That night, Azrael had forfeited his soul, and now only shadows remained.

"You look lousy. Couldn't sleep?" Bronn said, stretching his muscular arms, yawning loudly.

Azrael tensed, distracted by another time and place. Over the past week, his mind kept replaying the Dunstead raid—the Spectrals' turbulent emotions, the young man's head rolling along the cobblestones, the girl with flowers trembling in her hand who reminded him of his sister, Jaida. The serum created havoc within him, taking him places he didn't want to go, mentally or emotionally. For someone who lived and breathed combat, who felt anxious without it, the war raging inside him left him exhausted. He still wasn't sure how to suppress the unwanted feelings. He'd thought about wearing one of Drexus's collars, but now that he'd experienced the power, he didn't want to let it go. He'd already grown accustomed to the strength and speed that pulsed through his body.

Azrael shook his head. He'd had enough; he needed to focus on the mission.

"Is everyone ready?" Azrael asked, his gaze fixed on the horizon.

Bronn nodded and pointed at the village below. "My sources say the steward is in that cottage with a dozen guards. Shouldn't be a problem for the Angel of Death."

Azrael ignored his lieutenant's sarcastic tone, admiring the sunrise one more time before turning to retrieve his weapons. Distria adjusted her crossbow, her face expressionless, while Sabine strapped on her armor, looking everywhere but at him. She had been quiet the entire trip, not her usual flirtatious self. Azrael shrugged. He'd rather battle twenty soldiers than try to figure out a woman's changing moods.

"Our assignment is simple," he said. "Bronn and I will ride in first. Distria and Sabine, you take out anyone who tries to escape. Once we've disposed of the steward and his guards, Bronn will set the place on fire. No masks—it's imperative this looks like a Fire Spectral killed the steward."

Azrael was about to pull himself onto his horse when Sabine spoke. "Are you sure this is a good idea?" Bronn's head shot up. She continued, "Have we thought through the repercussions?" Her eyes darted between Bronn and Azrael.

Azrael frowned. Sabine wasn't one to show trepidation before a job. He glanced at Bronn, whose jaw twitched, the morning light making his blond hair appear white.

"It's not your place to question orders, Sabine," Distria said, her eyes cold.

Sabine's face paled, and she looked away from Distria, focusing on her weapons belt.

"Drexus has a plan, one that will better Pandaren." Azrael squeezed Sabine's shoulder. "It'll be fine, just no witnesses."

Azrael mounted his horse, noticing Bronn shrug while Distria shook her head. He rode down the hill thinking about Sabine. What repercussions was she so worried about?

Halfway through the clearing, a searing pain tore into Azrael's back. He twisted, his eyes darting from the vibrating shaft of an arrow to the top of the hill. His stomach dropped. Bronn and Sabine watched from their horses while Distria knocked another arrow in her crossbow.

He immediately felt the effects of the Brymagus plant, remembering the day in Nigel's forge with the arrowheads and sweet-smelling liquid on the worktable. He tried to reach the arrow lodged into his back, but Distria's aim was perfect.

Angry shouts invaded the quiet morning.

Azrael tore his gaze from the three Hunters, focusing on the villagers barreling toward him. The blade of betrayal cut deep as a second arrow whizzed through the air, lodging into Azrael's thigh. He tried to yank it out when another bolt struck his shoulder, the force knocking him from his horse.

Azrael rolled out of the fall, crying out as the shaft in his back snapped in half. Blood oozed from his shoulder and leg. He reached with his uninjured arm and retrieved his sword, steel flashing in the morning light. Drawing upon thirteen years of training, he crouched into his fighting stance and faced the oncoming mob.

The Angel of Death welcomed the rage and conceded to the darkness, cutting down every villager in his path. Blood splattered his face and gore dripped from his sword.

Azrael grunted mid-strike as a blade sliced his leg, causing him to lose his footing. He turned and stabbed the man in the chest. Out of the corner of his eye, metal flashed. Azrael yelled; a sword pierced through his armor into his side, and he fell to his knees, panting, blood soaking the ground. A roar of victory sounded as Azrael blocked an array of kicks and punches.

Familiar boots walked toward him, parting the crowd.

Gritting his teeth against the pain, Azrael tried to lunge forward, but someone wrenched his arms behind him. A kick in the ribs had him gasping for air.

Bronn knelt and grabbed Azrael by the hair, yanking his head back. Azrael sucked in a breath, the muscles in his neck corded with fury, and glared into Bronn's dark eyes.

"Why?" Blood dripped down Azrael's face, into his mouth. If he could pull free, he'd rip out Bronn's throat with his bare hands.

"Because you're a failed experiment," Bronn sneered. He twisted the arrow in Azrael's shoulder. Azrael swore through clenched teeth. "With you out of the way, I'll be second in command. As it should've been."

Azrael's upper lip curled, his muscles shaking. "You're betraying me because you're second best?"

Bronn's smugness melted into rage. Stars exploded as his fist connected with Azrael's jaw, whipping his head to the side.

Azrael glared, spitting blood onto Bronn's shiny boots. Bronn punched him again. And again. Azrael's head hit the ground, his eyes swelling and jaw pounding.

Bronn gripped Azrael by the throat, pulling him off the ground. "If it's any consolation, Drexus regretted losing his precious Angel. Gave me strict orders not to kill you." Azrael struggled to breathe as black spots floated in his vision. Bronn released his grip, leaving Azrael on his knees, gulping for air, and threw a bag of gold to someone in the crowd. "The Angel of Death is all yours," he said, turning on his heel and walking away. In the distance, Distria lowered her crossbow, her face blank. Sabine's mouth drew into a thin line, her eyes never leaving Azrael's.

"I will kill you!" Azrael yelled, struggling against the hands holding him, the arrowheads digging deeper into his skin. "I will kill you all!"

The hilt of a sword crashed down onto his head.

⚙ ⚙ ⚙

Drip.

Drip.

Drip.

Water—at least, Azrael hoped it was water—dripped onto the stone floor, and a scream sounded in the distance. Azrael hung from the ceiling, his arms numb, metal cuffs digging into his wrists. A rodent skittered by, grazing his toes which barely skimmed the ground. He tried to inhale to clear his head and immediately winced, the smells of the dungeon assaulting him: sweat, rot, and death.

Guards arrived with moldy bread and foul-tasting water at varying times, so Azrael had lost track of the days. One thing remained constant, though: Every day, they hoisted him up and let him hang, sometimes for hours, before a guard used his tattered body for punching practice.

Pain is inescapable; suffering is a choice.

Azrael tried to repeat the mantra he had spoken so often at the Watch Guard to help him get through the grueling training and the beatings, but with the Hunters' betrayal the words seemed meaningless. He now understood Sabine's uneasiness. *Have we thought through the repercussions?* They had no idea the torment coming for them, the nightmare that would destroy them. Drexus should have ordered his death, for he would make Bronn, Sabine, and Distria pay for their treachery. And after Azrael killed the Hunters, he would deal with Drexus—if he didn't die in this filthy prison.

Azrael's head swam from the blood loss caused by the gashes in his thigh and side. Blood-soaked bandages covered the lacerations, but the broken arrowheads remained embedded in his body. Someone, and he guessed it was Drexus, told whomever held him captive that the arrows suppressed magic. They wanted him alive, but powerless.

Azrael swore. "You're still the Angel of Death. Act like it."

Boots thumped down the stone corridor. His last visit from the guard—a smelly man who delighted in punching his enormous fists into Azrael's wounds—had left him unconscious for hours.

A short, heavyset man stopped in front of his cell, nodding at Smelly to open it. Two other guards flanked him. Four against one were usually good odds. Usually.

"It's never a good sign when prisoners talk to themselves," the man said in an oily voice as he entered the cell. "We can't have you losing your mind yet."

"Who the blazes are you?" Inwardly, Azrael grimaced at the weakness in his voice.

Smelly's fist came out of nowhere, connecting with Azrael's jaw. Blood dripped from his mouth.

"Manners, please," the man said, staring up at Azrael with watery brown eyes. "My name is Phillip Gallet, warden of Bradwick Prison. My guards tell me you're not talking, except for an array of swear words." Phillip paced, his hands resting on his beefy backside. "If you don't tell me what I want to know, then you leave me no choice."

Azrael spat a glob of blood onto the warden's boots. Pain exploded in his side and blood gushed through the bandages, splattering on the floor. It took everything Azrael had not to cry out. Smelly wiped the blood off his knuckles, yellow teeth peeking through his crusted lips. Azrael glared at the guard, his vision swimming.

"How did you become a Spectral?" Phillip asked. "That's the rumor—and based on the warning regarding those arrowheads, they must be true."

"I'm not a Spectral."

The warden inclined his head. "You have magic, therefore you're a Spectral."

Azrael scowled, wanting to smack the smug look off his face.

"Did something go wrong? Why would Drexus surrender his Angel of Death?" Phillip started pacing again, his boots thudding along the stone floor. He waved his hand lazily in the air. "You see, I like to dabble in this sort of thing, experimenting if you will. What if we could choose to have magic? Then we would all be equal. No more Spectrals against Naturals." He stopped in front of Azrael, his sagging cheeks flushed. "So I will ask again. How did Drexus do it?"

Azrael lifted his chin and glowered at the man. Loyalty to the Watch Guard ran deeper than the tattoo inked on his arm. He wouldn't tell the warden anything. Once he did, the warden would have no reason to keep him alive.

He just needed a little more time. Soon, a guard would make a mistake and Azrael would escape. He breathed deeply, readying his mind for the pain that would come.

"Very well. We'll try again tomorrow." The warden nodded to Smelly, who retrieved a whip from the other guard. Phillip paused at the opening of the cell. "You *will* tell me, Angel of Death. I promise you that."

The sound of retreating boots faded as the whip sliced through the air.

⚜ ⚜ ⚜

A rock skittered down the stone path and flickering torches distorted the two approaching shadows. Whispers floated through the air as the shapes grew larger. Smelly had left Azrael hours ago, leaving him hanging from the ceiling, blood and grime covering him. Besides the agony of the serum transfusion, Azrael couldn't remember ever being in this much pain.

"Just a bit further," a male voice said.

"I know the layout just as well as you," another voice replied, this one female.

"Oh, shut it."

"You shut it."

"How about you both shut it?" Azrael said, his voice gruff. He flexed his hands, trying to get his blood to flow against gravity.

"Well, there's gratitude for you," the man said, placing a torch in the sconce on the wall, his features hidden in the shadows. He was easily six-four and had bulging muscles. He wore a black tunic with a leather baldric laden with throwing knives strapped across his broad chest.

A woman nudged the man out of the way. "We don't have much time."

"Watch it," the man said, gripping the hilt of his sword.

She knelt before the cell door, pulling two metal sticks from her black hair and sliding them into the lock. She looked a few inches shorter than Azrael, wearing a dented and scratched metal chest piece, her sword hanging on her hip. Azrael frowned, contemplating the metal gauntlets covering parts of her hands and wrists.

"Azrael, we're here to rescue you from this nasty hole. So please don't give us a hard time. I don't want to knock you out," the man said.

Azrael grunted, but based on his injuries and the man's size, he was at a considerable disadvantage. "Who are you?" His voice sounded like he had swallowed knives.

"Both of you be quiet," the woman said as she unlocked the cell, gripping her metal sticks. If Azrael could get those, a strike to the jugular would quickly and silently do the trick. The large man entered the cell, his features coming into view. Green eyes scanned Azrael's body, his lips a thin line above a chiseled jaw. Short black hair stood in all directions as if he had just battled a windstorm. His kind face contradicted his menacing form.

"Heal him now, or wait till we get out?" the man asked.

"Let's wait. If we're lucky, he'll die on the way to Paxton," the woman said, crossing her arms and sighing as the man frowned.

"We've been over this a hundred times, so knock it off." The man looked pointedly at Azrael. "You won't be any trouble now, will you?"

"Define trouble. And I'll ask again, who are you?" Azrael swiveled his head to watch the woman working on his cuffs. His stomach tightened, unable to stop staring at her green eyes, similar in color to the man's. She had a thin nose and a full mouth, which had him licking his lips. She was beautiful, in an angry sort of way.

The woman maneuvered her metal sticks into the lock. Her eyes flitted to his, narrowing when she found him staring. "Let's knock him out so I don't have to listen to him."

"Yeah, well, I don't feel like carrying him up all those stairs. Do you? He's lost a lot of blood, still has open wounds and . . ." He strolled behind Azrael. "Huh" was all he said.

Azrael's right arm fell heavily to his side as his feet fully touched the ground. He pivoted to keep the man in view and thought about neutralizing him—a quick strike to the nose and throat—but when his other arm fell free, it took everything he had not to collapse to his knees.

The woman quickly stepped back, twisting her wrists. A blue light pulsed through the gauntlets and her eyes remained narrowed as she watched Azrael shake out his hands. He flinched when the man grabbed his arm and threw it over his shoulder, lugging him out of the cell.

Azrael focused on each step as they climbed, his muscles quivering. He wished the man had knocked him out. They passed a few guards, alive but unconscious, and his fingers itched for his dagger.

"Easy there," the man said, looking at Azrael's twitching fingers.

"Why didn't you just kill them?"

"Because we aren't like you," the woman said. "Now please, shut up."

After what seemed like hours, the heavy door to the dungeon opened and brisk night air washed over Azrael's face. The stars shone brightly against a moonless sky. He breathed in the sweet smell of pine, cleansing the putrid scent of the dungeon from his nose.

"Where are we going?" Azrael stumbled, his vision blurring.

"Can you ride?" the man asked, leading Azrael to the edge of the forest.

"Of course." He wanted to roll his eyes, but even that tiny movement hurt.

Three horses waited in the shadows, pawing the ground. The man lifted Azrael as if he weighed nothing, which was impressive considering Azrael's size. If Azrael had to fight him, he'd have to rely on his magic, which was still, regretfully, absent. His mind instinctually formed combative scenarios, replaying each of his rescuers' movements, cataloging their weaknesses to use when the time came to escape.

Ropes wrapped around Azrael's body, securing him to the horse with his hands bound in front of him. The woman, already on her horse, trotted over and double-checked the ropes.

"Just in case I try to escape?"

"Just in case you fall off," she said, smirking. She looked over her shoulder as bells rang in the distance.

"You should've killed them."

She rolled her eyes. "Let's go." She kicked her horse forward, the blue glow of her gauntlets a reassuring beacon as they rode through the trees.

"Don't mind her," the man said. "She gets a little testy when she's skipped a meal. I'm Kord Haring, by the way. And that's my younger sister, Kenz."

Azrael gripped the reins, his knuckles white, every movement excruciating as the horses raced through the woods, the darkness of the forest swallowing shouts from the prison.

CHAPTER 5

Azrael woke to the sounds of whispers. He kept his body motionless, despite the irritating pebble poking through the blanket, denting his cheek. He barely remembered the ride through the forest, blood loss and pain battling his need to stay awake, and although he'd never admit it, he was thankful for the ropes that had tethered him on the horse. Without them, he would have fallen off, and he didn't know which would hurt more, the embarrassment or colliding with the ground.

He parted his eyes to take in his surroundings. They were in a large cave; bedrolls and satchels littered the floor, and swords leaned against the stone wall. The warmth from the fire made it hard to stay awake, but he forced himself to remain alert, listening to the voices nearby.

"It seems the Watch Guard has developed a new weapon against us," the male voice said. Kord was his name, if Azrael remembered correctly. And his sister, Kenz. He had no idea who they were or why they risked their lives to rescue him.

"What is it?" Kenz said, her feet shuffling closer.

"Here, feel it."

Kenz gasped. "Is that—?"

"Yep, these arrowheads have the Brymagus plant infused into them."

"Why would they use them on him?" Kenz said. "Unless . . ."

"Looks like the rumors are true. The Angel of Death has magic—I can feel it." Kord said, his hand resting on Azrael's arm.

"We should kill him now," Kenz whispered.

Azrael tensed and assessed his body, preparing to defend himself, then paused. He didn't feel any pain in his side or leg.

"That's not what Amycus wants," Kord said.

"He was almost unstoppable before."

Someone rummaged through a bag, and Azrael inwardly swore when metal cuffs locked around his wrists.

"These will suppress his magic," Kord said.

"Do I need to remind you he's still a trained killer?"

"I know that, Kenz. I'll keep a close eye on him." Kord sighed. "I know this is hard for you, but you have to trust Amycus." Kord cut through Azrael's tunic. "I need to get this disgusting thing off." Cold air fluttered over Azrael's back.

Someone gasped.

"What the blazes?" Kord said, his voice slicing along the cave walls.

"Who would do that to him? Not that he doesn't deserve it."

"Does anyone deserve this?"

Azrael bit down when fingers drifted along his back. He tried counting to ten as Kord's hands began another perusal over his scars.

"All right, knock it off." He swatted Kord's hand and pushed himself up, trying to see past the spinning room to his rescuers. Kenz jumped back and lifted her hands, the glow from her mysterious gauntlets filling the cave with a blue hue.

"We aren't going to hurt you," Kord said, his green eyes wide.

Azrael huffed and frowned at his side, running his fingers along the closed wound that looked days old. He examined the shiny metal cuffs, then glanced at Kord and Kenz.

"Feel better?" Kord knelt, examining Azrael's body.

"Much," Azrael said, his voice gruff from lack of water. Kord handed him a flask that he took greedily, gulping down the refreshing liquid.

"Is he healed enough to travel?" Kenz stood beside her brother, placing her fists on her hips.

"Yes, after he's had some nourishment." Kord walked to his pack and pulled out some dried meat and bread. He tossed both to Azrael.

"Well, make it quick. We've lingered here too long." Kenz grabbed her sword and stalked to the cave's opening.

Azrael sat against the stone wall and chewed the meat slowly despite his hunger, not wanting to throw it up later. "What day is it?" Azrael asked, taking a bite of the hard bread.

"Monday, almost dawn. As far as we know, you were in that dungeon for three days." Kord sat, placing the fire between them and resting his arms on his knees. Azrael squirmed under Kord's penetrating gaze.

"Three days." Azrael traced the tattoo on his right arm, sorting out the events leading to his capture: Hunters standing on a hill, arrows hammering him, villagers attacking, Bronn's eyes shining with triumph. *With you out of the way, I'll be second in command, as it should've been.* Azrael's nails dug into his palms, and he eyed Kord's sword leaning against the wall. They would all die, slowly.

"You need to calm down. You've only just healed, and we still have a long way to go," Kord said, watching him with those keen eyes.

Azrael forced his hands to relax and took another drink from the flask. He stared at the metal cuffs. "What are these for?"

"A safety precaution, since you have magic."

"You could've left the arrows."

The corner of Kord's mouth lifted. "That would've been rude."

Azrael pressed against his side where the blade had sliced him open; only a twinge of pain remained. "I'm assuming you're a Healer."

"You assume correctly."

"You must be powerful. I've never seen wounds heal this fast."

Kord shrugged.

"And her powers?" Azrael said, nodding toward the cave entrance.

Kord looked over his shoulder. "Kenz is a Shield, so don't get any ideas."

"What sort of ideas?"

"Oh, I don't know." Kenz's voice floated toward them. "What you do best—maim, kill, destroy. Those sort of ideas." She walked into the light, not sparing a glance in Azrael's direction, and slung her pack over her shoulder. "We need to go."

Azrael rose to his feet, keeping one eye on Kord. "I take it you don't like me much?"

"What's there to like? You're a Hunter, murderer, and traitor," she said through clenched teeth, hatred hardening her eyes.

"The first two are correct, but I am no traitor." Azrael stepped closer, Kord stiffened, resting a hand on one of his many blades. "And why rescue me? Why heal me?"

"If it were up to me, I'd kill you right now," Kenz said.

"You could try." His gaze traveled down her body, a jolt of longing trembling in his gut. His eyes drifted back to hers, and his hand twitched for his missing dagger, for he could see that she did, in fact, want to kill him. He understood the look too well, often mirrored in his own eyes.

Kord stepped between them. "Our orders are to bring you back alive. So there will be no killing, from either of you." He looked over his shoulder at his sister. "Got it?"

Kenz glared at Azrael for a moment, then turned on her heel and left the cave. Azrael relaxed his muscles, disengaging his fighting instincts. Any renewed strength dwindled.

"Now, do I have to knock you out or will you come peacefully?" Kord handed Azrael a clean tunic, pants, and boots.

"Do you knock people out a lot?"

A line etched between Kord's brows. "No, why?"

"That's twice you've threatened it."

Kord chuckled.

"Where are we going?" Azrael asked, eyeing the clothing.

"Paxton. It's a four-day ride, so we best be on our way." Kord turned, grabbing his pack and sword, and left the cave.

⚶ ⚶ ⚶

Azrael ached after riding all day, and even though his wounds had healed, his body still felt weak. Kord untied the ropes from the saddle and held the end as Azrael slid from his horse and stretched his arms and back.

After securing Azrael to a nearby tree, the siblings efficiently set up the camp. Even if they didn't have the same black hair and green eyes, he would have been able to tell they were related by how they moved. Azrael leaned his head against the tree, his long legs stretched out before him. At least they hadn't tied his hands behind his back.

"This isn't necessary," Azrael said, nodding at the ropes.

"Yes, well, we can't have you running away in the middle of the night, can we?" Kord said with a mischievous grin.

"Or slitting our throats while we sleep," Kenz muttered.

Azrael chuckled. "What's the age difference between you two?"

Kord glanced at Kenz. "Five years. I'm thirty. You?"

"Twenty-five."

"That's pretty young to be second in command of the Watch Guard, isn't it?"

Azrael shrugged, using the movement to hide his hands. "Not when you're the best."

Kenz rolled her eyes, mumbling something Azrael couldn't hear. Kord chortled.

"Look, if I'd wanted to escape, I would have." Azrael held up the rope that had bound his hands. He still hadn't worked out how to get the cuffs off but noted a small keyhole.

Kenz jumped up and grabbed her sword. Blue light pulsed through her gauntlets.

"And why haven't you?" Kord said, resting his hand on the hilt of his dagger.

"The Hunters betrayed me and Drexus has probably heard of my escape, so it wouldn't be wise to stay in Opax. I'm not at full strength yet, plus I need these cuffs off." Azrael's gaze drifted toward Kenz. "And curiosity. Why did you rescue me?"

"Why haven't you killed us?" Kenz retorted, her sword still raised.

The side of Azrael's mouth hitched up. "You got me out of that dungeon and most likely saved my life. Seems a poor way to repay you, don't you think?"

Kenz frowned. "You're the Angel of Death."

Having freed himself from the rest of the ropes, Azrael nodded and stood, wiping off his pants. Kenz lifted her other hand and indigo light from her shield flashed around him.

Azrael raised a brow, running his finger down the glowing barrier, smiling when she shivered. "Interesting." He took a step back, raising both hands. "I promise I will not escape." His eyes slid to Kenz's. "Or slit your throats in your sleep. And when I make a promise, I keep it."

"Please." Kenz rolled her eyes. "Do you actually think we'd let you roam free?"

"You can't keep that shield up all night."

A breeze rustled the leaves on the ground, bringing the fresh scent of pine and sap.

"How about a compromise?" Kord said, breaking the silence. "We only tie you up when we sleep."

"What? You seriously believe this killer?" Kenz said, her eyes wide.

Kord chewed the inside of his cheek, surveying Azrael. "I do."

Azrael crossed his arms and tapped his finger. "Deal," he finally said, his curiosity growing. He still didn't understand why they rescued him when it was obvious Kenz wanted him dead. He thought about his last conversation with Nigel. He meant what he'd said; he didn't have anywhere else to go, and the idea of leaving Opax appealed to him. He needed time to plan his revenge on Drexus and the three Hunters, and maybe find the Fire Spectral that had changed the course of his life.

⚘ ⚘ ⚘

The forest thinned the next day. They camped on the outskirts of the Desert of Souls, filling everything that could hold water. Crossing the desert would take two days, and on the other side lay Paxton, known for its mountains and lush forests.

Sparks from the fire floated into the night sky while Azrael absently traced the Watch Guard tattoo on his arm, wondering if Drexus had promoted Bronn to second in command, if the other Hunters celebrated Azrael's fall from grace. Anger and revenge, his constant companions, sparked to life as he replayed Bronn's betrayal.

But another feeling had emerged that day, rippling through his hatred, one he hadn't expected. Relief. No more looking over his shoulder or striving to stay on top, having to prove himself. A weight he hadn't known he carried lightened, and for once he could breathe easier.

"Is that *his* mark?" Kenz said, her voice dripping with venom. "Drexus and his mighty Hunters?"

Azrael dropped his hand and peered into the forest that had come alive with the chirps of crickets, nocturnal animals skittering on the ground, and the smell of sage mixing with the smoke. He remembered the day he received the tattoo with the other recruits, forcing himself not to cry as the needle carved into his skin. Drexus told them it was a mark of brotherhood.

So much for brotherhood. He pictured the silhouettes of three Hunters on the hill.

"This is the mark of the Watch Guard." Azrael looked at the three words circling a crossbow—loyalty, honor, and obedience. "Drexus brands recruits when they first arrive at the compound."

"How old were you?" Kord asked.

Azrael carved a line in the sand with the heel of his boot. "Twelve." His voice sounded hollow.

Kenz's eyes widened. "You were just a little boy."

Azrael laughed. "Don't pity me, Kenz. Hate me, loathe me, despise me. But do not pity me."

Kenz got to her feet, her eyes never leaving Azrael's. "I don't pity you, and I never will. You are evil, and people will celebrate when you're dead." She turned on her heel and stomped from the campsite.

"Kenz," Kord called after her retreating form, the darkness of the forest swallowing her. He looked back at Azrael and winced.

"She's not wrong," Azrael said, continuing to carve the line in the sand.

On the third evening they camped near a rocky outcropping that provided shelter from the wind. Azrael sat in the sand, rubbing his temples. He still felt weak, something he hadn't experienced in a long time. He tugged at the silver cuffs weighing heavily on his wrists.

Swords clashed together, accompanied by laughter as Kord and Kenz sparred on the other side of the campsite, the fire reflecting off their blades. Kenz's lithe body moved gracefully, her speed an advantage over her brother's strength. Azrael observed how her brows furrowed in concentration, trying not to focus on her teeth biting her bottom lip.

"What are you staring at?" Kenz's voice cut through the darkness.

"A beautiful woman." Azrael chuckled as both Kord and Kenz stiffened. "Actually, you're favoring your right side, leaving the left unprotected. And you're a bit heavy-footed. But other than that, you have decent fighting skills."

Kenz's eyes narrowed while Kord groaned, rubbing his forehead.

"Heavy-footed?" Kenz said, baring her teeth. She wrenched Kord's sword out of his hand and marched toward Azrael.

He stood, positioning himself near the firewood and evaluated the way she held both swords, the knuckles whitening on her right hand. Just before she reached him, Azrael flicked his foot under a smaller log, skillfully grabbing it with one hand while stepping forward to block her oncoming strike. He used her momentum and sidestepped, flinging her around him and swatting her on the back.

Kenz stumbled and swore, her knees hitting the packed earth. Azrael pivoted, keeping one eye on Kord, who stood frozen with his mouth open.

"If you let your emotions control you, you will lose yourself, and therefore lose the fight," Azrael said to Kenz as she stood, her face red, murder flashing in her eyes. "Rage and hatred are powerful, but you still need to be in control."

"Shut up." She approached him cautiously, throwing Kord's sword to the ground.

"Hey," Kord said, watching his sword land in the soft sand.

Azrael nodded. "Good. It's important to know your strengths and understand your weaknesses."

"I said, shut up!" Kenz swung her blade at Azrael's head, but not fast enough. Even weak and drained, years of relentless training commanded his body and mind. He gracefully dodged her strikes, his movement effortless, only raising his makeshift weapon to defend himself. She continued attacking as Azrael led her around the campsite, until he had her near the large boulders. Sweat dripped down her face and the vein in her neck throbbed.

"Now," Azrael said, smashing the log onto her forearm, the sword falling harmlessly at her feet. He spun and dropped to one knee, smacking the wood across the back of her legs, sending her to the ground. Azrael flipped through the air, landing behind her, holding the stick against her throat. "You're dead," he whispered.

"Azrael," Kord said, his voice calm. "Please release my sister." He took a step forward, gripping his sword.

Azrael tossed the wood onto the fire, creating sparks that fluttered into the darkness. "Like I said, heavy-footed." He turned his back on Kenz and walked to his bedroll.

"You arrogant, murdering—"

"Kenz, stop," Kord said, interrupting what might have been an impressive display of swearing.

"You're upset because you lost. It's understandable." Azrael admired her beauty, the way her chest heaved, the flush creeping up her long neck. Silky tendrils of hair had escaped her braid.

"Please don't bait her," Kord said, reaching to help Kenz up. She shook off his hand, striding away from the campsite and muttering under her breath. Kord sighed. He sat near Azrael and stared into the fire, mumbling something about a crazy mission.

"She seems to hate me." Azrael stared after Kenz. "I mean, more than the normal person. It seems personal. But I've never seen either of you before."

The sound of crackling wood filled the silence. Azrael cringed as Kord stoked the fire with his sword.

"The Hunters attacked a village two years ago, killing her fiancé and his family. She feels guilty she wasn't there to protect them," Kord said.

Azrael heard the protectiveness in Kord's voice, recognizing a brother's love. He stared into the fire, wondering what life would have been like if his sister had lived. What *they* would have been like. As for the Hunters attacking Kenz's fiancé's village—well, that's what they did.

"You have nothing to say?" Kord focused on the flames.

Azrael peered into the night; the Desert of Souls stretched out before him. "Is there anything I could say that would bring them back or change the past?"

Kord sighed and shook his head. "True. Brutal, but true."

CHAPTER 6

If Azrael never saw sand again, it would be too soon. It was everywhere—places sand shouldn't be—and all he longed for, besides a decent meal, was a bath. A bucket of water would do, he wasn't picky; he just wanted to be free of the sand. He wouldn't mind a break from the siblings' constant bickering either. After four days of their squabbling, his eye had begun to twitch.

Azrael didn't mind Kord's company; his light-hearted manner and entertaining stories had Azrael smiling more than usual. Kenz was another matter. He had kept his distance ever since she stormed off after their skirmish, although he caught himself watching her more than he wanted to. He understood her hatred of him and the Hunters. As a Shield, her primary purpose was to protect, and to feel you failed—well, he could relate. However, if she had been there when the Hunters attacked her fiancé, she would most likely be dead.

The sun beat down on the travelers, the desert turning into a sparse forest. Wooden cottages with tin roofs came into view. A large fountain, surrounded by stalls for the weekly market, indicated the center of town.

"Welcome to Carhurst," Kord said. "Kenz and I were born here." He lifted his chin, smiling over the village.

Azrael scanned the area, noticing soldiers patrolling a large manor on the outskirts of town. A flag with a symbol Azrael didn't recognize snapped in the breeze.

"That's Lord Rollant's residence," Kord said, following Azrael's stare.

"Is he sympathetic to the Watch Guard?"

"Not really. Like all lords of Paxton, he answers to Steward Brenet, but those are his soldiers; the Guard doesn't have a presence here. Lord Rollant usually travels north this time of year, so we shouldn't have any issues." Kord clicked his tongue to get his horse moving. "You should lie low, though, just in case."

"Unless Rollant's soldiers trained at the Bastion, they won't recognize me. I'm not concerned."

Azrael felt eyes boring into the back of his head and turned in his saddle to see Kenz glaring at him, her gauntlets glowing blue. He kept sneaking glances at the familiar metal encompassing her wrists, but any time he asked her about them he received a scowl.

"How do those gauntlets work?" Azrael asked, swiveling back to Kord.

Kord peeked over his shoulder, chewing on the inside of his cheek. "They focus her magic, allowing her to manipulate the shield. When they are blue, her power is ready, so to speak."

Azrael turned back around and gave her a wink, chuckling as her body went rigid and her eyes narrowed to slits.

"Please don't bait her."

"It's so satisfying, though," Azrael said, the corner of his lips lifting.

Kord yawned. "You two have a lot in common, both hot-tempered and exhausting."

"Do your powers have limits?"

Kord's healing was unprecedented. When most Healers used their magic, it took hours or days for wounds to heal where Kord's magic worked in minutes. Drexus would be very interested in acquiring him. Azrael wasn't sure of Kenz's magic, but since the two were related, he assumed she was just as powerful.

"Yes. Just like your magic doesn't have an endless supply, neither does ours."

Kenz rode past, her shoulders tight. "Why don't you just reveal everything, you babbling idiot?"

"Angry little thing," Azrael said, admiring the way her body kept time with the horse's movement. Desire pulsed through him, his fingers cramping as he squeezed the reins. He noticed Kord staring at him and cracked his neck, uncomfortable with his body's reaction and the older brother next to him.

Kenz hopped off her horse in front of a large cottage with smoke billowing from the chimney. Azrael glanced at the anvil and hammer symbol etched above the front door and walked in, blinking to adjust his eyes, his hand instinctively reaching for his dagger. Kenz walked past a cluttered desk, wove between two overstuffed chairs, and disappeared into another room, where the sound of clinking metal reverberated down the hall. The smell of smoke and hot steel tickled his nose.

Kord edged by Azrael, placing his bag near a bookshelf lining the far wall, and fell into a chair behind the desk. The hammering stopped. Azrael glanced around the room, locating potential weapons and placing himself near the exit. He inclined his head and listened to the muffled voices and the sound of footsteps growing louder.

An older man emerged from the doorway wearing a leather apron over his tunic, his rolled sleeves revealing muscular forearms. His brown hair, streaked with gray, was tied back, and scars decorated his strong hands. Kord rose from the desk and placed himself near Azrael.

The man smiled. The soot lodged in his wrinkles brought out the blue of his eyes. He removed the apron and wiped the grime off his face. "Hello, Jasce,"

Azrael tensed. He hadn't heard that name in years; it was one he had tried to forget. Blood rushed through his ears as memories assaulted him. *Jasce, wait up!* a sweet, youthful voice rang out as he ran through the trees, the wind ruffling his hair. His mother, calling him to dinner. His father, eyes glossy, slurring his full name—Jasce Liam Farone.

"My name is Azrael," he said through gritted teeth, not mentally prepared to reunite with his past or the onslaught of images he'd buried. He pushed away from the door, drawing nearer to Kord and his dagger.

The man inclined his head. "Actually, no. It's Jasce. Jasce Farone."

"How do you know who I am?" Azrael said, his voice like molten iron.

Sadness flashed across the older man's face. "It's been a long time."

A war of emotions raged inside Azrael—painful memories, betrayal, torture, desire—all combined into unleashed fury. His eyes darted to Kenz's gauntlets. He didn't know how long it took for her magic to engage, but he only needed seconds.

Azrael smashed his elbow into Kord's face while grabbing his dagger. He launched across the room and pressed the knife against the older man's throat, using him as a shield. Kenz swore, jutting out her hands, the gauntlets igniting.

"Stand down," Azrael said, his eyes darting to Kord. Blood poured from his broken nose.

The man held up his hands and looked at the siblings. "It's all right. He won't hurt me."

"Don't hold your breath," Azrael said in his ear. "I want answers now. Who are you? How do you know my name? And what do you want with me?" Azrael dug the knife into the man's throat, making him wince. Kenz drew her sword and stepped closer as a line of blood slid down the blacksmith's neck.

"Stay right where you are, sweetheart. You don't want this to get messy." Kord groaned.

"Sweetheart?" Kenz's eyes flashed. "You arrogant son of a—"

A gust of wind rushed through the cottage, propelling Kenz against the wall, holding her inches above the ground. Azrael's hair blew around his face, and his eyes widened as an unseen pressure forced the knife away from the man's throat, allowing him to turn.

Azrael's lungs burned. He gasped for breath, scolding himself for letting the Air Spectral face him.

"Kenz, I need you to control your emotions. Can you do that?" The man's eyes never left Azrael, who dropped to his knees, struggling to breathe, his knuckles whitening on the hilt of the dagger. Kenz mumbled a yes, and she lowered to the ground.

"Jasce, I will answer your questions once you return the knife to Kord," the man said, his voice even. "Please."

Black spots floated in Azrael's vision. He bit back his fury and slid the knife along the ground to Kord. The minute the blade left Azrael's hand, air rushed into his lunges. He focused on the colorful pattern of the rug and drew in a deep breath, his knees stinging from hitting the stone floor. Balling his fists, he peered through the curtain of hair that fell over his face. Kenz leaned against the wall, giving him a satisfied smile.

"Wonderful," the older man said, sitting in one of the two chairs. "Please, sit."

Azrael glanced at Kord and winced at the blood dripping down his chin, soaking his tunic.

"Sorry about that," Azrael mumbled, getting to his feet.

"No worries," Kord said. "I'm sure I'll be repaying you soon enough." Kord held a hand over his nose and a crack punctuated the silence. He slid to the floor, his face ashen, and rested his head against the wall. Kenz rushed over to wipe the blood away with a rag, her eyes shooting daggers at Azrael.

Kord waved her away. "I'm fine. Quit acting like a mother hen."

Kenz smacked him on the head. "Idiot." Her face lit up as she smiled at her brother, and Azrael's stomach flipped. He tore his gaze from Kenz and stared at the older man, who watched him intently, his blue eyes sparkling.

Azrael plopped down in the comfortable chair and almost groaned. Seven days of torture and traveling had taken its toll. He sighed, rubbing his temples, and leaned into the cushions.

"I bet you could use a drink," the man said.

"You read my mind." Azrael opened his eyes. "You can't do that, too, can you?"

The man laughed, reaching for a decanter full of amber liquid and two glasses. "No, I cannot read minds. My dominant power is manipulating the air, obviously, but I can wield the other elements." The man poured two drinks and handed one to Azrael, who swallowed it in one gulp, savoring the smooth, smoky flavor.

"I didn't think that was possible."

"Oh, it's possible, but at a cost. Most Elementals can manipulate all the elements—air, fire, water, and earth—but choose to focus on their primary ability." The man took a sip of his drink and placed it on the table, his eyes darting to Kenz and then focusing on Azrael. "My name is Amycus, by the way. Amycus Reins."

Azrael leaped from his chair and smacked into a wall of indigo light. Kenz stood next to her brother with her hand raised, her shield enclosing around Azrael. He glared at Amycus. His mind had been too hazy when he woke in the cave, but now he remembered Kord mentioning the name. It was common enough, but he should have known. He should have put the pieces together. Who else had the nerve to send two Spectrals into Bradwick Prison to rescue the Angel of Death?

"You're wanted for the murder of King Valeri," he said. Azrael couldn't believe the man who started the war between the monarchy and the Spectrals sat before him, sharing a drink.

"I know that's what you've heard," Amycus said, his palms raised. "But please let me explain. Then, if you want to take me back to Opax, you may."

"What?" Kenz said, her eyes wide. "You can't mean that, Amycus. Why would you even offer that?"

Kord rose to his full height, his nose healed, and crossed his arms. "That's not going to happen. If he doesn't like what you have to say, then he dies. Not you."

Amycus raised his brows. "That's not like you, Kord."

Kenz pointed at Azrael. "He's a Hunter, a murderer. His life isn't worth anything. You're too important to sacrifice yourself."

Azrael frowned, trying to ignore the sting of Kenz's words, and took a deep breath, considering the situation. If he didn't like what Amycus said, he could take him to Drexus. He might regret killing Kord and Kenz, but returning a wanted criminal would put Azrael back on top. The queen might even offer him command of the Watch Guard. Either way, Drexus wouldn't doubt his loyalty to the mission or think him a liability. It was a win-win. All he had to do was listen and then take the traitor back to Opax.

Kord and Kenz were still arguing when Azrael interrupted. "Will you two shut up?"

Their mouths dropped open.

"Lower the shield, Kenz," Amycus said, his eyes never leaving Azrael's.

"I don't think that's a good idea," Kenz said.

"It will be fine, I promise."

Kenz lowered her hand and the indigo light disappeared. "You breathe wrong and I will kill you. Understand?" Kenz pointed her sword at Azrael's chest while Kord walked to Amycus's side, removing his sword from its sheath.

The corner of Azrael's lip turned up. Three powerful Spectrals against one lethal assassin could be interesting. He settled into the chair, crossing his ankle over his knee. "Tell your story, old man. And it better be good."

Amycus leaned back, his fingers steepled under his chin. "You had to have been around eight when the conflict began. I'm sure you're familiar with its history."

"After the Vastane's fled, you killed the king. Because of you, the steward issued a decree for the Watch Guard to tag, capture, or kill Spectrals. Does that sum it up for you?"

Amycus's eyes hardened. "I did not kill King Valeri. I would never dream of hurting Dietrich. Not only was he my king, but also my friend." Sadness filled his voice. "Someone falsely accused me."

"Guilty people always say that." Azrael held Amycus's penetrating stare. "Okay, for argument's sake, who accused you?"

"Drexus Zoldac."

Azrael huffed out a laugh. "What does Drexus have to do with you?"

"I worked as a blacksmith in the palace, but the king didn't know I was a Spectral. I had also forged a strong friendship with Drexus. We were like brothers, but he didn't know of my magic either. It was a different time then." Amycus poured Azrael another drink. "Anyway, Drexus had this idea of using the Brymagus plant to subdue Spectral powers. I helped with his research."

"Why would you do that?"

"I wanted to keep track of Drexus's progress, and I honestly didn't think he would do anything to harm Spectrals. He was just curious—brilliant too. Then the Vastanes invaded, and I revealed my magic, offering my services to the king. When Drexus found out, he felt betrayed, and our friendship ended." Amycus traced the scars on his hand. "During the war, Drexus developed an insatiable need for power. He obsessed over magic. When the war ended, he found the perfect opportunity to take the power he craved and blamed me for the king's murder."

"But why?" Azrael asked.

Amycus's eyes darkened. "Because Drexus killed the king."

Azrael's mouth dropped open. "Drexus is commander of the Watch Guard, sworn to protect the royal family."

"With Dietrich's death, he could put himself in a position of power. Who do you think pushed for Steward Brenet to take control, suggesting the queen, because of her grief, wasn't fit to rule? The steward is weak, easily influenced. I'm surprised Drexus hasn't had him assassinated yet."

Azrael kept his face blank and reached for his drink. The alcohol warmed his throat but couldn't thaw the ice spreading through his veins. He knew Drexus craved power; he had told him in their last meeting when he ordered Azrael to kill the steward.

"I believe Drexus wants to rule Pandaren, and he has the ear of the steward and the entire council. The only people who could oppose him are Spectrals, which is why he needs to get rid of us," Amycus said.

Azrael stood and paced around the room, his mind a jumble of impossible notions. He shook his head. "How do I know you're not lying?"

Kenz huffed. "Because he's an honest man, unlike you."

Kord sighed and shook his head, turning away.

"One," Azrael said, stopping in front of her, forcing himself not to look at her mouth. "I've never lied to you or your brother. And two, why are you still here?"

Kenz crossed her arms and glared as Azrael continued pacing. He couldn't deal with her hatred right now, or how his body kept betraying him when she was near.

"I have no reason to lie to you, Jasce," Amycus said.

Azrael pointed at Amycus. "It's Azrael. Do not call me Jasce." Amycus leaned back in his chair as Azrael paced circles around the room. He thought about the map in Drexus's study and their last conversation. *I will rule this kingdom with you by my side, if you so desire.* Azrael refilled his glass and drank it in one swallow. Had Drexus killed the king and started this war between the Watch Guard and Spectrals? Could he believe Amycus? His story made sense. Drexus's desire for power was blatantly obvious, as well as his hatred of Spectrals.

Azrael rubbed his hand down his face, thinking about the Watch Guard and the tattoo branded on his skin. Loyalty, honor, and obedience. What did those words mean anymore? If Drexus had killed the king, then he was a traitor, and Bronn had betrayed Azrael for power. Where was the honor or loyalty? And the Angel of Death had performed the role of an obedient servant without thinking twice. What exactly had he fought for these past thirteen years? He had more questions than answers.

Azrael's eyes darted around the room, his anger escalating again, the walls closing in. Amycus stood, worry etched in the creases around his eyes.

"I need to get out of here," Azrael said, and strode out the door in search of the nearest tavern.

CHAPTER 7

The Iron Glass Tavern, one of two taverns in town, was located across from the large fountain Azrael had seen when first riding into Carhurst. Noisy patrons occupied the tables and most of the barstools, and the smell of roasting meat made his stomach rumble. He found a secluded spot along the bar that gave him an unobstructed view of the room. In his search for a tavern, he had located a stable and dunked his head in the trough to wash away the grime and sand. If only it were that easy to cleanse himself from the earlier conversation. Water dripped down his back as he frowned into his glass, searching for answers floating in the golden liquid.

Was Drexus capable of killing the king? Azrael snorted into his drink. Of course he was. Killing and placing the blame on someone else sounded precisely like something Drexus would do. But could he trust Amycus? Of the two, Amycus hadn't caused him any harm, going to dangerous lengths to rescue him, where Drexus had left him to die.

Azrael tossed back the rest of his drink, bitterness settling in his gut as he thought about the three words that had dictated most of his life: loyalty, honor, obedience. He would continue to honor his promise to kill the Fire Spectral and those who betrayed him, but he would devote his loyalty to himself. He would never be someone's pawn again, blindly obeying orders. He tapped his finger on the bar, the metal cuff clinking on the sticky surface. He grimaced and glared at his empty glass.

He needed to get these cuffs off.

"What do you hope to find in there?" asked a pretty barmaid with blonde hair and warm brown eyes.

"A reprieve."

"From what?" She smiled, sitting on an empty stool.

Azrael's eyes slid down her body. The alcohol adequately numbed his brain, but a little female companionship could make him forget everything, at least for a while.

"What's your name?" he asked.

She opened her mouth to answer, but a balding man squatting on the other side of the bar interrupted her, a dirty rag slung over his shoulder.

"Linnette, I don't pay you to sit!"

Linnette rolled her eyes. "Yeah, all right, Garin." She hopped off the stool, giving Azrael an apologetic smile.

He grabbed her hand. "How about a bowl of stew and your company when you get a break?"

Linnette grinned, wiping away a water droplet that slid down Azrael's neck. "You got it."

Azrael admired her swishing hips as she sauntered past a table with four men who also took in the scenery. Their attention shifted to Azrael, their looks of appreciation transforming into scowls. A muscular man sneered. His neck was so thick that Azrael didn't think he could wrap his hands around it.

Muscles might be a challenge, but the other three were a waste of breath. A beefy man, his love for drink evident in the gut hanging over his pants, had ale dripping down his curly beard. Next to Beefy sat a mousy man whose eyes darted from Muscles to Azrael. The third was short, bald, and looked too drunk to stand.

Azrael grunted and turned his back on the table.

Linnette returned with the stew while Garin poured him another drink. Azrael placed two coins on the bar, having nicked them from an unsuspecting patron when first entering the tavern. In his rush to leave Amycus and the siblings, Azrael had given little thought to where he'd sleep. He hadn't any money; it was another problem he needed to solve.

"Thank you, Linnette," Azrael said, the meat and gravy in the stew making his mouth water.

"You know my name, handsome. What's yours?"

Azrael was about to answer when a hand fell on his shoulder, giving it a forceful squeeze. "It's Az," Kord said. "How're you doing, Linnette?"

"Oh, hi, Kord. Keeping busy. Can I get you anything?"

"Ale, please." Kord sat, giving Azrael a big smile.

"What do you want?" Azrael asked, turning back to his stew. He wasn't in the mood for company, at least not Kord's. He'd had enough of him and his sister over the last few days. Of course, he'd expected one of them to show up. There's no way they'd leave a Hunter to run around town unsupervised.

"Thought I'd come check on you, plus a drink sounded like a good idea." Kord lifted his tankard and tapped it to Azrael's glass before taking a long swig.

Azrael shrugged and went back to eating, sneaking glances at Linnette whenever she walked by. His eyes followed her movements and crossed paths with the four men from earlier, who were still glaring at him.

Kord followed his gaze. "Those guys are trouble, especially when they're drinking."

"They're idiots." Azrael turned back to the bar, his words slurring. His shoulders loosened, the alcohol and food warming his belly.

"How much have you had to drink?"

"Don't know. Don't care." Azrael lifted his empty glass to get the barkeep's attention. Garin shrugged his stocky shoulders and poured him another drink. Azrael relaxed into the sound of clinking glasses and the low rumble of voices mixed with laughter.

Kord shook his head and was about to say something when two men a few stools down caught Azrael's attention.

"That's what I heard. The Angel of Death is wanted for treason," one man said.

"Who has the nerve or steel to go after him?"

"Well, he got caught once, or so the rumors go. But he escaped and the Watch Guard is after him, along with those Hunters."

"As long as they stay on their side of the desert, who cares?"

"One day they'll cross the desert."

Azrael instinctively surveyed the room, searching for the Watch Guard uniform or, magic forbid, the grinning skull mask. One question answered, at least. Drexus knew he had escaped. And now, instead of being the hunter, he was the prey. The silver cuffs, his ever-present prison, clinked menacingly on the bar.

"I need these off," Azrael said, pulling on one.

Kord shook his head, "Too dangerous."

"Too dangerous? For who? If the Hunters find me, I'll need my magic."

"Don't worry. We left a few false trails and rumors of our own. There's even one where you're dead. Sorry." He winked. "Oh, and another where you sailed to the Far Lands."

Those rumors wouldn't hold off the Hunters for long. Eventually, they would cross the desert, and Bronn would want to finish what he started, despite any orders Drexus may or may not have given. Azrael gripped his drink, the veins in his hand protruding through his skin as he visualized the betrayal, Distria shooting arrow after poisoned arrow into him. The glass in his hand shattered.

Kord swore and grabbed a rag from Garin, trying to staunch the blood dripping onto the bar.

Linnette's raised voice broke through Azrael's thoughts. She struggled to get out of Beefy's lap as he tried to kiss her while the other three laughed. Azrael pushed away from the bar, ignoring the blood dripping from his hand, his lips curling.

"Not a good idea," Kord said as Azrael stalked toward the table.

"You got a problem?" Beefy said, sweat dripping down his face, his arm tightening around Linnette.

"I have four problems," Azrael said, his words slurred. "Let her go."

"What's a drunk fool like you going to do about it?" said the mousy-look-ing man.

Azrael grabbed Mouse's head and slammed it onto the table, the force knocking over their drinks. A loud cry rang out as Mouse held his nose, tears streaming down his bloody face while the other three jumped up and knocked Linnette to the floor.

Azrael surveyed the men, his brain foggy and sluggish. A wise person would advise against fighting three men in his condition, but the events of the last few weeks stoked his anger like a spark landing among dried leaves. He rolled his neck and a satisfying crack echoed in his ears.

Baldy charged. Azrael dipped his shoulder and flipped him over his back, lunging away from Beefy's jab. Fists flew and furniture sailed through the air, and even in Azrael's drunken state, he knocked Baldy and Beefy unconscious. Then Muscles approached, cracking his knuckles.

"Finally, a challenge," Azrael said. They exchanged punches, to the delight of the gathered crowd. Another man joined the fight, landing a punch to Azrael's jaw. Azrael spun with an off-balanced kick to the man's face, hearing a gratifying crunch when his foot connected. He staggered, not moving fast enough to avoid Muscle's punch to the stomach, which knocked the air out of him.

"Watch out!" Linnette yelled.

Azrael turned toward the barmaid, her eyes wide, a hand covering her mouth. Stars exploded as someone hit him on the head with a bottle, and he dropped to a knee among the shattered glass. Azrael growled, trying to stand when a chair crashed against his back. In seconds, Muscles had him by the throat, pressing him against a table while fists pounded into his face and body.

Kord's voice drifted through a muddled tunnel of pain, blood, and alcohol. "All right boys, he's had enough."

CHAPTER 8

The sun gleamed through a window, making Azrael groan and cover his eyes with a pillow. The last thing he remembered was the pretty blonde with warm brown eyes and a chair crashing into his back.

He sat up and winced, looking around the sparsely decorated living room. An intricately carved wooden table separated him from two tan overstuffed chairs, similar to the ones at Amycus's. A mantle hung over a fireplace, covered with little pots containing what he assumed were herbs. He ran his hand over the bright swatches of color in a quilt covering his legs.

Azrael inhaled the vanilla and cinnamon smell wafting from down the hall. He tried to stand and hissed, a blinding pain stabbing him in the back of his head.

That would be from the bottle some coward hit him with. He winced when he felt the bump.

He dropped his head into his hands. Even though he drank too much and his body hurt, he no longer felt like he was going to explode. Hand-to-hand combat, especially against four at the same time, had released the week of suppressed magic and anger.

Azrael sensed another presence in the room and looked up slowly. A boy around the age of ten stared at him, his green eyes narrowed. He was tall, with black wavy hair that touched the top of his shoulders. The two appraised each other until the silence became uncomfortable.

"Hello," Azrael said.

"Mom! He's awake!" the boy yelled, never taking his eyes off him. Azrael moaned and dropped his head back in his hands.

"Sorry about that," a pleasant voice said.

A beautiful woman with long red hair and sky-blue eyes smiled from the hallway. Azrael's mouth dropped open.

"Easy there, that's my wife you're gaping at," Kord said, walking out of the kitchen with a pastry and mug in hand.

"Your wife?" Azrael asked.

Kord chuckled, wrapping an arm around the woman. "Yes, this is Tillie and my son, Maleous. Haring family, this is, um . . ."

"You don't know his name?" Tillie said, tapping her toe.

"Yes, I know his name, or should I say names." Kord raised his eyebrows at Azrael.

"Az," Azrael said, rubbing his temples and frowning at his bare feet.

"Nice to meet you, Az." Tillie turned to Kord, kissing him on the cheek. "Maleous and I have to get to the bakery, so we'll see you later." Maleous waved as he walked out the front door. Azrael leaned around Kord to get a better look.

"Stop gawking," Kord said, smacking Azrael on his head; the sudden pain made him gasp. "You look dreadful, by the way." He placed the mug and pastry on the table and sat across from him.

"I feel dreadful," Azrael said, massaging the back of his neck.

Kord laughed, causing Azrael to wince again and drop his head into his hands. A bitter sweetness tickled his nose.

Azrael looked up, a sudden idea bursting through his clouded brain. "Could you take care of my headache? You know, with your magic?"

"I could." Kord smiled. "But I won't. These are the consequences of over-indulging and being stupid. One doesn't learn if one doesn't suffer through the pain."

"One shouldn't give life lessons this early in the morning," Azrael mumbled, eyeing the steaming mug of black liquid.

Kord chuckled. "It's mid-morning. We let you sleep in."

"Let me?" Azrael frowned. No one *let him* do anything. He was second in command to the most lethal force in the land. Or had been. His position, title, and reputation were destroyed thanks to Drexus and Bronn. He had been a member of the Watch Guard for thirteen years—that was all he had known. Who was he now that he wasn't one of them, one of the feared Hunters?

Azrael took a tentative sip of the brew, sighing as a jolt of energy ran through his system. He bit into the pastry, uncomfortably aware of Kord's scrutiny. He moaned, the delicacy melting in his mouth.

"This is really good," Azrael said, shoving in another bite.

"I'll be sure to tell Tillie you enjoyed her pastries." When Azrael raised his brows, Kord continued. "She works at the bakery down the road—has made quite a name for herself."

"Beautiful and talented," Azrael said, a smile tugging at his lips.

Kord shook his head. "Come on. Amycus wants to see you. There's a change of clothes in the washroom down the hall. Clean up first, you stink."

In the village, a hive of people buzzed around the town square. Vendors in colorful stalls sold their wares and mothers conversed, keeping a watchful eye on their children who played in a nearby fountain. Azrael inhaled the smells of spices, fruits, and roasting meat drifting through the autumn air.

Kord stopped at a booth that sold chairs and tables similar to the ones in his house. He talked with the man behind the counter while Azrael leaned against a post, his eyes scanning for any threats.

"You got another order for a bookcase and they want Kenz to do the scrollwork," the man said.

Azrael observed the Healer out of the corner of his eye. Kord never mentioned that he and his sister worked in the carpentry trade. But why would he?

A talented family.

Kord finished up his business and continued toward Amycus's.

"So, you and your sister are carpenters?"

Kord nodded. "Yes. Well, I do most of the carpentry. She's more into the detail work and runs the booth. Our parents used to own the business, but they died years ago, so Kenz and I took it upon ourselves to follow in their footsteps."

"How did they die?"

Kord shoved his hands into his pockets, sadness filling his eyes. "They died fighting the Vastanes. Mom was a Water and Dad an Amp."

Azrael thought about this as they continued through the marketplace. No wonder Kord and Kenz were so strong, with both parents having magic. They had been young when they lost their parents in the war, but at least they had each other.

Many villagers greeted Kord with smiles and friendly hellos while giving Azrael a cursory glance. They had no idea the Angel of Death lurked among them, but without his mask, swords, or armor, he appeared common. Normally, he felt powerful when people saw him—relied on it. Now he was overlooked, an insignificant leaf fluttering in the wind.

Part of Azrael relished the ambiguity—no responsibilities or expectations, no one knowing his hands dripped with blood. But a casual stroll through the marketplace couldn't eradicate the death clinging to him.

Kord looked back and slowed, a frown replacing his usual smile. "There's this dark cloud surrounding you. Can you feel it?" he asked, reaching out.

Azrael lurched back. "I prefer the shadows."

Kord lowered his hand with a low chuckle. "Well, that's dramatic." He continued walking toward the blacksmith's cottage, his broad shoulders quaking with laughter. Azrael glowered and trudged after him, the villagers unaware of the danger in their midst.

Inside the cottage, Kord sat and yawned and rested his feet on Amycus's desk. Azrael's hands relaxed at the sound of hammering and the familiar smell of hot steel. He walked down the hall to the forge, passing a bedroom overlooking a large courtyard.

Amycus beat an unfinished piece of metal into the beginnings of a sword, sparks flying while sweat dripped off his long nose. Well-loved tools organized into neat rows lined the walls next to sturdy worktables. The room reminded Azrael of the forge in Delmar where Braxium had taught Azrael the trade.

He picked up a sword, running his thumb along the dull blade. If his life hadn't changed so drastically, Azrael could have seen himself as a blacksmith, creating instead of destroying.

"I'm almost finished," Amycus said, dipping the sword into water and causing a cloud of vapor to form a misty barrier. His eyes darted from Azrael to the sword in his hand. "Make yourself at home in the other room."

Azrael lowered the weapon and returned to the living room, taking in the minor details he overlooked yesterday. The late morning light shone through the curtains, illuminating floating dust motes while a welcoming fire danced in the hearth. Kord dozed, his soft snores filling the silence as Azrael examined the haphazardly stacked books and trinkets crammed into the bookcase. He studied Kord and Kenz's handiwork, eyeing the intricate carvings along the wood, the attention to detail impressive. Azrael chewed the inside of his cheek. He could picture Kord crafting the pieces, but he had a hard time imagining Kord's sister carving the unique designs. Kenz didn't seem the delicate type.

He was scrutinizing a unique chunk of glass when Amycus walked in, wiping his face and hands with a rag.

"That's what happens when wet sand meets extreme heat," Amycus said, nodding toward the glass in Azrael's hand. "We were testing out one of my student's powers and got that as a bonus."

Azrael's grip tightened. "You have a Fire Spectral?"

"I *had* a Fire Spectral. Drexus killed her." Amycus shoved Kord's feet off his desk, and Kord snorted awake, mumbling an apology. Amycus sat in the chair from yesterday and poured himself some tea, offering the kettle to Azrael, who shook his head.

"Do you have any other Fires?"

Amycus frowned. "Yes."

"Do any of them have black fire?" Azrael tried to relax his hands.

"No, why?"

Azrael put the strange-shaped glass on the bookshelf, unsure if he felt disappointed or relieved.

He tried to imagine Drexus and Amycus as friends—young men working together, experimenting with magic. The war had taken each boy down a different path. One wanted to control magic, while the other tried to protect it.

As Watch Guard soldiers, you are the only ones who can protect the Naturals—capture and restrain, or exterminate. That is your job, your mission. Drexus always gave that speech to the recruits, and Azrael had stood by his side, the vigilant soldier. But ever since experiencing the emotions from the Spectrals, Azrael had questioned the Watch Guard's mission and Drexus's belief that all Spectrals were evil. Currently, he was the evilest one in the room.

Kenz stormed in, the door slamming against the wall.

Was the evilest. Azrael laughed to himself.

"A bar fight? Really?" Kenz marched to where Kord sat and smacked her brother on the head. "And I heard you watched the whole thing."

Kord pushed her away. "He needed to burn off some steam, and Terrell and his gang had it coming. Az was quite chivalrous."

"A chivalrous assassin? Oh, that's rich."

Azrael frowned as a shiver ran down his spine, not liking how his body kept reacting to Kenz, even when she was scowling, her green eyes flashing. Her black hair hung in a long braid and her cheeks were flushed. She wore a blue tunic and form-fitting pants. Azrael swallowed. Very form-fitting pants.

The siblings continued their argument while Amycus looked on with an amused expression.

"Do you ever suck the air out of their lungs just to shut them up?"

"It is tempting." Amycus waved his hand. A gust of wind rushed through the room, silencing the two. As entertaining as this was, Azrael wanted answers before the headache pulsing behind his eyes turned into a migraine.

"You claim to know me. I'd like to know how." Azrael crossed his ankle over his knee, tapping a finger on his thigh.

"Ah, yes. Well, for a time, I worked with Braxium in his forge in Delmar."

"I don't remember seeing you."

"No, you wouldn't have. I left when you were only a couple years old." He paused, his fingers steepled under his chin, eyes sad. "I knew your family. My heart broke when I heard what happened to Lisia and your sister."

Azrael maintained a blank expression, gripping the chair. Hearing his mother's name unleashed a flood of feelings he didn't want to confront, but no matter how far he shoved the memories down, his mother's gray eyes and his sister's screams continued to haunt him.

"I never heard what became of Barnet," Amycus said, retrieving a satchel and placing it at Azrael's feet.

"He's dead."

"I'm sorry to hear that."

"Don't be. I killed him." Azrael focused on the hatred in his heart, blocking out the pain from the past. Kenz's gauntlets sparked to life, her hand tightening on the hilt of her sword. Kord frowned and crossed his massive arms.

Good. They needed to remember who he is, what he's capable of.

The logs crackled in the fireplace while Amycus studied Azrael, his mouth turned down. Azrael looked away from the penetrating gaze and to the canvas bag at his feet.

"Open it," Amycus said, his voice wavering. "I helped Braxium develop that interlocking armor, you know."

Azrael's eyes widened. His black chest plate peeked out of the bag. "I thought the villagers took it when they captured me. You've had it this whole time?" He glared at the siblings.

"Did you think we'd actually give it to you?" Kenz said, shaking her head.

Azrael pulled the armor from the bag, brushing his fingers over the familiar metal. He had spent hours perfecting the design with Nigel at the Bastion. Bronn had often joked about Azrael's strange relationship with his armor. He ran a hand along the spot where the arrow had pierced his back and shoulder; he could see through the metal where the sword had stabbed him. He gritted his teeth, pushing down the rage.

"I see you've made improvements to the original design," Amycus said, staring at the intricate piece. "It's very well done. Thought you'd like to repair it in my forge."

"Thank you," Azrael mumbled, his eyes darting from Kenz to Kord. "For retrieving it."

"That hurt, didn't it?" Kord chuckled, putting his feet back on Amycus's desk.

Azrael started returning the armor to the bag and then stopped, noticing his mask lying on the bottom. He picked it up, tracing his finger over the white skull smiling at him.

"That thing is hideous, by the way," Kenz said, leaning against the desk, her lips pursed.

"It's supposed to be. After all, death smiles at everyone." His eyes flicked around the room. "And my swords?"

Kenz snorted. "Yeah, right."

Azrael scowled, wanting to strangle and kiss her at the same time. He shoved the items into the bag and stood. He had decided to believe Amycus; the pieces connected too conveniently, but the puzzle wasn't complete. Yet.

"I believe you didn't betray the king," he said. "However, if I find out you lied, I will kill you."

Amycus held his stare, the skin around his eyes tightening. Kord stood and walked behind Amycus's chair. Kenz's gauntlets glowed.

"I need to leave, so remove the cuffs."

"Where will you go?" Amycus asked, relaxing into his chair.

"Back to Orilyon, to talk with Drexus. Plus, three Hunters have a destiny with me and my hideous mask." Azrael sneered at Kenz.

"The Watch Guard is searching for you," Amycus said.

"Another reason for me to leave. Kord mentioned the false trails, but eventually, the Hunters will cross the desert and find me. I'm sure you don't want them raiding your peaceful little village."

"We can protect the village," Kenz said to Azrael, then she looked at Amycus. "We don't need him. There are plenty of us that . . ."

Azrael's head tilted as he slipped Kenz a curious glance.

Amycus held up his hand, regarding Azrael. "It would be in your best interest to stay."

"Why?"

"Because there is so much you don't know about your past. About your mother."

"What about my mother?" Azrael growled, gripping the handle of the satchel.

"Your mother was a Spectral."

CHAPTER 9

"What did you say?" Azrael whispered, blood pounding in his ears. He had to have heard Amycus wrong. It wasn't possible. He would've seen his mother's powers, wouldn't he? And why would another Spectral kill her? It made no sense.

Amycus stared into the distance. "Lisia was a Psyche. Her ability to move objects with her mind was quite extraordinary."

Azrael stood, hands clenched by his side. "Do not lie to me, old man." He strode forward, swearing as he crashed into Kenz's shield, the indigo light glowing around him.

"Why would I lie to you? I have nothing to gain. And I value my life," Amycus said with a lopsided smile.

Azrael glared, shifting his eyes toward Kenz. "Lower it."

"No." Kenz flicked her wrists, making the shield thicker.

Azrael pressed his hands against the indigo wall, his cuffs feeling like weighted irons. His mother couldn't be a Spectral. But if she was, and if that was why his father betrayed her, then he wished he had taken his time killing the man.

More lies, more deceit.

Azrael's body shook, his teeth bared as wave after violent wave of anger crashed into him. With a guttural roar, his fist collided with the shield. He pounded the wall again and again, and with every strike, he pictured his father, Drexus, the Hunters. With every hit, he released his fury.

Azrael panted, his knuckles bloody. He used all his strength for one final punch that made Kenz wince. Kord moved from behind Amycus's chair, glaring at Azrael.

Amycus frowned. "Are you finished?"

Azrael lowered his head, arms hanging at his side. His mind reeled. He had just started wrapping his brain around Drexus killing the king, and now this.

Why didn't his mother tell him? Why would she hide it?

Azrael closed his eyes and breathed deeply. Focus on the problem and not the why, he told himself. He ran trembling hands through his hair, retied it, and lowered himself into the chair.

"Tell me about my mother." His voice cut like sharpened steel.

Amycus sipped his tea and placed the cup on the table. "As I said, your mother was a powerful Psyche. After the assassination of King Valeri, Steward Brenet targeted the Spectrals he considered the most valuable or the biggest threat. Lisia aided an underground group helping them escape, and someone discovered her powers and involvement."

Azrael huffed. "One guess who."

Amycus nodded. "Yes, unfortunately, I think it was Barnet, but I don't think he ever dreamed . . ." Amycus shook his head.

Azrael thought back to the day men in black cloaks and masks attacked his village. Jaida had gripped his hand, her entire body trembling. Their mother knelt defiantly in the dirt, black fire circling her. "Was she involved in the king's assassination?"

He pleaded the opposite. Please don't be connected with his murder, don't be tied to Drexus. He couldn't imagine his mother working with the same man who created the Angel of Death.

Amycus shook his head. "No." Azrael sighed, relaxing his damaged hands. "Anyway, Spectral powers can be hereditary, though not necessarily the same gifting."

Kord straightened. "It's not for sure. Maleous has shown no sign of having magic, and he's almost eleven. He may be like his mother. It's just—not for sure."

Azrael frowned. "You don't want your son to be like you?"

"I don't want my son targeted because of me."

Kenz gave her brother a somber smile and held his arm.

Azrael nodded, looking at Amycus. "So, are you implying that I may be a Spectral?"

"I am."

Azrael laughed. "I would've known if I could move objects with my mind or control elements, or"—he waved his hand toward the siblings—"do what they do. And lower your blasted shield." He glared at Kenz, tired of hearing the echo of his words bounce off his glowing prison.

Amycus nodded and the indigo wall vanished. Azrael arched a brow as both siblings stepped closer with their hands on their weapons.

"That tattoo would have suppressed your magic, if you had any," Amycus said, staring at the two triangles on Azrael's arm.

"I don't understand."

"Lisia knew that I'd worked with Drexus. And where Drexus used the Brymagus plant to make the collars, I took the liquid form and incorporated it into ink."

Azrael frowned, pulling a loose thread from his tunic. "If she was helping Spectrals, why would one kill her? She was innocent."

Kenz laughed, the sound inconsistent with the hatred in her eyes. "Does anyone else see the irony? You kill innocent people all the time."

Azrael slowly rose from the chair. Kord stepped between them with his palms raised, a pleading look on his face.

Amycus also stood, wind circling the room. "Jasce, don't."

Restrained fury vibrated through Azrael, his nails leaving deep grooves in his palms. "You mock the death of my mother and sister?"

"She didn't mean it," Kord said, hands still raised.

"Don't you speak for me," Kenz said, but her voice wavered, the fire having gone out of her eyes.

Kord faced his sister. "For the love of all that's magical, stop! You don't know what he's gone through."

The fury drained out of Azrael. He couldn't remember the last time someone had defended the Angel of Death. With one last glare at Kenz, he went back to his seat, flexing his hands and not wanting to admit her words disturbed him. He had justified every capture and kill, convincing himself he was protecting the Naturals, but in reality, his life was a walking contradiction.

Kord led Kenz to the other side of the room, whispering to her, resting his hands on her shoulders. Her eyes darted between her brother and Azrael, then she nodded and leaned against the wall, folding her arms.

"I still don't understand why a Spectral would kill her," Azrael said, attempting to compose his tone.

"How do you know it was a Spectral?"

"Because normal fire isn't black, nor does it move the way this fire did. It slithered around the man who held a knife against my mother's neck."

The blood rushed from Amycus's face. "I didn't know," he whispered, rising from his chair. He walked to where he kept the alcohol and poured a drink, his hands shaking.

Azrael frowned. "What is it?"

Amycus shook his head, giving a smile that didn't reach his eyes. "Lisia would've done anything to protect you and Jaida." He drank the whiskey and returned to his chair.

Azrael ran his finger along the carvings in the chair, struggling to swallow the lump in his throat. He blocked the images of his mother's death and thought about the tattoo. "If the tattoo suppresses magic, then why am I able to use the Amp power? The transfusion shouldn't have worked."

Amycus steepled his fingers under his chin. "I designed the tattoo to dampen your inherent magic, but the serum, on the other hand, is not a natural part of you. Think of the Amplifier magic like a virus, which your tattoo wasn't meant to fight."

"Is there a way to find out if Azrael is a Spectral?" Kord asked, standing next to Amycus.

Amycus nodded. "We'd have to remove the tattoo to know for sure. But there's no record of anyone having multiple forms of magic. There's a risk, Jasce, and I'm not sure how it will affect you."

"What risk?" Azrael and Kord both said together.

"And my name is Azrael," he growled. Amycus's eyes glinted, a smile tugging at his lips. Kord looked from Azrael to Amycus while Kenz fiddled with her gauntlets.

"I believe that if a Spectral were to receive another form of magic, they'd either go insane or die," Amycus said. "But if you have magic, then it's dormant, therefore the serum wouldn't affect you that way. I think."

Azrael sat up straighter, a thought occurring to him. "When I received the serum, I began to feel Spectrals' emotions, like sorrow and regret." He lifted a finger, glaring at Kenz, who opened her mouth to speak. "Whatever you're going to say, don't. I may not feel guilt, but I'm certain you do."

"I'm not feeling guilty," Kenz said, averting her gaze.

"Your face reveals more than you think." Azrael turned to Amycus. "I had assumed the emotions were a side effect from the serum, but maybe it's because I have another form of magic within me."

Amycus frowned, staring at something over Azrael's shoulder. After a while, he nodded. "It might. Unfortunately, there is only one way to find out, and that's where Kord comes in. He should be able to protect you if something goes wrong."

Kenz approached her brother. "Is there any risk to Kord?"

"No, Kord will be fine."

Azrael looked at the tattoos covering his arm and ran his finger along the dagger splitting the two triangles. He was about to come full circle. For the sake of power, he had undergone the transfusion, knowing it might kill him. And now, because of magic, he was about to put his life in danger again.

He wasn't sentimental, but the tattoo was the only thing he had left of his mother. However, he had to know if he had magic, and removing the tattoo seemed the only option. He might as well approach this as any other battle—head-on.

"Just the one. The rest stay," Azrael said.

Amycus peered at the swirls of black ink. "Out of curiosity, why?"

"I have my reasons." Part of Azrael wanted Amycus to remove the Watch Guard tattoo as well, but it served as a reminder, as did the other symbols etched on his arm.

Amycus and Kord left to gather the needed supplies, and an awkward silence filled the cottage. Azrael wandered over to the window, noticing that Kenz had ignited her gauntlets.

"If I wanted you dead, you would be." Azrael stared at the village through the dusty glass. For reasons he couldn't explain, it bothered him that she thought he was a heartless killer. He'd never cared what others thought before; he was doing his job. But her words from earlier were right—his very existence was a paradox. He didn't want to think about how many children he left without a mother or father, either taken to prison or killed. How many boys or girls were planning their own revenge on the Angel of Death?

Kenz sighed, and glasses clinked behind him. "I'm sorry for what I said, and for what happened to your mother and sister."

She held out a drink, but Azrael shook his head, turning back to the window and rubbing his hand along his arm. It must have cost her to apologize, especially since she blamed him for her fiancé's death.

"Might take the edge off. That's a pretty big tattoo."

Azrael didn't want to take the edge off. Besides, the pain didn't bother him; he was used to it, which said a lot about how he grew up.

Amycus and Kord walked back into the room.

"If you please." Amycus nodded to the chair next to a table while Kord took the drink Kenz held and gulped it down. She smacked him on the shoulder and approached the table to help Amycus.

Azrael sat, staring at her green eyes, narrowed slightly, and her mouth, which drew into a thin line. He remembered how her face changed instantly when she smiled at her brother. His stomach trembled then, just as it did now. His nostrils flared and he took a deep breath.

"Nervous?" Kenz asked, regarding him with those hypnotic eyes.

"No." He wasn't nervous about the procedure and didn't want to name whatever he felt when she was near.

She gave him a sly smile. "This is going to hurt."

He chuckled. "Don't sound so pleased." He noticed the dusting of freckles on her nose, the pink in her cheeks. Kenz stared back for a second, then quickly straightened, striding to the other side of the room. Azrael studied her until he glanced at her brother, whose forehead creased, forming a deep line between his eyes.

As Amycus wiped a cold liquid over Azrael's arm, Azrael noticed a small ignitor around his wrist. "It doesn't take much of the plant to subdue a child's power," Amycus said, "but we didn't want to take any chances, hence the size of your tattoo."

Kord stepped closer, frowning at the image. "That must have been excruciating, especially for a kid."

Azrael looked away from the sadness filling Kord's eyes. "Pain is unavoidable; suffering is a choice."

"There will most likely be a scar," Amycus said.

Azrael shrugged. "What's one more?"

Amycus stared at Azrael, his blue eyes full of sadness, and perhaps anger; Azrael couldn't be sure.

"I am sorry," Amycus whispered.

Azrael was about to ask for what when Amycus flicked his ignitor switch and the compact blade glowed, sizzling against his skin. Azrael bit down and closed his eyes, trying to focus on something other than the sound and smell of burning flesh.

A gagging noise made Azrael open his eyes. Kenz covered her mouth, turning a light shade of green. She shook her head, mumbling something about waiting outside.

"She has a weak constitution," Kord said, smiling. He handed Azrael a wooden pole. "Squeeze this instead." He nodded to the fingernail marks in Azrael's palm.

Azrael gripped the pole, his knuckles whitening as the blade continued its path across his arm. He looked from the unnaturally hot instrument to Amycus's face, where a sheen of sweat had broken out on his forehead. Azrael hissed, the blade cutting deeper.

"Sorry," Amycus mumbled, continuing to erase the tattoo.

After what felt like hours, Amycus put the knife down and leaned back, sighing. A cool breeze blew through the cottage, taking the smell and heat with it.

Azrael took a deep breath, sweat dripping down his back and temples. "I'm assuming that was a demonstration of your fire magic?"

Amycus nodded.

"You mentioned there was a cost to being able to use all four elements." It wasn't exactly a question, but Azrael waited. At first, he didn't think Amycus would explain, but his eyes finally opened, the blue paler than before.

"Because I can manipulate all four, my power isn't as strong as those who only wield one, plus I weaken much faster—a price I didn't know I'd have to pay. . ." He trailed off, his eyes focused on his clasped hands.

Kord wiped away the blood, the skin beneath blackened and raw. "We need the cuffs off if you want me to heal him."

Amycus straightened. "Yes, and to see if Jasce is a Spectral." He removed a key from around his neck and inserted it into each cuff.

An unfamiliar current flowed through Azrael, spreading from his chest to his fingertips and surging to a sharp jolt, causing him to jump out of his chair. His heart pounded in his ears, drowning out the sounds from inside the cottage. Azrael's vision darkened around the edges and he gasped, gripping the back of the chair, dizziness overcoming him. He heard Amycus as if from a tunnel, telling Kord not to touch him. He dropped to one knee, his heart feeling like it would explode from his chest, and his hands vibrated, their edges disappearing.

What was happening to him? Were they trying to kill him?

He growled, struggling to stand, and reached for Amycus, but indigo light flashed and blackness swallowed him; the room pitched, the hard stone jarring his bones. The coolness from the floor nipped his cheek while his heartbeat slowed simultaneously with the magical current.

Fire surrounded him, burning his skin. His sister's screams rang in his ears. Rough hands shoved him to his knees.

Azrael thrashed, swatting at the hand holding him down. His vision cleared; bright blue eyes stared down at him. Kord knelt next to Amycus, brows furrowed, and Kenz had one arm raised, her shield encompassing him.

"What happened?" Azrael's mouth felt parched. An electric hum flowed through his system, more intense than the Amp magic alone. He looked at his hands, thinking he must have imagined them disappearing.

"You survived," Amycus said.

"No kidding."

Kord chuckled and Kenz pressed her lips together as she lowered her shield.

"I wasn't sure if your powers would ignite slowly or quickly. As it turns out, they manifested quickly." Amycus smiled and helped Azrael to the couch. "I couldn't have Kord touch you, as we needed the process to complete, but I needed Kenz to put a shield around you, for all of our protection."

"What do you feel?" Kord asked.

Azrael glanced at his hands. "A buzzing inside of me. I'm not sure if I imagined it, but I think my hands may have disappeared for a second."

Amycus sat across from Azrael, his fingers steepled under his chin. "Interesting."

"What's interesting?" Kenz asked before Azrael could.

Amycus leaned forward. "And possibly amazing."

Azrael angled away, opening his mouth to speak.

"What's amazing?" Kord asked.

Azrael glared at the siblings. Amycus ignored the questions. "Kenz, your shield," he said. "I'd like to try something."

Kenz's gauntlets ignited and Azrael shivered, feeling her magic pulse with his. He raised his brow, peering at her and wondering if she felt it, too, but her face remained blank.

"Azrael, focus on your hands, please," Amycus said.

Azrael frowned and stared. Nothing happened.

"Imagine them disappearing."

He flexed his hands and concentrated on the magic thrumming inside him, starting in his core, spreading to his arms and legs. Azrael felt a tug inside his chest, pulling him toward—something.

"Whoa!" Kord jumped back while Amycus laughed. Kenz's hands shook, her eyes wide. Not only had Azrael's hands disappeared, but his arms and part of his chest too. He quickly relaxed his hands and his magic settled into a comfortable hum.

"Kord, pour us some drinks," Amycus said. "And Kenz, you can lower the shield. Everything is fine."

Kenz frowned at Azrael, then looked at Amycus.

"It's fine," he said again. "Lower the shield."

Kenz twisted her wrists and the shield dissolved. Kord placed the drinks on the table, his eyes darting to Azrael, whose hand shook as he reached for the glass and took a long swallow. He leaned back, sighing. "I'm a Spectral, aren't I?" He already knew, but he needed to hear Amycus say it.

"Yes, Jasce." Azrael frowned when Amycus spoke his given name. Amycus continued, "And if I'm not mistaken, you're a Vaulter."

CHAPTER 10

"A what?" Azrael asked, staring into Amycus's smiling eyes. Even though Azrael had the Amplifier magic, he never once considered himself a Spectral. Until now. He couldn't deny the power; this magic felt natural, a missing part of him finally found.

"A Vaulter," Amycus said, smiling. "You can transport your body from one location to another. This is a rare and powerful gift."

"Gift?" The word was strange on his tongue. Since he wasn't dead, he supposed the magic was a gift. He would have to wait and see if he lost his mind. As far as anyone knew, he was the only Spectral with more than one type of magic. If Drexus knew this was possible? Azrael shuddered thinking of the experiments he would try.

"So, since he's alive, does that mean he'll go crazy?" Kenz asked, biting her lip.

Azrael forced himself to stop staring at her mouth.

"Let me heal you," Kord said, sitting next to him. His magic instantly moved through Azrael's burnt skin, a pleasant warmth radiating along his arm, healing the destroyed flesh.

Then Azrael groaned, gripping the front of his tunic and pulling away from Kord.

Kord reached out. "What is it? What's wrong?"

Azrael held out his hand, clenching his jaw against the wave of emotions engulfing him. His throat constricted, hairs rose on the back of his neck and arms, and his entire body shook. Azrael swore, dropping his head in his hands.

"What's going on?" Kenz asked.

"Back away, both of you." Amycus grabbed Azrael's wrists, quickly fastening the cuffs. The sensation was immediate—a blanket quieting the fear, resentment, and regret that had exuded from the others. Azrael drew in a shaking breath and fell against the worn cushions, the electric hum of his magic subdued.

"What happened?" Amycus leaned forward, concern etched on his wrinkled face.

Azrael swallowed and opened his eyes, glancing between Kord and Kenz. "I could feel it all. Too many emotions at one time." He looked away, not wanting to see the horror or apprehension on their faces.

"Is this similar to what you experienced before?" Amycus asked.

Azrael nodded, reaching a shaking hand for his drink, and considered the influx of emotions. The resentment he could handle—it had accompanied his anger for years—but he needed liquid courage to tackle regret and fear. He hadn't allowed himself to feel guilty for any of the atrocities he'd committed as a Hunter, and if he went down that hole, he would never survive. And fear? Watch Guard soldiers had fear disciplined out of them. He knocked back the whiskey in one swallow and grimaced, rubbing his forehead. The wall he had erected over the years crumbled, brick by brick.

Some mighty assassin.

He stared at his trembling hands then raised his head and studied the blacksmith. Amycus had figured out how to manipulate all four elements, something Azrael had never heard before. Maybe the old man could be useful.

"Can you teach me? Help me develop the magic and block these emotions?"

Amycus strummed his fingers on his thigh, his expression thoughtful. "Yes, I believe I can."

Kenz interrupted. "Amycus, may I have a word in private?"

Azrael drew in a long breath and poured himself another drink, trying to ignore how Kord peered at him like he was a mystery the Healer needed to solve.

"Kenz, you can say whatever you need to in front of Jasce. I trust him," Amycus said.

"Yeah, well, I don't." Kenz waved her hand in Azrael's direction and a sound-proofing shield surrounded him. He wanted to laugh at Kenz's silent tantrum, but weariness overcame him. It didn't take a genius to understand the gist of the conversation; he made out words like "powerful" and "get rid of."

He didn't blame her. If he believed Amycus, Azrael was the most powerful known Spectral. The thought filled him with a renewed sense of purpose. The Vaulter and Amp magic made him invincible, and he could easily enact his revenge on Bronn and the others—and overthrow Drexus. He smiled, staring at Kenz, who glared at him with her hands on her hips. He hadn't realized her shield was down.

"What are you smiling about?"

Azrael stood, his eyes surveying her lithe body, satisfied when she stepped back. Amycus remained sitting, his fingers steepled under his chin, while Kord settled onto the couch, still staring at Azrael with a deep crevice between his brows.

"Train me, and I swear no harm will come to any of you."

Kenz snorted. "Why should we believe the word of an assassin?"

"When I make a promise, I keep it. Besides, it's not *you* I want to kill."

"I have another option," Amycus said. "I will teach you, and in return, you will train these two in combat, and any others who wish to join, for one year. Then, at the end of that time, you are free to do whatever you wish."

"Amycus, we don't need his instruction," Kenz said.

Azrael huffed. "Remember the lesson in the desert with my stick?"

Kord sighed and shook his head. Kenz's face flushed, her nostrils flaring.

Azrael turned toward Amycus. "One year? I can't wait that long. Besides, I don't owe you anything." One year in the service of these three? If the magic didn't make him go crazy, that would.

"We rescued you from that prison, so technically you owe me your life." Amycus's voice was like the edge of a knife, his eyes hard. He rose to his feet, eye to eye with Azrael. "There's so much more for you to learn."

Azrael cocked his head. "Like what?"

Amycus smiled. "Do we have a deal?"

༺ ༺ ༺

They agreed on six months. Amycus offered Azrael the use of his spare room in exchange for helping in the forge, but he declined, needing his space.

He would assist the blacksmith to pay for lodging at the Whispering Pines, run by the Taulers, who knew how to mind their own business.

It had taken only minutes to unpack his meager belongings, his armor and mask lying in the bottom drawer of the dresser. Azrael stared at the Hunter mask, the skull sneering back at him. In the last two days his world had turned upside down, and thinking about it made him too antsy to sit in the cramped room, so he walked to the Iron Glass, acquiring his spot at the bar with an unobstructed view of the tavern and its patrons.

Town guards entered the tavern and Azrael reached for his dagger, swearing as his fingers brushing the empty sheath. One soldier surveyed Azrael, homing in on his cuffs, and by the insignia on his uniform, Azrael knew the guard was a captain.

The men he fought the night before sat at the same table. Terrell, the muscly leader, nodded at Azrael, while the other three focused on their card game.

Azrael didn't stay long, the weariness from earlier taking its toll; plus, his new role as instructor started at dawn. The shocked look on Kord and Kenz's faces when he told them when to meet made him smile. He would work them as hard as any recruit at the Bastion, hoping they would convince Amycus to shorten his sentence. He doubted he would be that lucky.

The next morning, Azrael leaned against the wall of the Whispering Pines with a cup of coffee, watching the clouds change from pink to fiery gold. Mrs. Tauler made decent coffee, but not nearly as good as Tillie's. Azrael's lip twitched thinking of the beautiful and talented redhead, envying Kord and wondering what it would be like to go home to someone every night.

Kenz lumbered around the corner, her eyes heavy with sleep, and an intense hunger punched him in the stomach, making him choke on the hot drink. Azrael forced himself to look away and focus on the sunrise.

"Is there a reason you wanted to run this early?" Kenz yawned, braiding her hair.

"Shhh," he whispered. "Here it comes."

"Here what comes?"

"The light chasing away the darkness." He snuck a glance at her from the corner of his eyes. Her hands had stopped midair, mouth partly open as she stared at him.

Kord jogged around the corner, smiling. "Sorry, had to kiss the wife." He winked and then frowned at Kenz. "What did I miss?"

"Nothing," she mumbled, and Kord shrugged. Azrael took one last look at the sun peeking over the horizon then led them down the street, jogging past Lord Rollant's compound where guards patrolled along the wall. Once they entered the forest, Azrael picked up his pace, the burn in his muscles pushing him faster as he left the siblings behind.

He waited in the courtyard, the rhythmic hammering of steel from the forge further relaxing his mind. Kenz finally arrived, holding her side. Sweat gleamed on her flushed face and she immediately went to the water barrel.

Azrael glanced out the gate. "Where's Kord?"

"Vomit," was all she could say between drinks of water.

Azrael laughed. They definitely needed to work on their endurance.

He felt at home training again—the clashing of swords, muscles firing, his mind settling into the familiar routine. Azrael instructed Kord first while Kenz worked on her strength and flexibility. He had to force himself not to stare when she stretched, her fighting leathers showing off every curve.

"Kenz, your turn," Kord said after a while, bracing his hands on his knees. Kenz leaned against the wall with her arms crossed, her face expressionless.

Azrael raised his brow in a silent challenge. "Have you been practicing?" Besides admiring Kenz's appearance, he enjoyed irritating her, amused by her fisted hands and the crease between her eyes.

"Let's find out." Kenz pushed off the wall, grabbing a practice sword while Kord wiped sweat off his forehead and stepped out of the sparring circle. Azrael and Kenz paced the outside of the ring, analyzing each other. He gave her a wink, chuckling when Kord groaned. Kenz bared her teeth and charged, swinging her sword at his head.

Azrael effortlessly parried her attack, watching how she moved. "That's better. You're not favoring your right side as much."

"So glad you approve." She lunged to her right, dodging Azrael's strike.

Azrael taught while they sparred, correcting footwork and arm position. Despite Kenz's hostility, she listened, eager to learn. At one point, he grasped her arm, placing a hand on her hip to help her perform the move he was teaching. She stiffened and he immediately let go.

Hours later, Amycus entered the courtyard and observed the siblings sparring Azrael. When they were through, Kord and Kenz both bent over, hands resting on their knees as they gasped for air.

"You're not even breathing hard and it was two against one," Amycus said, smiling.

Azrael shrugged and went to the water barrel. When most children had played or went to school, Azrael and the other recruits trained. They spent their time practicing, in medical getting stitched up, or in the dining hall. He had learned early on to function with very little sleep and to ignore pain, becoming a honed weapon with unprecedented stamina.

"Jasce, I'd like to begin your training," Amycus said. He walked to the center of the ring, pulling the key from inside his tunic.

"Azrael. My name is Azrael," he mumbled. How many times was he going to have this conversation? He suspected Amycus did it now just to irritate him, especially seeing the sparkle in his eyes.

"Wait," Kenz said. "You're going to remove his cuffs?"

"That's the only way he can learn to use his powers. You know that."

"We can trust him, Kenz," Kord said, giving Azrael an encouraging pat on the shoulder.

Kenz's gauntlets glowed blue. "One wrong move."

"Or what? We'll have another sword fight?" Azrael said, struggling between annoyance and humor.

"Or this." Kenz ignited her shield, slamming it into Azrael. Only years of training and quick reflexes kept him on his feet.

"Kenz, that's enough," Amycus said, trying not to smile.

Kenz smirked at Azrael, then lowered her shield.

Azrael wanted to rub the pain in his chest but kept his hands at his side, not giving her the satisfaction. "I didn't know Shields could do that."

"There's a lot you don't know about me."

Azrael wiped a fleck of dust off his shoulder. "I know you hate me and are fiercely protective of those you love. Speed and agility are your strengths, uncontrolled emotions your weakness. You're very talented with wood carving. I know you bite your lip when you're worried and fiddle with your gauntlets when you feel guilty. Your eyes flash when you're annoyed, which is often, and you have a beautiful smile." Azrael inwardly winced at that last remark. Why did he say that?

Kenz's eyes widened and heat rushed to her face. Kord took a precautionary step toward his sister, placing himself between her and Azrael.

Amycus cleared his throat, gripping the key. "Do I have your word not to harm anyone?"

Azrael stared at the silver key, hand flexed, his freedom within reach. He had tossed and turned all night, weighing his options, and decided he would be a fool not to take advantage of Amycus's expertise, and a bigger fool to pursue his revenge when his magic wasn't ready. Plus, he was curious—about a lot of things. The oppressive weight of the Bastion and expectations of the Hunters had lightened, and Azrael wasn't ready to give that up just yet.

"You have my word," Azrael said, ignoring Kenz's snort. His lip twitched when Kord punched her in the arm.

"Good." Amycus removed the cuffs and Azrael immediately straightened, the magic surging through every fiber of his being. Then he groaned, resting his hands on his knees, focusing on the cobblestones.

"Give it a moment—you'll level out," Amycus said.

Azrael's magic pulsed and emotions bombarded him, making his breath hitch and body tremble, goosebumps forming on his arms. He held his head, trying to focus on one emotion at a time, but too many sensations flooded him. With a moan, Azrael dropped to his knees.

"Are you all right?" Amycus knelt, his gaze flitting over Azrael's face. Kord's wide eyes darted between them both and Kenz raised her arm, the gauntlet shaking and glowing blue, her anger swirling with fear. He understood the anger. It was the fear that left him breathless, his mouth going dry and throat constricting, making it difficult to swallow.

Azrael shook his head. He spent years learning to block out weak emotions, whether through practice or from Drexus's whip. And now he was drowning in them. He grabbed the cuffs lying in the dirt, his knuckles whitening, and counted to ten, breathing easier as the emotions subsided.

Azrael rose to his feet and nodded to the courtyard's far wall. "Stand over there," he said to Kenz and Kord.

"Excuse me?" Kenz said, placing her hand on her hip.

Azrael glowered. Kord grabbed her arm and walked to where Azrael indicated.

"Let's try this again," Azrael said, handing the cuffs to Amycus. The Vaulter and Amp magic buzzed through him, a welcoming hum of power. "You feel surprised or excited." Azrael rubbed his chest. "And also remorse."

Amycus raised his brows and nodded. Azrael focused on the siblings standing thirty feet away and felt nothing. He squared his shoulders. "Kord, come here, slowly."

Kord looked at Amycus and took a few steps forward. Kenz pushed off the wall.

"Only Kord. I'm pretty sure I know what you're feeling." Kenz rolled her eyes but stayed still. As Kord neared, Azrael felt the worry that matched the strained look around his eyes.

"You must find a way to quiet the emotions, otherwise they will impede your vaulting," Amycus said.

"And how do I do that?" Azrael cracked his neck, wanting to shove Kord's worry aside.

Amycus smiled. "Practice." Azrael bit back a sarcastic remark. "Try focusing on your magic, seeing it move through you, becoming one with you. The more comfortable you are with your power, the less you'll experience the emotions, in time blocking them entirely."

Amycus waved Kenz over, and her mouth drew into a straight line. Goosebumps raised on Azrael's arms and a tremble ran down his body, sweat glistening on his forehead. He balled his fists, fighting the urge to lash out with a sword, the fear and anger intensifying.

"Focus on your magic's essence," Amycus said.

Azrael raised his hand, stopping Kenz from coming closer, and closed his eyes, concentrating on the humming throughout his body. He envisioned the power energizing his muscles, pumping his heart, filling his lungs. He inhaled deeply and opened his eyes. The shaking and sweating stopped.

"Good. Now, let's begin. Kenz, create a shield from here to the edge of the courtyard."

Indigo light surrounded Azrael, her magic whispering across his face like a refreshing breeze.

"You don't need the shield. I gave my word."

Amycus laughed. "The shield isn't for our protection. It's for yours. We wouldn't want you accidentally disappearing somewhere, um, inconvenient. Now, vault from one side of the shield to the other."

"How exactly do I do that?"

"Picture the location in your mind and will your body to that spot."

"Will my body," Azrael repeated, trying to imagine himself disappearing. Nothing happened. He focused on the magic, on the power that had always belonged to him, dormant for thirteen years. What kind of man would he be if the tattoo hadn't blocked his magic? Could he have saved his mother and sister?

Azrael shook his head. There was no point dwelling on the past—he couldn't go back in time and erase the horrors that defined him nor the blood staining his hands.

Azrael forced himself to relax, blocking out everyone and everything. He closed his eyes, ignoring the sound of children playing nearby and the birds chirping. The smell of freshly baked bread made his stomach rumble, but he brushed it aside. He envisioned the power in his core expanding to his arms and legs, down through his fingertips and toes. An intense tug pulled from his stomach and darkness enveloped him.

A gasp followed by a chuckle had him open his eyes. A smile spread across Azrael's face. He had done it.

"Very good. Now come back."

Azrael wiggled his fingers and lowered his head, clearing his mind once again. The tug came faster, and he stumbled, breathing hard as if he had completed one of the Guard's training runs. Sweat trickled down his back. He estimated he only vaulted ten feet.

"I feel like I've been in a battle," Azrael said between breaths. "Is that normal?"

"You're just out of shape," Kord said, smiling.

Azrael frowned, his fatigue not making sense. His body and mind were in peak condition.

"You need to develop the muscle of your magic," Amycus explained, "and at first, it will drain your strength. But with time and practice, your ability to vault will become second nature. You won't tire as quickly, and you may even learn to take someone with you."

Azrael nodded, running his hands through his hair and taking a deep breath. "Again," he said, and he disappeared. He pushed himself as he would in any training, testing the limits of his focus and endurance until finally, with the last vault, he dropped to his knee. Sweat poured off him and his body shook. He felt Kenz's shield disappear and heard footsteps running toward him.

"I'm fine," he said, holding up his hand.

"You're done for today," Amycus said. "Draining your magic will leave your mind and body vulnerable."

The emotions he felt earlier tried to claw their way up to the surface. He swallowed, fighting against the trembling and goosebumps.

Kord handed him a cup of water, which he guzzled. The sky had darkened, stars twinkled, and a breeze wafted through his sweaty hair. He had spent hours training with a sword and magic, and even though he was exhausted, he felt relaxed, his mind clear—something he rarely experienced; a feeling that quickly dissolved when metal clicked around his wrists. Kenz stared into his eyes as she locked the final cuff in place.

"You still don't trust me?"

"Trust is earned, don't you agree?" Kenz stepped back, her face unreadable, arms hanging loosely at her side. To the untrained eye, she looked unconcerned, but Azrael could see the rapid pulse in her neck.

"Agreed," Azrael said, his voice tight. He could drown in those green eyes. She nodded and walked away, her hand on the hilt of her sword.

Kord's hand landed on Azrael's shoulder. "I bet you're hungry."

"You have no idea," Azrael mumbled.

CHAPTER 11

The days turned into weeks, and Azrael fell into a routine with early morning runs, combat training, and magic practice with Amycus. Life in Carhurst was so different from the Bastion, where one rarely heard laughter, and being the best was all that mattered. In the Watch Guard, mistakes were corrected harshly and praise was rare. But here, he had the freedom to teach the way he always wanted to, developing strengths and helping others understand their weaknesses and how to improve. The vise around Azrael's chest continued to loosen.

The training regimen Azrael created for Kord and Kenz was demanding, physically and mentally, but neither sibling complained nor gave up, both improving every day. They no longer fell behind during runs, and they both got quicker and stronger. Not that Kord needed to get stronger—when Azrael and Kord grappled, it took every ounce of strength and training to defeat the Healer. If Azrael didn't have to wear the magic-suppressing cuffs, however, Kord wouldn't have stood a chance.

Azrael got along well with Kord—his easy-going personality made it difficult not to. His sister was another matter entirely. Her eagerness to learn made her an excellent student, but if Azrael had to guess, her motivation was simple. She wanted to finish what they started in the desert but with him on his knees and her knife pressed against his throat.

Normally, if Azrael had an enemy like Kenz, he'd either work her into submission or kill her. But he couldn't do either. One, he'd promised no harm would come to any of them; and two, his desire grew every day as he watched Kenz train. The intense concentration on her face, the way she bit her lip, how her body moved—the thought of being on his knees before her tempted him in a very uncomfortable way. Unfortunately, she hated him. He could feel it every time they removed his cuffs, and the hostility he sensed from her, combined with his own anger living just below the surface, made him more volatile than normal. His magic also reacted differently with hers than with her brother or Amycus, as if an unseen force drew their powers together.

The combination of her bitterness and the strange connection between their magic made vaulting difficult when she was near, but with Amycus's instruction and patience, Azrael's endurance and distances increased. The next phase of his training included vaulting with external distractions, but Azrael wasn't sure what Amycus had in mind. He worked comfortably with the older man, having similarities in how they taught; it was such a contrast to Drexus and his punitive methods.

Azrael spent his evenings in the Iron Glass Tavern or in his room, having borrowed a few books from Amycus. He kept his distance from most of the villagers, especially the town guards, who monitored his movements with wary eyes. Linnette waited on him whenever she worked, which was most nights. She was beautiful and friendly enough, but green eyes and midnight hair haunted him.

After three weeks, loneliness crept in. During a momentary lapse of judgment, he finally agreed to have dinner with Kord's family.

Rain splattered on the window, pinging on the tin roof. Azrael's leg bounced in time with his finger tapping on the well-worn kitchen table as he scolded himself for accepting the invitation.

Kord's son, Maleous, snuck glances at Azrael while his mother served the food, the spices in the stew making his mouth water. He couldn't remember the last time he'd had a home-cooked meal.

"Kord, where's your sister?" Tillie asked, setting freshly baked bread on the table.

Kord shrugged. "We can start without her. I'm starving."

Azrael's leg stopped shaking. "Kenz is coming?"

"Yeah. She lives here. Didn't I tell you?"

"No." Azrael's stomach flipped, but he kept his face blank.

"Well, not exactly here, but in the apartment next to the shop out back. Our parents gave me the house when they died since I was the oldest." Kord scooped stew into his bowl.

"Maybe this isn't such a good idea. I don't want to intrude." Azrael started to rise when the door opened.

"I can smell that deliciousness all the way out—" Kenz's smile faded and her eyes narrowed as they met Azrael's. "What is he doing here?" She swiped at the rain on her face.

Azrael hovered over his chair, caught between sitting and standing. Kord pushed him down and stood. Tillie halted by the stove, her eyes darting between her husband and Kenz.

"I invited him," Kord said.

"Well, uninvite him."

"Kenz, living room. Now," Kord said, walking out of the kitchen.

Kenz huffed out a breath, her eyes shooting daggers at her brother's back.

"Hi, Auntie," Maleous said, smiling.

"Hey, Mal." Kenz messed his hair, then followed her brother.

Azrael watched her leave and then looked at Tillie. "I think I'll go." He got up from his chair, but Maleous cut in.

"Please stay. We haven't had any visitors for a long time. Except for Amycus, but he's boring. Anyway, Dad and Auntie always fight. It's actually really funny."

"Maleous, that's rude." Tillie squeezed his shoulder before sitting at the end of the table. "Kenz is like a fierce storm that rages quickly and calms into a gentle breeze."

Azrael slid a curious glance at the kid while reaching for his drink, taking in his surroundings—having already located any potential weapons and exits—and listening to the rain splatter on the roof. He was about to ask about the potted herbs near the window when loud voices came from the other room.

"You didn't ask me."

"I don't need your permission for who I invite to dinner. He has no one, Kenz, and I honestly wonder if anyone has shown him kindness in a long time."

"Only a trusting fool would show an assassin kindness."

Tillie's face paled and Maleous's spoon froze inches from his mouth.

"Kord didn't tell you?" Azrael said. Tillie shook her head, her eyes flicking toward her son, whose mouth hung open. Azrael set his wineglass on the table and looked toward the door.

"You don't have to leave," Tillie said. "If Kord trusts you, then so do I." Maleous grinned and resumed shoveling food into his mouth.

Azrael heard the restraint in Kord's voice as it floated down the hall. "We are trying to get him on our side. Or have you forgotten?"

"Have you forgotten what he's done to me? Training is one thing, but sharing a cozy meal is pushing it."

Kord's words softened to where Azrael couldn't hear them anymore. He wasn't sure what made him more uncomfortable, Kenz's rage or her despair, remembering what Kord had said about the death of her fiancé at the hands of the Hunters.

Tillie cleared her throat and quickly poured a glass of wine for herself, then filled Azrael's empty one. He proceeded to tap his finger on the table.

Tillie smiled at the twitching finger. "Amycus does that, too, when he's nervous or bothered by something."

"Does what?"

Tillie nodded to his finger. Azrael immediately stopped.

Kord walked in with a forced smile, followed by Kenz, who looked everywhere but at Azrael. She took a deep breath and loaded her bowl with stew. Kord and Tillie stared at each other, engaged in that silent communication that only married couples do. Thankfully, Maleous told stories from the marketplace, oblivious to the tension in the room. Kord asked questions, his eyes flitting from Azrael to Kenz. Azrael focused on the meal, wondering how quickly he could leave without being rude.

"So, how's the training going?" Tillie asked, buttering a piece of bread.

"Great," Kord said. "Az is an exceptional teacher and has made some impressive progress with his magic." His eyes shone as he looked at Maleous. "He's a Vaulter."

"A what?" Maleous asked around a spoonful of stew.

Azrael gulped his wine, barely listening while Kord explained Vaulter magic. He snuck glances at Kenz, who pretended he wasn't sitting across from her. Azrael pushed up his sleeves as a drop of sweat ran down his back.

"Wow, that's a lot of tattoos," Maleous said, staring at Azrael's arm. Azrael paused, his drink halfway to his mouth. "Do they all mean something?"

Intricate designs coiled around his forearm. Only his hand remained bare, the space reserved for the Fire Spectral. Maleous looked expectantly at Azrael, who took a sip of wine, wishing for something stronger.

"Each tattoo represents a . . ." Azrael's eyes shifted toward Tillie. "A job."

"A job?" Maleous asked.

Azrael sighed. "A kill."

Maleous's eyes widened as he peered at Azrael's arm. Tillie's spoon clattered in her bowl while Kord rubbed his face.

"I'm surprised only one arm is covered," Kenz said, smirking.

"Yes, well—" Kord started.

"Well what? You're the one who invited a Hunter to dinner," Kenz said.

Kord grabbed a piece of bread. "We've already discussed this."

"You're a Hunter?" Maleous asked, his green eyes sparkling. "Can I see your mask?"

Azrael blinked then looked at Kord, who coughed, choking on the bread.

Tillie frowned at her son. "Maleous, you're excused."

"What? Why?" The boy's face fell, looking from his mother to his father.

"I don't hurt children," Azrael said, his voice like steel.

"It's not you," Tillie said, nudging the boy with her foot. "Our son is acting rude."

Kenz huffed. "So assassins have a moral code now?"

Azrael leaned back in his chair, balling his fists under the table. "How do you think I ended up in that dungeon? One of the reasons Drexus betrayed me was because I wouldn't whip a recruit. He considers compassion a weakness and couldn't afford a merciful assassin."

Kord cleared his throat, looking apologetic. "So, what's for dessert?"

"Oh, how noble of you," Kenz said, her face turning red. "But what about those who just want to defend their village, their homes? Any mercy for them? You and your Hunters strike them down without a thought. Slashing his throat, leaving him to drown in his own blood—" Her voice hitched.

Azrael tensed at her choice of wording. "What was the name of your fiancé's village?"

"What?" Kenz asked through her teeth.

"Hunters killed your fiancé. That's what you're talking about, right?"

Kenz's mouth dropped open. She turned to her brother, her face red. "You told him about Ven?"

Kord shot a look at Azrael then faced Kenz, raising his palms. "I'm sorry. He asked in the desert after your fight."

"You guys fought? Who won?" Maleous asked, his eyes shining.

"That's not important," Kord said. Maleous huffed and slouched in his chair. Tillie took a long drink, staring at the ceiling.

"Your aunt is a talented warrior," Azrael said, the tension in the room making his head hurt.

"The last thing I need is your approval." Kenz glared at Kord. "You had no right to tell this monster anything about me or my past!"

Azrael pinched the bridge of his nose, took a deep breath, and addressed Tillie. "I don't think this storm's going to calm down anytime soon." He stood and walked toward the door, giving one last look to Kenz, and stepped outside. He looked up, letting the rain wash over him, cooling his temper. Or was it shame? A fine mist obscured the main road, enveloping the village in an eerie glow.

Azrael raked his hands through his wet hair and pulled up the hood of his cloak. If he had gone with his gut, he would have avoided this disaster. He didn't fit in at the family table with ordinary people, nor did he know how to handle Kenz's grief. All he knew was that her fiancé died two years ago, murdered by Hunters. Apologizing would be ridiculous; that was his job—or had been.

He groaned.

Why did he tell the kid that Kenz was a talented warrior? He never learned.

He knew Kenz didn't want anyone protecting her. He recognized the pride and a burning need to prove something. So why did he keep trying? She infuriated him, but this strange need to defend her kept surfacing out of nowhere.

He peered at the village through the rain and shook his head. This wasn't him. He didn't deserve friends who invited him to dinner or the kindness that Kord and Amycus had shown him. Even Tillie had welcomed him into her home, knowing what he was. He needed to leave. The sooner he could enact his revenge on the Hunters and confront Drexus, the sooner he could—what? If he didn't stay in the Watch Guard, what would he do? He'd meant what he said to Nigel that day in the forge: He had nowhere else to go. He looked over his shoulder at Kord's home. He couldn't stay here either—his very presence a reminder to all that Kenz had lost.

Monster. Killer. Murderer.

Azrael marched toward Amycus's home and barged into the cottage. Water dripped onto the stone floor as he shoved off his hood.

"Forget our bargain. I need these cuffs off now."

Amycus slowly lowered his book onto the desk. "It's only been a few weeks. What happened?"

Azrael sank into the chair across from Amycus's desk. "My presence here only causes hardship."

"I take it dinner with Kord's family didn't go well?"

Azrael grunted and rubbed his temples. He wasn't sure how Amycus knew where he'd been, but he didn't care. "Look, I don't belong here. I need to return to Orilyon. I can't get any answers if I stay."

"You will get your answers, Jasce."

Azrael glared at the man, who simply smiled back.

"But," Amycus continued, "you need to be patient. You haven't fully learned to use your magic or protect yourself."

"I'm not a patient person."

Amycus chuckled. "No, but you may find so much more during the waiting."

"Like what?"

"Like who you truly are."

Azrael trudged back to the inn and sat on the edge of the bed, holding his Hunter mask. Was he a monster? Azrael huffed. Of course he was. He killed his own father, murdered innocent people, captured Spectrals with no remorse. All he had wanted was power and revenge, and he hadn't cared who he hurt along the way. But what about now? Amycus was right—his entire world had shifted and he didn't know who he was.

He threw the mask into the drawer, the white skull grinning menacingly. Monster. Killer. Murderer.

CHAPTER 12

Azrael spent the evenings assisting in the forge, content to listen to Amycus's stories rather than sitting alone in his room where the weight of the Hunter mask suffocated him. While they worked on perfecting his armor alongside crafting pieces for Lord Rollant's soldiers, Amycus reminisced of his time in Delmar as a blacksmith. Often, Azrael would catch Amycus staring at him, his lips parted like he wanted to say something, but whenever Azrael asked about it, Amycus shook his head, saying it was nothing.

Azrael began working on a pair of throwing knives for Kenz that would fit her hands. Her innate skill and precise aim made her formidable, but the practice blades weren't balanced properly. With these, along with her crossbow, she would be lethal. Of course, based on the encounter at Kord's he would probably end up with the blades lodged in his chest.

Azrael sighed. His thoughts gravitated toward Kenz more than he liked, and they were driving him crazy. He enjoyed her quick wit, even when it was at his expense. He had stopped by the siblings' woodworking shop to talk to Kord and couldn't keep his eyes off her, watching how she painted the scrollwork, thinking she'd make a great tattooist. Her ink-black hair and piercing eyes mesmerized him to where she was becoming a distraction. During a training session, her laugh had caught him so off guard that Kord almost sliced him in two.

"You're here early," Amycus said, causing Azrael to jump, cutting his hand with the newly sharpened blade.

He swore and grabbed a rag to staunch the bleeding.

"Sorry about that," Amycus said, lowering himself onto a stool. "What are you working on?"

"Throwing knives."

Amycus leaned closer to look at the details on the hilt. "Those are excellent. A little too small for you, though."

Azrael frowned, placing both knives on the worktable. "They aren't for me."

"Ah, I see."

Azrael took a deep breath, wrapping his hand tightly with a bandage. He needed to clear his head, and working in the forge wasn't getting the job done. "I'm going to train for a few hours."

"I've invited some Spectrals to a meeting this afternoon," Amycus said. When Azrael raised his brows, he continued, "Kord and I are recruiting, and I wanted you to meet and possibly train them. If both parties are willing."

"Did you tell them who I was?"

"Well, no."

Azrael snorted. "This will be interesting."

He walked to the courtyard, rolling his neck from side to side, and heard a satisfying crack. He focused on the mastery and form of each exercise, pushing the thoughts of Kenz out of his mind. As he trained, he wondered what Amycus had up his sleeve if he was actively recruiting. He also thought about Amycus's idea of training other Spectrals, doubting the visitors would want to be in his presence let alone learn combat skills from him once they knew who he was. Until a month ago, Azrael was a Hunter and their enemy.

Kord entered the courtyard grinning and strolled over to the water barrel, a fine layer of sawdust coating his tunic. Azrael envied his calm happiness, wondering what it would feel like to have such peace that your everyday expression was a smile.

"Hey, Az. Looks like you got a good workout in," Kord said, giving Azrael a look from head to toe. "Something on your mind?"

Azrael slid him a guarded look and raked his fingers through his hair despite the bloody bandage on his hand.

"What did you do?" Kord asked, grabbing Azrael's hand before he could pull away.

"Got distracted in the forge." The cut on his hand mended together, leaving only a red line.

"You know, one man's distraction is another man's haven," Kord said, that grin still on his face. Azrael frowned, shaking his head. Some of Kord's sayings left him baffled.

"I hear we're going to have visitors," Azrael said.

"Yep, they're already here."

"Anything I need to know?"

Kord tapped his chin. "There are two Element Spectrals—one Earth, one Fire—and another Shield."

Azrael stiffened. "What color is the Fire?"

Kord's smile faltered. "Green. He's not the one you're looking for. Anyway, two of them are friendly enough."

"And the other one?"

"I'll let you judge that for yourself." Kord winked, turning as Kenz walked into the courtyard. "Hey, sis."

Azrael choked on the water as Kenz's smile transformed her face. She wore a black tunic with gray pants, her boots laced up to her knees. Her hair, hanging to the middle of her back, looked like crushed velvet.

Kord slapped Azrael on the back. "You okay? Wouldn't want you to choke to death."

"We could only be so lucky," Kenz said, walking past Azrael toward Amycus's cottage.

Azrael couldn't help but laugh, having missed her sarcastic remarks. They had kept their distance over the past week, acting like the disastrous dinner at Kord's never happened.

"She'll soften up over time."

Azrael smiled. "I certainly hope not."

Amycus cleared his throat when they entered the cottage. "Good, we're all here."

Azrael scanned the newcomers, immediately locating the Fire Spectral by the ignitor contraptions on his wrists. The man looked Azrael up and down, his amber-colored eyes hardening. A woman with short white hair stood next to Kenz donning similar gauntlets, obviously designed by Amycus. That left the Earth Spectral—a tall, thin man with shaggy brown hair and a long nose.

Azrael leaned against the wall and crossed his arms, the clinking of the metal cuffs echoing in the strained silence.

Amycus stood behind his desk and smiled. "Flynt, Delmira, Slater, I'd like to introduce you to Jasce Farone."

Azrael's jaw tightened. "The name is Azrael."

Delmira gasped, her gauntlets glowing a bright yellow. Flynt jumped out of his chair, sliding his wrists together creating a green flame, and Slater stood slowly, his hands fisted. Azrael was pretty sure he felt a slight tremble through the floor.

"Azrael, as in the Angel of Death?" Flynt asked, the flame dancing between his fingers. "The one the Watch Guard is looking for?"

Azrael smiled, baring his teeth. "The very one, and unless you plan to burn down the place, you should put that out."

"Not helpful," Kord murmured out of the corner of his mouth.

"Amycus, what is the meaning of this?" Slater asked.

"Everyone, relax, please," Amycus said, moving to the center of the room. "Flynt, Slater, please sit down. I'm asking you to trust me." With a final glare at Azrael, they sat, Flynt fiddling with the hilt of his dagger.

"I told you this was a bad idea," Kenz said, smirking at Amycus.

"Shut it, will you?" Kord said. Kenz's mouth dropped open and Azrael pressed his lips together, stifling a laugh even though he agreed with her. Amycus should have told these three who they were meeting before coming face-to-face with him.

Kenz snapped her mouth shut. The tension in the room was like a taut bowstring, the arrow notched and ready to fly.

Amycus said, "I have learned that the steward has ordered the Watch Guard to cross into Paxton." A collection of gasps filled the silence.

Azrael remained motionless, recalling the map in Drexus's study. The Guard didn't have the numbers to conquer Paxton. Or did they? Who knew what else Drexus was hiding?

Questions poured in from the Spectrals.

"When?"

"Why?"

"What are we going to do?"

Azrael chuckled.

"Something funny?" Slater asked, his brown eyes hard.

"Yes, I find the level of panic funny."

"Again, not helpful," Kord said.

Azrael slid his eyes toward Kord and then back to Amycus. "How did you come across this information?"

"I have my sources," Amycus said, avoiding Azrael's stare. "We need to gather our forces and be ready when the time comes. We can't let the Watch Guard capture, or worse, slaughter us. We need to train and take the fight to them." Amycus dropped a fist into his other hand, his cheeks red.

Flynt stared at Azrael and then looked at Amycus. "What does *he* have to do with any of this?"

"I've asked him to train you."

"You want the Angel of Death to train us?" Slater asked, his brows disappearing under his shaggy brown hair.

Azrael looked at Amycus with an *I told you so* kind of look.

"Isn't the Watch Guard looking for him?" Delmira glanced at Azrael. "That's the rumor, at least."

Amycus sighed. "Yes, they are, but that's not the only reason they're crossing the desert. Drexus is experimenting with magic. I won't go into the details, but we aren't safe."

"What kind of training?" Flynt asked, a sliver of flames twirling through his fingers. Of the three, Flynt was the only one who kept a level head.

"Combat."

"Why do we need him?" Slater asked. "You could teach us how to fight."

Azrael uncrossed his arms, frowning at Amycus, who shifted his attention to his desk.

"Drexus has developed a new weapon." Amycus passed around the laced arrowheads. Slater gasped, dropping the arrow onto the rug, and Flynt swore when his fire sputtered out. Delmira took one, her lips pursed, and held it like it was something foul. "You need other skills besides your magic, and Azrael can teach you. I assure you, his training works. Kord and Kenz have already benefited from their time learning from him."

The three visitors looked at the siblings; Kord smiled while Kenz gave a reluctant nod.

"How do we know he won't betray us?" Flynt asked, a muscle twitching in his jaw. Slater nodded. The only sound came from Amycus tapping his finger on the desk.

"I trust him," Amycus said.

Kord placed his hand on Azrael's shoulder. "So do I."

Azrael stepped away from Kord, not wanting to think about how easily they trusted him. Flynt was right; he could betray them. Drexus would kill to know Amycus's location and get his hands on a Healer like Kord.

Focus on the problem, he told himself.

"What's the timeline?" Azrael asked. If Drexus and the Guard crossed the desert, Azrael would need to master his magic to defeat them.

"I'd guess less than a year," Amycus said. "As you know, the Guard also needs to recruit members. I want to scout the other garrisons to see how close they are to having enough soldiers."

"Impossible." Azrael scanned the room. Amycus raised his brows while Flynt and Slater glared. "First, it would take years to get them into even decent fighting shape to go up against the Hunters. Second, we don't have the numbers."

"And third?" Amycus said.

Azrael stepped forward, feeling the vein pulse in his neck. "What's in it for me? I'm not a part of your crusade. I'm here to master my vaulting, and once these cuffs are off, I'm gone."

"You're a Vaulter?" Delmira said.

Azrael slowly turned, and she took a step back, knocking into the wall.

"Out of everything he said, that's what you got out of it? That he's a Vaulter?" Slater asked, shaking his head.

"It's just that I've never met one before," she said, her voice wavering. "I thought they'd all been killed."

"Azrael, think about it," Amycus said. "Our goals are similar. You need us as much as we need you."

"What makes you think I need any of you?"

Kenz huffed. "You really are an arrogant brute, you know that?"

Kord sighed and rubbed his face. Delmira covered her mouth, stepping away from Kenz, and Flynt chuckled as Slater's eyes darted between Azrael and Kenz. Amycus got to his feet, his body rigid.

Azrael stalked over to Kenz, his anger bubbling to the surface. Any calm gained from his earlier training vanished. He sensed Kord and Amycus moving closer, heard a click of metal, and knew Flynt had ignited his fire. The frustrations of the way she plagued his thoughts, how she reacted to him, her utter disdain, made him want to lash out in rage. Kenz swallowed as he whispered in her ear. "Do you feel that?" He relished the panic that swam in her wide eyes, the stiffness of her shoulders, her shallow breathing. "That's fear. I could kill you with my bare hands. Remember that the next time you insult me."

He turned his back on her and walked out the front door.

CHAPTER 13

Two days had passed since the meeting. After Azrael had stormed out, the Spectrals debated, finally agreeing to allow Azrael to train them as long as he wore the cuffs. Azrael bristled at the thought. He hadn't earned the title of Angel of Death because of magic.

Amycus and Kord left to visit neighboring towns before Azrael gave the blacksmith his answer. If he decided to do this, to train his former enemy, then he had sealed his fate. The option of rejoining the Watch Guard was off the table, and Drexus would never forgive him. Of course, he could always lead the Spectrals into a trap and get back into Drexus's good graces, but that idea repulsed him. What would happen to Tillie and Maleous if Kord was killed? And the thought of handing Kenz over to Drexus made his skin crawl. He'd only known Amycus, Kenz, and Kord and his family for a short time, but he felt closer to them than he ever had with Bronn or Sabine. Well, not Kenz—she still hated him.

It was late afternoon on market day when Azrael strolled through the town on his way to the tavern. He nodded at a group of ladies standing at a nearby stall selling fresh fruit and vegetables. The booth, awash with colors and smells, tempted him, but the glint of metal reflecting the sun caught his eye. The corner of his mouth lifted. He had known the minute he entered the marketplace that Kenz was following him. She may be excellent with throwing knives and her crossbow, but she was horrible at shadowing. Maybe he would add stealth to their training program. For now, he let her tail him, pretending to be unaware.

He stopped at a stall selling knives and swords, missing the weapons he had made at the Bastion with Nigel, the quality of those superior to the ones here. Even the blades he and Amycus made for Lord Rollant's soldiers were better than these. Azrael assumed the blacksmith was from another village as he surveyed the table, running his fingers over the sharpened steel and wondering what it would be like to have his own forge, to have a different life where he worked at something he loved and went home in the evening to a wife with sparkling green eyes. He snorted—those were the aspirations of a fool, a dream he didn't deserve.

"Put it down."

Azrael rolled his eyes, placing the weapon on the table. Kenz leaned against the stall, her crossbow peeking over her shoulder. Her hand rested on the hilt of her sword, which was belted around her trim waist. Her green tunic, exposing her slender throat, turned her eyes into emeralds, and the form-fitting pants made his stomach tighten. He wished she would wear something baggier.

He leaned against the table, crossing his arms. "Hello, Kenz. Do you enjoy following me?"

"No, I don't. But someone has to keep an eye on you."

Azrael smiled. "You can keep an eye on me any time. Maybe we could take turns." He pushed off the table and stepped closer, unable to stop his eyes from traveling down her body.

Kenz huffed but didn't back away. "You really are arrogant."

"A woman like you needs a confident man." Azrael winked, smiling at the flush that spread up her neck.

Kenz tried to shove him but he grabbed her wrists, anchoring them behind her back.

"Let me go," she said through clenched teeth.

"Why? Do I make you nervous?" Azrael's pulse thudded as he pulled her closer, knowing he needed to push her away. Her breath hitched, and he couldn't hide the shiver that ran down his spine when she licked her lips. She pulled her hands free and pressed against his chest, his racing heart betraying the desire coursing through him. Her eyes darted to his mouth and he smiled, the redness now brightening her cheeks.

"What you make me is—"

The sound of a warning bell echoed through the town. Azrael squinted into the distance while she pushed away and turned toward the forest. Dust swirled and hooves pounded as ten hooded soldiers rode toward Carhurst. No skull masks in sight, just the Watch Guard emblem on their cloaks.

Villagers hurried toward their homes and vendors locked up their stalls. In the chaos, Azrael seized a throwing knife, tucking it into his boot while picking up the dagger. His eyes darted down the main road.

Where were the town guards?

Azrael stepped into the middle of the empty street, facing the Watch Guard as they dismounted. His hand tightened around the hilt of his dagger as he analyzed the movements of each soldier, their faces obscured.

"Your people, I assume?" Kenz said, her voice tight. Azrael was grateful to see her crossbow already loaded.

"Not exactly." He wasn't a member of the Watch Guard anymore, even though he still had the tattoo inked into his arm. He also wasn't accepted as one of the Spectrals. He didn't have a people. It was just him, which is what he always thought he wanted. He didn't want to think about the sudden relief he felt when Kenz joined him in the street.

"I need these cuffs off. Do you have the key?"

"No, it's with Amycus."

"Well, you may just get your wish then," Azrael said, walking toward the soldiers, squeezing the dagger. "Feel free to start shooting anytime."

The soldiers ran forward as Kenz let loose arrow after arrow, her technique flawless as she took down three guards.

Seven to go. Azrael crouched into his fighting stance.

The soldiers broke formation, two rushing toward Kenz, whose gauntlets glowed as she gripped her sword. She jutted out her chin and positioned herself just like he taught her. Azrael quickly snatched the knife from his boot and flung it at the soldier closing in on her. He swore when it missed the soldier's neck, hitting him in the chest instead. Still, it would slow him down and give Kenz a chance. She glanced at him; her brow furrowed.

Five against one and all Azrael had was a dagger. His cuffs were debilitating shackles chaining him to almost certain death. Hopefully, he'd given Kenz enough time to get help. He peered down the street, again wondering where the town guards were.

"We've been looking for you," the lead soldier said, pulling back his hood to reveal a scarred face. Azrael didn't recognize him or the others as they removed their cloaks.

"Here I am," Azrael sneered, holding his arms out as if welcoming them.

Two of the soldiers charged. Azrael used the first's momentum, dodging his attack while side-stepping, grabbing the man's sword arm, and using it to block the strike from the other soldier. Azrael landed a kick in the second man's chest, sending him backward. In one fluid movement, he elbowed the first warrior in the nose, broke his wrist, and wrenched the sword from his useless hand. Azrael only had time for a shallow slice to the man's body before the other soldiers attacked.

Weapons clashed, legs swept, and fists flew as the remaining soldiers tried to surround him. Azrael moved his feet, leading the men away from the marketplace, constantly keeping his attackers in view while sneaking a glance at Kenz. One soldier was down, the other was fighting viciously. Kenz used her shield simultaneously with her sword. Sweat dripped down her face.

Azrael swore as the sting of a blade slashed his arm. He instinctively raised his weapon in time to block the strike aimed for his neck, his teeth clenching at the vibration thrumming through his injured arm.

"You've gone soft." The lead soldier stepped into the fray, a mocking sneer on his face.

"Just making this a challenge."

Years of training, muscle memory, and instinct kept him alive. Azrael blocked another blow, sideswiping one of the attackers and knocking him off his feet. He sheathed his dagger and picked up the fallen sword, twirling the two blades and ignoring the blood running down his arm. He twisted and stabbed a man in the chest, but another soldier snuck under Azrael's guard, steel slicing across his leg. He hissed, backing away from the soldiers.

His right arm and leg burned, his hand was sticky with blood, a drop of sweat stung his eye. He pivoted, tracking the soldier behind him while watching the two in front. His eyes flicked to the man on the ground and he turned slightly, trying to locate the other one when an intense pain slashed through his back, forcing him to his knee.

"Look, men. The mighty Azrael kneels before us," the lead soldier said, laughing.

Azrael groaned, gritting his teeth against the searing pain. Kenz stood twenty feet away, the two soldiers dead and her sword hanging at her side. He recognized the look in her eyes. She was finally getting what she wanted—him dead at the very hands of those whose mission it was to destroy Spectrals. It was fitting, really, being killed by the Watch Guard. He regretted never finding the Fire Spectral or the vengeance he so desired, but at least he would die knowing that for once he was the protector instead of the Angel of Death.

Azrael nodded at Kenz and struggled to his feet. He needed to take down as many soldiers as he could to give her a better chance. He blocked another strike, fighting the pain in his back, blood spilling to the ground. Metal gleamed as the whine of a sword slashed through the air.

This was it.

The death blow crashed into a solid wall of indigo light. The lead soldier's eyes widened, then burned with hatred as Kenz sprinted toward them.

"What are you doing?" Azrael growled.

"Saving your life." Kenz's shield surrounded them.

Azrael gathered himself to full height, relying on the adrenaline coursing through his veins. The smell of copper stung his nose as sticky wetness traveled down his broken body. He didn't have much time.

The shield dissolved and blades clashed, Kenz fighting behind him as they took on the remaining soldiers. All the training and lessons clicked into place—they fought as one, anticipating each other's moves, and within minutes it was over.

Azrael stared at the carnage, blood dripping down his face and off his swords.

The world tilted.

His grip loosened, swords clattering to the ground, and with a final groan, Azrael fell.

Kenz gripped his shoulders. "Hold on. I've got you."

ॐ ॐ ॐ

Azrael lay on his stomach, focusing on the scratchy wool against his cheek and taking controlled breaths to block out the pain. Kenz rustled through the bottles on Amycus's bookshelf, mumbling under her breath.

The door crashed open and Linnette rushed in, her hands covering her mouth. "What happened?" she asked, her voice barely above a whisper.

Azrael grimaced, his vision blurring. "What does it look like?"

"Linnette, I need you to have Tillie or Mal ride out to Hillford and find Kord. Then come back and help me stop the bleeding." Kenz sounded like a commander barking orders.

Linnette nodded and ran out, leaving Azrael alone with Kenz. The sound of dripping filled the silence. Azrael closed his eyes, trying to ignore the puddle of blood beneath him.

A chair scooted closer and he opened his eyes. Kenz placed bottles and rags on the table, her face pale. He remembered Kord mentioning her weak constitution when his tattoo was burned away.

"You don't have to stay," he said.

"If I don't stop the bleeding, you'll die."

"Isn't that what you want?"

Her eyes met his, her mouth set in a hard line. She shook her head. "I thought I did."

"What changed your mind?"

Kenz tied bandages along his arm and leg and removed a knife from the sheath on her thigh. Azrael tensed, then relaxed at the sound of tearing fabric as Kenz cut away his tunic. He sucked in a breath as she dabbed at the wound across his back.

"I don't want to be like you," she said, methodically working on his back. "You deserved to die after all the people you murdered." Her eyes brimmed as she stared at his back. "But then I saw the look on your face."

"What look?"

She shrugged. "Understanding, I suppose. You knew I wanted you dead, and you accepted your fate. Instead of feeling gratified, I felt ashamed." She shook her head slightly and continued mopping up the blood. "Kord warned me that bitterness would eat me alive. It almost did. I wouldn't be able to live with myself if I watched you die, knowing I could've prevented it."

When their eyes met, he couldn't look away. They held hope, something he hadn't seen in a long time. He slowly reached out to touch her hand; her skin was soft and warm. She looked down at his fingers but didn't pull away.

"Kenz, I—"

The door burst open again. "I found Maleous," Linnette said, rushing to his side. She gasped and he turned his head, not wanting to see the revulsion on her face. He knew what his back looked like—a crisscrossing of scarred flesh.

"Good," Kenz said, and she gave more instructions to Linnette. Azrael peered at the fire, mulling over Kenz's words. She had made a choice, in a matter of seconds, to not become a monster like him. He didn't want to think about the choices he'd made over the past thirteen years—choices that created a man consumed by revenge to the point of killing his father, justifying the wrongs against him. What would his mother or sister think if they knew what had become of him? He closed his eyes. They would be ashamed.

"I need to clean the wound and stitch it back together," Kenz said, interrupting his thoughts. "This is going to hurt."

"Pain is unavoidable; suffering—"

"Yeah, yeah. I know. Suffering is a choice," she said.

Azrael's chuckle turned into a groan when she poured alcohol along the wound. He gripped the edge of the cot, his knuckles turning white.

"Here, have some." Linnette offered a bottle to Azrael, who gulped the contents down.

"Where is Kord when I need him?" Kenz muttered, focusing on the needle and thread. "Better bite down on this." She handed him a wooden dowel.

"Do you know what you're doing?"

"No."

He swiveled his head, frowning.

"Yes, I know what I'm doing. Amycus taught us wound care, just in case we were without Kord's magic."

Azrael nodded and bit down on the wood, wishing the alcohol's numbing effects would kick in. His muscles twinged when the needle went through his flesh. His jaw ached and sweat dripped down his face as he silently repeated his mantra every time the needle pierced his back.

Pain is inescapable. Suffering is a choice.

Linnette wiped his forehead, pushing the hair off his face.

"You're blocking the light, Linnette," Kenz said, her voice hard.

Azrael moaned, trying to stay conscious. His fingers twitched, reaching again for the bottle.

"Almost done," Kenz said.

Finally, she let out a sigh of relief and tied off the last stitch. Azrael stared at the blood-soaked rags covering the floor, trembling as she gently rubbed an ointment on his back. Linnette gathered up the rags, saying she'd be back later with food.

Kenz walked to the window, her hands shaking while she lit the candles. The sun dipped below the horizon and the sky glowed a deep orange.

"Are you all right?" Azrael asked, his voice strained.

"I need to look at your other wounds but thought you could use a break."

"Kenz," Azrael whispered. "You should sit."

Her shoulders tensed. "You're in no position to tell me what to do."

"Your face is pale and your hands are shaking." Azrael took a deep breath, wincing. "Please, sit. Have a drink."

Kenz sighed and turned from the window. She sat near Azrael, drinking straight from the bottle. The room darkened and the candlelight flickered. Kenz rolled the bottle back and forth between her palms.

"I don't blame you," he said, his voice slurred. "I wouldn't want to be like me either." He took the bottle, taking a long drink, and handed it back to her. "I wasn't always a cold-blooded killer. I had a family once, a little sister I adored. I used to dream about being part of something special, being a hero." He sighed, surrendering to the oblivion of the alcohol.

"That's a wonderful dream, Azrael."

"It does me no good to dream. I'm not worthy . . ." As his voice trailed off, he felt the gentle caress of her fingers wipe the hair off his face.

CHAPTER 14

Azrael's eyes fluttered open and a soothing warmth tingled down his body as Kord's hands drifted over his back, humming a familiar tune. The fire illuminated the room with a soft glow, the smell of burning wood a reprieve from the blood that had permeated the cottage. The last thing he remembered was sharing his longing for a normal life with Kenz, expressing feelings that had risen from the deepest part of him as if the blade that had slashed across his back opened more than just his skin. He groaned, remembering his last words.

"You okay?" Kord asked.

"Yeah." Azrael's voice sounded tired and raw.

"You had us worried there for a bit."

"Us?"

Kord chuckled. "Yes. Amycus, Kenz, and myself. Even Tillie. You actually looked like the Angel of Death when I got here. I could feel how close you were to dying. But your pulse is strong and you're getting color back into your face."

"How long have you been here?" Azrael asked, unaccustomed to having people worry about him. As a Hunter, all anyone cared about was completing the job, and failure was not an option.

"For a few hours. I sent everyone else home to get some rest."

Azrael squeezed his hands to get the blood moving; his entire body ached. "I need to get up."

"In a minute. Kenz did a great job sewing you up, but it's going to take longer for your back to heal, so you need to be careful." Kord's finger grazed one of Azrael's many scars. "Who did this to you?" he whispered.

Azrael tried not to flinch. "It's part of the training and the Guard's way of disciplining. You learn at an early age not to cry out or show pain. Otherwise, the whip keeps striking."

He tried to relax, focusing on breathing while Kord worked his magic. He rubbed something on Azrael's back that smelled faintly of lavender.

Kord chuckled. "I'm really thankful you don't train us like that."

Azrael laughed, then grimaced.

"Try to relax—you're easier to heal when you're unconscious. I have to work around the stitches, I don't want your skin mending over them. It will take longer, so no training for a while." Kord worked for a few more minutes, then placed his hands in his lap. "Okay, you can get up now. Slowly."

Kord put his hand under Azrael's shoulder and helped him into a sitting position. Azrael swayed and closed his eyes, waiting for the room to stop spinning.

"Probably from the blood loss and the alcohol. How much did you and my sister drink?" Kord asked, smiling.

Azrael snorted. "Too much, I'm sure. Thankfully, she did her drinking after she stitched me up." He did a quick inventory of the rest of his body. The wounds on his arm and leg were healing, and a comfortable humming buzzed through his system. Azrael frowned at the cuffs lying on the table, trying to suppress the worry emanating from Kord.

Kord rubbed the back of his neck. "The cuffs block the healing process, so I had Amycus remove them."

"I bet Kenz wasn't happy about that."

"Actually, she accepted it, but she was also exhausted and drunk. I'm sure when she comes back later today and sees them off, she'll have a fit." Kord stared at the cuffs, a curious look on his face. "Tillie said the entire village is talking about the fight against the Guard. Ten of them, huh?"

"I don't know if they got lucky and found me or knew where I was." Azrael hoped the former. He didn't want the Watch Guard or Hunters knowing his location and putting Kord and his family at risk. Or anyone else. Although he complained about being coerced into staying in Carhurst, a sense of belonging had emerged. His daily routine of training and working in the forge had settled his mind, and the tension abated from his chest, the vise loosening, allowing him to breathe.

"Thank you for protecting my sister," Kord said, pulling Azrael out of his thoughts.

"She protected me. I'd be dead if it weren't for her."

Kord raised his brows. "All Tillie told me was that you two fought brilliantly together. Or at least, that's what the villagers are saying."

The corner of Azrael's mouth turned up. They had fought well together. Like a dance, they had moved fluidly, guarding each other's backs. Even with Bronn and all the hours they trained together, he never felt that connection.

The night sky slowly turned from black to purplish-gray. Azrael stood finally, wincing, and walked toward the door leading to the courtyard.

"Where do you think you're going?" Kord asked, getting up from his chair.

"Just need some fresh air." He looked over his shoulder. "I'm fine. Go home and get some rest." He opened the door and breathed in the crisp morning air. He felt Kord watching him as he sat on the bench and stared at the brightening sky. He could enjoy another sunrise because Kenz had chosen not to allow bitterness and anger to control her fate. She was a braver warrior than he ever was.

๑๖ ๑๖ ๑๖

Azrael spent most of the day making himself comfortable on Amycus's couch, reading and savoring Tillie's coffee and pastries. At one point, needing to stretch his legs and settle something in his mind, he walked to the end of town, past Lord Rollant's manor. Only two soldiers guarded the closed gates, and the flag he had seen earlier was lowered. He stared past the men into the empty courtyard.

"What do you want?" one guard asked.

Azrael cocked his head. "Where were you yesterday?"

"That's none of your business."

"My blood staining the ground in the marketplace says otherwise. The Watch Guard attacks and the soldiers responsible for protecting the town are strangely absent? Where's your captain?"

The guard stepped forward, removing his sword from its sheath. "Again, that's none of your business. I suggest you move along."

Azrael glanced over the guard's shoulder. This soldier obviously didn't know who he threatened, that his life could end in seconds, even with Azrael's wounds still healing. But he didn't need another enemy right now. He would get his answers soon enough.

Azrael had just settled himself back on the couch, his body aching more than he would ever admit, when Amycus emerged from the forge, wiping sweat off his forehead, and sat in a nearby chair. He laid the poisoned arrowheads on the table between them.

"These are quite ingenious, and effective. Wouldn't you agree?" Amycus twirled an arrowhead around his fingers, his brow furrowed.

Azrael nodded, reaching for one and immediately feeling its effect. He handed the arrowhead back and released the hold on his magic, sensing confusion flowing off Amycus. "What are you thinking?"

"I just can't figure out how Drexus created the serum. Do you know?"

"No. I was simply the test subject."

"Do you regret it? Getting the serum, I mean?" Amycus's eyes scanned Azrael's face.

"Who wouldn't want more power? I became invincible once I received that serum, so no, I don't regret it."

"Almost invincible. Something so insignificant defeated you." Amycus focused on the arrowhead he twirled in his fingers.

Azrael leaned back and winced. At the time, he had felt honored to be the first to receive the serum, but now he knew he was expendable, just another cog in Drexus's wheel of dominance.

Amycus walked to the window and rubbed his hands down his face. "If I know Drexus, he will recreate the serum now that it's successful and give it to the Hunters and Watch Guard. We can't let that happen."

Just then, Kord and Kenz came in, surveying Azrael and Amycus. Kenz frowned at the discarded cuffs, her eyes darting to Azrael. He swallowed, remembering her fingers on his skin and his alcohol-induced confession. Vulnerability wasn't a comfortable emotion. He practically heard the crack, a rift splintering through the wall he'd spent years building. He breathed deeply, dampening the part of his magic that experienced emotions, unable to contend with them right now. But with his cuffs off, he couldn't lessen the way his magic pulsed when Kenz was in the room.

"Amycus, I need to leave," Azrael said.

Amycus turned from the window, his face expressionless. Kord stopped mid-stride and Kenz's shoulders stiffened.

"You haven't fulfilled your end of the bargain," Amycus said.

"Kord and Kenz can continue the training and teach any other recruits."

"May I ask why the sudden desire to leave?"

Azrael's eyes flitted to Kenz, who lowered her gaze, shoving her hands in her pockets. "I'm putting you all in danger." He stood, wincing from the pain in his back. Kord immediately went to his side, but Azrael brushed him off. "The Guard may know where I am, and it's not safe for me to stay, for any of you." He couldn't keep from looking at Kenz, her face unreadable.

"You're in no condition to travel right now," Kord said.

"I've been in worse shape."

Amycus moved from the window and sat, his fingers steepled under his chin as he stared at nothing. All three of them waited. Azrael steadied himself on the side of the couch, his legs shaking. Kord grabbed his arm and forced him to sit, giving Azrael a knowing look.

"The Guard crossing the desert is more worrisome than if they know where you are. That means Drexus is getting close to making his move," Amycus said. "We need to see what he's up to."

"What's your plan?" Kenz asked, finally moving from the wall. Azrael didn't miss that she avoided looking at him.

"I need you two to check out the garrisons across the desert and gather information," Amycus said, his eyes meeting both Kord's and Kenz's.

"Are you serious?" Azrael said. "You want to send them to spy on the Watch Guard?"

"And why not us?" Kenz said, finally looking at him, her eyes like emeralds.

"That's a suicide mission and you know it."

"That's why you will go with them. I'm not letting you out of our bargain. Plus, you haven't mastered your vaulting," Amycus said.

"I'll learn as I go."

Amycus huffed. "You haven't successfully vaulted out of the courtyard and still struggle with distractions. You aren't ready."

Azrael tightened his fists, his anger growing. How dare anyone suggest he wasn't strong enough. With the cuffs removed, no one could stop him from leaving, and he didn't need their blessings.

Amycus leaned back in his chair. "I'll tell you what. You vault out of this room and I will consider our bargain fulfilled."

"What?" Kord said. "No, Amycus, he hasn't healed enough—"

Amycus raised his hand, silencing Kord.

"Fine." Azrael stood, keeping his face blank, hiding the pain radiating through his back. He focused on the courtyard, concentrating on the humming in his body, the magic flowing through him. Then he shivered, feeling Kenz's magic swirl with his, recalling the softness of her touch as she brushed his hair off his forehead.

Focus. He scolded himself, trying to envision the courtyard, the training obstacles he helped create, the bench where he watched the sunrise. Azrael reached for his power, feeling the tug. His body vibrated and darkness enveloped him.

Azrael yelled in pain as he crashed into the door and dropped to his knees, feeling his stitches open and blood trickle down his back. Kord swore and rushed to his side, pressing his hand to his injuries.

"I think that answers our question." Amycus rose from his chair and retreated into the forge, weaving the arrowhead through his fingers.

"Well, that was entertaining," Kenz said, chuckling and leaving the cottage without looking back.

Kord helped Azrael stand, leading him to the couch. "You're an idiot, you know that?"

Azrael's laugh turned into a groan.

"What's so funny?" Kord asked, rummaging through Amycus's healing ointments.

"I'm used to your sister calling me that, not you."

Kord snorted, twirling his finger to indicate Azrael should lie down. He dabbed at the blood and rubbed salve along the stitches. "You shouldn't leave. I appreciate you not wanting to put us in danger, which, I have to say, is quite the opposite of the Angel of Death. But we need you."

Azrael looked over his shoulder to find Kord staring at him, his green eyes so similar to his sister's. Azrael didn't want to tell Kord the real reason he needed to leave. It wasn't just to protect them. It was to protect himself.

CHAPTER 15

When Azrael wasn't helping plan the reconnaissance mission, he worked in the forge creating weapons and improving his armor to keep his mind off his failure to vault out of Amycus's room. He started training again, his back almost healed, but he still wasn't ready for battle. They received news that the Watch Guard had searched a village in northern Paxton, shortening the timeline; Amycus wanted them scouting the Ironbark Garrison within the week.

Azrael finally succeeded in blocking Spectral emotions, but he still kept his distance from Kenz, his magic seeming to call out to her, their powers interacting in a way he didn't experience with anyone else. He wasn't sure if she felt it, too, and there was no way he would ask her, having already left himself vulnerable, revealing more to her than he wanted. He needed to shore up the wall that had cracked the minute she touched him. Wearing the magic-suppressing cuffs would stop the sensation, but he didn't consider that an option—he'd grown accustomed to the power to the point of craving it.

Azrael leaned over Amycus's desk, staring at the drawing he had made of the Ironbark Garrison, still questioning the validity of this plan and how easily he'd agreed to lead the mission. Kord, Kenz, Amycus, and Flynt peered at the map.

"The garrison hedges up to the Linden Forest, and if memory serves there are two entrances. We can ride through the forest along the Berg River and camp here." Azrael pointed to the map, chewing the inside of his cheek.

Flynt, who had volunteered to go with them, frowned. He had remained mostly silent during their meetings but didn't hide the caution in his eyes. "How do we know you aren't leading us into a trap?"

Azrael raised his head, his eyes narrowed. "You don't."

Amycus sighed. "According to my source, the Guard has orders to kill Azrael on sight. This mission is more dangerous to him than it is to you."

"My point exactly. He could easily turn us over to clear his name." Flynt crossed his muscular arms, the light from the candles making his red hair shift to bronze.

"You don't have to go," Azrael said.

"Oh, I'm going. I've known Kord and Kenz longer than you. Someone needs to watch their backs."

Kord lifted his hands. "I think it's time for a break."

Amycus nodded, his eyes darting between Azrael and Flynt. Azrael frowned when Kenz gripped Flynt's arm. She pulled him from the table to pour him a drink.

Azrael cracked his neck. "I need some air."

He pushed away from the table and walked outside, grabbing a practice sword and hoping the repetitive motions would settle his mind. He hadn't known he had a death sentence, most likely Bronn's doing if he assumed Bronn was now second in command. Not that this information changed anything. Flynt's doubts were understandable, but he still irritated Azrael, especially when Kenz touched the Fire Spectral, how comfortably they responded to each other. He wondered if Kenz and Flynt were together. A Shield and a Fire made more sense than Kenz choosing an assassin. Azrael laughed bitterly. Why would she ever choose him, and why did it matter? He would be leaving once they completed this mission.

Azrael relaxed his shoulders and focused on his footwork—stepping, lunging, and twisting while weaving the sword through an elegant dance. He concentrated on his breathing, losing himself to the movements, releasing all thoughts of the mission, of magic, of Kenz.

"That's beautiful."

Azrael faltered, and the sword paused mid-strike. He lowered the weapon and turned.

Kenz rested one hand on her hip, her head cocked. "Why haven't you taught us that?" She walked toward him, their magic interlacing as she approached. His knuckles whitened on the hilt of the sword.

"I have. But in parts." He twirled the sword and relaxed his grip. Kenz stared at his bare wrists, a flicker of fear crossing her face.

"I'm not going to hurt you."

"Is this the same man who said he could kill me with his bare hands?"

Azrael winced. "I never thanked you for saving my life." He tried to keep from staring at her body. Tried and failed. A black leather belt cinched the waist of her white tunic, accentuating her lithe form.

Kenz surveyed him. "I'm sure you would've done the same."

Azrael raised his brows, the side of his mouth flicking up.

Kenz laughed. "Maybe." She traced a line in the sand with the toe of her boot. "How are you feeling?"

Azrael returned the sword to the rack. Pain twinged down his back and he still felt weak, but he wouldn't admit to either. "Better. Kord's abilities are truly amazing."

Kenz huffed.

"So are yours," Azrael said.

"Sometimes I wish . . ."

"Wish what?"

Kenz hugged herself and looked over the courtyard. "That I didn't have magic. To just be ordinary, I suppose. Not having to watch my back for fear of the Guard capturing me. Having this responsibility to protect . . . it's exhausting."

Azrael reached for her hand, smiling inwardly when she didn't flinch, and traced the intricate design of her gauntlet, his thumb grazing the inside of her wrist. His eyes met hers when she shivered.

"Even without magic, you'd never be ordinary." Heat rushed to her face and Azrael restrained from trailing his finger down her cheek, across her bottom lip. Birds chattered in the trees and a soft breeze ruffled her hair. He inhaled her clean, citrus scent, his eyes dropping to her mouth. Their magic spun in an awkward dance, and he felt her pulse thump under his thumb. She licked her lips, and desire punched him in the gut.

"Hey, you two, the meeting's starting," Kord said, making Kenz jump. Azrael released her hand, taking a step back; he hadn't realized how close they stood. She gave him a small smile, a flush brightening her cheeks, and walked to the cottage.

Kord arched a brow as he glanced between his sister and Azrael.

Azrael shook his head. So much for rebuilding his wall.

❧❧   ❧❧   ❧❧

Azrael strapped on his armor, savoring the way it melded to him like a second skin. The improvements he and Amycus made using interlocking leather and metal plates provided more protection, especially against arrowheads. He slid on the arm and leg guards, thinking about this first mission, about collaborating with the enemy he had fought for so many years. Now he was leading the Spectrals, and if things went wrong, he would be the one to protect them. The internal battle warred—what he had known for thirteen years versus what he had learned and experienced during his time in Carhurst.

Azrael was sitting on his bed, lacing his boots, when his mask caught his attention, the skull grinning from the bottom of the drawer. He slowly slid it over his face and shuddered.

The Watch Guard had saved him, made him. The Spectrals destroyed his family. The mask told him to kill them, line up their corpses as leverage, and take back what was his.

Azrael ripped off the mask and slammed the drawer shut. His fingers trembled as he tied back his hair, catching his reflection in the mirror— haunted blue eyes stared back at him. He ran his hands down his face, feeling the stubble along his jaw, and breathed deeply. He anchored his emotions to the magic flowing through every fiber of his being and allowed the soothing thrum to silence the voice in his head.

Everyone waited in the courtyard, and the different expressions on the Spectrals' faces made Azrael chuckle. A gleam sparkled in Amycus's eyes, Flynt's jaw tightened, and Kord grinned. Azrael stopped mid-stride when he noticed Kenz staring at him; her mouth dropped open as she perused his body slowly, a flush creeping up her neck. Azrael raised his brows and closed the distance between them, admiring the black fighting leathers which fit every curve snugly.

"If it's any consolation, you look really good too," he said. He walked past her to the weapons rack.

"Oh, shut up," she said. She crossed her arms, trying to hide her smile.

116

Azrael winked at a glaring Flynt, who mumbled a curse under his breath. He searched for an adequate sword, sighing at the worn and chipped weapons and longing for the two he'd forged. When they returned from this mission, Azrael would remake his lost swords.

When he felt a tap on his shoulder he turned. Kord handed him a leather-wrapped bundle, familiar black hilts pointing out the end.

"You look so pathetic," Kord said, the corner of his eyes crinkling.

Azrael slowly unwrapped the swords and ran his hand down the smooth steel. "You've had them this entire time?"

"Well, we weren't comfortable giving an assassin not one, but two excessively sharp swords. But we can't have you going on this mission unarmed."

Azrael smiled and took the swords, sliding them into the scabbards along his back. He straightened his shoulders, inhaling deeply. "Thank you."

"You know, I'd say you have an unhealthy relationship with your accessories." Kord nodded to the armor and hilts visible behind Azrael's shoulders.

Azrael laughed as he slid a dagger into the sheath on his leg. "They're a lot less complicated than a woman, that's for sure." His eyes instinctively found Kenz across the courtyard talking with Amycus. Under Kord's inquisitive stare he immediately fiddled with his armor.

"Yes, well, time to go," Kord said, walking toward the stables.

They rode for two days and crossed into the Linden Forest at dusk. Azrael pulled his cloak tighter against the chill and the layer of fog covering the ground. They secured their horses near the campsite and walked the rest of the way to the Ironbark Garrison.

After being warned numerous times to stay out of sight, Kenz and Flynt left to scout one side of the compound. Azrael smiled, recalling Kenz as she rolled her eyes and said, "Thanks for the tip."

Azrael and Kord hid behind a boulder, surveying the stone and wood structure residing on a grass-covered hill surrounded by tall cypress trees. Azrael squinted into the dark, spotting only two guards standing watch at the arched entrance where flickering torches illuminated the open gates. Four more guards patrolled on the wall, each armed with crossbows. He assumed more soldiers covered the west side of the garrison, where a side entrance led to the sleeping quarters. Scaling the north wall would keep them away from most of the guards if they needed to get inside.

"Do you have a plan?" Kord asked, kneeling next to him and blowing into his hands.

"Yes, but let's wait for the others to see what they have to say."

Kord lifted a brow.

"What?"

"Just figured you'd take command and expect people to follow."

Azrael shrugged. "A good leader isn't afraid to hear other opinions." Azrael crawled backward, out of the soldiers' line of sight. Kord followed, and minutes later they entered their campsite with no sign of Kenz or Flynt.

"They should be back by now," Kord said, his voice tense.

Azrael scanned the forest, trying to detect movement. He lowered his protective measures against emotions to sense Kenz's or Flynt's magic. Nothing. "You wait here, just in case they return."

He headed in the direction they'd gone, mindful of where he stepped, the ground littered with pine needles and fallen leaves. He thought about vaulting to the other side of the garrison, but he didn't have a visual of where he wanted to go and the distance was greater than anything he'd ever tried. Azrael picked up his pace, moving like shadow and wind through the trees, his breath clouding in the air.

The torches on the other side of Ironbark revealed two soldiers leaning against the wall, their crossbows secured behind their backs. Azrael crept closer.

"She makes me nervous, is all I'm saying. Why is she even here?"

The other guard shrugged. "Everyone's on edge since Joren's team went missing. I guess having a Hunter stationed here is to give us more protection."

Azrael stiffened, the hair lifting on the back of his neck. Either Sabine or Distria was here. He squeezed his fist, hoping it was Distria as he sprinted to another set of trees, looking for a way inside. If Kenz was captured . . . he shook his head.

A muffled yelp from behind him made him drop to his stomach. Azrael peered into the dark, a familiar power beckoning him. He slowly crawled toward it.

"Well, what do we have here?" a voice said in the distance.

Azrael hid behind a bush and slid his dagger free. Kenz knelt in the dirt. Distria used one hand to press her knife against Kenz's neck while using her other to point her crossbow at Flynt, whose green fire swirled through his fingertips.

"Put out the fire, you Spectral piece of filth, or she dies," Distria said.

Azrael's breath hitched, an image of his mother kneeling among black flames flashing through his mind. His jaw tightened as he focused on Distria, standing thirty feet away in a clearing surrounded by trees. He needed to vault before she alerted the guards. His power hummed through his system as he squeezed the hilt of his dagger, and visualized himself appearing behind her.

The tug of magic intensified and the darkness swept him away.

In less than a heartbeat, Azrael had his knife pressed to Distria's exposed throat.

"What the—?" Distria partially turned and gasped, the blade digging deeper.

"Hello, Distria," Azrael said, relishing the fear pulsing through the traitor's neck, a trickle of blood dripping down her skin.

"Azrael? How?"

He yanked her head back and she swore, dropping the sword and crossbow. Azrael nodded to Flynt to pick up her discarded weapons. He did a quick scan of Kenz, who stood, her gauntlets glowing.

"Are you all right?" Azrael asked, his voice like a taut bowstring.

Kenz nodded.

Azrael gave her one last look and then nudged Distria. "You breathe too loud and I will gut you." She hissed as he held her wrists, practically grinding the bones together while keeping the knife pressed to her throat. They trudged through the woods to their campsite, Kenz leading the way, Flynt walking alongside pointing the crossbow at Distria.

Kord paced around the campfire, halting when Kenz emerged through the trees. His shoulders lowered. "You okay? What happened?"

Kenz and Flynt dropped their gear near the fire. Kord's eyes darted between them and Distria.

"We're fine," Kenz said, shaking her head. "She got the jump on us when we were scouting the area."

"Who is she?" Kord asked.

"A Hunter," Azrael growled, shoving her to the ground. She landed hard on her knees.

Flynt sat on a stump, rubbing the back of his head where dried blood crusted his hair. "What do you plan to do with her?"

"Kenz, I need a sound shield," Azrael said. He scowled at Distria, who glared back. It would take considerable time and pain to get her to talk, but he had all night.

Kenz bit her lip, her face pale as she looked to her brother, who grimaced.

Azrael sighed. "We need information. If you don't like it, you can leave." He knelt before Distria, tracing the knife along her cheek. The vision of her shooting arrows while the villagers attacked made his anger surge. Finally, he had a chance for revenge, starting with the one who had left him powerless. "You will give me what I need. How quickly is up to you." He smiled when her eyes widened.

"There's no turning back from this, Az," Flynt said. "You torture a Hunter and they will never stop looking for you."

"I'm counting on it." Azrael looked over his shoulder at Kenz. "Shield, now."

Kenz swallowed and raised her hand, igniting the shield. Distria swore and spit in his face, and Azrael wiped it away, baring his teeth. "Slow it is. I've imagined this moment ever since you shot those arrows."

Screams echoed off the indigo wall, shimmering with every yell of pain as the night slowly turned to dawn. Azrael lost himself to the darkness. The Angel of Death dominated reason and decency while he questioned her, methodically torturing her. Sweat and blood dripped down his face, and though Kenz's shield remained stable, she had turned away. Kord left the campsite, and Flynt stared into the fire, still as a statue.

Finally, Azrael had what he needed from Distria, who lay groaning on the ground, clutching fingers twisted in different directions. Blood covered her, except for the tracks on her face left by tears. She glared up at him. "I was obeying orders," she panted. "What would you have done?"

"What happened to loyalty and honor?" Azrael asked, his voice guttural.

He wiped his blade on the grass, leaving a dark red streak, and motioned to Kenz to lower the shield. She flicked her wrists and the sounds of the forest filled his ears.

He frowned, sliding his sword from the scabbard on his back. "Turn away, Kenz." She shook her head, hands covering her mouth. "Kenz," he said through gritted teeth. Finally, she turned. Azrael's sword sliced through the air and Distria's head rolled down the hill, away from the rest of her damaged body.

One down.

Adrenaline coursed through him as he picked up Distria's head and marched toward the garrison—ready to send a clear message from the Angel of Death.

CHAPTER 16

The steady rhythm of the horses' hooves accompanied Azrael's thoughts on the ride back to Carhurst. His hands, still splattered with blood, gripped the reins as the forest rushed by. He had ignored the conflict within him while he tortured Distria, his magic writhing and pleading for him to stop. Walking back to the campsite after delivering Distria's head to the garrison, he'd fallen to his knees and retched, his stomach heaving over and over until it left him hollow. Seeing the disgust on Kenz's face made him sick, and for the first time, ashamed. He imagined what his mother and sister would think. Would he be able to torture someone in front of them? He didn't think so.

Azrael ordered his team to ride straight through, ignoring the pained expressions on both Kord's and Kenz's faces. The Ironbark guards would soon find Distria's head and the message it carried. It hadn't been safe to linger at the smoldering camp where only ashes remained. Azrael had sighed with relief when he'd returned to the site and Distria's body was gone, thankful Flynt had taken care of it.

The information he pulled from Distria left him both relieved and concerned. Drexus didn't know Azrael's location but suspected he was in Paxton; those suspicions were confirmed when the soldiers who attacked Carhurst never returned. He also learned that Bronn, now promoted to second in command, remained in Opax at the Bastion Compound. Distria told Azrael about the new Amplifier serum developed in the medical facility at the Desert Garrison, but she hadn't known if it was ready or who would receive the transfusion, though all the Hunters had volunteered. Azrael suspected Bronn would be the first.

They arrived at Carhurst in the early evening, exhaustion lining their faces. Smoke from the forge billowed into the sky, but Amycus was the last person Azrael wanted to see. He was positive the old man wouldn't approve of his interrogation tactics.

He agreed with Amycus that the Hunters could not receive the serum. Spectrals wouldn't stand a chance against a team of assassins with magic—Azrael had already proven that. Destroying Drexus's serum and facilities took priority over his need for revenge against Bronn and Sabine. Azrael strode from the stable without uttering a word to his team and returned to his room, desperate to wash the blood from his skin, get a drink, and sleep.

A knock on the door had Azrael opening his eyes. He groaned at the bright light flooding the room and the burning in his left arm. The bed shifted. He lifted his head, swallowing the nausea from too much alcohol, and frowned at the head of blonde curls next to him. Azrael swore as the knocking continued and stumbled out of bed.

"What?" he said as he opened the door, his voice gravelly with sleep.

Kenz's eyes widened as they traveled down his partially naked body. Azrael, too tired to care, leaned against the door, blinking to clear his vision as Kenz frowned at a spot on his left arm that was now marked with a tattoo of a crossbow.

"That's new," Kenz said, her mouth drawn into a thin line.

Azrael sighed. "Is there something you need?"

Her eyes flicked to his and she took a deep breath. "I just wanted to see if you were—" The color drained from her face as she stared over his shoulder. Azrael turned and swore. Linnette sat on the bed, hair tousled, smiling sleepily at Kenz.

"You're here awfully early. Is it training time already?" Linnette said, stretching, thankfully, fully dressed. Azrael rubbed the back of his neck, remembering she had gone with him to get the tattoo and then walked him back to the inn. After that, nothing.

"Never mind," Kenz said, turning on her heel.

Azrael grabbed her arm. "It's not what you think. Nothing happened." He turned to Linnette. "Nothing happened, right?" Hurt flashed through the barmaid's eyes.

"I don't care what you do in your spare time, Azrael," Kenz said, trying to pull away. Azrael tightened his grip, his stomach lurching. She had come to check on him.

Kenz glared at his hand and he let go.

"Amycus wants to see you as soon as you're decent." She stomped down the hall, calling over her shoulder, "I guess he'll be waiting a long time."

Azrael rubbed his hand down his face and leaned against the closed door. One day of reprieve. Was that too much to ask? Could he just have time to, what? Wallow in self-pity? Drown the memories of blood and screams? Enjoy the company of a woman? Linnette watched him with her wide, brown eyes, and she smiled, patting the bed. The problem was that the woman currently occupying his bed was not the one he wanted—that one had marched down the hall full of fire and heat.

He sighed and plopped into a chair, resting his feet on the bed, staring up at the water-stained ceiling. Disappointment lined Linnette's face, but he couldn't bring himself to care.

She left soon after and Azrael crawled back into bed, wanting to sleep the day away. A knock on the door had him groaning.

"Now what?" he said, loud enough for the person on the other side to hear.

"May I come in?" Amycus asked, his voice muffled.

Azrael sighed. "Yes."

Amycus entered, his eyes traveling around the cramped room. Only a bed, dresser, and chair fit; even Azrael's quarters at the Bastion were bigger than this. The room often felt claustrophobic, especially now.

"The offer to stay in my spare apartment is still available." Amycus wore his usual brown tunic and pants, minus the blacksmith's apron. He sat, his fingers steepled under his chin, eyes holding a hint of sadness.

"I don't need handouts."

"The work you're doing in the forge would pay your rent, and I need an assistant, especially one so talented."

Azrael grunted and got out of bed, trying to find a clean shirt. His jaw clenched when Amycus's breath hitched; he knew the look of horror he would see on the man's face. He pulled on a black tunic and sat on the bed, pinching the bridge of his nose.

Amycus's eyes welled up. "I'm so sorry for the suffering you have endured."

Azrael huffed. "Suffering is a choice. Besides, it's not your fault."

Amycus opened his mouth then snapped it shut, clearing his throat instead. "Anyway, did you ever give Kenz those throwing knives?"

Azrael arched a brow. He didn't recall telling Amycus they were for her. "I don't think that would be wise. She'd probably just throw them at me."

Amycus chuckled. "Smart move."

Azrael laced his boots while Amycus stared out the window, the blue sky mocking Azrael's mood.

"Kord told me about the mission," Amycus said, his voice quiet.

Azrael scratched a flake of dried blood off his knuckle. He thought he had washed it all off last night. "Your Spectrals don't approve of my methods."

"Do you?"

Azrael's head shot up.

"I just meant, was there another way?" Amycus asked, raising both hands.

"I don't know any other way." Azrael laced the other boot. "This is what I do, how I operate. If they can't handle it, then they shouldn't tag along."

Amycus's piercing blue eyes surveyed Azrael. "I've seen you teach others with patience and encouragement. You create beautiful works of art in the forge."

"Your point?"

"I believe there is more to you than a killer, Jasce."

Azrael cringed at the sound of his name, and again felt shame at what he had done. What he had become. Disappointment emanated from Amycus like a wave crashing on the shore, eroding the wall Azrael had so carefully built during his time in the Watch Guard.

Amycus rose from the chair and placed his hand on Azrael's shoulder, giving it a light squeeze, then silently left the room.

Usually, after a successful mission, Azrael would receive pats on the back or praise on a job well done from his fellow Hunters. He never thought he craved such accolades until this morning. He had felt none of those things from Amycus—no respect or admiration—and for some reason, Azrael cared what he thought. Somewhere along the way, Amycus's approval started to mean something.

Azrael stared around his room, the claustrophobic feeling making his skin crawl. He needed a change of scenery, so instead of training he saddled his horse and rode toward the neighboring village of Hillford, nestled at the base of Roden Peak.

Halfway through the forest, his shoulders stiffened; someone was following him. He darted off the path and slid off his horse, drawing his dagger. He waited until the stranger passed, then leaped from behind a tree and yanked them off their horse, a high-pitched yelp sounding underneath their hood. Azrael wrenched it back and Maleous's big green eyes stared up at him.

Azrael shoved his dagger into the sheath on his thigh and helped the boy to his feet. "Why are you following me?"

"I just . . . I just wanted to see what you were doing," Maleous said, his bottom lip trembling.

Azrael frowned at the boy and crossed his arms. "Did your father put you up to this?"

Maleous shook his head. "No. He doesn't know where I am. Or Mom."

"Great." Azrael looked at the sky and sighed. He'd probably be accused of kidnapping now. The two stared at each other for a minute, then Azrael clicked his teeth for his horse. "I'm going to Hillford. If you want to come, you better keep up and not irritate me."

"Yes, sir," Maleous said. He hopped on his horse, a huge grin spread across his face.

Hours later, the sun dipping below the horizon, Azrael and Maleous rode back into Carhurst, smiling and covered in dirt. Maleous flaunted a black eye and Azrael a split lip. The day spent with the kid had made Azrael feel normal—just two guys enjoying a festival, eating sweets, joining in the competitions. And despite the minor injuries, a weight had lifted from his shoulders.

Until he saw Tillie with her hands on her hips, tapping her foot, a frown marring her beautiful face. Kord paced in front of his house, his hair standing up in all directions. He froze when he saw them walking up the street. Maleous sighed and focused on his shuffling feet.

Azrael patted Maleous on the head. "Don't worry, kid. I'll take the blame," he murmured. Kord's shoulders sagged when he saw them, his eyes shining.

"Maleous, where have you been? I was worried sick," Tillie said, marching toward him. She stopped short when she noticed his black eye, then pushed his hair off his forehead and glared at Azrael. "What happened?"

Before Azrael could answer, Kenz's indigo shield blew him back, and if not for his training, he would have ended up on his back. He bared his teeth and glared at her, all thoughts of worried parents evaporating. She marched toward him, dropping her shield right before she shoved him.

"What did you do to my nephew?"

"You think I did this?"

She shoved him again. "I asked you a question."

"Careful," Azrael said, his voice like velvet-wrapped steel.

"Or what?" Kenz raised her hands to shove him a third time, but Azrael used her momentum to flip her over his back. She grunted as she hit the ground.

"Or that." Azrael automatically reached for his sword, and Kord stepped forward, his eyes wide. The fear radiating off Kenz made Azrael freeze. He took a deep breath and stepped away.

"It wasn't his fault, Auntie," Maleous said, standing between Azrael and Kenz. He looked up at his parents. "I followed him through the forest. We went to Hillford, and they were having a festival, and there was a boxing ring, and Azrael taught me how to fight. Please, don't be mad."

Kenz, her butt still on the ground, glanced between Azrael and Maleous, then at her brother. Azrael reached out to help her up, but she brushed him away and got to her feet. Kord looked contemplatively at Azrael, his mouth curving into a smile.

"Sorry we worried you," Azrael said to Tillie and Kord. "He's got a mean right hook." He ruffled Maleous's hair, and the boy grinned up at him. Azrael's chest expanded upon seeing his accepting smile. The last person to look at him with such adoration had been Jaida. The thought made his heart hurt. "I'll see you around, kid," he said and began walking down the street.

"Wait!" Tillie said, the side of her mouth hitching up. "I bet you two are hungry." Kord also smiled. Azrael was about to accept the offer when he noticed Kenz scowling at her sister-in-law.

With one last look at Kenz, he said, "Maybe some other time." He walked toward the tavern, to his familiar barstool and comforting drink, even though the last thing he wanted was familiar or comforting.

CHAPTER 17

The following day, Azrael met with Amycus to discuss the information he'd gathered from Distria, both agreeing that the Desert Garrison was their next target. Amycus didn't mention Azrael's interrogation tactics, but a sadness lingered in the man's eyes. That sadness encouraged Azrael to work on strengthening his internal wall, blocking Spectral emotions entirely—he struggled enough with controlling his own. The anger fueling him churned under the surface, but other emotions had risen and he didn't know what to do with them, having spent years suppressing feelings considered weak.

After the meeting, Azrael continued his training with Amycus, forcing his magic to become second nature, combining his two powers and making them act as one. He vaulted in the courtyard while discussing how best to sabotage Drexus's facility and obtain a sample of the serum for Amycus to study, but using one part of his mind to strategize and the other to vault caused him to materialize in locations he hadn't aimed for.

Azrael's lessons intensified every day as he dodged flames and sandstorms while vaulting to marked circles around the courtyard. His experience and discipline as an assassin merged with the magic, creating a lethal combination, and Azrael transformed, becoming what he always wanted: invincible. Nothing and no one would stop him from overthrowing Drexus, destroying Bronn, and finding the Fire Spectral.

During one of Azrael's trainings, a small crowd gathered. Two new Spectrals joined Kord, Flynt, Delmira, and Slater, who all loitered against the wall observing as Amycus blasted water from the barrel to where Azrael stood. From the courtyard, Azrael smirked, catching Slater and Flynt exchanging coins, hoping whoever bet against him lost a considerable sum.

Suddenly, Azrael wheezed, falling to one knee. Black spots floated in his vision as he reached for his throat. Amycus had both hands raised, his forehead glistening.

"Come on, Az, you can do it!" Kord called from across the courtyard.

Azrael closed his eyes, blocking out the feeling of suffocating, and focused on the power humming within him, seeing himself appear behind Amycus to get out of his line of sight. The familiar tug yanked him into the void with a force he hadn't experienced before. A light appeared suddenly and pain radiated through his shoulder as he gasped for air, lying on his side. The tree behind Amycus had fallen over. Its trunk was splintered and a carpet of dead leaves covered the ground.

"That was one of my favorite trees," Amycus said, wiping sweat off his brow.

Azrael got to his feet and rubbed his shoulder, frowning at the damaged tree. "How long would you have kept going?"

"Until you lost consciousness. You hesitated and then panicked, and based on the tree, your Amp magic influenced the vaulting. You need to disappear the second you feel the air pull at your lungs."

"I never panic."

Amycus chuckled. "The tree would say otherwise."

Kord jogged across the yard. "I knew you could do it," he said. Azrael swore when Kord smacked him on the shoulder. The other Spectrals lingered against the wall, some whispering, others staring with wide eyes. Dirt swirled around Slater's feet while Flynt smiled, counting coins.

Azrael walked to the water barrel, where Flynt joined him. "Well done," Flynt said, twirling a coin through his fingers.

"I thought you would've bet against me."

"I may not like you, but I'm not a fool." Flynt waved the two newcomers over. "This is Aura and Vale. Aura is an Air and Vale is an Earth. They're coming with us to the Desert Garrison."

Aura's long white hair wafted as if in a constant breeze, her gray eyes reminding Azrael of a stormy sky. "You did well fighting through Amycus's magic," she said. "You'll have to try it with me sometime."

Azrael raised a brow. He'd fought other Air Spectrals in the past, but Aura's power radiated off her. She would give him a challenging workout if he didn't pass out first.

Vale, who looked to be in his teens, ran a hand through his unkempt brown hair. He bounced on his toes; eyes wide with excitement. "That was amazing! I've never seen a Vaulter before."

Slater shook his head, mumbling under his breath. Azrael glanced at Kord.

"They know," Kord said.

"And you're okay working with the Angel of Death?" Azrael asked, staring at Aura and Vale. Aura's eyes narrowed slightly and Vale swallowed.

"I trust Amycus, therefore, I trust you," Aura said, closing the distance, her magic rustling her dress and the leaves swirling at her feet. She glanced at Azrael's chest and his lungs tightened. "Don't make me regret it."

Flynt stepped closer, resting his hand on the hilt of his sword while Vale's eyes darted between Aura and Azrael. Amycus stared from across the courtyard, a line of sweat dripping down his temple.

Back at the Guard, if someone had been foolish enough to threaten him, they'd find themselves on the ground, bleeding. He relaxed his hands and counted to ten—his fight wasn't with them, but he could use their magic.

"I need practice vaulting with distractions," he said, inadvertently scanning the courtyard for Kenz.

Kord crossed his muscular arms. "What did you have in mind?"

For the next hour, Azrael trained harder than he had in years, physically and mentally. He sparred with Kord while Flynt threw fireballs, which forced Azrael to block Kord's strike and vault away from the flames while Amycus gave instructions between attacks. At one point, Aura extracted the air from his lungs while Vale and Slater hurled rocks, compelling Azrael to trust his training and surrender to his magic. He dodged and lunged, swords clashing as he vaulted, sweat dripping down his face and back. Once a separate entity, his magic became a part of him—body, soul, and spirit.

Azrael crossed swords with Kord while Vale and Aura created a dirt cyclone and spun it toward him as Flynt ignited another ball of flame. Time slowed and a shiver ran down Azrael's spine, his magic fluttering.

Then Kenz walked into the courtyard, her hair shining like black silk in the midday sun. She frowned, glancing around until her eyes met his. She opened her mouth, eyes wide when a glint of metal caught Azrael's attention.

A searing pain erupted as Kord sliced his sword across Azrael's thigh. A ball of fire smacked into his chest as the cyclone launched him across the yard.

Azrael blinked at the wisps of clouds floating overhead, struggling to breathe, the rough cobblestones digging into his back. His chest burned and blood ran through his fingers as he clutched his leg.

"Az!" Kord sprinted over, placing his hand on the wound. A tingle of warmth radiated through Azrael's thigh and shadows fell over him, blocking out the sky. Amycus and Flynt knelt next to him while Vale apologized profusely. Aura, Delmira, and Kenz looked on in surprise.

"Blast it, that hurt," Azrael groaned.

Amycus chuckled and helped him to a sitting position. "Thankfully, the dirt in the cyclone extinguished the fire." He looked over Azrael's body, his leather chest piece scorched by the flames. "What caused you to lose focus?"

Azrael's eyes flitted to Kenz, and her cheeks reddened. He swallowed. "Just tired." Kord removed his hand and the pain in Azrael's leg vanished.

"I think that's enough training for now," Amycus said.

Vale whispered to Slater as they walked back to the cottage. "Did you see that? How fast he moved, the vaulting? Amazing."

Azrael dusted himself off, frowning at his bloodstained pants. He didn't understand why his magic behaved the way it did when Kenz was near or why the sensation continued to intensify, but he needed to figure it out soon; otherwise, she would get him killed.

⚸ ⚸ ⚸

The Desert Garrison resided on a hill, a stronghold of shadows against the setting sun. Guards patrolled the tall stone wall and in front of the portcullis blocking the entrance bordering the Desert of Souls. Azrael, Flynt, and Kenz hid behind a dune, timing the guards' rotations.

"There's a separate entrance to the medical facility on the west side of the compound, with guards posted inside and out," Azrael said, motioning to the stone wall.

Kenz pointed to a long, rectangular structure. "What's that building over there?"

"Edgefield Prison." Azrael kept his eyes fixed on the garrison, feeling Flynt's and Kenz's stares.

"How many?" Flynt said.

"It can hold up to a hundred prisoners but hasn't been at full capacity in a while. I don't know how many Spectrals are in there now."

Flynt flexed his hand, his ignitor visible on the inside of his wrist. "We need to free them."

"That's not part of this mission," Azrael said, edging back from the dune. Freeing the Spectrals added complications to an already risky mission—destroying Drexus's worksite and getting out alive was challenging enough. He didn't want the responsibility of extricating the captives as well as protecting the lives of his team.

He had never worried about his fellow Hunters during raids; he'd only cared about himself. Now all he could see was Tillie hugging Kord, threatening him if he didn't return home, and the anxious look on Amycus's face as he sent them off.

Back at the campsite, Flynt told the others about the prisoners, suggesting they split up and rescue the Spectrals. Azrael argued with them, but when he was outnumbered, he finally gave in.

"Fine, you win," Azrael said. He reformed his strategy, studying the map of the garrison and prison and locating the easiest ways in and, more importantly, out. His breath froze in the air and he pulled his cloak closer. "Once you get them out, you'll want to cross the desert at its narrowest section. The prisoners will have magic-suppressing collars and won't be much help if a fight breaks out." Azrael tapped at the best location, nodding to Kord. "You'll lead that group; they'll probably need your magic the most once you're clear. Aura, Delmira, Kenz, and Slater will go with you. I need Flynt to blow up the site." He pointed to Vale. "And you will stay here. If anything goes wrong, we need you to alert Amycus." Vale opened his mouth to argue but snapped it shut at Azrael's glare.

Kenz squared her shoulders. "I'm going with you and Flynt."

"Still don't trust me?" Azrael said.

"Kord doesn't need two Shields."

"Flynt and I don't need a Shield."

"You have no idea what you'll find in there. I can protect you both and fight."

Azrael rubbed his hand down his face. He was running out of excuses. Strategically, she was correct, but he couldn't allow what occurred in the courtyard to happen during the mission, and he hadn't figured out how to block her magic from interacting with his. It could get them both killed.

Azrael crossed his arms. "Then, I'll take Delmira."

Kenz narrowed her eyes, anger hiding the hurt that flashed across her face. "I'm the stronger fighter and you know it," she said, poking him in the chest.

Azrael stared at her finger and ignored the shiver that ran down his back. He grabbed her wrist. "I'm leading this operation and I won't have my orders questioned."

Kenz twisted her arm out of his grasp, her face turning red. "You're acting like a stubborn mule."

Someone gasped. Kord and Flynt stepped closer, and Slater swore under his breath.

Azrael's nostrils flared. "And you're behaving like a childish fool."

"Give me one good reason you'd pick Delmira over me."

Delmira chewed on her lip. "I'm fine going with—"

Azrael raised his hand, cutting her off. "I don't have to give you a reason."

"Because you can't."

Azrael inhaled and counted to ten, fighting the urge to grab Kenz and shake her. A wolf howled and a breeze blew dead leaves across the ground. He counted to ten again; Kenz waited with her arms crossed.

Azrael closed the distance, trying not to get lost in her mesmerizing eyes or the way their magic wove together. "You will do as I say. Is that clear?"

He turned on his heel, his teeth grinding at her satisfied smile, and walked to the other side of the campsite. So far, this mission wasn't going as planned. The team was splitting up, and the one distraction he'd tried desperately to avoid was now going with him. He really hoped his luck would change; he'd already lost two battles and they hadn't even left the campsite.

They waited until just before dawn when the nighttime guards rotated with their early morning replacements. Azrael looked to the east, where the stars twinkled in the midnight sky—another sunrise, and some of his team might not live to see it. He had grown fond of this group in the short time they'd trained together, especially Kord and Kenz. He didn't want to dissect his growing attraction for Kenz, not entirely sure what to do or how to stop it; and her brother, with his warm smiles and forgiving nature, was becoming a genuine friend, something Azrael hadn't experienced since he was young. Azrael stared into the distance, squeezing and relaxing his fists, battling the worry swirling in his gut.

Gravel crunched under boots. "Couldn't sleep?" Kord said.

"Never can before a battle." Azrael glanced once more to the horizon and turned to see Aura and Kenz sliding on their armor and Delmira fiddling with her gauntlets. Flynt placed the compact bombs he had made into his bag and double-checked his wrist ignitors. Slater talked quietly with Vale, placing a reassuring hand on the teenager's sagging shoulder.

Azrael strode toward his gear, sheathing his swords and dagger and quickly tying back his hair. He caught Kenz staring at him, a flush in her cheeks, and his stomach tightened, unsure what that look meant.

They circled around the smoldering fire, looking to Azrael. But he wasn't one for long, encouraging speeches. "Wait for our signal. Be smart, watch each other's backs, and get in and out as quickly as possible." Azrael's eyes met Kord's in a silent plea. "And stay alive."

ᐬ ᐬ ᐬ

The woods behind the compound came to life as green flames slithered like serpents between the trees and devoured the dry brush along the ground. Flynt joined Azrael and Kenz, a hungry smile on his flushed face, as shouts rang out and soldiers ran to the edge of the forest, leaving one to stand watch while the fire blazed closer. Azrael felt the tug of his magic and disappeared into the void, appearing behind the unsuspecting soldier and quickly snapping his neck. He scanned the area, the smoke making his nose twitch. Kenz's and Flynt's silhouettes were black against the flames as they sprinted across the clearing.

Kenz readied her shield while Flynt melted the lock on the door. In the distance, the soldiers' shouts competed with the roar of the fire engulfing the trees. Azrael pulled his dagger from its sheath and focused on the hum of his magic, ignoring the way it called to Kenz, who glanced at him and frowned.

Azrael pushed the door open and swore. Bronn lay unconscious, strapped to a table with tubes sticking out of his arms and legs. They were too late; the Hunter had already received the serum. Drexus's head shot up, surprise followed by anger flashing across his face. He barked orders for the guards to attack while his assistant squeaked and ran to the other side of the table. Azrael used his Amplifier magic and sprinted across the room to dispatch three guards, who crumpled to the ground. The remaining soldier escaped into the central area of the compound. Kenz threw her shield around Bronn and Drexus while Flynt ran to the far side of the room, already retrieving the bombs from his satchel.

"We don't have much time," Azrael said over his shoulder as he strode to the assistant. Drexus yanked the tubes out of Bronn, and the Hunter's eyes blinked open.

"Azrael," Drexus growled, reaching for his sword; his hand grabbed thin air. The forgotten weapon lay near the open doorway.

Azrael pulled one of his swords from his back and pointed it at the assistant while monitoring Drexus, still trapped inside Kenz's shield. "Where's the remaining serum?" His voice sounded like liquid steel. The assistant yelped as Azrael flicked his blade across the man's cheek. "Where is it?"

The assistant's eyes darted to the corner, sweat and blood dripping down his face.

"Kenz, over there." Azrael pointed to the other side of the room.

"You coward," Drexus said, glaring at the man.

Azrael closed the distance, the assistant holding up his hands and stepping back into Kenz's shield.

"Please, don't, I—"

Azrael's blade cut through the air, silencing him forever.

"No!" Drexus pounded on Kenz's shield while Bronn struggled against his restraints, his teeth bared, hatred and pain contorting his face.

"Kenz, lower your shield," Azrael said, his eyes flicking to where Flynt remained busy setting his explosives as smoke billowed from the far corner of the room. They were running out of time.

Azrael stalked to the table, his knuckles whitening on the shaft of his dagger, his sword pointed at Drexus's chest. He glared at Bronn. "You left me to die, you traitorous snake. Should I return the favor?" Azrael drove the blade through the middle of Bronn's leg, pinning him to the table. Bronn roared, gripping the hilt.

"Azrael, stop!" Drexus yelled, his face turning red.

"Do they know?" Azrael pressed the tip of his blade into Drexus's chest. "About the king?" The anger churning under the surface bubbled to the top— the betrayal, the lies, the whippings. Thirteen years of brutality churned inside of Azrael as he glared at the man who had caused so much pain.

Drexus released a harsh laugh. "You would believe Amycus over me?" His eyes darted to Kenz, who was loading the remaining vials into her satchel.

Azrael's hand tightened on his sword. "Did you kill the king?"

Drexus's lip curled. Bronn panted, still trapped on the table. Smoke filled the room as Flynt's fire melted the equipment, the assortment of chemicals setting off minor explosions.

"Hurry!" Flynt yelled. Kenz ran to the exit, using her shield to block the main entrance.

Drexus snarled. "You've chosen the wrong side, boy."

"I don't think so." Azrael pushed Drexus into the counter and pressed the sword tip deeper into his chest. Blood stained his tunic.

Flynt's green fire coiled up the back wall. The air rippled in the intense heat, and Bronn's eyes widened as flames crawled up the legs of the exam table. Bronn ripped the dagger free, his yell echoing through the smoke, and sliced the remaining restraints. He rolled off the table and crumpled to the ground, the bloody dagger skimming along the floor.

"I want answers," Azrael said. He lifted Drexus off his feet and pushed him back until the fire ignited his cloak. "Did you kill the king?"

Drexus grabbed Azrael's wrists, his face turning red. Bronn crawled away from the flames toward Drexus's sword as guards pounded against Kenz's shield.

"Azrael, let's go!" Flynt yelled. Smoke obscured the exit.

Drexus's mouth curved into a smile. "You want answers?" he croaked. He released Azrael's wrist and reached back, submerging his hand in the blaze.

Azrael loosened his grip, transfixed on the flames that swirled through Drexus's fingers.

Green fire shifted into black.

"No," Azrael whispered, stumbling. It couldn't be. The fire clung to Drexus like a lover. His arms rose and the flames immediately obeyed; a blaze of curling fingers reached for Azrael. Drexus smiled and shot a fireball at Kenz, who leaped to the side. Her shield vanished and soldiers filed in with swords drawn. Bronn leaned against the wall, the color drained from his face and his eyes shining with surprise as he watched the black flames shift into living shadows. Explosions burst from the back of the room as soldiers formed a barrier between Azrael and Drexus. Azrael choked on the smoke-filled air, sweat running down his face and back.

For thirteen years, Azrael had obsessed over the Spectral who had killed his mother and sister. All this time, it was the man who trained and groomed him to rule by his side.

His entire body shook with rage as the Angel of Death broke free, desperate for blood. Soldiers cried out. Blood spattered the walls.

Azrael's sword was shadow and death, slicing down the guards who stood between him and vengeance. He swung his blade at Drexus's head, but instead of the sound of severed flesh and bone, metal clanged.

Bronn sneered, blocking Azrael's sword; the serum had already transformed the Hunter, infusing him with the Amplifier magic. Azrael used his strength and slammed Bronn into the burning exam table. Instruments crashed, disappearing into the black flames that slithered on the floor and walls.

Drexus waved his hand, maneuvering the firestorm away from Bronn. "You're just like your mother. Lisia chose Amycus over me, too, a decision that cost her dearly."

"Don't you dare speak her name," Azrael growled, reaching for his second sword and glaring at the man who took everything from him.

"I thought I whipped that sentimental nonsense out of you," Drexus snarled.

Azrael charged forward, but an impenetrable wall of heat blew him back. Drexus smiled through the black flames.

"Azrael!" Kenz's voice broke through his rage, her shield glowing brightly as soldiers flooded in and recoiled from the smoke. Flynt used fire and steel as he battled with the guards trying to enter through the back entrance. Azrael swore. Flynt's bombs would explode any second.

"Now you die," Azrael said. With one last look at Drexus, he sprinted toward the exit, slashing through the remaining guards like paper. They cleared the door and were halfway through the clearing when the explosion launched them forward. Azrael hit hard, using the momentum to roll to his feet. Fire engulfed the compound as soldiers ran from the other side of the building.

"We need to go," Flynt said as more soldiers advanced.

Azrael saw Drexus through the inferno, a cocoon of flames protecting him and Bronn from the blast.

Flynt grabbed Azrael's arm. "Azrael, now."

Azrael looked over his shoulder, his teeth bared. Flynt backed away, eyes wide, hand gripping his sword.

Kenz shook her head. "Azrael, no."

Azrael faced the compound and the man who had turned his life to ashes. The Angel of Death stalked toward the approaching soldiers, succumbing to the darkness that seduced him like a greedy lover. Hatred and destruction defined him and unleashed the monster within, his lust for blood consuming all thought, all reason. He commanded his magic to obey, felt the tug, and vaulted.

Guards dropped with each violent slash of his swords, falling at his feet and leaving carnage in his wake. Blood and gore covered him. With every kill, darkness penetrated his soul.

Kenz yelled his name, but he didn't care, he couldn't stop. He lost himself in the killing, his magic drowning in blood.

Indigo light wrapped around him, halting his attack.

"We need to leave!" Kenz's hands were raised, her eyes pleading. Flynt stood by her side; his knuckles were white on the hilt of his sword.

Dead soldiers spread out before Azrael, and through the smoke and flames, a silhouette loomed, surrounded by black fire. A guttural roar tore through Azrael, the revenge he craved within his grasp.

He glared over his shoulder. "Drop the shield." His voice dripped with malevolence. Kenz slowly shook her head. She used her shield to drag him away from the compound and another squadron of approaching soldiers. Azrael's feet gouged the blood-soaked ground as she pulled him back.

Azrael yelled, slashing the impenetrable wall with his swords. Kenz winced and blood dripped from her nose. He dug into his remaining strength, drawing from years of pain, and pounded against the shield. With a cry, Kenz fell, the indigo barrier disintegrating. Azrael trudged through the slain bodies toward Drexus, vengeance so close he could taste it.

Blinding pain dropped him to his knees, and stars flashed in his eyes as Flynt struck a second time with the hilt of his sword, sending him into oblivion.

CHAPTER 18

*F*ire snaked along Azrael's body, destroying everything it touched, the smell of burning skin suffocating. A young girl's screams echoed in the darkness and lifeless gray eyes stared at him accusingly. Laughter . . . maniacal laughter ripped through the shadows. Rivers of blood carved the desolate ground. A voice calling his name pulled him from a pit of death, and magic beckoned him like a beacon shining through the night—a safe haven, his salvation.

Azrael's body rocked side to side with the steady rhythm of his horse, the movement accompanied by the gurgling of running water. He lifted his head, blinking against the bright sun, and tugged at the rough cords of ropes restraining his arms and hips. Silver cuffs gleamed on his blood-encrusted wrists.

The last thing he remembered was a silhouette surrounded by black fire, blood dripping from Kenz's nose, her shield trapping him. He had used his magic and rage to break free of her shield, then the indigo light disappeared and was replaced with a blinding pain to the back of his skull.

Flynt. He ground his teeth. Drexus would be dead if it weren't for him.

He turned his head and grimaced. His entire body ached and an emptiness he had never experienced threatened to overwhelm him. Kenz rode next to him, her brow furrowed and gauntlets glowing blue. She stiffened and turned to see him staring. Her eyes, smudged with shadows, scanned his face, and her mouth drew into a straight line.

He smelled the blood covering him. He must have looked like a monster.

Kenz faced forward. "I'll remove the cuffs if you promise not to go back to the garrison or harm Flynt."

He twisted in the saddle and bared his teeth. Flynt glared back, his coppery eyes hard, his body rigid.

"Why did you stop me?" Azrael asked, facing forward, his voice sounding like broken glass.

"Because you could've died and gotten Flynt and me killed in the process," Kenz shot back.

"I have searched for that man for years, and you stole my revenge. If I had died, so be it, as long as I took him with me."

"And what about Flynt and me? Would you sacrifice us for your vengeance?"

Azrael clenched his teeth and looked away. He'd been blinded by rage and hadn't even thought of their safety. Disjointed thoughts and emotions ravaged his mind. He had relished the soldiers lying dead at his feet, the copper smell of blood overflowing his senses, the violence empowering him. But now, all he felt was broken. A chasm of defeat lay before him. He dropped his head and lost himself to the motion of the horse.

When they stopped by a stream, Kenz untied Azrael's ropes while Flynt stood behind her, his sword drawn. Azrael was too tired to care; a part of him wanted Flynt to run him through just to end the nightmare. He slid off the horse and peered into Kenz's eyes, which were brimming with wariness.

"Do I have your word?" she asked.

Azrael nodded. She held his gaze, then unlocked the cuffs. He closed his eyes, inhaling deeply as the hum of magic rushed through him. During the battle, his power had recoiled from the violence, draining with every vault, every slash of his sword. Now, it stormed through him and left him gasping for air. He rested his hands on his knees and drew in a long breath, his stomach convulsing at the smell and feel of dried blood.

"I have to get this off," Azrael said, tugging at his armor covered in blood and gore. He stumbled into the river, the icy water rushing past his knees and sending a shiver up his spine. He swore, his hands shaking violently, unable to unclasp his chest plate.

"Let me help you," Kenz said, stepping into the stream. He jerked his head to stare through a curtain of hair, frozen and helpless.

Her steady hands released each buckle. Azrael inhaled as the chest piece fell away. She continued removing each section of armor, rinsing them and placing them gently on the shore. Azrael counted the freckles across her nose, captivated by the pink in her cheeks. The panic subsided, replaced by desire. He wondered if she could hear his heart thumping, if she knew what she was doing to him. Her magic caressed his—a calming balm to his broken soul. She shivered slightly as she peeked up at him under her lashes.

"Do you have an extra one?" she asked, frowning at his filthy tunic. He nodded. Somewhere along the way, he had lost the ability to speak.

He sucked in a breath as she lifted the tunic over his head, her knuckles scraping his chest. Goosebumps flared across his body and heat exploded in his core. She rinsed the soiled shirt in the water and stood on her toes to wipe the blood off his face. He slowly lowered to his knees, sinking into the sandy riverbed as the cool water rushed over his waist. Azrael closed his eyes, leaning into the gentleness of her touch; the way her fingertips pushed back his hair, ran along his jaw, skimmed his lips. He grabbed Kenz's arms, halting her torturous hands.

"Stop, please." He kept his eyes closed, swallowing the yearning, wanting more yet fearing it. He slowly lifted his head and his breath hitched. Her irises darkened to a forest green color, and she bit her lip as she stared at his mouth. He imagined pulling her to him, crushing his mouth against hers, feeling every curve of her body. He wanted to run his tongue along her lip and drown in the taste of her.

Flynt cleared his throat, looking in the other direction. "We need to keep moving."

Kenz's face flushed as she seemed to remember they weren't alone. Azrael had forgotten about Flynt too. He released her wrists and brushed a piece of escaped hair behind her ear, thankful for the frigid water extinguishing his need.

"Thank you." He couldn't hide the huskiness in his voice.

She nodded and took a shaky step toward the shore. He slowly followed, water dripping from his wet hair and down his naked chest. He gathered his clean armor and walked past Flynt, who grabbed his arm. Azrael glared at the hand and then met Flynt's stare.

"I'm sorry," he nodded to Azrael's head. "But I had to. You understand that, right?"

Azrael looked back at the man's hand and Flynt quickly let go. Azrael nodded and turned, stopping when he heard Flynt swear.

"Who did that to you?"

"The monster you kept me from killing," Azrael said, striding toward his horse. He understood why Kenz and Flynt had interfered. If the situation were reversed, he would have done the same. But the justice he'd sought for so many years had slipped through his fingers, and that made him want to break his promise to Kenz and ride back to the Desert Garrison. His magic shuddered against the bloodlust bubbling to the surface. He relaxed his hands, concentrating on the ebb and flow of his power like gentle waves lapping the shore.

"We still have a day's ride to meet up with the others," Flynt said, climbing onto his horse. Azrael ran his fingers through his wet hair then swung himself into his saddle, Kenz following suit.

They arrived at the campsite as nighttime fell, and Azrael's shoulders relaxed when he saw Kord, alive and unharmed. Kenz jumped off her horse and ran into her brother's embrace as Azrael scanned the campsite. Delmira sat by the fire, her head in her hands.

"Where's everyone else?" Azrael asked.

"We got separated." Kord's eyes darted to Flynt's. "Slater didn't make it. I'm sorry." Flynt swore and pulled Delmira into his arms.

"And the prisoners?" Azrael asked.

"We rescued fifteen. Aura and Vale are leading them to Rochdale."

"Only fifteen?" Even when the raids had slowed, Edgefield Prison held more prisoners than that. Azrael glanced at Kenz, who was leaning into her brother, his arm wrapped protectively around her. Flynt cradled Delmira, who cried quietly into his chest.

"What about the facility?" Kord asked.

"Destroyed," Azrael said. "We retrieved a few samples of the serum, but Bronn had already undergone the transfusion." He turned from Kord to stare at the fire. During their trek through the forest, Azrael had thought about the years he'd served Drexus. All that time, the man he had searched for had been within his reach. A nagging thought kept recurring, too, one he didn't want to contemplate—had Amycus known Drexus was a Spectral? Azrael remembered Amycus's expression when he first mentioned how his mother died.

And now another Hunter had the Amplifier magic, and despite the extra samples Kenz had retrieved, he knew Drexus would have more than one worksite. They couldn't allow any more Hunters to receive the serum.

Kord rested his hand on Azrael's arm. "We don't need to dissect everything now."

Azrael stepped out of his reach. "We need to keep moving. They can grieve later."

"What happened?" Kord asked, looking from Azrael to his sister.

"The commander of the Watch Guard is a Spectral," Kenz said.

"What? Drexus has magic?"

Kenz nodded. "And powerful. His fire protected him and the Hunter from Flynt's bombs."

Kord raised a brow, staring at Azrael. "What am I missing?"

Azrael lifted his chin. "He killed my mother and sister." The words tasted like ash.

"Drexus is the one?" Kord's eyes widened. "I'm so sorry, Azrael."

"Don't call me that," Azrael said through bared teeth. "He gave me that name." He turned away from the pity on Kord's face and trudged into the woods.

He meant it too. He would no longer go by Azrael, but his given name, the one his sister and mother had called him.

Jasce.

Amycus would be pleased. The thought made him bitter.

He stumbled, remembering how Drexus had encouraged him to search for the Fire Spectral, secretly mocking him.

He roared, punching a nearby tree with all his might, the split wood slicing through his knuckles. He hit the tree again, damaging his other hand. He wanted the pain, needed it. He may have excused Drexus for lying to him about the king or leaving him for dead because he understood the Hunters' methods. Until last night, Jasce hadn't even made up his mind about killing Drexus. But he would never forgive the man for murdering his family. The betrayal left him breathless. His only mission now was to destroy Drexus and take everything from him, as he had done to Jasce. And then he would make him beg for death.

A branch snapped. Jasce reached for his dagger, his fingers brushing the empty sheath. He closed his eyes and listened for movement. A bush rustled nearby.

"We need to work on your stealth," Jasce said. Silence followed, then a loud sigh as Kord emerged from behind a tree and stood next to Jasce, both of them peering into the forest. An owl hooted in the distance, and the moon created twisted shadows among the tall trees. Jasce shoved his hands into his pockets, breathing in the fresh smell of pine with a hint of snow.

"What do you want?" he finally asked.

Kord remained still, an anchor of fortitude. "I'm here if you want to talk. Or not."

Jasce didn't talk about his problems or his feelings. It wasn't how trained killers operated. The other Hunters couldn't know what you cared about or one day they would use it against you, like the young Spectral girl in the village holding wildflowers or the recruit kneeling in the dirt, bleeding. The scars along his back proved that.

Jasce shivered, not wanting to discuss what happened outside the compound. He recalled the blood running down his face and tasting it as it dripped into his mouth, gore hanging from his sword, cries from wounded soldiers echoing through the clearing, his boots squishing into the blood-soaked ground.

Jasce's stomach seized. He stumbled away from Kord and vomited, squeezing his eyes shut, purging his thoughts as he repeatedly retched until only dry heaves remained. All the while, Kord stayed vigilant by his side.

Finally, Jasce stood, wiping his mouth on his sleeve. "So many," he said, his voice hoarse. "I slaughtered all of them. Every soldier bore Drexus's face. And I killed them all." Jasce ran his hand down his face. He had killed before and often, but never had he felt so lost and out of control.

Jasce told Kord about how Drexus manipulated the fire, about when he'd seen its blackness slithering toward him. He recounted the day Drexus killed his mother, the same fire circling them as the knife slashed her throat; he had screamed while blood pooled around her, sightless eyes staring at him. He talked about the Spectral girl that reminded him of his sister, the decision to let her and her brother go. The whipping in the courtyard, taking the young recruit's punishment. Jasce emptied himself and Kord remained a silent stronghold, never judging or recoiling at the horrors.

145

Jasce finally let out a sigh and looked up at the stars. The night seemed brighter, his shoulders less heavy.

"Thank you for telling me," Kord said, laying his hand on Jasce's shoulder. For the first time, Jasce didn't flinch.

They returned to the campsite. Delmira and Flynt were asleep by the fire, and Kenz's green eyes reflected the hypnotizing flames. Kord sat next to her and pulled her into a hug. Jasce didn't move until she patted the ground and smiled. He had always wondered what it would be like to be on the receiving end of her smile. His magic quivered as he sat next to her and stretched out his legs. He leaned back on his hands to admire the stars.

Kenz reached out. "Hi, my name is Kenz Haring."

The corner of Jasce's lip hitched. He stared at her slender hand, remembering the way she'd touched him at the river. His hand engulfed hers and he gave it a gentle squeeze. "Jasce Farone."

CHAPTER 19

They traveled through the day, only stopping to water the horses, and arrived in Carhurst late in the evening. Jasce battled the images swirling through his mind, replaying the events at the Desert Garrison. The lightness he felt after talking with Kord faded, replaced by the lies Drexus had spewed and which had defined Jasce's life as a Watch Guard soldier and Hunter. He was neither now. Black fire had turned the Angel of Death into ash. And now, he had no idea who he was. Drexus had ripped from him everything he had known and loved, and for the last thirteen years, his thoughts had revolved around hatred and revenge. The darkness surrounding him was impenetrable—or had been until two siblings and a blacksmith entered his life. Pinpricks of light had punched through Jasce's wall.

Regret, something he couldn't remember feeling before, had washed over him when he stood in that stream with Kenz. He had checked to make sure his defenses were still up and was shocked to learn that the emotion wasn't coming from her, but him. He regretted annihilating those soldiers and losing himself to darkness and hate, and only the sound of her voice and the feel of her magic had brought him back.

Jasce wasn't worthy of her forgiveness or Kord's friendship, and their acceptance had left him speechless. He could still feel the blood covering his hands, running down his face, and he knew more blood would spill, because he would not stop until Drexus was dead, until he had his revenge on Bronn and Sabine. After he defeated them and his mission was complete, he might be worthy of a life with friendship, and maybe love. But until he saw the light leave Drexus's eyes, that life would have to wait.

A glow from Amycus's cottage welcomed them, and even though Jasce desperately needed sleep, he wouldn't rest until he knew for sure. He couldn't stop wondering if Amycus had known about Drexus's power, and the closer he got to the village, the more that familiar anger increased, churning inside of him.

Jasce stood in the shadows of the stables, watching Delmira and Flynt enter the Whispering Pines Inn while Kord and Kenz headed to their home, Kenz giving Jasce a concerned glance over her shoulder.

He snuck through the back entrance of the cottage, finding Amycus sitting in his chair, transfixed on the drink he held, lost in thought.

Jasce pulled the knife from his boot. "Did you know?"

Amycus whipped his head around and sighed. "You've returned. Is everyone all right?"

He took a step closer, squeezing the hilt. "Did you know?"

Amycus stared at the knife and frowned. "Did I know what?"

"That Drexus was a Spectral?"

Amycus swallowed, placing the forgotten drink on the table and getting to his feet slowly. "I did."

"What magic does he have?" Jasce's voice was like jagged glass.

"He's a Fire."

Jasce's jaw pulsed with fury. "And what color is his fire?"

Amycus looked up, his eyes pleading.

"You knew, didn't you? You've known all this time that Drexus was the one who killed my mother and sister." Jasce stepped forward, his entire body trembling. "You knew!" Rage blinded him as he lunged for Amycus, the knife aimed for his throat.

A wall of air slammed into him. His lungs burned. Jasce glared at the blacksmith as he tried to vault free of the invisible shield. The door of the cottage flew open and Kord and Kenz took in the scene. Kenz's gauntlets ignited and Kord reached for his sword.

Amycus raised his hands. "You need to understand—"

Jasce wheezed, unable to draw in a full breath. "What I understand is that you are a liar, just like Drexus, and everything in me wants to kill you. That's what I understand."

Amycus stumbled back into his chair, his face pale, the lines around his mouth deepening. Kenz rushed to his side, glaring at Jasce.

"You're right, Azrael, and I'm sorry," Amycus said, the wall of air disappearing. Breath rushed into Jasce's lungs.

"I'm no longer Azrael."

Kord edged toward Jasce, staring at his knife. Jasce didn't need his magic to sense the fear and disappointment emanating from both siblings. Sorrow surrounded Amycus, the light from the fire shining on the gray streaks in his long dark hair as he stared at his scarred hands.

Would he have killed Amycus? Was he that lost to the darkness, that broken?

Jasce took a deep breath through his nose and slid the knife into its holder, his body vibrating with suppressed anger.

"Why didn't you tell me?" he asked.

Amycus took a deep breath. "What would you have done if I had told you when we first met?"

Jasce paced around the room, ignoring Kenz's flinch when he passed. Whatever ground he had gained with her disappeared the minute she came into the room and witnessed him holding a knife over Amycus.

What would he have done if Amycus had revealed Drexus's secret?

Jasce sighed. "Most likely kill you."

"Exactly. You would never have learned about your mother, or that you had magic." Amycus nodded at his arm. "You wouldn't have developed genuine friendships or seen your potential."

"Right. So, you lied to protect me? To help me become a better person?" Jasce's laugh sounded harsh even in his ears.

"Jasce, I won't apologize for lying. There's more at stake than your feelings."

Jasce stared at the old man. "Well, that's brutally honest."

"I am, however, sorry that Drexus killed Lisia and Jaida. I wasn't totally sure until you told me how they died." Tears lined Amycus's eyes, and he took a sip from his drink, his hands shaking. "I am curious how you discovered the truth."

Jasce told Amycus about the mission—the destruction of the site and that Bronn had received the Amplifier serum. Kenz removed the vials she had stolen and handed them to Amycus.

Jasce sat, resting his face in his hands. He was so tired, not just physically but emotionally. It seemed like every time he got his feet steady, the ground split open and swallowed him whole.

Kord described the rescue of the captive Spectrals and of Slater's death. Amycus hung his head and sighed at the news. Kenz sat on the couch next to Kord, everyone lost in their own thoughts.

A banging on the door had Jasce and Amycus jumping to their feet. Jasce removed his knife from his boot, Kenz's gauntlets glowed, and Kord reached for his sword. Amycus walked to the door and opened it to four guards.

"Can I help you?" Amycus asked.

"Lord Rollant requests the presence of that man," one soldier said, pointing to Jasce.

Jasce's neck tensed. He recognized the man from the tavern, the one with the captain's insignia on his cloak.

"Why?" Amycus said.

The captain glared at Amycus. "It's none of your business, and unless you want to spend the night in the dungeon, you'll step out of the way."

Kord stood next to Amycus and sheathed his sword. "Hello, Reed."

The captain shook his head and sighed. "Hello, Kord."

"What's going on?"

"Lord Rollant wants to meet our newest town member."

"Now? It's awfully late."

"Yes, now." Reed stared at Jasce. "Leave your weapons here."

Jasce stared at the four guards, his lips curling to show his teeth. Two guards stepped away as he removed the swords from his back and handed them to Amycus. He had hidden the knife in his boot, just in case. If they didn't properly search him, that was their fault.

"I'm going with him." Reed opened his mouth to protest, but Kord continued. "As a representative, which is allowed by town law."

Reed pinched the bridge of his nose. "Your weapons stay too."

Kord nodded and handed his sword to Kenz, along with the five knives on his baldric and two daggers on his thigh.

Reed swore. "What have you been up to, Kord?"

"Preparation and victory go hand-in-hand," Kord said, a mischievous glint in his eyes.

Kenz dropped Kord's weapons into Amycus's arms. He stumbled back under the weight of steel as she said, "I'm going too."

Reed hesitated. "Now look, Kenz. I realize you two are inseparable, but only one representative is allowed."

Jasce frowned at Kenz. "I'll be fine."

"It's not you I'm worried about," she mumbled.

The captain gripped his sword. Jasce snorted and walked into the night with Kord on his heels. Reed and another soldier led the way to Lord Rollant's manor while the other two guards followed.

They arrived at Lord Rollant's home and walked through the gates, passing more guards who saluted Reed.

"Is this normal, Captain, to bring visitors to meet the town lord?" Jasce asked, their boots echoing off the cobblestones. The torches illuminated the rough stone and Jasce had already calculated the height of the wall. It wouldn't be a challenge to climb.

Reed stopped, analyzing Jasce. "It is when said visitor gets into a fight with ten Watch Guard soldiers."

"Yeah, and where were your men when they attacked?"

A shadow flickered in Reed's eyes, but he kept his face expressionless. He turned without answering, leading them through wooden doors into a foyer two stories tall. An enormous chandelier lit the room, and four candelabras, which could be potential weapons, lined the wall. They entered an office where a wiry man with sandy blond hair sat behind a substantial desk covered in papers. He looked up with a smile that immediately faded when he saw Kord.

"Why is Mr. Haring here?"

"He insisted on acting as a representative," Reed said, nodding to the guards to fan out around the room.

Lord Rollant's brown eyes narrowed, then he forced a smile, stood, and walked to the front of his desk. "So, it seems you've made a name for yourself, Az. Is that correct?"

"No," Jasce said.

Rollant's brow furrowed, glancing at Reed. "No, you haven't made a name for yourself or—"

"My name is Jasce Farone," Jasce said, cutting Rollant off.

The man pursed his lips as he gazed over Jasce, who hadn't changed before confronting Amycus. His leather pants had splotches of dried blood and dirt, and his tunic was filthy after two days of traveling. His scraggly hair scraped his shoulders and he was positive he still had blood on his skin.

Probably not the best first impression.

"Yes, well, Mr. Farone, as I am lord of Carhurst and Hillford, I am therefore responsible for the town's safety, and I have a few questions."

"I have a few questions of my own," Jasce said. Kord sighed.

A muscle in Rollant's jaw twitched as his eyes flicked from Kord to Jasce. "Where are you from and how long are you planning on staying in Carhurst?"

"Orilyon, and undecided."

Rollant chuckled and leaned against his desk. "You're a man of few words, I see. I understand there was a fight at the Iron Glass a couple months ago, with Terrell and his men."

Kord stepped forward. "I can vouch for Jasce. Technically, Terrell's gang started it."

Rollant waved his hand in the air as if shooing away a fly. "I'm not concerned about that. But what does worry me is the fact that you killed ten Watch Guard soldiers. Can you explain that?"

Jasce squeezed and relaxed his hands. On the walk over, he figured Rollant would inquire about the incident with the Guard, especially if he aligned himself with Steward Brenet. Jasce didn't have enough information about Rollant and hated being unprepared.

"The Guard attacked and your soldiers were strangely absent, so I handled it." He felt Reed stiffen behind him.

"One against ten is quite impressive," Rollant said, his sculpted brows raised.

"I had some help."

"Do you know why the Guard would visit Carhurst?"

"No, but I would assume to check on you."

Rollant stared, chewing the inside of his cheek. He nodded, then sat behind the desk. "And are you aware that one of the Watch Guard's Hunters is wanted for treason?"

Jasce kept his face blank. "I've heard the rumors."

"They are more than rumors. The Angel of Death was spotted in Paxton." Rollant leaned back in his chair, his eyes never leaving Jasce's. "Thankfully, it seems he's returned to Opax, so it's no longer my concern." He nodded to Reed, who stepped beside Jasce. "I hope your little stunt with the Guard doesn't cause me problems, Mr. Farone."

Rollant returned to the papers on his desk, not giving Jasce a second glance.

Jasce and Kord were almost through the door when Rollant spoke again. "Oh, and Mr. Haring, please tell Tillie I need to meet with her regarding the Winter Celebration." Kord glared over his shoulder, his jaw tight. The smile on Rollant's face reminded Jasce of a wolf stalking its prey. Jasce grabbed Kord's arm and led him out of the manor. Neither man spoke until they were clear of the gates and halfway through town.

"Want to tell me what that was about?" Jasce asked.

Kord shook his head. "I'll see you tomorrow."

Jasce stood in the center of town as Kord strode down the street to his home. He didn't know what to make of Lord Rollant but suspected the man knew who Jasce was. Why Rollant and his soldiers were missing during the attack remained a mystery, one Jasce intended to solve, but not now.

Jasce sighed and trudged toward the Whispering Pines, longing for sleep and to turn off his mind. His feelings were a jumbled mess: Drexus's betrayal, Amycus's lies, the incident with Kenz in the stream that made him uncomfortable in more ways than one, and whatever was going on between Kord and Lord Rollant. And now, it seemed Rollant's watchdog was following him.

"Good night, Reed," Jasce called out as he entered the inn, snorting when he heard Reed swear.

Jasce lumbered down the hall and froze. His door was standing open. He wrenched the knife from his boot and closed his eyes, trying to get a sense of who was in his room. Then he let out a breath, feeling her magic, and inwardly swore at her citrus scent filling the room.

Kenz sat on his bed, staring at the Hunter mask in her hands. Her head shot up when Jasce entered, her eyes shifting to the knife in his hand.

"I'm tired, Kenz. What are you doing here?" He put the knife on the dresser and sat in the chair across from her to remove his boots. He rubbed his face and leaned back, crossing a leg over his knee and giving off a look of calm irritation. Thankfully, she couldn't hear the way his heart thumped. Having her in his room was dangerous to both of them.

"I need to understand," she said, looking from the mask to Jasce.

"Understand what?"

"Would you have killed Amycus? I realize he shouldn't have lied to you, but your first instinct was to take his life."

Jasce tapped his finger on the chair. How much should he tell her?

"When I was twelve, Drexus and his men raided our village and killed my mother, dragging Jaida away." He swallowed and shut his eyes. "Her screams still haunt my nightmares." He rose from the chair, needing to move. "They left me outside the Watch Guard compound in Orilyon. At first, I tried to fight back against their training, against their methods and ideals. But all I had was fear and anger. I didn't want the fear, so I surrendered to the anger and used the Guard to develop my skills, surpassing the other soldiers, and joined the Hunters. I would never be helpless again as I vowed to have my revenge."

Jasce peered out the window into the night, feeling Kenz's stare. "You called me a monster," he finally said, turning. She opened her mouth, but he held up his hand. "I let them turn me into a walking nightmare, and I don't know how to be anything else. I can't just turn it off, Kenz."

The bed squeaked as she stood. "I have tried so hard to hate you, and sometimes you make it easy. But I believe you can be so much more than just an assassin." She handed him the mask and opened the door, pausing at the threshold. "If you truly want revenge on Drexus, then don't become like him."

After she left, Jasce sat on the bed, the covers still warm from where she sat. He stared at the mask. She was right. He wouldn't let Drexus win—in this war against Spectrals or the battle for his soul. He lit a fire and watched the kindling ignite, then grabbed his knife. Shadows and darkness may have consumed him, but he didn't have to behave like a monster. The most honorable victory—one that he, and possibly Kenz, could be proud of—was overcoming himself and allowing that pinprick of light to chase away the darkness.

His knife cut through his hair. Strands fell next to the grinning skull as it melted in the flames.

The Hunter mask turned to ash.

જ⁂ જ⁂ જ⁂

Jasce moved into Amycus's spare apartment the next day, his decision made. To prevent another war, the Spectrals needed to eliminate Drexus and those who stood with him. Jasce had chosen his side and who he wanted to be.

"I'll be your apprentice to pay my way," Jasce had said, leaning against the forge entrance. "And continue to train the Spectrals. I will help you stop Drexus and his war, but do not lie to me again." Amycus had opened his mouth to say something, snapped it shut, and nodded.

That evening, after working in the forge crafting swords and spears, he went to the Iron Glass Tavern searching for Kord. Jasce hadn't seen him training in the courtyard and heard from Flynt that he was in the tavern and "not in a good mood."

Jasce scanned the room, inhaling the comforting smells of Garin's cooking; he'd enjoyed many bowls of the barkeeper's stew during the past months. He nodded to Terrell and his companions, having also spent time with the men he once fought after they'd come to an understanding. Captain Reed and two of his soldiers sat at their usual table, joined by the guard who had followed Jasce into the tavern.

Kenz, Flynt, Delmira, and Vale sat around a table laughing and drinking. Jasce frowned, noticing how close Flynt sat to Kenz. He nodded at Vale's enthusiastic wave as he approached Kord hunched over the bar cradling a drink, his face downcast.

Garin placed his usual glass of whiskey in front of him as he sat next to Kord, who looked from Garin, to the glass, to Jasce.

"I come here a lot," Jasce said, taking a drink.

Kord grunted and went back to staring at nothing. Jasce tapped his finger on the bar, avoiding a sticky spot, and waited. He glanced in the mirror behind the bar, not comfortable with his back to the room, and his eyes landed on Kenz, who laughed at something Vale said. Flynt's arm rested on the back of her chair. Jasce ground his teeth.

Linnette delivered a bowl of stew, placing her hand on Jasce's arm and leaning close so Jasce could smell her perfume.

"You cut your hair," she said, pouting.

"Yeah, it was time for a change." His eyes flicked to the mirror, catching Kenz staring. She quickly looked away.

Linnette looked at Kenz and frowned. "Well, you just let me know if you need anything else." She gave his arm a squeeze and sauntered off to another table.

Kord, still as a statue, seemed content to glower at the bar. Jasce sighed, then drained Kord's drink along with his own. "You ready to talk about it?"

"Talk about what?"

"Whatever has you in such a mood." Jasce took a few bites of stew, wondering if Kord would talk. He had never seen Kord like this and wasn't sure how to help.

Kord rubbed a hand through his short hair and frowned at his empty glass. "Tillie and I argued."

"About?"

Kord watched Garin refill their empty glasses and then took a long drink. "Lord Rollant continues to make unwanted advances on my wife. You saw how he was last night, wanting to meet with her to discuss the festival. He owns the bakery and has desired my wife for too long. Tillie insists she can handle him and to stay out of it. We exchanged words and she called me an 'intolerable domineering male' and kicked me out."

Jasce looked away, hiding his smile while imagining Tillie telling Kord precisely that. He drained the contents of his glass. He didn't like seeing Kord distraught and knew only one way to get him out of the mood.

"Well, you can't blame Rollant. Tillie is beautiful," Jasce said.

Kord turned, the muscles in his neck taut. "Not helping."

"I could kill him, if you'd like."

Kord sighed. "You know, death isn't always the answer."

Jasce shrugged, his eyes flicking back to the mirror, meeting Kenz's gaze again. He winked, then chuckled when she rolled her eyes and turned away.

"Why do you have to irritate her?" Kord asked, looking into the mirror.

"It's so easy to do." Jasce tapped the bar again. "She's quite beautiful too."

Kord slowly turned, snarling. "First my wife and now my sister?"

"Can't a man appreciate beauty?" The corner of Jasce's mouth lifted. "They are both very desirable." The lost look in Kord's eyes disappeared, replaced by a slow-building fury. "All I'm saying is that if you need pointers on how to satisfy your woman, let me know."

Jasce saw the fist and braced himself. Kord knocked him off his stool, and he landed hard at Kord's feet. He had forgotten Kord's strength and should have had one more drink to lessen the sting. Jasce blinked, focusing on the wooden rafters, waiting for the stars to disappear. The bar was quiet—the smell of ale, smoke, and sweat crinkled Jasce's nose.

Kord glared at Jasce, his hands shaking at his sides. "You stay away from my sister and my wife, or so help me—"

"Kord Haring!"

Kord's face went blank as his wife approached. "Tillie?"

Jasce rubbed his jaw and got to his feet.

"What are you doing here?" Kord asked, keeping a wary eye on Jasce.

"Bringing you home, you insufferable man." Tillie raised her brows at Jasce and turned back to her husband. She reached up to cup his face, smiling. "I'm sorry, and I love you."

Kord's shoulders relaxed. Jasce patted his back and gave him a knowing smile, then Tillie grabbed Kord's hand and led him out of the tavern.

Jasce stood alone at the bar, rubbing his throbbing jaw. A better man would have handled that differently, but irritating Kord was the only thing he could think to do. The man had walked beside Jasce through many of his moods; he'd wanted to return the favor, and his method was painful but effective.

He sensed Kenz's magic long before she made it to the bar. She stared at the closed door. "Thank you."

"For what?" Jasce asked, leaning against the bar.

"For helping Kord." She smiled. "Few men can stand after taking one of his punches."

Jasce looked around the tavern, at the many patrons staring in their direction. Captain Reed gave a disapproving frown and Terrell raised his tankard.

"Seems like you've earned the respect of Terrell and his degenerate crew."

"And what about you?" Jasce continued staring straight ahead, unsure why he asked or if he wanted the answer. He expected her to say no, but what if she didn't? "Don't answer that." He forced a smile, focusing on the crease between her eyes to avoid staring at her mouth.

She chuckled and glanced at his head. "I like the hair. It makes you look dignified." She ran her fingers through the shortened locks and he bit back a groan. When he took a quick step back, she lowered her hand.

Jasce swallowed, his eyes scanning the tavern. Most of the patrons had gone back to their business. Flynt drummed his fingers on the back of the vacant chair while Delmira smiled into her drink. Linnette shot daggers from her eyes at Kenz's back.

"Uh, yeah, well." Jasce rubbed the back of his neck. "Wouldn't want me dignified now, would we?" He gave Kenz one last look then walked away, pulling up a chair at Terrell's table and joining the card game his men were playing.

He envied Kord for having a woman who would caress his face and tell him she loved him, take his hand and lead him home. Jasce didn't want to think of what he could've had if his life hadn't changed so drastically all those years ago. He couldn't imagine anyone loving him like Tillie loved Kord. His eyes flicked to Kenz, who was deep in conversation with Delmira.

After the massacre at the Desert Garrison, Kenz had taken care of him when he could not. No one had shown him kindness like that, not since he lost his family. He remembered her hands unstrapping his armor, wiping away the blood and gore. He tried to stop his mind from replaying the feel of her fingertips along his bare chest, and just now as she'd run her hand through his hair. He waved to Linnette, needing another drink to extinguish the fire growing inside him.

Kenz deserved someone better. Someone who wasn't responsible for the death of her fiancé, whether or not he'd dealt the killing blow. She might think he had more to offer than his skills as an assassin, but she deserved someone who hadn't left a trail of corpses in his wake—a man who was whole, not some broken warrior.

He shook his head and drank down the contents in his glass. Better to drown in alcohol than hopeless dreams.

CHAPTER 20

The weather grew colder as winter approached. A light dusting of snow covered the courtyard and snowflakes stuck in Jasce's hair. He wasn't used to the shorter length, often catching himself wanting to tie it back. Peering through the steam from his coffee, he watched the sunrise, the clouds turning from purple to gold, and he lifted his face to inhale the cold air. In a few hours, he would ride to the Eremus Garrison for another recon and possible rescue mission. And he wouldn't be going alone.

His shoulders tensed when he smelled the familiar citrusy scent. Kenz's boots crunched on the frozen ground as she walked toward him. She wore traveling gear and a wool cloak and was armed with her sword and crossbow, her gauntlets peeking out from her sleeves. A shiver went down his spine as her magic tangled with his.

"What is it with you and sunrises?" Kenz asked, standing next to him.

"Good morning to you too." Jasce closed his eyes, feeling the sun warm his face.

Kenz heaved a sigh. "Good morning, Jasce."

Jasce's chest tightened when she spoke his given name. Her black hair hung down her back, twisted into a braid, a few tendrils escaping around her face. Snowflakes clung to her eyelashes.

"I have something for you," Jasce said, reaching into an inside pocket to retrieve the throwing knives he'd made. Kenz's eyes widened as she looked from the blades to Jasce.

"You made these?"

Jasce nodded, struck silent by her beauty. The chill in the air made her cheeks blush pink and her green eyes sparkle.

"They're beautiful. Thank you." She studied the intricate markings.

Jasce rubbed the back of his neck. "They'll fit inside your boot."

Her eyes met his. "Why?"

"Why will they fit in your boot?"

She laughed. "No, why did you make them for me?"

Jasce gripped his mug to keep from brushing the snow off her hair. "The practice blades are dull and not fitted to your small hands. These will work better."

"My small hands?" Kenz asked, the corner of her mouth lifting.

He couldn't help it. He took hold of one, rubbing his thumb along the inside of her wrist. "Very small hands," he said, his voice gravelly. His heart pounded in time with the pulse in her wrist, their magic swirling together faster. "Do you feel that?"

"Feel what?" she asked, her voice a breath in the air.

Jasce stepped closer, his eyes drifting to her mouth. "Our magic. I don't understand it, but I can always sense yours interacting with mine."

She swallowed. Jasce tucked a piece of hair behind her ear, his hand lingering near the soft skin. He needed to step away, remind himself she deserved better. Kord's furious voice still rang in his ears, commanding Jasce to stay away from his sister. He slowly lowered his hand and stepped back. Confusion flashed through her eyes.

Jasce cleared his throat. "You should practice with those, get a feel for them."

Kenz looked at the knives, then lifted her head, her face clear of any emotion. "Thank you."

Jasce shoved his hands into his pockets and walked toward the forge. How was he supposed to go on this next mission with her, alone? He couldn't even be in her presence for two minutes without wanting to touch her.

He strode into the forge, finding Amycus bent over a chest plate he had created, its lines delicate yet strong.

"I've been thinking about the mission," Jasce said by way of greeting. "We need to change the groups." The heat from the forge had him pulling at his collar, a line of sweat already dripped down his back.

"Why is that?" Amycus asked, holding up the armor to inspect it in the light.

"Because . . ." Jasce started, and then realized he hadn't thought up a good reason. He couldn't say his desire for Kenz could compromise the mission or that his feelings for her grew despite his best efforts. He couldn't tell Amycus that he had almost kissed her. No matter how hard he fought, his thoughts always circled back to Kenz, and he was very close to losing the battle.

The light shimmered off the armor, a blue tint swirling through the metal. "What did you do to that chest piece?" Jasce said instead.

Amycus turned and smiled. "I've infused the outer layer with Brymagus to protect the wearer from any surprise weapons that Drexus may have conjured. I've pondered this ever since I saw those arrows, and thought if he could make a weapon out of the plant, why not make something to disable it? Kenz's armor is compromised, and her shield is too valuable to have her magic extinguished by a silly arrow. This will protect her."

"But won't the infused plate affect her magic?" Jasce held up the armor, impressed by how light it was. He could see her in it, the image in his mind jump-starting his heart, heat spreading through his body. He closed his eyes and took a deep breath, placing the chest plate onto the worktable. He was in trouble if a piece of armor got his blood flowing.

Amycus studied him, a line etched between his brows. "No, I've created a barrier on the interior of the plate to keep her magic protected. I'm hoping to create more for the rest of us. Now, why did you want to change the groups?"

"I can handle the recon mission by myself. I don't need Kenz."

Amycus's eyes widened, staring over Jasce's shoulder. Jasce stared at the ceiling, then turned. Kenz stood in the doorway glaring at him, her hands balled into fists. She looked at Amycus. "Vale is waiting for you."

"Kenz, wait," Jasce said. She turned on her heel and stalked out.

Amycus raised his brows, looking from the empty doorway to Jasce. "Flynt, Delmira, and Aura left last night for the Ferox Garrison, wanting to get ahead of the storm. I'm sending Vale and Kord to Torrine to recruit more Spectrals, which leaves you and Kenz to go to Eremus. It's not safe for you to go alone. So, whatever's going on, deal with it."

Jasce ran his hands through his hair and down his face. That was the problem. He didn't know how to deal with "it."

⚘ ⚘ ⚘

Snippets of small talk filled the silence during the three-day ride south to Eremus. Jasce preferred Kenz yelling or insulting him to the cold shoulder she gave him. He had hurt her with his comment and had tried coming up with an apology, but every version in his head sounded ridiculous. The only way he could explain his behavior was to tell her how he felt, which wasn't an option. So every night they both kept busy collecting firewood or hunting food, in opposite directions. Sleeping had become impossible. He couldn't get his mind off her as he listened to her quiet breathing. On the third night, he gave up trying, and stalked into the woods swearing, grabbing his flask as an afterthought.

When he returned to camp, he found Kenz awake and poking at the fire, her breath coming out in small puffs of air. Jasce handed her the flask when she shivered.

She looked from the flask to him and then took a quick drink. "Thanks." She rubbed her hands up and down her arms.

"Can't you create a shield around you and the fire to keep warm?" Jasce asked, sitting across from her.

"I could, but that would drain my magic." She stabbed a stick into the flames. "Why didn't you want me to come with you?"

Sparks drifted into the sky, the smell of snow mixing with the smoke from the fire. Heavy clouds clung to the tops of the Arakan Mountains, blocking out the stars.

"Is it because I'm not strong enough? Not a good enough fighter?" she asked, finally looking at him.

"Kenz, you're the best fighter in the group."

"Then why?"

Jasce stood and walked to a large tree. He kept his back to her, placing his hand along the trunk and dipping his head. "Because you're a liability." He winced. That wasn't what he meant, and by the sound of her marching boots, he had made her angry. Again.

"Excuse me?" She grabbed his shoulder, turning him. Her green eyes sparked. "I'm a what?"

"That wasn't the right word. I just meant you're a distraction."

"A distraction?" She crossed her arms. "Is your mind so weak that you can't focus?"

Jasce looked toward the dwindling fire, and she shoved him into the tree. He leveled his gaze, his jaw tight.

"Answer me," she said, moving to push him again.

Jasce grabbed her hands and spun her so her back was against the tree. "Don't."

She lifted her chin. "Or what?"

Jasce placed his hands on either side of her head, standing close enough to feel her breath caress his face. "Or I might do something you'll regret."

Her eyes widened and she leaned back, her hands flat against the bark. Her pulse thumped in her neck.

Jasce dropped his head. "You don't need to be afraid of me. I would never hurt you."

"I'm not afraid of you," she said, her voice tight.

He lost himself in her eyes. "Maybe you should be." He stepped closer, her body soft against his. He placed one hand on the back of her neck and the other gripped her waist. She swallowed and licked her lips.

He was about to cross a line.

"Stop me, Kenz."

She barely shook her head as he leaned down, and her eyes fluttered closed when his lips met hers. They were soft and yielding, fitting perfectly against his. He groaned and deepened the kiss, parting her lips with his tongue, pulling her against him. She gasped, feeling his desire, her hands clutching his shoulders as if her knees would buckle. Their magic erupted, interlacing as the kiss deepened. He couldn't get enough of her—the taste of her, the way her body felt against his. He lifted her tunic and ran his knuckles up her side, her skin soft and warm. She moaned and Jasce lost himself in the sound. He grabbed her legs and wrapped them around his waist, needing to get closer, to feel her heat. His lips trailed down her throat, licking at the spot where her pulse throbbed.

A branch snapped and Jasce froze.

He removed Kenz's legs from around his waist and lowered her to the ground, sliding one of her knives out of her boot. Her eyes were wide as she looked over his shoulder.

Jasce turned, placing himself between her and the armed men across the campsite.

"By all means, don't stop on our account."

CHAPTER 21

"Geleon," Jasce said, scolding himself as he surveyed the Hunter. Only a fool would lose himself in the touch of a woman a mile from the enemy's garrison. Geleon sneered, his sword at his side. Two Watch Guard soldiers aimed their crossbows.

"We've been looking everywhere for you," Geleon said. "You've caused some trouble, what with Distria and destroying the Desert Garrison." He tapped the sword on the tip of his boot. "I didn't believe it when Bronn told me. Azrael, the Angel of Death, a traitor. Obviously, I was wrong."

Jasce stepped forward, hiding Kenz's knife in his sleeve, and considered Geleon. The Hunter was loyal to Bronn and, therefore, had to die.

"I know what you're thinking, Azrael, that you could take all three of us, but I have the Amplifier serum now. All the Hunters do."

Jasce contemplated Geleon's words, feeling the cold steel of Kenz's knife along his forearm as he formulated his attack. His eyes flashed to his discarded weapons.

Geleon followed his gaze. "Tsk, tsk. You're getting complacent. The Azrael I knew would never be without his precious swords." Geleon leered, looking Kenz up and down. "This one must give it good to make a warrior like you so careless." Geleon licked his lips. "Boys, don't kill her. We can have some fun first."

Jasce growled.

"I'd like to see you try," Kenz said, stepping beside him, her gauntlets glowing blue.

Jasce's rage intensified; he feared what Geleon and his soldiers would do to Kenz if he failed. Images of men dragging his sister away had him gritting his teeth. Jasce let the anger fuel him, focusing on the humming inside his body, forbidding his magic to shy away from the rage. He needed both right now.

"Slow or quick?" Jasce asked. "It's your choice." He took another step forward, feeling the familiar tug.

Geleon snarled. "You're an arrogant son of a—"

Jasce vaulted across the clearing. Geleon swore, his eyes wide as he watched the first soldier fall, a slash across his chest. Jasce kicked the soldier's sword up into his hand and turned to Geleon.

"You were saying?" Jasce said. Out of the corner of his eye, he saw arrows bouncing off Kenz's shield.

Geleon twirled his blade and charged. Jasce smiled—his first fight with an amplified Hunter. Finally, a proper challenge. Swords clashed, the shock of contact rippling up Jasce's arm. They moved back, each evaluating the other. Jasce stepped into a low stance, tightening his grip on Kenz's knife while holding the sword.

"You always were impatient, Geleon."

Geleon attacked again, using his speed to get under Jasce's guard. Jasce lunged to the side, pivoted, and swiped his knife across Geleon's stomach. Geleon bent over, using his free hand to clutch the wound. Jasce grabbed him by the back of the head and thrust his knee into the Hunter's face. A loud crunch sounded, followed by a gush of blood. Geleon snarled like a wounded beast.

"I'm going to kill you," Geleon said, slashing his sword at Jasce's neck.

Jasce vaulted again, landing behind Geleon and thrusting his sword through his back, the tip exploding out the front. Geleon gasped for breath as he stared at the sword protruding from his chest, dripping with blood.

"You were saying," Jasce whispered in Geleon's ear.

"Jasce!"

The other guard stood behind him, sword raised for the killing blow. Jasce raised his dagger to block the attack, but a knife sank into the man's throat. The guard dropped to his knees, blood gurgling from his mouth.

Jasce pulled his sword from Geleon's chest and turned. Across the clearing, Kenz panted, a dark stain forming where an arrow protruded from her shoulder. Jasce looked at the first guard, who was lying on his side with his arm shaking, aiming the crossbow at Kenz. Jasce stabbed him in the back and the weapon disappeared into the snow.

"Blast it, Kenz," Jasce said, striding to her. "You didn't need to protect me."

"Obviously I did," Kenz said, her face pale. "That guard was about to skewer you while you whispered in the Hunter's ear."

Jasce's jaw tightened as he examined her shoulder. "I need to get the arrow out and clean the wound." He grabbed his flask and tore off a section of his tunic. Gently, he tried to twist the shaft. Kenz cried out, shoving her fist in her mouth.

"It's lodged in the bone." Jasce's voice cut like steel. He ripped the fabric of her shirt away from the shaft and froze. Moments before, his lips had pressed against the surface of her neck, feeling her blood pulse through her veins. Now it dripped down her shoulder and chest, the bright red a stark contrast on her pale skin. His hands shook. He had seen members of his team injured before, but he never felt like this, never felt fear. She had lowered her shield to protect him and paid the price.

She gripped his hand, which was now stained with her blood. "You know what you need to do."

Jasce swallowed and grabbed his dagger, holding it to the flames and dousing it with the whiskey from his flask. The only way to pull the arrow free was to enlarge the entry wound so it wouldn't cause more damage.

"This is going to hurt," he said, squeezing her hand. Her face was pale, her freckles resembling splatters of blood.

She nodded and took a long pull from his flask.

"Deep breath," he said as he carefully widened the opening around the shaft, her blood warming his fingers. She swore, turning her head. Jasce gave her a minute before he dug his finger into her shoulder.

Kenz screamed and her eyes rolled back as she fell limp at his side. Jasce pulled the shaft free and poured alcohol on the wound, then pressed the piece of torn tunic against it to staunch the bleeding. His body trembled—seeing her in pain, blood dripping down her chest and covering his hands. After securing the makeshift bandage with part of a torn blanket, Jasce placed her by the fire and spread his cloak over her. He pushed her hair from her face, remembering she had done the same to him after he'd almost died from the Watch Guard attack. His hands still shook; he needed to keep busy. Geleon and his soldiers lay on the other side of the campground. Jasce dragged the bodies from the campsite, not wanting them nearby when she woke.

He kept watch and paced, his eyes darting to Kenz every minute, making sure her chest still rose. He put another blanket on her as the temperature dropped further and snowflakes began drifting through the air. He tried to focus on Geleon's last words, that all the Hunters had received the serum. Geleon had seemed surprised by Jasce's ability to vault, which meant Drexus didn't know of the dual powers. It was an advantage—one they would need.

Kenz moaned in her sleep and Jasce's thoughts turned to the kiss. The passion and heat, the way her legs wrapped around him. She fit against him perfectly. He rubbed his hand down his face, knowing he shouldn't have kissed her. He had struggled to keep his thoughts under control before—what was he supposed to do now?

Focus on the job. Put the mission first, above all else. Drexus's voice trespassed in his mind and Jasce shook his head, wishing Kord were there. He groaned and lifted his face, snowflakes melting on his cheeks. What would Kord think of him kissing his sister? Jasce sighed, shoving his freezing hands into his pockets.

"You're going to carve a trench if you don't stop pacing," Kenz said, her voice tight.

Jasce rushed over and helped her sit. She hissed as she moved her arm.

"How are you feeling?" he asked, handing her the flask. "Do you think you can ride? We need to put some distance between us and the garrison."

Kenz looked at her chest and shoulder, frowning at her damaged tunic. "This was one of my favorites," she said, taking a drink.

Jasce chuckled. "Glad to see you still have your priorities straight."

Kenz slowly got to her feet, trying to hide her grimace. "We still need to check out the compound. I didn't ride all this way for nothing."

"I'll go." Jasce strapped on his scabbard and slid the two swords along his back. He had already put on his armor, wanting to be ready in case there were any more surprises. Plus, it helped keep him warm, which he would never admit. His dagger, cleansed of Kenz's blood, was secure against his thigh.

Kenz shook her head. "No, I'm going with you."

Jasce frowned. "Is there any chance you won't argue with me?"

"Nope," she said. A cry of pain escaped when she tried to braid her hair.

"Let me help you." His fingers ran through the silky strands of her hair, revealing the soft column of her neck. He skimmed his thumb along the delicate skin, her pulse throbbing with her magic and making his breath hitch. Jasce forced himself to focus on the task, blocking out the images of wrapping his arms around her, kissing the side of her neck, finishing what he started against that tree.

"I need to secure your arm to prevent further damage," he said, his voice husky. She turned, her eyes burning with passion or pain, he didn't know. He stared at her bloodstained shirt.

"Hey!" She slapped his hand as he tore a piece of fabric from the bottom of her tunic.

"It's already ruined, so shut it." He anchored her arm across her chest.

"Shut it?"

"And you're wearing your armor. No arguments." Jasce walked to where her bag lay, shaking his head when she mumbled something about overbearing males.

Riding with Kenz's injury and in the dark, made the one-mile ride take longer than it should have. Jasce squinted through the falling snow, barely making out the borders of the Eremus Garrison. He couldn't see any guards, and the air smelled like smoke.

"Something's wrong," he said, sliding off his horse. "Stay here. I'm going to take a closer look." He took five steps when a branch snapped. Kenz crept after him, mouthing, *Sorry.* Jasce shook his head and drew his knife as they entered the deserted compound.

The barracks were empty, along with the kitchen and dining hall. Not a soul, and nothing to indicate a battle had transpired. The smell of smoke and death grew sharper as they moved through the complex.

Jasce's stomach lurched. "Kenz, please go back to the horses." Ignoring him, she peered down one hallway, and her eyes widened. She ran toward the stench of charred flesh.

Jasce swore, sprinting after her and stopping in front of the prison cells. He swallowed the bile rising in his throat. The Watch Guard had locked the Spectrals in cages and set the chamber on fire. Kenz turned away from the carnage, burying her face in his chest. Jasce wrapped his arms around her, not sure who he was comforting. Face-to-face combat was one thing, but this? It was cowardly and cruel. And it sent an obvious message.

Jasce grasped Kenz's hand and led her away from the cells, stopping at a closed door. He frowned and pushed it opened, the smell of smoke and burnt metal making his eyes water. Two exam tables stood in the center of the room, and on top of one lay a charred corpse, still chained to the surface.

Another worksite—one that Jasce hadn't known about. How many more were there? He thought back to Edgefield Prison, how Kord and his team had only rescued fifteen Spectrals, how he'd thought that number was low. Now he knew why. Drexus had transferred the captives to different garrisons to perform his experiments.

Kenz, still pale, walked around the room and turned to him. "Is this what I think it is?"

Jasce nodded and walked to a glass case that had escaped the fire; it held several bottles labeled with different types of magic. Jasce frowned at one bottle marked *Psyche*. According to Amycus, his mother was the last. Had Drexus found another? He frowned at the chains along the wall, the dark stains on the floor.

Jasce put the vials in his pocket. "Let's go. There's nothing else to see."

Snow stung his face as they galloped along a ravine, putting distance between them and Eremus. Jasce stopped when he saw how pale Kenz's face was, and the blood seeping through her bandage. He led the horses to a nearby stream, catching her as her knees buckled.

"You need to rest," Jasce said, setting her against a tree. The snow continued to fall and the wind picked up, the temperature dropping rapidly. "I'm going to build a fire and figure out some sort of shelter."

This mission was going from bad to worse—Geleon's attack, Kenz injured, the devastation at Eremus. Now the weather.

Jasce lit a fire and brought the horses near to help block the wind. He removed their bedrolls and rigged up a covering while layering the blankets on Kenz. He shivered and sat as close to the fire as possible.

"We need to share body heat," Kenz said, her teeth chattering. He didn't realize she was awake. How long had she watched him?

"I don't think that's a good idea."

"Why not?"

"It should be obvious, considering what happened the last time you were against a tree."

She smiled, but it didn't reach her eyes. "Would you rather freeze to death? I promise to keep my hands to myself."

She was right, of course. The wind howled through their makeshift shelter. They would stay warmer being next to each other. Jasce swallowed and slid next to her, pulling the blankets over them both. "It's not your hands I'm worried about."

Kenz chuckled. "Do you want to talk about it?"

"Not really." Jasce pulled her close, careful not to nudge her shoulder. A shudder ran down his spine, feeling her body fit against his.

"Hmm. Okay, tell me about when you were young."

Jasce's eyes slid to hers. He didn't want to discuss that, either, but of the two options, he'd take the latter. He figured one day they would have to discuss that incredible kiss, how amazing it felt. But not when his body pressed against hers under layers of blankets. He felt every curve, her body and magic melding to his.

So Jasce told her about growing up in Delmar, running through the forest with Jaida pretending to be heroes battling the Vastanes. He talked about working in the forge and how, one day, he would like to have his own. His voice grew thick when he told her about his mother, her beauty and fierceness. Kenz's breathing evened out, and soon she was asleep in his arms. Despite everything that had happened, a peace he'd never known crept into the recesses of his heart. He shut his eyes, allowing sleep to take him.

CHAPTER 22

Jasce pounded on Kord's door, not caring it was the middle of the night or who he woke. The last day of riding had weakened Kenz, and based on the heat radiating from her body, the wound was infected. Jasce adjusted her in his arms and knocked again. "Kord!" he yelled, about to kick the door down.

Kord swung it open, the light from inside illuminating the sword in his hand. He had been asleep—his hair mussed, pants unbuttoned, barefoot. His face paled as he lowered his weapon.

"Is she—?"

"She's alive," Jasce said, striding past Kord and laying Kenz on the couch. Kord's heavy footsteps followed.

"What did you do?" Kord asked, his voice tight, pushing Jasce aside to examine his sister.

"What makes you think I did this?"

Just then Tillie came into the room, tying the sash of a robe around her waist. "What happened?" She kept her voice low. Kenz's face shone with sweat, her cheeks flushed.

"Shot by an arrow, trying to protect me," Jasce said through gritted teeth. "I cleaned it, but I think it's infected."

Kord ripped open Kenz's shirt, and Jasce quickly turned. The wound had started bleeding again; the bandage was soaked with blood. He raked his hand through his hair and caught Tillie staring at him, her brows raised.

"I had to widen the opening to pull the arrow out safely. The tip was lodged between her chest and shoulder."

"You did good work." Kord kept his eyes focused on his sister. Already, Kenz's breathing was leveling out as Kord used his magic. Jasce's shoulders lowered. He had wished for Kord's gift as they'd traveled to Carhurst—the last fifteen miles had been torture. Kenz had almost fallen from her horse, so Jasce had her ride with him, his arm wrapped around her waist as he tried to keep her head against his chest. He had told her every mile to stay with him, trying to keep his panic at bay.

173

"I'll go get some water," Tillie said, backing out of the room, mouthing, *She'll be fine.* Kord grunted while his hand rested on Kenz's shoulder.

Jasce let out a breath and walked toward the door. She was safe, she would survive. That was all that mattered.

Kord stood, reaching for Jasce's arm. "Jasce, I . . . I didn't mean . . ."

"Forget it." Jasce glanced once more at Kenz's flushed face, her body covered with a quilt. She looked so young and peaceful. Beautiful.

"Jasce, wait—" Kord said as Jasce shut the door.

He rubbed his forehead, releasing a heavy sigh.

What did he think would happen? Jasce stalked down the road, leading the horses to the stables near the forge. Kord's first reaction was that Jasce had harmed his sister. He was shocked at the disappointment and hurt he'd felt when Kord blamed him. In a way, Kord was right. If Jasce hadn't been so careless and proud, he would have taken care of the other guard instead of savoring Geleon's death. Though Jasce hadn't shot the arrow, it was his fault Kenz was injured.

And things would get worse if what Geleon had said was true, about all the Hunters receiving the serum. He couldn't put Kenz in jeopardy again, or Kord.

A stone skittered along the road. Jasce stopped, reaching for his dagger as he scanned the nearby alley. "You may as well show yourself."

Reed swore and marched onto the road, holding his sword.

"Your stealth skills need some work."

Reed's brows furrowed as he studied Jasce, who had dried blood on him from the Watch Guard and Kenz. "You were making quite a racket a few minutes ago. Where have you been?"

"None of your business." Jasce went to move around the soldier but stopped when Reed raised his sword.

"Lord Rollant has made it my business. I'll ask again, where have you been?"

"I'm really not in the mood."

"I don't care." Reed stepped forward, pushing the tip of his sword into Jasce's chest. Within seconds, Jasce vaulted and spun, appearing behind Reed with his dagger across the captain's throat.

"Do you care now?" Jasce held him for a second and then let go. "This is a battle you will lose."

Reed turned, his face red. "I know you're the Angel of Death."

"Not anymore." Jasce returned his dagger to its sheath. He didn't have the energy or desire to fight the captain. "What are you going to do?"

Reed lowered his sword. "You protected the town, even though they were probably looking for you, so for now, nothing. But if you take one step out of line, you're mine."

Jasce shook his head, and the soldier disappeared into the shadows.

⧫⧫ ⧫⧫ ⧫⧫

Jasce worked in the forge the next morning, hammering metal that would eventually turn into a helmet, his left arm stinging with each strike. The tattooist hadn't been happy to see Jasce in the middle of the night, but the bag of gold had changed his mind. Jasce had two tattoos inked onto his left arm, one for Distria and now one for Geleon.

"What did that metal ever do to you?" Amycus asked from behind Jasce.

Jasce saw the dents and sighed, tossing the ruined piece into a pile. He pinched the bridge of his nose.

Amycus held two steaming cups of coffee. "I didn't realize you returned last night. How did it go?" He nodded at the discarded pile. "Based on your appearance and frustration, I'd say not well."

Jasce leaned against the worktable and crossed his arms. The discovery at Eremus had kept him awake most of the night; the other half was spent tossing and turning, thinking of Kenz. He had drifted off only to wake drenched in sweat, his hands still covered with her blood.

"Besides being attacked by a Hunter and two Watch Guard soldiers, Kenz getting injured—she's fine," he quickly added, seeing the concern on Amycus's face. "Eremus was abandoned and the prisoners had burned to ash, and we got caught in a snowstorm. So, no, it didn't go well."

Amycus handed Jasce a mug and sat at the worktable. "The other team had a similar experience at the Ferox Garrison."

"Somehow they knew we were coming." Jasce frowned, staring into his coffee. "Who knew, besides our team, where we were going?"

"No one, except Tillie. You honestly don't think—"

"No. Of course not, but someone warned them. Lord Rollant?"

Amycus sighed. "I'll look into it. But in the meantime, tell me everything."

Jasce went over the mission, leaving nothing out—except kissing Kenz. He didn't want to know what Amycus thought about their relationship, or whatever was going on between them. He handed Amycus the retrieved vials.

"You said my mother was the last Psyche."

Amycus frowned at the label, then lifted it to the light, swirling the liquid inside. "As far as I knew, she was. Both her power and yours are extraordinary."

"It seems Drexus may have found another."

"You said the Hunter had Amplifier magic?"

Jasce nodded. "If what Geleon says is true, then all the Hunters have received the serum." Ten lethal assassins with speed and strength at their disposal. Even if the Spectrals had the numbers, it would be a bloodbath. "Three of Drexus's facilities are destroyed, but I'm positive he has another one. I can't remember seeing anything on the map from his study to indicate where it might be. You knew him. Do you have any ideas?"

Amycus took a sip of his drink, frowning. He placed the vial on the table and walked toward the fire, staring into the flames. "I might," he finally said. "I'll check in with my source—see if they know anything."

"Who is this source of yours?"

Amycus continued to stare into the fire. Jasce wanted to know the identity of Amycus's informant—if they were trustworthy—but that was a problem for another time.

"We need to figure out what he's doing. There were other vials labeled with different types of magic. He's up to something." Jasce rubbed the back of his neck. "It's like he's creating an army of Spectrals."

Amycus slowly turned, his eyes wide.

Jasce swore. "That's it, isn't it? Drexus is creating soldiers to overthrow the steward and destroy any Spectrals that stand against him so he can rule

Pandaren." Jasce paced around the room, recalling the last three missions. "Drexus has perfected the serum for Naturals, like the Hunters, and he'll give it to the Watch Guard. So why the other vials?"

Amycus sat at the table, tapping a finger against his coffee mug and staring at the rising steam. "Amplifier is the only magic that is closely aligned to the human body, making it the easiest one to assimilate. Maybe he's trying to transfer the other types?"

Jasce frowned and took a long drink of coffee, the liquid burning his throat. "We have another problem. Reed knows who I am."

Amycus sighed. "Does Lord Rollant know?"

"Does Rollant know what?"

Jasce's head shot up. Kord filled the entryway, his arms crossed.

"Shove over," Kenz said, pushing past her brother.

Jasce stopped himself from going to her. She moved a little stiffly and had shadows under her eyes, but otherwise seemed fine.

"Are you all right?"

"Yes, except for my overbearing brother wanting me to stay in bed."

"In bed sounds good," Jasce said, then blanched. Kord and Amycus stared at him, their eyes wide. "I mean, *you* should be in bed. Resting. Alone."

Kord frowned as he glanced between the two of them.

Kenz's cheeks flushed as she stared at a spot over Jasce's shoulder. "I'm fine. Now, what's this about Lord Rollant?"

"Let's talk in the other room. It's a little hot in here." Amycus gave Jasce a knowing look and stood, motioning the siblings out the door.

Jasce stared at the scarred worktable and shook his head. What a blundering fool he had become. A surge of relief had filled him when he saw Kenz in the doorway, followed by a longing he didn't want to contemplate, especially with Amycus and Kord staring at him like he had two heads. This had to stop. He couldn't pursue Kenz, not with Kord's reaction or the threat of amplified Hunters searching for him.

Jasce entered the main room. Amycus was already sitting at his desk, his fingers steepled under his chin, while Kord and Kenz settled into chairs. Jasce drained his coffee then filled the mug with whiskey from Amycus's stash.

Kord raised a brow. "It's a little early for that, isn't it?"

Jasce scowled at Kord and swallowed the alcohol in one gulp. He recognized the feelings swirling in him when Kord had appeared in the doorway, and the hurt and disappointment from last night came rushing back. Kord had become a friend, or so Jasce thought. But his response to Kenz's injury made Jasce wonder if Kord would ever fully trust him. And if Kord knew Jasce had kissed his sister? If he had any idea of Jasce's feelings, despite his best efforts to suppress them . . . ?

He shook his head and poured another drink. "Last night, Reed essentially threatened me, claiming he knows I'm the Angel of Death. I don't know if Lord Rollant knows or not. If he does, then there's a good chance the Watch Guard is on its way. Which means I need to leave."

"We have some time," Amycus said. "Drexus is regrouping after the destruction of the garrisons, and Lord Rollant is busy with the Winter Celebration. But we do need to figure out what to do about Reed."

Jasce paced, thinking of options. "Killing the captain will cause more suspicion, but I could make it look like an accident." He stopped, looking around the silent room. A smile tugged at Amycus's lips, Kord rubbed a hand down his face, and Kenz shook her head.

"What?"

Amycus stood and patted Jasce on the shoulder. "There *are* other options than killing the man."

"Well, what's your plan?"

"I was thinking of having Kenz feel out Reed to see what his intentions are."

"Excuse me?" Kord said just as Jasce said, "No way!"

Amycus smiled at Jasce. Kord's head swiveled from Amycus to Jasce, his eyes narrowed to slits.

"I think that's a great idea," Kenz said, getting to her feet. "Better than killing the guy."

Jasce and Kord objected, but Amycus silenced them both with a raise of his hand. A gust of wind whipped across their faces.

"It's a solid plan," Amycus said.

Jasce shook his head. "I could question Reed, even Rollant, if I need to."

"No, we've seen the way you question people," Kord said.

Jasce slowly turned, squaring his shoulders. "You have a problem with how I do things?"

"Yeah, I do. Especially when your methods bring my sister home bleeding and unconscious."

"Kord," Kenz said, grabbing her brother's arm.

Jasce's jaw tightened. Any hope he had disappeared with Kord's reaction, and the last thing he wanted was another fight. He pushed past Kord to the door.

"Where are you going?" Amycus said.

"To scout out the area, make sure everything's clear."

"You're an idiot, Kord," Kenz said as the door closed. Jasce was halfway through the courtyard when Kenz jogged up behind him. "Jasce, wait."

Jasce stopped, keeping his back to her. "He's right, you know. If it hadn't been for my arrogance, you wouldn't have been injured."

"Why did you kiss me?"

Jasce stiffened. He was about to hurt her, again, but it was the only way to protect her. He removed all emotion from his face, ensuring she would only see the assassin she despised. He slowly scanned her body, his eyes taking their time. "I had an itch, sweetheart, and you were available." He winked and continued walking, trying to ignore the pain that washed over her face. He reached the exterior gate, and a whoosh of air brushed his cheek, the knife he made vibrating in the wooden doorframe inches from his head. He looked over his shoulder.

Kenz gripped the other one, tears welling in her eyes. "Keep your gift."

The second blade landed with a resounding clang, and something fractured in his chest. But it was better this way. Jasce wasn't the hero of her story, just the hired killer.

CHAPTER 23

Carhurst bustled with excitement with the beginning of its annual Winter Festival. An enormous bonfire lit up the town center and musicians played a lively tune, and everyone was in a festive mood—except Jasce. He leaned against the stone wall of the Iron Glass Tavern, glaring at the holly berries and pine boughs draped along pillars and rooftops. Villagers danced and merchants sold their wares; bonfire smoke and the promise of snow filled the air.

Jasce had worked all day in the forge trying to burn off his irritation, but his mind held fast to the thoughts plaguing him. He needed to find Drexus's hidden compound, stop his experiments, and kill the remaining Hunters. But he had no idea where to start his search and was running out of time. News of the Watch Guard raiding Torrine in search of the Angel of Death had spread like wildfire. They would eventually ride to Carhurst, and Jasce couldn't allow that. There were too many people in this town he cared about, especially the woman across the square with firelight shining off her ink-black hair and reflecting in her green eyes.

Jasce tore his gaze from Kenz, instead observing Tillie and Maleous working in their booth. They sold pastries and hot beverages while Lord Rollant hovered nearby, a crooked smile on his face. Jasce tightened his fist, wanting to smack the grin off the weasel, but Kord walked over, placing a muscular hand on Rollant's shoulder and whispered in his ear. The man paled and sauntered off to another booth.

Jasce hadn't spoken to Kord since their argument at Amycus's, and the tension didn't sit well with him. He wanted to fix things before leaving but hadn't found the words or the right time. It seemed fate was about to force his hand. Tillie looked at Jasce and said something to Kord. His lips drew into a straight line and nodded, walking through the crowd in his direction.

"Hey," Kord said, leaning next to Jasce, scanning the crowd of partygoers.

Jasce arched a brow. "Hey."

Kord scraped his boot on the ground, carving a line in the sand. "Look, I acted like an idiot, and I'm sorry. I shouldn't have said those things."

"I understand why you did."

"No, I don't think you do."

"I'm the Angel of Death, an assassin who only knows how to kill. It's understandable to think the worst or not trust me."

"Do you believe that about yourself?"

"It doesn't matter what I believe, does it?"

Kord chuckled. "Touché." They stared at the crowd, and Kord sighed. "I love my family so much it hurts, and I would do anything to protect them. Sometimes I forget Kenz is a grown woman who can take care of herself. When I saw her bleeding in your arms, I lost myself to fear and jumped to conclusions. And then this thing with Lord Rollant and Reed . . . I've been stupid."

"I bet Kenz tore your head off." Her name tasted bitter on Jasce's tongue. He couldn't erase the words he said or the hurt he caused.

Kord laughed. "Still trying to find it."

Jasce snorted. He noticed Lord Rollant talking with Reed across the square, periodically glancing over his shoulder. "What's going on with Rollant? Did Tillie set him straight?"

Kord stared where Jasce indicated. "You know Tillie. I should never have doubted that she could handle this better than I could. I would've pulled a Jasce and threatened the guy, which could have put her out of business." Kord nudged Jasce, who laughed. That *is* how he would have handled the situation, and he would not have stopped at threatening.

"What do we know about Reed?" Jasce asked. Kenz sat with Delmira, Aura, and Flynt near the bonfire. He hadn't been thrilled with the idea of Kenz "feeling out" Reed, as Amycus had said, though he knew she was more than capable of taking care of herself.

"Kenz said Reed would keep his mouth shut. He cares more about the village than getting the bounty. Reed won't tell Rollant either. Rollant isn't a fan of the steward and doesn't agree with how the Watch Guard does things, but he isn't a pillar of strength. Best to keep him in the dark regarding who you were."

Jasce didn't miss the emphasis Kord put on *were*. He could have easily said *are*.

Jasce felt the tension drain from his shoulders. Kord believed in him, or who he could be. It seemed Amycus did, too, and Kenz—even if she currently despised him. She could never know how much he had treasured her words to him that night in his room. *I believe you can be so much more than just an assassin.* He wanted to prove he was worthy of their trust, and the only way he knew to do that was to protect them. The urgency to stop Drexus pulsed through him.

"Kord, I need to leave."

Kord sighed, his eyes scanning Jasce's face. Jasce fought the urge to turn away from his probing stare. "One, this whole mess isn't your responsibility. You need to wrap your head around the fact that we are in this with you."

Jasce opened his mouth to argue.

"And two," Kord interrupted, "tonight is a night to celebrate."

"This is foolish with the Watch Guard closing in. People should be preparing to fight or flee. Anything but this." He pointed to the people dancing around the bonfire. "You need to take your family and go somewhere safe."

"Lord Rollant warned the people. Besides, if we don't stay, who will protect them? If we can't celebrate the joys in life, take time to dance and love, then what are we fighting for?" Kord patted Jasce's shoulder and walked to the fire to join his family and friends.

Kord sat next to Amycus and Kenz, and soon all three were drinking and laughing. Maleous ran to Kord, handing out pastries along the way; a huge grin spread across his face as Kord wrapped him in a tight hug. Even Reed joined the group, talking with Flynt and Aura. He looked up once, catching Jasce's stare, and nodded. It seemed everyone had a reason to celebrate. Part of Jasce wanted to join them—to drink and dance his cares away, but another part feared the emotions that came with the relationships: fear, vulnerability, love.

Jasce's stomach dropped. He couldn't fall in love with Kenz. Even if she believed there may be more to him than an assassin, she deserved a man whose hands weren't stained with blood.

The bonfire burned brighter, sparks drifting into the night air. A lone snowflake landed on Jasce's arm. Heavy clouds hid the stars, promising more snow would soon follow. Jasce's jaw clenched as Flynt grabbed Kenz and led her into a dance around the bonfire, her head thrown back in laughter. That was a better match; it was safer for Kenz to be with Flynt than him. Jasce longed for something out of reach, his fingertips scraping a future that wouldn't be his. The regret felt like knives lodging into his heart.

"Why don't you join us?" Tillie asked, leaning against the wall, flour dusting her cheek. Jasce hadn't even heard her approach, but the vanilla and cinnamon smells that seemed to be a part of her made his mouth water.

"Not in the mood," Jasce said, focusing on Kenz.

Tillie turned toward him, her eyes searching his. "You really should let your hair down. By the way, I like it shorter."

Jasce forced a smile and looked away. Villagers danced to an upbeat tune and laughter rang out through the square. "How do you do it?"

"Do what?"

"Love someone while fearing you might lose them."

Tillie smiled and watched her husband play a game with Maleous that involved hiding a coin in one hand. "Do you regret loving your mother and sister?"

Jasce spun, narrowing his eyes. She stared straight ahead, a sad smile on her face. "Kord told me bits and pieces of your past."

"No, I don't regret loving them," he said finally. "But I don't know if I can go through that kind of pain again. I didn't handle their deaths well and became someone I'm not proud of." He ran his hand down his arm, visualizing the tattoos. "What if something happens to Kord? Who would take care of you and Mal? Or Amycus? He's like a father to them. What if that arrow had been a few inches to the left?" Jasce's jaw ached when he remembered Kenz's blood running through his fingers as he dug the arrow out of her chest.

"Jasce, you can't live your life by what-ifs. You will never truly live, constantly controlled by the unknown." She squeezed his hand. "Every time Kord goes on a mission, I worry I won't see him again. But I refuse to live in fear. Instead, I try to love him as much as I can while we are together. I can't ask him not to go—he's not one to stay behind. Neither are Kenz nor Amycus.

They believe in what they're fighting for, and you can't take that from them." She gave him a warm smile and a light kiss on the cheek, then handed him a pastry. She walked to her husband and son, and soon all three were dancing around the fire.

Kord was lucky to have a woman so wise, so full of life and love. And who could bake like no other. He licked the sugar from his fingers, his eyes finding Kenz. She dropped her gaze, listening to something Aura and Delmira were discussing. Jasce thought about what Tillie said. Living a life of what-ifs was not living, only surviving, a slave to fear and worry. The night he threw his Hunter's mask into the fire was the night the first link of the chain broke. He had tasted freedom and would never allow himself to be a prisoner again.

His stomach somersaulted, knowing what he had to do. Why was apologizing to Kenz harder than going into battle? He couldn't leave until he made things right with her. He felt ashamed for hurting her during their last conversation and trying to convince himself he was protecting her. He was a bloody coward.

Kenz left the bonfire and meandered to a booth selling ale. Jasce pushed off the wall, setting his shoulders, and made his way through the crowd. He placed her knives on the counter next to her drink.

"I'm glad you have excellent aim," Jasce said, signaling the barkeep.

Kenz stared at the knives and looked up. "Yeah, well, I missed." She turned on her heel and walked past the booths, the noise from the party fading.

"Kenz, wait." Jasce pocketed the knives and grabbed her arm, dragging her to the nearby stable.

"Let go."

"I will, I just—"

"Just what?" She glared at his hand.

He loosened his grip and cleared his throat. "It's better for you to not be with me."

"For the record, I'm *not* with you. Remember? I'm just an itch." She crossed her arms, scowling at him.

"I'm sorry I said that."

"Why did you?"

Jasce rubbed the back of his neck. This wasn't going as he planned. "To protect you."

"What is it with you and my brother?" She huffed, staring over his shoulder. "And what are you protecting me from?"

Jasce concentrated on her freckles, the crease that formed between her eyes whenever they argued. "Me."

He stepped closer, her magic a magnet drawing him in. Her eyes darted to his as she bit her lip.

"Please don't do that," he said.

"Do what?" she whispered.

Her pulse thumped in her neck as he traced his finger along her jaw. "I can't stop thinking about the other night. How you felt, how you tasted."

What was he doing? He needed to leave but was unable to pull himself away.

Kenz swallowed. "I do feel it, you know. The way our magic reacts. I've never felt that with anyone before." She held his wrist and he knew she could feel his heart pounding. "What if I don't want to be protected?" She stood on her toes and kissed him lightly, running her tongue along his lower lip.

Jasce moaned and pressed her against the wall, heat flooding his body. She wrapped her arms around his neck, deepening the kiss. He should push her away, apologize and leave, but all he wanted was to stay in this moment forever, lost in her touch. He longed to explore every curve, needed the feel of her skin. He inched a hand under her tunic and splayed his fingers along her ribs, his thumb caressing the soft skin below her breast. Her back arched and every nerve ending ignited when she sighed his name. His lips trailed down her neck, moving the fabric aside to kiss her collarbone, licking the spot where the arrow had pierced her soft flesh. He shivered as her hands slid up his back and didn't shy away as she touched his scars, her fingers sending sparks of heat to his core.

"Kenz," Jasce whispered, finding her mouth. Their tongues and magic joined in a seductive dance that left him aching for more.

"Ahem."

Jasce swore and straightened Kenz's tunic as her fingers stilled on his back. She peeked over his shoulder and groaned.

Kord stood at the entrance of the stables, his hands fisted and face scarlet.

"I suppose you want to hit me again," Jasce said.

"You have no idea."

"What are you doing here?" Kenz asked, her hands on her hips.

"I think the question is, what are *you* doing here, with him?"

"I would think that had been obvious, you nosy, overbearing mule."

Jasce rubbed his forehead. He had just smoothed things out with Kord, and now Kord caught him kissing his sister in the stable. It would have been funny if not for Kord's red face and the muscle threatening to explode from his jaw. But he was fortunate, at least, that Kord came in when he did; that kiss was quickly turning into something not appropriate in public.

Kord stepped forward, his massive frame blocking the entrance to the stable. "She's my baby sister."

"What happened to the grown woman who can take care of herself?" Jasce pointed out, then winced as Kord slammed him into one of the stall doors.

"Kord, you're acting like an idiot," Kenz said, trying to pull her brother off Jasce. Kord pushed her and shoved Jasce.

Anger boiled to the surface, extinguishing the desire from moments before. "You get one shot," Jasce said.

"One's all I need." Kord's fist flew.

Pain exploded in his cheek as the skin split open and blood spilled down his face. Jasce tapped into his magic and used his strength and speed to grab Kord's arm and twist him. In less than a heartbeat, Kord lay flat on his back. Jasce lodged a knee into his chest, knocking the air out of him. One hand gripped his tunic while the other one rose, ready to strike. Jasce froze as his blood dripped onto Kord's face.

He blinked. Two Kords were on the ground and the stable swayed. Kenz's voice sounded miles away. Jasce toppled off Kord, gingerly touching the cut on his face, his eye already swelling.

"Dad!" Maleous ran to his father, his wide eyes darting between Jasce and Kord.

"What happened?" Amycus asked as he rushed in, followed by Tillie.

Jasce shook his head, trying to clear it while Kord got to his feet, his face still red.

"My brother is what happened," Kenz said, kneeling by Jasce, lifting his chin to look at the gash on his face. "Kord, look what you did."

Tillie arched a brow. "Kord Haring, explain yourself."

"Dad, you shouldn't hit your friends," Maleous said, inching closer to Jasce.

"My friend had his dirty hands all over my sister, practically eating her face."

Maleous gasped, his eyes bulging out of his head as he looked at his aunt's face. Jasce cleared his throat, Kenz giggled, and Tillie covered her mouth, trying to hide her smile while Amycus examined the walls of the stable.

"It's not funny," Kord said.

"It's kind of funny," Jasce said, then hissed, touching his cheek. Kord pressed his lips together, trying to hide a smile of his own.

Maleous's brow furrowed and he reached out, his fingertips touching Jasce's cheek. A warmth radiated through the cut and the pain lessened.

Tillie gasped and Kord shook his head, fear flashing through his eyes. Tillie looked from Maleous to Kord, the color leeching from her face. Kenz, still kneeling beside Jasce, stared at her brother, her mouth open.

"Did you see that?" Maleous said, grinning wide, staring at his mother and father. Kord remained motionless. Tillie gave the boy a weak smile.

Jasce stood and rubbed Maleous's head. "Thanks, kid." A drop of blood trickled down his face, but the swelling and pain had lessened. He glanced at Kord, who still hadn't moved. Jasce rested his hand on Kord's shoulder. "It will be all right," he murmured.

Kord stared between Maleous and Jasce.

A horse whinnied from outside the stable, and someone called Jasce's name. Amycus ran toward the exit, almost colliding with Reed, who yelled, "Hillford's under attack!"

CHAPTER 24

Reed marched into the barn, his face hard as he glared at Jasce. "Lord Rollant just received word that the Watch Guard is raiding Hillford."

"Do you know what they want?" Amycus asked, though Jasce assumed they all knew the answer. Flynt, Delmira, Aura, and Vale entered, their eyes wide.

Reed pointed at Jasce. "Him, plus any other Spectrals they can find."

This is what Jasce had feared, people injured or killed because of him, and it was why he had wanted to leave sooner. He should have left the minute he figured out Drexus's plans, but because of his selfishness, wanting a taste of normal life, people were in danger. Jasce strode for the stable's exit.

Amycus grabbed his arm. "Where do you think you're going?"

Jasce scowled at the scarred hand. "Take one guess."

"You don't need to do this by yourself, Jasce."

"It seems Drexus regrouped faster than we thought, and I've wasted enough time." Jasce shrugged out of Amycus's hold and continued out of the stable. Footsteps sounded behind him.

"We're coming with you, and don't you dare try to talk us out of it." Kenz marched past him toward her home.

"Everyone, get your gear and meet at my place." Amycus stood next to Jasce. "There's no point arguing with her. You should know that by now."

Jasce huffed and caught Kord's stare. He mumbled something to Tillie, ruffled Maleous's hair, and followed Kenz.

Jasce donned his armor, sliding his swords and daggers into their scabbards. He raked his hands through his hair—nothing was going according to plan. He was supposed to leave Carhurst and forget Kenz and whatever was happening between them. But after that kiss, he couldn't imagine being away from her for a single moment. He closed his eyes. Those thoughts and feelings were selfish, and now he was putting everyone at risk again.

Jasce emerged into the courtyard and stopped short. Amycus wore armor similar to Jasce's, his dark hair tied back and fire sparking in his blue eyes.

Amycus handed Flynt and Delmira newly crafted chest pieces. They smiled at each other, strapping them on immediately.

Jasce approached, pushing past Flynt. "You're not coming with us," he said to Amycus.

"Your concern for my safety is endearing, but I assure you I've done this before. I'm not just a blacksmith, you know." Amycus retrieved his scimitar, gave it a twirl, and slid it into the leather sheath along his back. The hilt of the curved sword peeked over his shoulder.

Jasce frowned, uncomfortable with the worry plaguing him as Kord, Kenz, Aura, and Vale walked into the courtyard, all wearing fighting leathers and armed to the teeth. He had never worried about his Hunters when going into battle, only about himself and the mission. In the past few months he'd realized he didn't like the man he had been—selfish, ambitious, and blood thirsty—but if he was honest, going into battle not caring about those around you was much easier than this.

Kenz frowned as she approached, her eyes darting between Amycus and Jasce.

"What?" Jasce asked, double-checking the strap on his armor.

Kenz shrugged. "Nothing, you two just seem—"

"Kenz, have you picked up your new arm plates?" Amycus asked, leading her away from Jasce to hand out more armor to those who had just arrived. Jasce and Amycus had worked tirelessly on the new protective coverings for the Spectrals. He hoped it would be enough.

Soon, everyone was ready. The horses' breaths turned into icy puffs in the wintery air as they rode to the outskirts of the village, where Reed and his guards waited.

Jasce nodded as Reed rode up beside him.

"Let's hope you're as good as everyone says," Reed said, gripping the reins.

Jasce squinted, focusing on the dark road stretched out before him. "Any updates?"

"Just that they're under attack and the Watch Guard is searching for the Angel of Death." Reed's hard eyes burned into Jasce.

"They're about to find him." Jasce kicked his horse, leaving Carhurst and the celebration behind.

ᡝᡝ ᡝᡝ ᡝᡝ

They stopped on the edge of Hillford, where flames lit up the night sky. Everyone waited, staring at Jasce.

Amycus nodded. "You know the Guard best."

Reed's face was expressionless as he gripped the hilt of his sword, his men behind him.

Jasce took a deep breath. The lives of these men and women rested on his shoulders. They needed to trust him if they were to follow him. But why would they? Until recently, he was a Hunter and Drexus's second in command.

"I have not earned the right to lead you in this battle—I'm not worthy of the honor. But know that I will do everything in my power to defend you and protect the people." Jasce lifted his chin, bracing himself as Kord stepped forward.

"Jasce, despite what you did—" He waved his hand, his eyes darting to his sister. Kenz frowned but couldn't hide the flush in her cheeks. "We are a team," Kord said. "You are one of us, and we trust you."

Jasce's shoulders relaxed. He grabbed Kord's forearm, nodding his thanks, and Kord returned the gesture but pulled Jasce close.

"We're still going to have a little chat," Kord whispered, patting Jasce hard on the shoulder.

Jasce pinched the bridge of his nose. He turned and addressed the warriors before him. "Reed, you and your men protect the villagers, get them out at all cost. Once they're free, circle back around. The rest of us will attack." Jasce stared at each Spectral. "Kenz and Delmira, use your shields as weapons—the Guard won't expect that. Work together, combine your magic, and remember: You cannot show mercy, for you will receive none. Is that clear?"

Jasce stared at Kenz, memorizing every detail of her face. Then he shoved his feelings aside, drawing instead from his magic, training, and the anger that had fueled him for so many years. Kenz's eyes widened when she saw the hardness in his eyes, his face like stone. The killing calm settled over Jasce as he entered the village.

The scene was all too familiar—kneeling villagers, some bleeding, some crying, some already dead. Jasce recognized the Tracker from his previous raids, her scraggly white hair blowing in the wind as she walked through the people and searched for Spectrals. A dozen soldiers surrounded the town square and a Hunter stood on the edge, the skull mask grinning in victory.

Jasce looked over his shoulder at his team. "Change of plan. I'll take the Hunter; you focus on the Guard." He scanned the rest of the square, searching for more skull masks or black fire.

"Tracker!" Jasce yelled, his arms outstretched. Villagers lifted their heads in surprise while the Watch Guard trained their crossbows on Jasce. The Hunter raised his hand to stop the soldiers from shooting.

The old woman turned, her white eyes crinkling around the edges. She shuffled toward him, her chains rattling on the cobblestones, and sniffed the air, inhaling deeply when she neared. She smiled, her yellow teeth peeking out beneath chapped lips. "Your magic is finally free," she whispered. "Now, kill me."

"What?" Jasce leaned back, keeping an eye on the Hunter making his way across the square.

"Kill me. I will not be a slave any longer." She yanked Jasce's dagger from its sheath and aimed for his chest. Instinct took over. He grabbed her wrist, twisted, and plunged the blade into her heart.

She gasped in pain and fell into Jasce, her blood drenching his hand.

Shouts rang out as Reed and his men charged through the square. Yellow light burst from Delmira's gauntlets, her shield igniting to protect the villagers while Kenz's shield pushed the Hunter back. Firebombs, rocks, and tornados crashed into the guards as Jasce's team ran into battle.

Jasce looked at the woman in his arms. "Why?"

"Drexus can't finish what he's started," she whispered, blood bubbling from her mouth, grasping his bloody hand.

"Tell me what he's doing."

The woman swallowed, her eyelids closing. Jasce shook her. "Please, tell me."

Her lids fluttered open. She licked her lips, dark blood stark against her white skin. "He has a Psyche," she breathed. Her head drooped to the side, her hand releasing his.

Jasce clenched his jaw and lowered her to the ground. This wasn't what he wanted. He hadn't wanted to kill her, could've stopped himself and easily disarmed her. Rage vibrated through him and he tore his gaze from the dead Spectral, directing his hatred at the approaching Hunter.

Swords clashed and magic filled the air. Spectrals battled the Watch Guard soldiers, who each seemed to have the Amplifier magic. But even with their new powers, his team worked together, driving them back. Flynt shot fireballs while using his sword to cut down any soldiers that got past his flames. With her shield, Kenz pushed soldiers into either Flynt's fire or Vale's rocks. Many guards fell to their knees, grasping their throats as Aura and Amycus worked side by side. Reed had freed the villagers, and half his men now circled back to join the fray.

Jasce gripped his two swords and approached the Hunter.

The Hunter growled and removed a longsword from its sheath. "You will pay for what you did to Distria and Geleon."

Jasce recognized the voice. "I don't want to kill you, Lyon, but I will."

Lyon's eyes hardened and he swung his sword in a mighty arc. Jasce blocked the blow with both blades, the strength of the attack vibrating up his arms. His mind automatically focused on the Hunter's movements, searching for weaknesses—he spun and flipped in the air, his swords a blur, slicing across the Hunter's chest. Lyon cried out, dropping to his knee, and slashed his sword. Jasce blocked it easily, then cursed as Lyon jammed a dagger into Jasce's thigh. Jasce stumbled back.

Blood poured down Lyon's chest as he struggled to his feet, gripping his sword with both hands.

"Surrender," Jasce said.

Lyon's lips drew back in a snarl and he charged, his blade cutting through the air.

Jasce felt the tug inside him and materialized beside the assassin, using his sword to remove Lyon's head. He squeezed his eyes shut and yanked the dagger free of his skin, then ripped his tunic to tie around his leg.

A cry rang out through the square. A soldier maneuvered around Delmira's shield and threw her, her body crumpling against a burning building. Aura yelled, snuffing out the fire and running toward Delmira. The soldier sprinted for Kord, whose back was turned as he fought another guard. Without Delmira's shield to protect them, more soldiers approached.

"Vale, over there!" Jasce yelled, pointing to the soldiers. Kord turned just as Vale sent a dust storm at the approaching soldiers, ripping cobblestones off the ground to drive the men back. Jasce vaulted to Vale's side, cutting down the remaining guards.

"Nicely done," he said, patting Vale's back.

"Watch out!" Kord yelled. A glint of metal flashed and Jasce veered away, dodging the incoming arrow. A yelp from behind had Jasce spinning. The arrow meant for him sliced Vale's neck; blood seeped through his fingers.

"No!" Jasce grabbed the boy before he fell and yelled for Kord. He looked in the direction where the arrow had come. The Hunters stood next to Drexus, who smiled, his arms crossed. He was flanked by Sabine and Bronn.

Bronn loaded another arrow into his crossbow, aiming for Kord, who knelt next to Vale.

"Kenz, shield Kord!" Jasce traversed through the darkness and slashed his sword down onto Bronn's crossbow. Bronn swore and stepped back, reaching for his swords. Jasce faced Drexus, whose eyes widened then quickly turned to stone. The other Hunters aimed their crossbows at Jasce.

Drexus ignited his fire, black flames dancing between his fingers, making the clear gem in his ring glow. "You're a Vaulter? How is that possible?"

"Long story."

Drexus's eyes narrowed. "I want him taken alive," he ordered the Hunters. Bronn jerked his head, gaping at his commander.

Jasce pointed his bloody sword. "You and your Hunters will die."

Sabine's eyes, just visible above the grinning skull, widened.

Bronn pulled his mask off and laughed. "It's ten against one, you arrogant traitor. Even you aren't that good."

Drexus scanned the clearing, snarling. "What a waste. You could've been ruling by my side. Instead, you've joined them."

Bronn's eyes flicked to Drexus, a muscle in his jaw throbbing.

"I will never allow you to rule Pandaren," Jasce growled.

"You think you and your little band of Spectrals can stop me?" Drexus looked over Jasce's shoulder, his eyes going cold as Amycus walked toward them, fire swirling along his curved sword.

Jasce bit back a curse as Amycus stood beside him and said, "Drexus, it's been a long time."

"Indeed." Drexus transferred fire from one hand to the other while the Hunters stood shoulder to shoulder, an impenetrable wall of lethality.

Jasce's hands tightened on his swords. A few months ago, he would have stood at Drexus's side, loyal and blind. Sounds of the battle raged behind him, and it took everything he had not to turn around.

Jasce glared at Drexus and Bronn. "Amycus, I'll handle this. You protect the others."

"I don't think so." Amycus twirled his flaming scimitar while dirt swirled around his feet. A Hunter gasped, grabbing his throat, trying to gulp in air.

Black fire slithered along the ground, circling Jasce and Amycus. Amycus tilted his head and waved, a cool breeze blowing the fire toward the Hunters.

"You've finally accomplished it, I see," Drexus said, redirecting his flames. "Manipulating all the elements. But I wonder at what cost?"

"Care to find out?"

Drexus peered at Jasce, his lip curling. "He's the reason your family is dead."

Jasce stiffened. "What?"

Amycus paled, the breeze disappearing.

"Oh, he forgot to mention that?"

Jasce lowered his swords and faced Amycus, whose jaw tightened. What was Drexus talking about? How could Amycus be responsible?

He needed to focus on the enemy in front of him. He would deal with Amycus later.

"Drexus, stop this madness," Amycus said.

Drexus laughed and stared at Jasce. "He never could grasp what I'm trying to do, what I can accomplish."

"You're experimenting on and killing your own kind," Amycus said.

"No! I'm creating a stronger Pandaren. One that others will think twice about before invading. The king was weak, and the steward is a fool for trying to negotiate peace with the Vastanes. With what I'm doing, we will never be at the mercy of anyone. Why can't you understand that?" Drexus's flames burned brighter, the heat causing sweat to trickle down Jasce's back.

Jasce's nostrils flared. "Loyalty, honor, and obedience. Or death for anyone who doesn't agree with you. Is that it?"

Drexus flexed his hands, the fire inching closer. Jasce's stomach dropped, remembering the flames circling his mother. Her dead, gray eyes staring at him. His sister's screams.

"Never again," Jasce said, his voice like steel. He vaulted through the flames, bringing his sword down. He swore as his weapon crashed into Bronn's.

"I've been waiting for this moment for a long time," Bronn said, pushing Jasce back.

Jasce snarled and settled into his fighting stance, protecting his injured leg.

Bronn circled Jasce, baring his teeth. Steel clanged as the two warriors battled. Bronn maneuvered inside Jasce's guard and pain burned across his waist.

Jasce swore, lowering his arm to protect his injured side. Bronn laughed, stalking his prey, smelling blood.

"You've gone soft."

Jasce retreated a step, sneaking a glance at the battle occurring behind him. He needed to keep the Hunters distracted, give his team time.

Drexus and Amycus fought with whips made of flames. The heat of the colliding magic sent ripples through the air. Sabine continued to guard Drexus's back while the remaining Hunters strode toward the Spectrals.

"Kenz, the Hunters!" Jasce yelled, taking another step, leading Bronn away from the fight. Amycus shifted his attention to Jasce, and a blast of fire knocked Amycus off his feet. Drexus raised his hands in the air, sending a spear of fire toward Kenz's shield. Aura and Flynt flanked Kenz, with Reed and his men behind them. Vale sat on the ground, pale but alive, and Kord stood, twirling his sword with Vale's blood on his hands.

"Stop!" Drexus yelled to his Hunters, his gaze piercing Kord. He smiled and pointed. "Bring me the Healer."

Jasce inhaled, limping around Bronn, blood running down his leg and side. He needed to stop Drexus and the Hunters—now. Swallowing the pain, he surrendered to the anger, allowing the bloodlust to ignite inside him, losing himself to the darkness.

He charged Bronn, feinting one way and slashing the other. Bronn hollered as Jasce attacked, each swipe of his sword pushing him back. Jasce elbowed him in the face and grabbed his neck. He held Bronn in the air, squeezing the Hunter's throat.

"Look out!" Amycus yelled.

Jasce barely had time to drop Bronn before he felt Sabine's sword slice through his arm. He roared as bone peaked through the ravaged flesh. Bronn crawled to his knees, coughing and holding his throat, while Sabine struck again. Jasce lifted his uninjured arm, blocking the blow, wincing as he swung his sword. She gracefully darted out of the way.

Drexus sent a ball of black fire at Amycus, launching him through the air. Jasce heard Kenz yell as he lifted his sword. His arm felt like it moved through mud, and exhaustion was consuming him, his magic fading.

He glanced at his team. More time. They needed more time. He gritted his teeth, fighting past the pain and fatigue, and faced Sabine and Bronn, knowing he wouldn't survive if they both attacked.

"No!" Drexus yelled as Bronn brought down his sword. It stopped inches from Jasce's throat. "I told you, I need him alive." Fury twisted Bronn's face, his sword shaking. "Bronn, step away. You too, Sabine."

Drexus approached Jasce, his eyes scanning him, calculating. "You are quite valuable now, with your two types of magic. You can tell me how you did it or I can carve you apart later."

Jasce growled, stumbling forward and blindly swinging his sword. Drexus punched him so hard that Jasce fell backward, his head smacking on the cobblestones. Blood poured from Jasce's wounds, his vision blurred. Drexus pulled a collar from inside his cloak.

No.

He eyed the collar and commanded himself to get up.

Jasce got a knee under him and reached for the dagger in his boot, waiting for Drexus to get closer.

The pounding of hooves broke through the sounds of battle as Reed and his men charged forward. It was all Jasce needed. He struggled to his feet and slashed his dagger across Drexus's chest. The ground disappeared as a fireball blasted into Jasce's body, hurling him through the air. Pain exploded in his head when he landed. A blanket of smoke and darkness covered him.

Voices yelled from the courtyard. Jasce focused on Kenz's, ordering him to get up. He rolled over, trying to get to his knees, struggling to breathe. His chest burned. He lifted his head to see Sabine dragging Bronn away, the other Hunters protecting Drexus, who stared at Jasce with a wicked smile lining his face before sending a stream of fire toward Reed's men. With a twirl of his cloak, he fled into the night.

The black flames crashed against Delmira's shield causing her wall of yellow light to quiver. Footsteps thumped through Jasce's head. Someone dropped to their knees and rested a hand on his shoulder. Familiar blue eyes peeked through the darkness. Jasce tried to get to his feet, needing to go after Drexus. He couldn't allow him to escape again.

But the world shifted, failure and fatigue dragging him into the shadows.

CHAPTER 25

Warmth tingled through Jasce's skull as Kord's hands cradled his head, the darkness receding along with the blinding pain. The sun crested over the hills and the woodsy smell of smoke drifted through the morning air. Voices mumbled in the distance as Jasce opened his eyes.

Kord smiled, sitting back on his heels. "That was quite a knock to the head. Even I was worried. How are you feeling?"

Jasce rubbed the back of his head, scanning the square. "I'm fine. Vale?"

"He's stabilized." Kord sighed. Dark shadows stood in stark contrast to his green eyes.

Jasce saw Kenz patching up Delmira.

"She's fine," Kord said, seeing where Jasce stared.

The people returned to the village, faces smeared with ash and tears. Many embraced the Spectrals for protecting them from the Watch Guard. Reed shied away from one of the older women, who clung to him, sobbing. He untangled himself and walked toward Jasce and Kord. Flynt, Aura, and Reed's soldiers helped clear debris and extinguish fires around the square. Amycus stared in the direction Drexus had gone, sparks of flames swirling around his closed fists. He turned as if feeling Jasce's glare, his eyes holding Jasce's captive.

What had Drexus meant about his mother's and sister's death being Amycus's fault? Jasce rubbed his hands over his face. He was so tired of the lies and betrayal, of not knowing who to trust. He tried to remember Amycus's recounting of his time with his mother, but his brain was fuzzy, his body ached, and his wounds throbbed. Kord's magic must be depleted if Jasce wasn't fully healed, but Vale and the others needed him more. Jasce was used to pain.

He laughed bitterly. Pain is inescapable; suffering is a choice.

"What's so funny?" Reed asked, massaging the back of his neck.

Jasce shook his head. "You and your men were invaluable. Thank you."

Reed snorted. "That must have been hard to say."

Jasce stared at the dirt and blood covering his hands. "How many did you lose?"

"Four." Reed's voice was tight.

Jasce nodded. The extra soldiers had helped, but they were no match for the amplified Watch Guard. He could understand why Drexus wanted to create a special force of soldiers with magic—total domination. Only Spectrals standing against Drexus could protect Pandaren. They needed to find more who were willing to fight.

Kenz watched him from across the square, her face smudged with dirt, a fine layer of ash covering her hair. He had been so relieved to find her unharmed. Relieved they were all safe.

"Why didn't the Hunters attack? It seemed Drexus was waiting for something," Reed said.

"At first, he wanted me alive, and when he saw Kord heal Vale, he wanted us both. He couldn't risk us getting caught in the crossfire." Jasce met Amycus's eyes as the man sat across from him in the dirt.

"He saw you vault, didn't he?" Amycus asked.

Jasce nodded. "He was intrigued by my two types of magic. The snake threatened to carve me open." His nails pierced his palms. "What did he mean about it being your fault?"

Amycus shook his head. "Jasce, I . . ."

Rage and failure swelled inside Jasce, needing a release. He stood, grabbing Amycus by his tunic, and yanked him to his feet. "I told you not to lie to me again."

Reed and Kord jumped up, both pushing against Jasce's chest. Amycus's eyes filled with tears.

"Jasce, let me explain."

Kenz jogged over, her eyes wide. Jasce dropped Amycus and shoved Kord and Reed aside. "You mean it's true? You're the reason they're dead?"

Amycus raised his hands. "I don't know . . ."

"You don't know?" Jasce's voice was a lethal caress. He reached for his dagger, but a wall of indigo light separated him from Amycus.

"Jasce, settle down," Kenz said, her hand raised. Kord's mouth pursed and Reed drew his sword.

So much for being a team. They obviously didn't trust him now, and he didn't blame them. He wanted to kill one of their own.

No. He wanted to kill one of *his* own.

He turned, unable to stomach the looks on their faces.

"Jasce, wait," Amycus said, reaching forward.

Kord held him back. "Let him be."

Jasce picked up his fallen swords, returned them to their scabbards, and mounted his horse. Kenz grabbed the reins, but he sighed and looked away. His eyes met Vale's and he grimaced at his pale skin and the bandage speckled with blood tied around his neck. The kid had almost died because of him.

"What?" Jasce said, looking down at Kenz.

"Where are you going?"

"Away from you. All of you."

"Why do you always run when things get hard?"

Jasce looked away from the flash of anger in her eyes, the set of her jaw. Right now, he didn't care, his failure suffocating him. He didn't want to deal with Amycus's lies or the disapproval he saw on his team's faces. He couldn't believe he was face-to-face with the man who ruined his life, and he'd escaped again, along with Sabine and Bronn. He didn't want to sit around the fire and talk it out. He wanted to be alone.

He ripped the reins from Kenz and kicked his horse, but he'd only gone a few yards when Kenz called out, "You're a coward! You know that?"

Jasce's shoulders stiffened. He slid off his horse mid-stride and strode back to Kenz, who glared at him.

"What did you call me?"

"You heard me."

Jasce reached for his swords.

"What? You want to kill me too? Is that your answer to everything?"

Jasce's hand froze. The rest of the group were on their feet, some with mouths opened. Flynt clicked his ignitor and fire twirled through his fingers while Kord edged forward, placing himself between Jasce and his sister. Amycus's shoulders hunched, pain filling his eyes. Jasce's magic had dwindled to an ember, and he didn't have the strength to stop the flood of emotions filling him. Goosebumps spread along his skin and his breath hitched, dizziness overcoming him as fear, regret, anger, and disappointment crashed into him.

Jasce stumbled back and closed his eyes, breathing deeply, blocking the feelings. He retreated to his horse and glared at his team. "You aren't worth it. None of you are." He turned from the hurt flashing across Kenz's face and mounted his horse. Riding away, he gripped his chest as something in his heart snapped.

৩৵৹ ৩৵৹ ৩৵৹

The Dry Gulch Inn on the outskirts of Carhurst catered to those needing an escape. Jasce blended in with the murderers, thieves, and misfits. Alcohol poured freely and women loitered nearby, eager to help patrons forget their troubles.

Jasce finished another drink, his mind and body numb, no longer caring that he was covered in dried blood and dirt. His appearance kept anyone with nefarious desires at bay. He tried to focus on the conversation at the table, where a hairy man—Jasce couldn't remember his name—spoke of his voyage across the sea to the Far Lands. Jasce wondered what it would be like to sail away and no longer be chained to Pandaren's magic and deceit.

Jasce smiled sloppily at the barmaid, who came by with drinks, and wrapped his arm around her waist. A gust of cold air tickled his cheek and he swiveled his head, uttering a string of profanity that startled the woman. The candles flickered and the glow from the fireplace illuminated Kord's face, his glare intimidating anyone with half a brain. Thankfully, that part of Jasce's brain was drowned in liquor.

Kord's eyes locked onto him. Jasce swore again, releasing the barmaid as Kenz, Amycus, and Reed entered the seedy tavern too.

"Excuse me," Kord said to the patrons at the table. "I need to borrow my friend." Kord grabbed Jasce by the back of his armor and hefted him out of the chair.

Jasce wobbled on his feet. "Why can't you people leave me alone?"

"Because we're your friends, you imbecile." Kord dragged him outside, where the twilight sky was dotted with stars and the cold felt like a smack in the face. He couldn't believe he had spent the entire day in that tavern. Jasce blinked, trying to clear his vision as Kord led him to the stables, beelining for a large barrel of water.

"Don't you dare—" Jasce inhaled as Kord dunked his head, the shock of the freezing water clearing his muddled brain. He tried to reach Kord but his armor restricted his movements. Seconds passed before Kord finally hauled him from the barrel.

Jasce sputtered, spinning out of Kord's grip. "You son of—" Stars flashed as Kord's fist connected with Jasce's jaw. He fell against the barrel, his mouth filling with blood.

"Kord," Amycus said, frowning.

"Don't worry, Amycus. He's too stubborn to be hurt."

"What's the matter with you?" Jasce shook his head, water dripping down his face and back, indignation replacing his alcohol-induced stupor.

"*You* are what's the matter with me! How dare you just ride off, drowning in self-pity. You aren't the only one who's suffered in this world, Jasce. You aren't the only one who's been lied to or had someone close to them die. True warriors don't run from their problems. A true warrior rises from adversity."

"Don't you dare lecture me on what a warrior is or isn't." Jasce stepped forward, jabbing Kord in the chest. "Your biggest concern is, what? Whether some man is flirting with your wife? You have a wife, Kord. You have a family. I have nothing!" Jasce's entire body shook.

Kord's face softened. "You could have a family if you would just allow us in."

Jasce snorted and pushed past Kord, longing for another drink. He didn't want to listen to the sentiment, and he certainly didn't want to process his confession. He hadn't meant to reveal those feelings, especially to the man who blocked his path.

"Get out of my way," Jasce said to Amycus. Kenz stood next to the blacksmith, her gauntlets glowing blue and her face expressionless as she watched Jasce.

"I will not until you listen to me," Amycus said. "Then you can go back to drinking your problems away. But not until you've heard what I have to say. Is that clear?"

Reed covered his mouth, trying not to laugh.

Jasce glowered at him and spit blood into the dirt. "What are you doing here?"

Amusement flickered in Reed's eyes. "Backup. Not that they need it."

Jasce leaned his head back and sighed. The sooner he could get this conversation over with, the sooner he could have another drink. His head pounded and the wounds in his leg and arm throbbed. "Fine. Have it your way."

He limped out of the stables and into the inn, heading upstairs to his room with four sets of footsteps following him. He grunted, too tired and now too sober to care.

The pocket-sized room accommodated a bed, chair, and dresser. Kenz leaned against the door while Amycus fell into the chair, lowering his head and rubbing his temples.

Jasce unstrapped his armor and let it drop to the floor. Kenz gasped, frowning at the gash in his arm. The jagged wound, only partially healed, revealed a sliver of bone protruding through flesh. Now that he had sobered up, the pain from his injuries returned with a vengeance. He plopped onto the bed, wincing and retied the blood-soaked fabric around his thigh.

"Oh, that's lovely," Kord said, stomping over to Jasce, and grabbed his arm. "Why didn't you tell me?"

Jasce let out a string of expletives as he tried to pull free. "Your bedside manner sucks, by the way."

Kord snorted and pressed his hands against Jasce's arm and leg. Immediately, warmth flowed and the wounds knit together. Kord inspected Jasce's side and healed that too.

Jasce turned from the kindness in Kord's eyes, but there was no safe place to look. Amycus stared, hope and sadness lining his face. Reed stood near the window, his brows raised as he eyed Jasce's healed arm while Kenz frowned and then turned away.

He had hurt her. He had hurt all of them with his cruel words. Jasce sighed and removed his bloody tunic, throwing it in the corner and fumbling in his bag for a clean shirt.

Reed swore, his lips pursed in disgust. "I've heard rumors of Drexus's discipline, but never imagined . . ."

Jasce kept his face expressionless, staring at Amycus. "Say what you need to say, then let me be."

Amycus nodded and focused his gaze on his clasped hands. "You remember me saying I apprenticed to the blacksmith in your village? That's when I met your mother. I convinced her to join the underground group hiding Spectrals. I guess Barnet felt betrayed by your mother and blamed me, and he must have alerted Drexus." He took a deep breath and continued. "Drexus attacked your village to draw me out. But I didn't know. I was on the other side of Opax. When I returned, I heard you were all dead."

Jasce paced the room, deep in thought. He tried to relax his hands, but the familiar anger thundered inside him.

"I had no idea you'd survived until years later when I heard rumors of Drexus's Angel of Death. I needed to investigate this new threat, and that's when I saw you. You had removed your mask, and I knew you were Lisia's son." Amycus took a deep breath and sat up a little taller. "So when I heard about your capture, I sent Kenz and Kord to rescue you. I had to make things right for Lisia. For you."

"Why didn't you tell me when we first met? Or after I discovered it was Drexus who killed my family?" Jasce strode forward, his face warming. "I told you to never lie to me again."

Indigo light flashed in front of him. He stopped before smacking into it. "You need to quit doing that," Jasce said, scowling at Kenz.

"You need to control your temper."

Jasce inhaled and retreated to lean against the dresser. He arched his brow and Kenz lowered her shield.

"I wanted to tell you, Jasce," Amycus said. "I tried to, many times. But I was afraid."

"Afraid of what?"

"At first? I was afraid for my life and those that stood with me. Then I was afraid you would leave." Amycus stood, taking a small step forward. "I feared you'd never forgive me."

Jasce frowned. "I don't understand."

Amycus sighed. "Drexus killed Lisia and Jaida, captured you, made you into the most lethal warrior of all time, to make me pay. Your family is dead because of me."

A knot formed in Jasce's stomach. Drexus had murdered his family, taken Jasce, and turned him into a monster, all to make Amycus suffer. The fury drained out of him as he slid to the floor, resting his arms on his knees and lowering his head. Amycus sniffed and moved back to his chair. Reed sat on the creaking bed next to Kord.

Jasce wanted to be angry at Amycus. He wanted to blame him for the way his life turned out. But it was Drexus's fault. And his own. Jasce chose to become the Angel of Death. He chose to let hatred and revenge define him. He had chosen this life.

He lifted his head and stared at the stained ceiling. The self-pity, which he would never admit to, subsided, replaced by a desire to make things right. This was no longer about revenge, but justice. Drexus needed to pay for his crimes.

Amycus stared, his blue eyes lined with silver. Jasce nodded, looking at the people who wouldn't give up on him. "I'm sorry for what I said earlier." His eyes met Kenz's, who stood by Amycus holding his hand. "You're worth more than you know," he said.

Kenz's mouth curved into a smile and Kord sighed, rubbing the back of his neck. He pulled Jasce to his feet and draped an arm around his shoulders. "Come on. It's time for that little chat." Kord gave his sister a knowing look as he led Jasce from the room.

CHAPTER 26

The next day Jasce, Amycus, and Reed met to discuss plans to stop Drexus. Reed had updated Lord Rollant on the battle in Hillford, which made Jasce uneasy. He didn't fully trust Rollant, unsure where his loyalties lay.

Jasce had spent the night at the inn, pacing and listening to the revelry in the tavern below. He hadn't wanted to return to the forge and chance talking with Amycus, which would just reopen wounds from the past. He wasn't ready to discuss whether Amycus was to blame for the deaths of his mother and sister, or the reasons he'd kept that information hidden. In the end, it was Drexus who had slashed the knife across his mother's throat. He didn't want to think about what happened to Jaida, only remembering her screams, and then the silence.

He had tried to focus on the problem of Drexus and Hunters with Amplifier magic, but his mind kept returning to that kiss with Kenz and her brother's reaction. The conversation with Kord had left him baffled.

"Care to explain what's going on between you and my sister?" Kord had asked once they received their drinks.

"I don't know. I've tried to stay away from her, but I can't. I'm drawn to her in a way I can't explain. Even our magic reacts differently."

Kord raised a brow and nodded his head, both hands gripping his tankard of ale.

"That's it?" Jasce asked after a few minutes. He had expected a lecture, or worse, another punch to the jaw, which still throbbed.

"She's a grown woman. And you know she isn't one to be controlled—she makes her own decisions." Kord swirled the liquid in his mug, his face thoughtful. "I don't know if she truly loved Ven. I think she wanted a normal life, wanted what Tillie and I have, and Ven was the first to ask. And then she failed in protecting him and his family. It's been guilt more than love these past two years." Kord sighed and took a sip of his drink. "She's different with you. Anyone can see that."

"But?"

"I know you won't stop, not where Drexus is concerned. You rush into danger, thinking of revenge over anything else. I understand why, but I don't know if she can protect you."

"I don't need protection."

Kord smiled, but it didn't reach his eyes. "Yes, you do. You need protection from yourself. And I don't know how she will react if something happens to you. I don't want to see her suffer as she did before."

Jasce ran his finger along a gash in the stained bar top. "I assume you've already had this conversation with her?"

"I have."

Jasce had grown to care for both of them, and he didn't want to cause them pain or suffering. Kenz deserved better than a bloodstained assassin driven by revenge. But maybe after he killed Drexus, assuming he survived, he could attempt a life worthy of her, a life where she didn't have to protect him, where her light chased away his darkness.

Sunlight now filtered through the window, illuminating a dried speck of blood on Jasce's boots. He rubbed his temples and groaned, the lack of sleep catching up to him as Reed and Amycus discussed the Watch Guard.

Jasce lifted his head. "We've been over this a hundred times. We don't know how many received the Amplifier serum, but let's assume all of them. There are still nine Hunters and Drexus to deal with. We need Rollant's soldiers and every Spectral who can fight." He filled his mug with coffee and fell into the chair, staring at the fire.

"We were successful yesterday against Drexus and his Guard," Reed said, jutting out his chin.

"Drexus was simply gathering information, learning what kind of magic we had. He didn't unleash the Hunters or his full power on us. If he had, we wouldn't be sitting here."

Reed chewed on his thumbnail. "What's bothering me is how he knew you and your Spectrals would come."

Amycus stared at Reed, his fingers steepled under his chin. "Are you thinking the raid was a setup?"

"It's possible."

Jasce swore and stood, staring out the window. "That would make sense and fit with Drexus's schemes. Who told Rollant about the raid?"

"I don't know," Reed said. Jasce glared and Reed got to his feet. "But I'm going to find out."

Jasce watched him walk down the street. Something wasn't adding up, and the lack of sleep made it difficult to think clearly. "Drexus has vials of different magic. The Tracker said he had a Psyche too—he must have them hidden, but why? He wants me because I have two types of magic. But why does he want Kord? Why a Healer?"

Amycus jumped to his feet, knocking over his mug and shattering it to pieces. "He's combining magic—or trying to. He doesn't want the Watch Guard to just have the Amplifier magic, but other powers as well. You're proof it's possible."

Jasce rubbed his face, focusing on the wood beams in the ceiling. "He won't stop with the Guard. He'll want more magic for himself too. But I still don't understand why he wants Kord."

"Think about it," Amycus said. "We know two types of magic in one Spectral could kill the person. But what if you had a powerful Healer to counteract the effects?"

Jasce let loose a string of profanity and paced around the room. Amycus knelt to pick up the broken pieces of his mug.

"I have to stop him," Jasce finally said.

Amycus shook his head. "He can't get his hands on you or Kord. Can't you see that? You're the last person who should go. Right now, he's guessing. But if he has either of you?"

"Are you seriously asking me to stay out of this?" The muscle in Jasce's jaw pulsed and the headache hiding behind his eyes threatened to return with a vengeance.

"Yes. Kord, Tillie, and Maleous need to go into hiding, and so do you."

"I don't hide."

"If you care about any of us, or ultimately the survival of Spectrals and Pandaren, then you will put your selfish agenda aside and let someone else handle this."

"Someone else?" How dare Amycus ask this of him and then call him selfish. "I have searched for years for the man who killed my mother and sister, and you want me to let someone else handle this?" Jasce clenched his fists, keeping himself from reaching for his dagger. Kenz's words had cut him; he didn't like that his first instinct was to kill. That was Azrael, the Angel of Death, Drexus's pawn. It was not Jasce.

Amycus stared into the fire. The wood crackled sharply. "Do you see the irony? Your quest for revenge makes you dependent upon Drexus. Do you think your pain will end when Drexus is dead? That your wounds will suddenly heal? You've given your enemy power over you."

Jasce's mouth fell open. He had never thought of it that way. His need for vengeance had consumed him, and he supposed that did give Drexus power over him. But could he trust others to do what needed to be done?

Jasce relaxed his hands and made himself sit. "What's your plan?"

Amycus returned to his desk. "I will go."

"What? That's ridiculous. *You* are going to stop Drexus? Can you kill him, if faced with the choice?"

Amycus arched a brow. "Why do you doubt me?"

Jasce opened his mouth and shut it. He didn't know. All he knew was that he couldn't see Amycus defeating Drexus. Amycus wasn't a killer.

Kord and Kenz walked into the cottage. They both froze, their eyes darting between Jasce and Amycus.

"What did we miss?" Kord asked.

"Yeah, we just saw Reed storming down the street." Kenz sat in the chair next to Jasce. He curled his fingers. Her hair flowed down her back in soft waves, and he wanted to run his hands through it. He couldn't stop the rush of feelings cascading through him nor block the way their magic swirled. He sprang out of the chair to refill his coffee, blaming his shaking hands on the caffeine running through his system.

Kord sat in the vacant chair. "So, what's going on?"

Jasce focused on the flames in the fire, letting Amycus talk.

"You, Tillie, and Maleous, along with Jasce, need to go into hiding."

"What?" the siblings said at the same time.

"Drexus needs your abilities, Kord—and Jasce's. We can't allow him to get his hands on either of you. We figured out what the extra vials mean and what experiments Drexus is doing. He's trying to combine more than one type of magic. Jasce is proof it can be done, but he needs a Healer to help with the process."

Kenz paled, her eyes darting between Kord and Jasce.

Kord crossed his arms, frowning at Jasce. "Did you agree to this?"

Jasce slowly turned and nodded. No, he didn't agree, but for now he'd play along.

"Where do you expect them to go?" Kenz asked.

"Opax," Jasce said, a plan forming in his mind.

"Why Opax?" Amycus asked.

"It's the last thing Drexus would expect. He knows we're close to Hillford, and it's just a matter of time before his Hunters come here."

Amycus leaned back in his chair, a crease forming between his eyes. "The idea has merit."

"We need to get word out we've left, to protect the people. Reed can help with that." Jasce walked toward the door without glancing back. "We leave tomorrow."

ᏬᎦ ᏬᎦ ᏬᎦ

Jasce sat on his bed, lost in thought. Water droplets slid down his back. He had spent the day and early evening working in the forge, finalizing the plan that had formed as he'd stared into the flames—a plan that could not include Kenz or Kord or anyone he cared about. If everything went smoothly, Drexus wouldn't be able to harm them again. He had left the forge, memorizing every detail. His own forge would look exactly the same, if he survived.

Jasce rose to a soft knock on the door, immediately feeling her magic. He leaned against the doorframe, suddenly very aware that all he wore were linen pants.

Kenz swallowed when she saw him, a flush brightening her cheeks. "Do you have a minute?"

Jasce nodded, holding the door open for her. She walked to the center of the room, keeping her back to him.

"What's really going on?" she asked.

"What part of Amycus's plan didn't you get?" He winced at the harshness in his voice. He would leave tomorrow, possibly forever, and he didn't want to hurt her again.

Kenz turned, hugging herself. "There's no way you'd agree to sit this one out. So, I want to know what's going through that thick head of yours."

Jasce forced a smile. "Thick head, huh?"

"Extremely thick."

Jasce leaned against the door. "It's a solid plan and will catch Drexus off guard when he realizes I'm not with Amycus and the rest of the Spectrals during the attack."

"I don't believe you."

Jasce sighed, staring at his bare feet. She was correct—he wouldn't sit by and allow someone else to enact the justice that was due him. He also wasn't sure he would survive. The only way to protect her was to put an end to whatever was happening between them. He kept telling himself this was better for her.

"Kenz, this needs to stop." The words tasted like ash in his mouth.

Her eyes narrowed. "I don't understand."

"You're better off without me. Trust me on this one."

"Are you trying to protect me again?"

He closed his eyes, breathing in her scent, feeling her magic call to him. "I'm trying to protect both of us."

She walked toward him and traced the tattoos on his arm, her fingers moving to his chest. He sucked in a breath. Desire burned in her eyes as her hands scraped along muscle.

Jasce grabbed her wrists. "Kenz."

"Shhh." She stepped closer, placing her mouth gently against his, sucking on his bottom lip.

"Kenz, I can't," he said against her mouth. "I won't be able to stop."

She ran kisses across his jaw and neck, her hands free to explore his chest. "Then don't," she whispered.

Logical thought dissolved from his mind. All he could think about was her, the way she kissed him, how her hands made his body tremble. With a moan of surrender, he picked her up, shuddering as her legs wrapped around him. He placed her gently on the bed, deepening the kiss, their tongues and teeth scraping. He needed skin, needed to feel the softness of her flesh. She lifted her arms as he slid her shirt over her head.

He froze, his eyes devouring her body. "You're beautiful."

She smiled and moved to take off her pants, but he grabbed her hand, tearing his gaze from her body to focus on her mesmerizing eyes. "Not yet." He ran his hands along every curve, his desire and magic pulsating as her body responded to his touch. She moaned and ran her fingers through his hair, making his breath hitch, igniting a flame that threatened to burn out of control. He savored every inch of her as his mouth trailed kisses along her silky skin.

Jasce lifted his head and smiled, black lace making his mouth water. "Absolutely beautiful."

"Jasce, please," she breathed under his teasing touch.

He ached, consumed by desire as he explored every part of her, her soft cries making his heart stutter. The flame inside him sparked brighter and burned hotter with each caress. He forced himself to take his time, to savor every moment, every kiss.

Kenz cried out as a shudder coursed up her body, her hands fisting into the sheets.

His muscles quivered as she ran her nails along his back, her gentle touch finally removing the barriers between them. The heat from his body clashed with the cold air whispering against his bare skin.

"Kenz," he whispered, shuddering under her intimate caress. Her flushed cheeks and swollen lips ignited his need. He hungered to be closer, to feel her body claim his. He kissed up her neck and along her jaw, finally capturing her mouth, and groaned as their magic converged and exploded. He lost himself as they moved together seamlessly. The light emitting from her flooded his soul, chasing away the darkness, and he surrendered to her—heart, body, and soul.

৯৩৯ ৯৩৯ ৯৩৯

Jasce woke the next morning, his arms wrapped around Kenz, her body fitting perfectly against his. They had made love through the night and he'd cherished every moment, knowing it might be their last. He rose from the bed and slid on his traveling gear, then stared at her, committing to memory every freckle, the sensual curve of her lips, the delicate arch of her collarbone. He had to leave now, while she slept, otherwise he didn't know if he would have the strength. If his plan worked, she would most likely hate him, but at least she would be safe.

He gathered his bag and weapons and quietly left the room without looking back.

Jasce walked to the stables, the sun still hidden behind the horizon. Tillie and Maleous waited on their horses while Amycus and Flynt talked to Kord and helped load the last satchel of supplies.

"Reed has sent some guards to the neighboring villages under the guise of searching for you," Amycus said as Jasce approached. "Drexus should hear about it and hopefully leave Carhurst alone."

"You should spread a rumor that you aren't here either," Jasce suggested. "I'm pretty sure Drexus hates you too."

Amycus chuckled. "Already done. A few Spectrals and I are currently meeting in the Linden Forest."

Jasce went through the timing of their attack one more time. "Figure at least one week to locate Drexus's hidden compound, devise a plan, and destroy it. Send word to the cave when it's finished. Remember, no mercy."

Amycus rested his hand on Jasce's shoulder. "I know. Trust me, I will handle this."

Jasce swallowed, looking away from the man's penetrating blue eyes. Aura and Vale entered the stables to wish them luck.

"Vale, how are you feeling?" Jasce looked him over. The wound on his neck had healed completely and his color was back to normal, but there was a hardness to his eyes that hadn't been there before. "You okay?"

"I'm fine." Vale glanced at Jasce and looked away.

Jasce gave last-minute instructions to Aura and Flynt. Kord peered down the street.

"Everything all right?" Jasce asked.

"Just wondering where Kenz is. She said her goodbyes last night before she met up with Aura and Flynt, but I just figured . . ." His voice trailed off.

Jasce swallowed the guilt churning in his gut. Kord would kill him, and have every right to, when he found out about last night. "You know how she hates early mornings."

"Yeah," Kord said, sending one last glance down the street.

They led their horses out of the stable, where Tillie and Maleous waited for them. Tillie's eyes filled with tears as she looked toward their home while Maleous fiddled with the reins.

"Reed should return soon with the soldiers from neighboring towns," Jasce said, trying not to sound worried.

Amycus stared up at Jasce. "It'll be fine. We won't do anything without his men."

Jasce gripped his forearm. "Protect them, stay safe." Amycus squeezed Jasce's arm and smiled. Jasce nodded a farewell to Aura, who blew a kiss on a cool breeze.

"See ya, kid," Jasce said to Vale, who smiled sadly. Jasce led the Haring family out of Carhurst, looking back once at Amycus's cottage, picturing Kenz asleep in his bed. A different pain shuddered through him as they rode toward the Desert of Souls.

As the day wore on, a sense of urgency filled him, the oppressive hand of the Hunters bearing down on them. He tried to keep from continually looking over his shoulder.

They camped the first night on the edge of the Desert of Souls, Jasce choosing the southern route, which was narrow enough they could cross it in one day. They would soon enter enemy territory and Jasce couldn't afford to let his guard down. Two more days of traveling and they would arrive at the hideout Amycus had used when he was on the run from the Watch Guard.

They finally arrived at the cave near the town of Dunstead. Jasce stood on a hill overlooking the village while Tillie set up camp and Kord and Maleous collected firewood. Jasce's breath misted in the air and he pulled his cloak tighter, the Camden Mountains in the distance covered in snow. A shiver ran down his spine. The sleeping village below is where his life had drastically changed. He wondered if the two children he let go were all right. He hadn't forgotten the Earth Spectral's name—Emile—and hoped she had stayed hidden, that her brother had kept her safe.

Cinnamon and vanilla wafted through the air, and dried pine needles crunched under soft steps.

"What aren't you telling us?" Tillie asked, standing next to Jasce.

Jasce focused on the village. Plumes of smoke drifted from chimneys and candlelight glowed through the windows.

"This village is where everything changed for me," Jasce said. Tillie looked from him to the town.

"What happened?"

"The serum was wreaking havoc on me—so many emotions I hadn't allowed myself to feel. It was overwhelming. I found a young girl and her brother hiding behind some crates in an alley. The girl, Emile, stood up to me, jutted out her chin." He chuckled, remembering her defiance. "She reminded me so much of Jaida. Her brother protected her, something I didn't do for my sister." Jasce scraped the toe of his boot through the dirt. Tillie rested her hand on his arm. "Anyway, Drexus discovered I'd let them go—Emile was a Spectral. He punished and then betrayed me."

"If you had known how it all would've turned out, would you do it the same?" Tillie asked.

Jasce lifted his head, shoving his hands in pockets. "Yes."

She nodded. "Are you going to answer my first question?"

Jasce turned. Tillie's red hair was tied back, her cheeks red with the cold. She was so beautiful and kind, and too perceptive for her own good. "No."

She nibbled on her bottom lip, looking again at the sleeping village. "Kord loves you, you know. You're the brother he's always wanted. I believe Kenz does, too, she's just not as quick to show it."

Jasce swallowed, thinking of last night, the way their bodies and magic molded together. "I don't deserve their affections."

"Jasce, I know you have a past you aren't proud of. But you can't let that define you. You deserve a life full of love and happiness too." Maleous's laugh carried through the trees as father and son returned with the firewood. Tillie squeezed his arm. "Don't give up hope."

Jasce watched her hug Maleous and disappear into the cave, Kord looking over his shoulder before following his wife and son.

The next morning, Jasce trudged up the hill from Dunstead, finding Kord waiting for him on the edge of their campsite.

"You were up early," Kord said.

"I've secured lodging on the outskirts of town. It's a barn, near a vacant home."

Kord frowned. "What's wrong with our lovely cave?"

"This is safer. You will need to stay hidden since Drexus got a good look at you. Your size alone gives you away. But no one knows Tillie or Mal. They can move through the village undetected."

"What about you?"

Tillie emerged from the cave, wrapping a blanket around her shoulders.

"Let's get you settled and then I'll tell you my plan."

Kord tilted his head and glanced at Tillie. Jasce knew Kord's first instinct would be to protect his family—he had counted on it.

Jasce led them to the barn, keeping to the forest line. Tension ached through his shoulders as time grew short.

The barn wasn't the most comfortable, but it was clean and larger than the cave, including a loft and a small room with a fireplace and cooking utensils. Tillie immediately set to work preparing breakfast while Maleous explored the loft, claiming it for himself.

Jasce looked at Tillie and Maleous one last time, then turned to Kord. "I need to make sure no one followed us." Tillie looked up, tears welling in her eyes.

Kord frowned. "Who would follow us? No one knows we're here. Right?"

Jasce stared into Kord's bright green eyes, so much like his sister's, and sadness seized his chest like a vise, knowing this might be the last time he saw his friend. "Just being cautious. Stay hidden and stay safe." Jasce grabbed Kord's forearm and left, riding swiftly back to the cave.

And waited.

Jasce jerked his head to the side as a twig snapped in the distance, glad he had never taught his team how to move with stealth. He stoked the fire and remained sitting, waiting for the traitor he knew would come.

CHAPTER 27

Vale emerged through the tree line holding his sword. He was followed by a Hunter and five Watch Guard soldiers.

Jasce kept his expression blank. "It took you long enough."

Vale stopped short and frowned. "What?"

"I knew someone on our team was working with Drexus, giving him our locations, luring us to Hillford. I thought it was Flynt."

"Flynt does seem more like the type, doesn't he?" Vale nodded to the guards, who surrounded Jasce.

The Hunter, Caston, approached, his dark eyes peeking out over his skull mask and his crossbow aimed at Jasce's chest. "Drop your weapons, Azrael."

Jasce stood, placing his two swords on the ground, shifting to keep one eye on the guards behind him. All of their swords were pointed at his back.

"The dagger too." Caston motioned his crossbow toward Jasce's right boot.

Jasce shrugged and slid it free, dropping it next to his swords. He hated leaving them behind, or worse, having a Hunter put their filthy hands on them. Vale walked toward Jasce, still frowning, and pulled a collar out of his cloak.

Jasce shuffled back, eyeing the silver ring. "What if I promise to come peacefully?"

Vale sneered. "I don't think so."

Jasce winced as Vale snapped the power-suppressing collar around his neck. "You didn't seem the type to betray your own kind."

Vale yanked Jasce's arms behind his back, securing his wrists with metal cuffs. "You should talk. Drexus is right. We are powerful and should never be at the mercy of anyone. Now move." Vale shoved him.

Movement out of the corner of Jasce's eye made him pause. He had a feeling Kord would follow him, and even though his stealth skills were still abysmal, he at least remained hidden from Vale and the Watch Guard. "We

218

could've accomplished so much more if I would've known you were working with Drexus," Jasce said, making sure his voice carried through the trees.

"What are you talking about?"

"Did you actually think I joined up with Amycus? I've been gathering information for the last few months. I've just been waiting for the opportune moment."

Vale's hands tightened around Jasce's wrists. Jasce snuck a glance to where he'd seen Kord and could only imagine the disappointment on his face. Hopefully, he'd get his family out of there and tell Amycus. Surely Jasce's betrayal would keep the Spectrals from attacking Drexus's compound. They knew they couldn't defeat Jasce, Drexus, and the Hunters.

"Yeah, well, we'll see." Vale pushed Jasce again. "Now, move."

Jasce spun and head-butted Vale. The kid cried out and covered his nose, blood running through his fingers.

"Don't shove me," Jasce said.

Caston grabbed Jasce by the wrists, squeezing until his bones creaked. "Let's go." He led Jasce through the forest and down the hill toward Dunstead, where their horses waited, Vale complaining the entire way about his broken nose. Jasce glanced back only once.

Drexus's hidden garrison lay near the coast of the Merrigan Sea, its dark gray water reflecting the heavy clouds, the smell of rain filling the air. Jasce shook his head. How many times had he ridden past this area, never suspecting it belonged to Drexus? Who knew how many secrets hid behind the tall stone walls?

They entered the compound through wooden doors large enough to fit three wagons riding side by side. Smaller buildings surrounded a central courtyard. Jasce counted the soldiers on the wall while identifying the structures; the garrison was similar to the Bastion in Orilyon but on a limited scale.

Vale, whose swollen nose had finally stopped bleeding, led Jasce into the compound, where soldiers trained on the far side of the courtyard. Bronn waited, a sneer lining his hard face. "Vale, whatever happened to you?"

Vale stiffened, his hand tightening around Jasce's wrists as the first drops of rain fell.

"Welcome to Arcane," Bronn said, stepping forward. Without warning, his fist connected with Jasce's jaw, knocking him flat on his back. Jasce rolled to his side, spitting a glob of blood into the dirt.

Bronn laughed. "Nothing to say?"

Jasce struggled to his feet, his hands still bound. "I don't need to waste my time with you. Where's Drexus?"

Rage twisted Bronn's face. Jasce doubled over as Bronn punched him in the stomach. He wheezed, grimacing, and tried to move, but Bronn's knee shot up, snapping Jasce's head back, stars filling his vision. Bronn spun and kicked Jasce in the temple, dropping him to his knees.

"Bronn, that's enough." Drexus strode through the courtyard with Sabine at his heels. Her face paled when she saw Jasce kneeling in a puddle of blood. Bronn wiped the spit from his mouth as rain drops splattered on the ground.

Drexus knelt, lifting Jasce's face. "I told you that you'd be mine. You were a fool to come back to Opax."

Jasce blinked, trying to clear his vision.

Drexus looked at Vale. "Well done, but by the look of your face he didn't come quietly." Drexus brushed the dirt off his knee as he stood. "Where's the Healer?"

"I'll find him. He couldn't have gone far."

Jasce kept his face blank and rose to his feet. "Kord left two days ago, through the Camden Forest to Wilholm."

Drexus crossed his arms, his eyes narrowed. "And why would you offer that information?"

Vale swallowed. "He says he's been gathering information on Amycus and the others."

Bronn raised a brow. "That's convenient."

"What's convenient is that you're a short-sighted idiot," Jasce said, snarling at Bronn.

Bronn's lips curled and he lunged for Jasce, but Drexus's arm shot out, blocking the Hunter. The sound of clashing swords ceased as soldiers gaped at their commander and second. Vale shuffled his feet, his eyes darting between Drexus and Jasce while Caston stood with his back straight, observing the confrontation.

Drexus stared at Jasce, his dark eyes hard as steel. "Caston, take him to the dungeon. Vale, find the Healer." Drexus turned and marched across the courtyard with Bronn and Sabine trailing behind.

Caston shoved Jasce into a cell and locked the rusty gate behind him. The echo of his boots faded down the corridor. The only light came from a torch illuminating a bed of straw in one corner and a bucket in the other. Jasce wrinkled his nose, the place smelling of waste and death.

His plan had gone smoothly, besides the beating he received from Bronn. He should've expected it from the grudge-holding oaf. He gingerly touched his face, wincing at the swelling around his eye and mouth, and swept his tongue along his teeth, swearing when he felt one missing.

He hoped Kord had grabbed Tillie and Maleous and fled to Paxton, the opposite direction of Wilholm and Drexus's soldiers. He prayed he bought Kord enough time.

He wondered what Kenz's reaction would be when Kord told her Jasce had been working for Drexus all along. She would be furious, but at least she'd be safe. They all would if everything kept going according to his plan.

Hours later, as Jasce lay on his straw bed with one arm resting behind his head, he finally heard the clomp of boots growing louder.

Sabine appeared, her brown hair looking black in the dungeon's darkness. She frowned as she scanned his body. "Drexus wants to see you."

"About time," he said, getting to his feet, swiping at the dirt and dried blood on his tunic and pants.

Sabine pursed her lips. "You stink."

"No kidding. It's not like someone gave me a bath and a clean bed of straw."

She twirled her finger, indicating Jasce should turn around, and reached through the bars, securing his wrists with metal cuffs. The cell door opened and Sabine's foot shot out, dropping Jasce to his knees.

"That's for Distria."

Jasce doubled over, swearing, trying not to retch from the pain. He couldn't speak—it felt like his balls were in his throat.

Sabine yanked him to his feet and pulled him down a long corridor with torches lining the wall. It led to a room with tables fitted with chains and tubes. A petite woman stood in front of a worktable wringing her hands, more equipment sitting neatly behind her.

Jasce limped inside, keeping a wary eye on Sabine, and cleared his throat. "Your new assistant is much easier on the eyes."

Drexus frowned. "Yes, since you killed my last one."

"I did you a favor. The man was spineless."

"Indeed." Drexus nodded to Sabine, who led Jasce to the table, unhooked his cuffs, and reached for the restraints.

"The chains aren't necessary," Jasce said. "I came here of my own accord. Or didn't Vale tell you?"

"By the look of Vale's face, I thought otherwise."

"He shoved me. Twice."

"Ah. And why would you come willingly after all you've done?"

"All I've done? I'm not the one who did the betraying. You can thank Bronn, Sabine, and Distria—if she still had her head—for that." Sabine flinched and pulled her dagger free of its sheath. Jasce continued, "You left me in that dungeon, allowed your enemy to rescue me, and then sent your Hunters to kill me. Because of you, Geleon and Lyon are dead."

"You're just stalling." Drexus nodded to Sabine, who pushed the blade into Jasce's side. His hand shot out. He twisted her wrist and had the dagger to her throat in seconds. Drexus stepped forward, his face red, his sword already pressed to Jasce's chest.

Jasce released Sabine and returned the dagger. "I've chosen to be here. Do you think Vale and Caston snuck up on me? I could've killed those five guards with my eyes shut. I'm more powerful than you could have imagined, and I'm offering my services."

Sabine looked from Drexus to Jasce, her eyes wary, while Drexus chewed on the inside of his cheek. "Why would you do that?" he asked.

"Answers." Jasce rested his hands on the table. "And power."

Drexus sheathed his sword and leaned against the counter. His assistant stood next to him, fiddling with a piece of equipment.

"Did you kill the king?" Jasce asked.

The woman's head shot up, but she quickly hid the shock when Drexus glanced at her.

"Yes," he said.

Cold spread through Jasce's veins. "Why did you blame Amycus?"

"He chose Spectrals over the Watch Guard."

"*You're* a Spectral."

Drexus pushed off the counter, his eyes hard. "I am a loyal soldier to Pandaren and the Guard. Being a Spectral has nothing to do with it. But Amycus couldn't see that. He was going to expose me and my plans to the king."

Jasce swallowed, his blood turning to ice as the cold intensified. "Why did you kill my mother and sister?" He noticed Sabine stiffen, but he kept his gaze locked on Drexus.

Drexus's nostrils flared. "Lisia belonged to a group that undermined my efforts and got caught in the middle. I had no intention of killing her, Azrael."

"Jasce." He wanted to rip out Drexus's vocal cords but instead choked down the rage at hearing his mother's name on the lips of the monster before him.

"Right. *Jasce.*"

"And why didn't you tell me?"

"Your anger and the revenge you sought made you the most lethal Hunter to have gone through the program. It gave you motivation, and I thought that was better than wallowing in self-pity."

Jasce laughed bitterly. "So you lied for my benefit?" Jasce remembered asking the same question of Amycus. It seemed these two had more in common than they would care to admit.

"And mine. I'd be a fool not to use such a powerful weapon."

Jasce lowered his head, hiding the anger festering inside him—so many lies, betrayal after betrayal. Drexus admitted Jasce was nothing but a pawn in his sick game for power and dominion, and he felt himself slipping into a pit where darkness eclipsed the trust and hope he had experienced over the last few months.

He straightened, lifting his chin. "I want command of the Watch Guard. You can rule Pandaren, do what you want with the steward—I don't care. But the Watch Guard, the training, and all the recruits are mine."

"What makes you think this is a negotiation?"

"It would be to your benefit to have me fighting at your side. Amycus and his insignificant Spectrals will think twice when they realize their greatest weapon is once again their enemy. As you said, you'd be a fool not to use me."

Drexus paced the length of the room, his hands behind his back, brow furrowed. Jasce forced himself to lower his shoulders and breathe.

"And all you ask for is my title?"

"Yes. Commander Farone has a nice ring to it. Oh, and one more thing: I want Bronn's head." Sabine's head jerked to the side, her eyes flicking to Drexus.

Drexus approached, staring hard at Jasce. "You'll forgive me if I don't immediately trust you. But if you prove loyal, and once I figure out how to combine magic, I will relinquish my command."

"And Bronn?"

Drexus's eyes narrowed. "He's all yours. But *not* until I am satisfied. And if you betray me, I will burn everything and everyone you hold dear."

Jasce forced his hands to relax. "Fine." They stared at each other for a few heartbeats.

Drexus turned to his assistant. "Maera, you may begin."

Jasce positioned himself on the table, wincing when Maera inserted the needle into his arm to begin extracting vials of his blood.

The room swayed when Jasce finally rose from the table. "Did you get enough?" he asked through gritted teeth.

Maera smiled, tucking a lock of blonde hair behind her ear. "I believe so. It will take a few days to analyze and isolate the magic."

Drexus focused on Jasce. "You have two days, Maera. Sabine, take him to the barracks and post a guard at all times." He strode from the room, his cloak trailing behind him like black wings.

CHAPTER 28

Jasce rubbed his arm where the needle had punctured his skin as Sabine led him through the garrison. They stopped in the mess hall, the din of metal trays and conversation deafening.

"Get in line, I need to check something." Sabine stationed two soldiers with him and walked to the other side of the room.

Jasce's stomach grumbled; he couldn't remember the last time he had eaten. He kept his eyes forward, progressing through the line as he marked the exits and how many soldiers patrolled the dining room. The soldiers led him to a table and stood behind him as he ate. A younger recruit snuck glances at Jasce, opening his mouth and shutting it in a way that reminded Jasce of a fish.

"What?" Jasce finally said.

"Is it true? The Angel of Death has returned?" The boy looked at his friends and then scooted closer to Jasce.

Jasce lowered his fork and stared down the table into eager faces. A few of the recruits winced as they moved, others had dark smudges under their eyes. The training and discipline were taking their toll. Jasce's jaw tightened. He didn't want to think about how Drexus brainwashed and beat his recruits into submission.

"So to speak," Jasce finally said. The recruits slid closer and the soldiers behind him stiffened, resting their hands on their swords. Jasce rolled his eyes. He could kill them both with his fork.

"I heard you'd been killed," a recruit said, eyes wide.

"I heard you sailed to the Far Lands," another piped in.

"Well, neither is true, obviously." Jasce took a bite of his cold eggs.

"Have you returned to train us? My brother said you were the best and didn't whip recruits."

Jasce grimaced. He hadn't lied when he told Drexus he wanted command of the Watch Guard. While working with the Spectrals he had discovered his talent for teaching. Molding future soldiers would give him a purpose, just like working in the forge—creating instead of destroying.

Jasce's neck tingled and he glanced around the dining hall, recognizing a boy four tables away who was glaring at him, his fork shaking in his hand. He was the brother of Emile—the Earth Spectral he had let go in Dunstead. The boy had bravely protected his sister, and by the looks of things, had paid the price with servitude to the Guard. Jasce's eyes darted around the room, searching in vain, realizing that as a Spectral Emile wouldn't be a recruit. He glanced back, but the boy was quickly slipping out the exit.

A female recruit tugged Jasce's sleeve. "Have you heard the rumor about Drexus's new project? He's supposedly got himself a Psyche."

Jasce's head whipped around. "What did you say?"

The girl's eyes widened and she shied away. "That's just what we've heard. He has a Psyche, a powerful one, but none of us have seen her." Her eyes darted to the soldiers behind Jasce.

Jasce remembered the vials he'd found at the Eremus Garrison and the words of the dying Tracker. He opened his mouth to ask for more details but Sabine strode to the table, frowning. The recruits lowered their heads and shoveled food into their mouths.

"Let's go." Sabine led Jasce out of the dining hall. He glanced at the young soldiers, whose eyes were wide as they watched him leave. He smiled, giving them a sarcastic salute that caused the recruits to laugh and high-five each other.

Sabine glanced at Jasce from the corner of her eye. "You've changed."

"How so?"

"I don't know. There's a light in your eyes that wasn't there before. You captivated those young recruits. It seems they would follow you anywhere."

Jasce shoved his hands in his pockets. He visualized Kenz in his arms and knew where that light had come from, or rather, from whom. Being back at the Watch Guard and among the recruits, he realized how much he truly had changed, but he couldn't afford to forget the role he was playing—the Angel of Death had returned.

Watch Guard soldiers stopped their drills as they entered the training grounds and barracks. Jasce scanned the yard and found Bronn sparring with Elliot. Bronn said something to Elliot, and the Hunter turned to stare. Bronn's smirk morphed into fury when Jasce winked.

Sabine stopped outside Jasce's room. "You shouldn't bait him, you know."

"It's so fun, though." He stepped back, holding his hands in front of his crotch. "You aren't going to kick me again, are you?"

She smiled, her eyes dropping to his mouth. "No, I didn't like Distria *that* much. Your room has a bath. Please use it."

Jasce's smile remained until the door shut; the lock thudded with finality. He sighed, taking in his surroundings. They were similar to his quarters at the Bastion, including the washroom. He quickly stripped, hoping the water would wash away the filth but doubted a hundred baths would eliminate the shame of siding with Drexus, of being his pawn again. But he would debase himself for those he cared about, even if it meant becoming the Angel of Death once more. He just needed to convince Drexus, who wasn't a fool and didn't trust easily. He thought he could get Sabine on his side, but not Bronn. He would be a problem.

Jasce thought again about Kenz. He wondered where she was, how angry she would be when she learned of his betrayal. He lowered himself onto his bed, wincing from the pain of Bronn's beating, and closed his eyes, hoping Kenz would forgive him—someday.

᪥ ᪥ ᪥

Maera finished isolating the magic from Jasce's blood forty-eight hours after she drew it, and he found himself once again lying on the cold table with tubes sticking out of him. An unconscious man lay on a table next to him, also with tubes in his arms and legs.

"Who's that?" Jasce asked.

Maera pushed up his sleeve to insert the final needle, straightening as Drexus and Bronn entered the room.

"Are we ready?" Drexus asked, inspecting the equipment.

Maera nodded. "We need to remove the collar and then we can begin."

"You can't take that thing off him," Bronn said, unsheathing his sword.

"The collar suppresses his magic. I can't perform the experiments with it on."

Drexus nodded, then glared at Jasce. "Remember what I said. You try anything and the people you care about will suffer."

Jasce stared at Drexus. "You have my word."

Jasce hissed as Bronn dug the tip of his blade into his side and a line of blood dripped down his skin. "Your word means nothing," the Hunter said. "I will run you through if you blink in a way I don't like."

Jasce only smiled, visualizing all the ways he could kill Bronn.

The equipment whirred and Jasce immediately felt his magic draining away, siphoned through the tubes. He squeezed his fists and tried to breathe through the discomfort of having a part of him sucked out.

The man next to him groaned awake as the machine pumped Jasce's magic into him. He cried out, his back arching, and Maera ran to him, frowning at the device.

Drexus leaned over her shoulder. "Adjust the flow."

She nodded and modified the equipment, and the man's body went still. Jasce squeezed his eyes shut against the spinning room, swallowing the queasiness.

Then the man screamed as flames exploded out of his mouth and eyes.

Maera yelled and jumped back while Drexus ignited a wall of black fire to protect them. Bronn swore, stepping away from the burning man as the tubes in his arms and legs melted alongside his skin.

Jasce turned his head, feeling the heat, and breathed through his mouth to block out the smell of burnt flesh.

Drexus extinguished his fire and glared at the smoking corpse. "We need to slow the flow of the transfusion." He turned to Bronn. "Get me another one. Try a Water or Air—they aren't as volatile."

Bronn nodded and walked out of the room. Maera's body trembled, her face drained of color. She unhooked Jasce, who lurched for the corner, fell to his knees, and vomited. He rested his hand on the wall, trying to stop the room from spinning as Maera gave him a bucket.

Drexus clicked the collar back around Jasce's neck. "When will he be ready?"

Maera swallowed, averting her gaze from the smoldering man. "Jasce's magic is completely drained. Do we have more healing tonic?"

"No. We used it all during the last set of experiments."

Jasce got to his feet shakily and leaned against the edge of the table, eyeing the blackened corpse. "What in the blazes just happened?"

Drexus ordered the guards to remove the body. "The Spectral's innate magic repels the foreign one, usually violently." There was a hunger in his eyes as he peered at Jasce. "This is why you're such a rarity, why your blood holds the key."

Maera rested two fingers against Jasce's neck and peered into his eyes. "The transfusion should have killed him, but for reasons I can't explain, his two types of magic co-exist," she said to Drexus. To Jasce she asked, "Did you not know you were a Spectral?"

"No."

Drexus stepped closer to Jasce, his eyes burning. "How was your Vaulter magic suppressed?"

Jasce lifted his chin. He didn't want to give Drexus any information, but he had to appear loyal. "The Brymagus plant was in the ink in my tattoo, which was given before I showed signs of magic."

Drexus laughed, staring at the scar on Jasce's arm. "Of course! I always wondered about that tattoo." He paced the room, tapping his bottom lip. "Brilliant."

Maera snuck a glance at Jasce and then looked away, her expression blank.

Drexus called for one of his guards. "Go to the forge and have Nigel bring me the Brymagus extract." The guard saluted and left while Drexus continued pacing. "Maera, let's try mixing the extract with Jasce's magic on the next subject. See what happens."

Maera gaped. "Sir, I should conduct a few experiments first before trying it on a Spectral."

Drexus turned slowly, his nostrils flaring. Jasce pushed back from the table, the room finally still. He knew that look in Drexus's eyes.

"Was I not clear with you, Maera, regarding your . . ." Drexus waved his hand, searching for the word, "motivation? Remember why, or should I say for *whom*, you are doing this."

Maera swallowed and nodded, her eyes wide.

Bronn walked in dragging a woman behind him, her sobs echoing off the walls. She thrashed and twisted and cried out as Bronn slammed her onto the table. One punch silenced her.

Jasce lurched forward, but Maera grasped his arm and pulled him back. She walked over to the unconscious Spectral. "Please keep your dog from beating my test subjects, Drexus." She glared at Bronn. "I have medicine that will render her unconscious."

Bronn bared his teeth, but Drexus raised his hand.

Maera inserted tubes into the woman's body as the soldier from earlier arrived with Nigel, his blacksmith apron still tied around his waist, soot and grime streaked across his face. His eyes widened when they met Jasce's, and sadness washed over his face when he spotted the collar around Jasce's neck.

"Did you bring it?" Drexus asked, pushing past Jasce.

Nigel shifted his feet. "Yes, but there's only a small amount left. You used the last batch on the sw—"

Drexus backhanded the man, who gasped in pain, covering his cheek. "Mind what you say," he growled, taking the bottle from Nigel.

Nigel held the right side of his face, bright red from the blow, and stared at the unconscious woman. "What are you planning to do?"

"That's none of your concern. You may return to the forge."

"You can't keep doing this, Drexus. Your plan will not work. Spectrals cannot have two types of magic."

Drexus turned slowly, his face expressionless. "Our Angel of Death is proof that it will work, and that's twice now you've disappointed me." He focused on Nigel. "Jasce, you have some talent in the forge, don't you?"

Jasce straightened, his eyes darting between Drexus and Nigel. "No, I'm not skilled like Nigel. I don't have—"

Nigel gasped as Drexus thrust his sword into his chest, the tip erupting through his back. Drexus pulled the blade free, and Jasce rushed to catch the man. Nigel stared at Jasce, blood oozing from his mouth. He squeezed Jasce's hand. "Don't give in to the darkness," he whispered. Then his eyes rolled to the back of his head, and he let out one last breath.

Jasce gently laid the man down and stood. Nigel's blood covered his hands. "You didn't have to do that."

Drexus nodded at a soldier, who dragged the body from the room; Jasce couldn't look away from the smear of blood left behind.

"Yes, Jasce, I did. Now you have something to keep you busy between experiments. You should thank me." He grabbed Jasce's tunic and yanked him close. "And do I need to remind you what happens when my soldiers question me?"

Jasce wanted to rip out Drexus's heart and shove it down his throat. For the sake of the mission and protecting his friends, he kept his mouth shut and lowered his gaze.

Drexus released him. "I'd say you've recovered enough."

Jasce's body trembled with rage as he lay on the table, gripping Maera's wrist to keep her from chaining him down. "I'm not going anywhere."

She gave him a small smile and gently placed the needle in his already bruised arm.

"Let's try again, this time with the Water," Drexus said.

Maera nodded and began the transfusion. The Water Spectral's body went rigid, her eyes snapping open and flooding with tears. Water dripped from her mouth, ears, nose—the whole time, she glared at Drexus, gritting her teeth.

Jasce groaned, again feeling the room spin, his body and magic growing weaker with every minute, the pumping of the machines matching his heartbeat.

Maera's voice drifted as if through a long tunnel. "He can't take much more."

"He's strong, give it another minute."

A scream reverberated through his mind as blackness clouded his vision.

He woke later in his room, having no recollection of how he got there or how much time had passed. He clenched his jaw to fight the bile that rose in his throat. He'd known the Brymagus plant wouldn't help; based on the woman's screams, he assumed she didn't make it—and Nigel had died for nothing. Jasce rolled over and dry heaved, his stomach raw. How many more

Spectrals would Drexus kill in his effort to combine magic? Jasce collapsed onto his bed, unsure even he could survive many more attempts.

CHAPTER 29

Jasce inhaled through his nose and gripped the reins of his horse as the village spread out before him. The Hunter's mask felt like a death shroud suffocating him. He couldn't believe he was searching for Spectrals in Dunstead—again. Drexus had ordered Jasce and Caston to find Healers, since it was taking longer for him to recover between experiments. It was another test to prove Jasce's loyalty.

Jasce rubbed the burns on his knuckles. For the past two weeks, when he wasn't being poked and prodded, he worked in the forge repairing the training weapons. It was in Nigel's sanctuary that Jasce formed his plan; he wouldn't let the old man die in vain. Recreating the bombs Flynt had used at the Desert Garrison was trickier than he thought, but he was making progress. He just needed a little more time.

"Azrael, you awake?" Caston stared at him, his eyes visible above the skull mask. Watch Guard soldiers waited patiently behind the two Hunters while townspeople scurried from the marketplace to their homes.

"It's Jasce," he said, getting off his horse.

Caston strode next to him, holding his crossbow. "Vale said he found a Healer hiding out in the Salty Merchant Tavern."

Jasce's stomach twisted into a knot. "Isn't Vale supposed to be in Wilholm?" Vale and a few soldiers had traveled to the town in search of Kord, and Jasce hadn't heard of their return.

"He's waiting for us near the town square." Caston grabbed Jasce's arm. "Look, I have orders to kill you if you try anything." Caston's eyes flicked to the collar around Jasce's neck. "It's amazing something so small can defeat the mighty Angel of Death."

Jasce scowled at the hand holding his arm and flicked his eyes to Caston's. The Hunter released Jasce and stepped back. "Your mistake," Jasce said, "is thinking that I'm defeated without magic."

Jasce strode down the street, his hands twitching for his swords. He didn't even have a dagger, but he wasn't defenseless. He just hoped he wouldn't have to kill Caston. They hadn't been close when Jasce was a Hunter, but he always thought Caston was different. Maybe he could become an ally, if Jasce could convince him.

Vale leaned against the wall across from the Salty Merchant, an oily smile on his face. Jasce frowned and the hairs on his neck stood straight. He scanned the marketplace. Something was wrong.

The town guards disappeared into the tavern and Caston readied his crossbow, his eyes trained on the door.

Vale sauntered up to Jasce. "Let's see if Bronn was right about you," he whispered.

Jasce jerked his head toward the tavern, his heart dropping as a soldier pulled Kord through the door, his tunic hanging off his shoulder, torn and filthy. Blood dripped from a gash on his cheek that was already healing. When he recognized Jasce behind the mask, Kord went rigid.

No. Blast it, what was he doing here?

Jasce quickly analyzed the scene. He could feign indifference and try to free Kord on the ride to the garrison, but Vale already suspected him. Plus, Vale's guards were somewhere near, and without his magic or weapons, he would never defeat both groups of soldiers and a Hunter.

All of Jasce's plans crumbled into a useless heap.

Vale crossed his arms, smirking at Kord as the soldiers dragged him across the square. Caston lowered his crossbow.

There was no way Jasce could allow Drexus to capture Kord. Drexus thought Jasce's blood and magic were key, but he only had half the equation. Kord's magic would give Drexus the power he so desperately wanted. Jasce had to act now.

He spun, elbowing Vale in the face and ripping his sword from its sheath. Vale swore as blood spurted from his nose. Jasce pivoted, his sword aiming for Caston's neck. The Hunter turned, eyes wide, and in half a heartbeat Jasce adjusted his grip and brought the hilt down on Caston's head. The Hunter crumpled to the ground.

Jasce sprinted for Kord, who fought off the soldiers.

An arrow slammed into Jasce's shoulder, twisting him around. Bronn emerged from an alley, loading another bolt into his crossbow. Watch Guard soldiers appeared from behind the stalls.

Kord yanked free of the soldier holding him and ran. Bronn leveled the crossbow and let the arrow fly.

"Kord!" Jasce yelled.

Kord stumbled, hitting the dirt hard as an arrow lodged between his shoulder blades. Soldiers ran toward him, jerking him to his feet.

Jasce yanked Vale off the ground and used him as a shield, pressing the tip of his sword into his back. "Bronn, drop it or he dies."

Bronn laughed as Vale strained against Jasce's grip, sweat and blood dripping down his face.

"You take mine. I'll take yours." Bronn waved a soldier forward, dragging someone behind him.

Jasce felt the blood drain from his face as the soldier shoved Kenz into Bronn's arms. He grabbed his dagger and pressed it to her throat, the tip piercing pale skin above a silver collar. Her eyes filled with hatred.

"I told Drexus not to trust you, and now I have proof." Bronn pulled Kenz against him. "Drop your weapon."

Jasce released Vale, who skittered away, and the sword hit the ground, clamoring with inevitability. His hands shook as he ripped off his mask, his eyes darting from Kenz to her brother.

Guards wrenched Kord's arms behind his back, causing him to cry out, the arrow still lodged into his body. Kenz struggled against Bronn, who grabbed her hair and yanked her head back. Jasce fisted his hands, stopping himself from charging Bronn and ripping out his heart.

Caston groaned and slowly got to his feet.

"You're lucky you still have your head," Bronn said, shoving Kenz in Caston's direction. Caston glared at Bronn and secured Kenz's hands behind her. He glanced once at Jasce, his eyes narrowing.

Blood ran down Jasce's shoulder, but he didn't notice the pain as he stared at Kenz, his hands hanging by his sides.

Jasce closed his eyes. "Why are you here?" he whispered.

"Take one guess," Kenz said, her voice full of disgust. "How could you do this, after everything?" Kenz tried to lunge forward, but Caston held her back. "I trusted you!"

Jasce flinched. Kord's eyes hardened to stone, the muscle in his jaw pulsing. Kenz's chest heaved as she struggled against Caston.

Bronn laughed as he drew closer. "Looks like whatever you were planning failed." Bronn gripped the shaft of the arrow and twisted. Jasce bit down against the pain and glared into Bronn's dark eyes.

"I will kill you," Jasce growled.

Bronn yanked the arrow out, ripping open Jasce's flesh. He couldn't keep from yelling as blood gushed from the wound. "I've heard that one before. And yet, here I am." He motioned to his soldiers, who hauled Kord and Kenz down the street.

Vale hobbled to where Jasce and Bronn stood. Bronn frowned at Vale's bloody face and shook his head.

"That's twice now," Vale said, launching rocks at Jasce's head. Jasce raised his arms, wincing at the pain in the shoulder as the projectiles pelted him.

"Knock it off," Bronn said. He shoved Jasce toward the waiting soldiers. Vale mumbled curses but obediently followed.

They arrived at the Arcane Garrison after sundown, the waves crashing on the shore a distant sound. Jasce tried to block out the throbbing in his shoulder and the fear that writhed in his gut. He remembered Drexus's warning: *If you betray me, know that I will burn everything and everyone you hold dear.* This couldn't be happening. Kord should be safe in Carhurst with his family, and Kenz should have been with Amycus.

Jasce swallowed the bile burning his throat, and as he tried to figure out how to fix this, the sound of clashing swords around him silenced. Soldiers stared as Jasce, Kenz, and Kord stumbled into the courtyard. The young recruits Jasce had seen earlier stood with their mouths open, their eyes darting between Drexus and Jasce. Emile's brother lingered near the wall away from the others, his mouth set in a thin line.

Drexus waited with his arms crossed, face as hard as the surrounding stone walls. Sabine stood at his side, expressionless. Her hand rested on the hilt of her sword.

"I didn't want to believe Bronn," Drexus said, "but it seems he was right about you."

Bronn forced Jasce to his knees while the other guards shoved Kord and Kenz forward. Drexus raised a brow. "Who's the girl?"

"A Shield. We caught her trying to sneak into the tavern." Bronn grabbed the collar around Kenz's throat. She twisted and kicked at Bronn, letting out a string of profanity.

Bronn laughed. "Quite the spitfire. Beautiful too."

The blood rushed in Jasce's ears but he forced his face to remain indifferent. He imagined all the ways he would make Bronn suffer, starting with cutting out his tongue.

"Keep your hands off her," Kord growled.

"She's Kord's sister," Vale said, pushing past Caston. He licked his lips, staring at Drexus.

Kord swore, lunging forward, and Vale scurried back, his eyes wide.

"Is she now?"

Jasce hadn't realized he'd been staring at Kenz, but he glanced away as Drexus walked past. He stopped and frowned at Jasce, then looked back at Kenz. A hideous smile formed on his face.

"She seems to be more than just the Healer's sister." Drexus turned toward Kord. "Ever since I saw you heal Vale—thank you for that, by the way—I've wanted you. You're the most powerful Healer I've ever seen. And as Jasce knows, I always get what I want."

Without warning, Drexus's fist flew and the entire side of Jasce's face exploded in pain, Drexus's ring gouging his cheek. He grabbed Jasce by the throat, pulling him to his feet. Jasce sputtered, clinging to Drexus's wrists.

Drexus's face twisted in rage. "You will pay for your betrayal." Spit peppered Jasce's face. Black spots floated in his vision. His heart pounded.

"Stop it!"

Drexus loosened his grip at the sound of Kenz's voice. Jasce landed on his knees, gulping air. Drexus frowned at Kenz. "You care what happens to this man?"

Kenz swallowed, staring at Jasce; a war of anger and fear battled in her eyes.

Drexus's lip curled as he dug his finger into Jasce's wound. Jasce tried not to yell, crushing his teeth together so hard he felt his jaw crack. The coppery taste of blood filled his mouth and his cheek and eye throbbed.

"Take the Healer and Jasce to Maera. The Shield too—she may prove useful," Drexus ordered.

Rough hands yanked Jasce off the ground and ushered him through the garrison and down the corridor. Kenz swore the entire way, struggling against the guards, but Kord walked silently, his chin lifted.

Maera jumped when they entered, her eyes wide. "What's going on?" She lurched out of the way as Bronn shoved Jasce onto the table, attaching the chains on his legs. Jasce groaned as Bronn secured his hands above his head, tearing the wound in his shoulder. Maera's mouth pursed as she stared at the blood dripping on the floor.

"Chain the Shield over there," Drexus said when he entered the room. A soldier forced Kenz to the wall, lifting her off the ground as she struggled. Bronn shook his head and strode over to her, a heavy thud sounding as he punched her in the stomach. She tried to suck in air as she fell to her knees.

Kord roared and pulled free from the soldier holding him, stealing his dagger and slicing it across the guard's chest.

"I'd rethink your next move," Drexus said. Bronn pointed his sword at Kenz.

Kord froze. His shoulders sagged, dropping the dagger. Jasce's body shook—never had he felt so useless.

Maera dabbed at Jasce's wound, mopping up the blood. She was his only hope of rescuing his friends.

"Help me," he whispered.

Maera's eyes darted to Drexus, then focused on Jasce. She leaned down, as if inspecting his shoulder. "My son," she whispered. "Drexus has him. He's a recruit. Promise you'll save him."

Jasce nodded.

Maera straightened and cleared her throat. "He's useless if he bleeds to death."

Drexus stepped away from Kenz and grabbed Kord, yanking him to the table. "Heal him."

Kord looked from Jasce to his sister, his face like granite, solid and immovable.

Drexus tilted his head. "Do I need to remove one of your sister's fingers?"

Kord paled and Bronn laughed, replacing his sword and tugging his dagger from its sheath. Chains rattled as he pressed his knife against Kenz's index finger.

Jasce lifted his head and stared at Kord. "One doesn't learn if one doesn't suffer through the pain." Recognition flashed through Kord's eyes.

Drexus looked from Bronn to Maera. "What is he talking about?"

"Well, he has lost a lot of blood. No thanks to your lapdog," Maera said, still dabbing at the wound.

"Quit calling me that." Bronn strode over to Maera, his knuckles whitening on his dagger.

Drexus sighed. "You two, play nice." Bronn continued to glare at Maera, who rolled her eyes and busied herself with the equipment. Drexus turned to Kord. "Heal him or your sister loses her hand."

The muscle in Kord's jaw thumped. "You need to remove the collar."

Drexus inserted the key, and with a click the collar unlocked. He handed it to Maera, who placed it on the counter. Drexus drew his dagger and rested it on Jasce's neck. "Bronn, if he vaults, kill the woman." He smiled at Jasce. "Her life is in your hands."

Jasce swallowed, the sharp edge of the blade stinging his neck. Bronn marched to Kenz, his knife pointing at her chest, an evil sneer lining his face. Kenz's eyes darted from Jasce to Kord.

Kord looked away and rested his hands on Jasce's wound.

Drexus gasped. "Look at that."

Warmth tingled through Jasce's body. The pain melted away, his shoulder knitting together while the swelling in his face diminished. Jasce's magic purred as his powers slowly returned.

"Maera, hook Jasce up and begin the process." Drexus pointed to the guard by the door. "Bring me the Earth girl from the village."

Jasce jerked his head, hissing when Drexus's knife slid across his skin. "Careful, Jasce, can't have you die yet. The experiment should work this time.

The girl is young, and with the Brymagus extract along with your magic, I should be able to replicate what your mother did, so to speak."

A scream echoed through the corridor.

No, don't let it be her.

A soldier shoved the girl into the room and Jasce recognized her immediately. Her blonde hair lay matted in greasy chunks, and tears carved through the dirt and grime covering her face. Her eyes widened when she saw Jasce strapped to the table, staring at her in horror.

"You," she whispered.

"Drexus, no. She's just a child." Jasce struggled against the chains, the knife cutting deeper.

The soldier led her to the table next to Jasce. Maera covered her mouth and shook her head. Kenz swore and Kord went pale.

Drexus looked from the girl to Jasce. "How do you know her?"

"That's the one he let escape," Bronn said.

Drexus's mouth curved into a smile. "Is that so? It seems all your conniving plans and sacrifice have amounted to nothing."

The girl thrashed as the soldier forced her onto the table and secured the chains. She looked so small and helpless.

"You can't do this. Please, I will do anything," Jasce said.

"What have I told you about compassion?" Drexus stared at Maera. "Drain him. I want all of his magic."

"That will kill him."

"The Healer can tell when he's close to dying." Drexus looked at Kord, who nodded. Maera hesitated, looking from Jasce to the girl. Drexus grabbed her by the arm. "Would you like your son strapped to the table instead? I'm sure I can have Rowan brought in from training."

Tears filled her eyes as she shook her head. She inserted the needles into Jasce's body. "I'm sorry," she whispered.

"Wait!" Jasce yelled. The only way to save the girl was to tell Drexus the truth. Kord would survive the procedure, but Emile wouldn't if Jasce didn't tell him.

"I'm done waiting. Maera, begin."

Jasce glanced at Kord, who gave a shallow nod and closed his eyes.

Jasce twisted to stare at Drexus. "The only way to combine magic is to use Kord's healing power alongside mine. That's why the other experiments haven't worked. You need both."

A grin slowly spread across Drexus's face. "Of course. Why didn't I think of it before? And you sacrificed all those Spectrals to keep your secret? I underestimated you, Azrael. You are the Angel of Death."

Jasce squeezed his eyes shut—more blood staining his hands. But he couldn't let Emile die, not when he knew how to save her.

His eyes found Maera's. "Save her, please."

"Maera, you may begin," Drexus said, his knife still pressed to Jasce's throat. Kord stood nearby, staring at the tubes sticking out of Jasce's arms.

Maera's shoulders sagged. She went to her equipment, the whirring sound filling the air. Jasce's breath hitched as his magic left his body.

"Emile, be strong." Jasce tried to move his head to see her face but could only make out her tiny frame, trembling. Her soft cries cut through Jasce like a dull blade.

"That's so endearing," Drexus said, snarling. "Increase the flow," he said to Maera.

Jasce groaned against the pull, his magic emptying at an alarming speed. His heartbeat slowed, his body going limp. He struggled to keep from vomiting, the room spinning violently. He heard Kord's voice from a distance.

"That's enough, you're killing him."

The whirring stopped.

Jasce's head sagged to the side. He was unable to move or speak. He felt like he was floating helplessly above the table.

Kenz cried out his name.

Metal scraped against stone, and then something bumped Jasce near his head. They had wheeled in another table.

"Your turn, Healer," Drexus said. The table squeaked and chains rattled. Kord's hands brushed against Jasce's.

"You're out of your mind!" Kenz shouted, pulling against her restraints.

"Sacrifice is needed for discovery. Now shut up, or I'll let Bronn have his way with you," Drexus said.

The whirring of the machines started again.

"Kenz, it'll be fine," Kord said.

Jasce's mind screamed, telling himself to get up, to move, to do something.

Emile cried out and Kord grunted.

Drexus's boots thudded as he walked away from Jasce. "Very slow, Maera. And keep adding the healing magic."

Emile whimpered.

Jasce felt a finger touch his knuckle and a familiar warmth rippled through him. He forced his body still and kept his eyes closed as Kord's healing power slowly awakened his magic.

Emile cried out.

They needed to hurry. He visualized his magic swirling through his body, filling every part of him. He embraced it, welcomed it as he grew stronger.

Emile screamed louder.

"Stop it!" Kenz yelled, then she grunted at the sound of a fist striking flesh.

Anger burned through Jasce, and this time his magic didn't fight it. He welcomed the rage and the two intensified, feeding off each other until Jasce felt the initial tug, a comforting darkness enveloping him.

Metal shattered as Jasce broke his chains and disappeared, reappearing behind Bronn and slamming his head into the wall. He grabbed Bronn's sword and slashed it down on Kenz's shackles before wrenching the collar off her neck. With both their collars removed, he immediately felt her magic swirl around his, filling a hole he hadn't realized was empty.

Drexus swore and ignited his fire, forming a whip that sizzled through the air. Jasce blocked the attack, wincing as the flames singed his hand. He tried to vault, but his magic wasn't strong enough—Kord's power had only healed him enough to get free.

"Kenz, get them out of here!" Jasce lunged forward, swinging his sword, slicing Drexus's cloak. Drexus snarled and launched a fireball at Jasce, who jumped out of the way.

Kenz ignited her shield, ramming the two soldiers into the wall, knocking them unconscious. Maera dashed to Kord, who groaned as the tubes ripped free, his restraints clanking onto the table. He rushed to Emile's side, sweeping her unconscious body into his arms.

"Go!" Jasce yelled. "I'll hold him off."

Drexus laughed. "Look at you, trying to play the hero." A spear of black fire shot across the room, glancing off Jasce's shoulder. He hissed, almost dropping his sword.

Bronn groaned, rubbing his head and trying to stand. Maera stood in the corner, her eyes wide with terror. Kenz sprinted to the unconscious soldiers and grabbed a sword. "Jasce, come on!" She pushed Kord, who held Emile, out of the room.

Drexus cackled, shooting firebombs at Jasce, who upended the exam table to use as cover. Black fire separated Jasce and Maera from the door. Kenz stood in the corridor, using her shield to push back the flames.

"Bronn, go after them!" Drexus ordered, maneuvering the fire to clear a path. Bronn struggled to get up, stumbling as he headed for the doorway. Maera took a step toward the exit.

"I don't think so," Drexus said, flinging his dagger into her chest.

Maera cried out in pain, sliding to the floor, shock in her eyes as she stared at the knife.

"No!" Jasce yelled. He tried to get to her but Drexus raised his arms and the wall of flames surged.

Bronn lumbered toward the door, grabbing the other guard's sword.

"Kenz, go!" Jasce yelled. She looked down the corridor and then back at him, her eyes filling with tears. Her shield faded as she disappeared with Bronn on her heels, both of them swallowed by the black smoke.

Jasce swore. He needed to kill Drexus—that's why he was here, why he'd surrendered himself. But now his friends were in danger.

An explosion erupted from the corner of the room. The metal table glowed, air rippling from the heat. Black fire coiled along the floor, inches from where Jasce knelt. He wiped away the sweat dripping into his eyes and dug deep for his magic; he just needed enough to get him to the corridor. Jasce focused on the tug, picturing the hallway he had walked down these past two weeks. Hatred filled his heart as he took one last look at Drexus and vaulted.

Jasce barely reached the door. Drexus roared, sending a stream of fire straight for him. He rolled out of the way and sprinted down the corridor after Bronn. Rage burned through him, unable to stomach the fact that he had let Drexus go again. If Kord and Kenz had just stayed away, then Jasce would have destroyed Drexus once and for all.

Light glowed from the end of the hallway and Jasce burst through the doorway into the courtyard.

"Jasce, watch out!"

A board swung out of nowhere, hitting Jasce in the temple and knocking him on his back. The air rushed out of his lungs as stars swirled in his vision.

Drexus's oily laugh sounded behind him, accompanied by the clomp of boots from the corridor. "Excellent. I knew I could count on my Right Hand," Drexus said, yanking Jasce to his feet as he snarled in his ear. "She's even better than you."

Jasce lifted his head, blinking. A young woman with golden hair lowered her arms, the board dropping to the ground. She wore a silver dress that made her gray eyes glimmer. Eyes Jasce hadn't seen in thirteen years.

Jasce's knees weakened as an image rushed into his mind of a girl running through the forest laughing, her tangled blonde hair flowing behind her, hands holding wildflowers, her cheeks smudged with dirt.

Drexus smiled at the woman and then turned toward Jasce. "Say hello to your sister."

CHAPTER 30

"Jaida?" Jasce shook his head, trying to make his brain catch up. "How?" Thoughts careened through his mind with memories of the day she died. He saw the men drag her away, heard her screams.

And then silence.

Darkness.

The rocking of the carriage taking him to the Bastion.

Jaida inclined her head, her cold, gray eyes surveying the scene. She raised her slender arms and Kenz cried out as she slammed into the wall, her arms pinned to her side. Kord, still holding Emile, took a step toward his sister.

"Don't move," Bronn said, pointing his sword and swaying on his feet. Sabine and Caston stepped into the courtyard, crossbows aimed.

Jasce stared at his sister. She was alive, after all this time. He lowered the protective wall on his magic, trying to sense her emotions. Didn't she know who he was?

He felt nothing.

His sword slipped from his grasp. He couldn't move, couldn't think. Cool metal clicked around his neck and the dregs of his magic winked out.

Drexus shoved Jasce toward Sabine. "Take them to the dungeon."

"Jaida?" Jasce said. He glanced over his shoulder as Caston and Sabine led them out of the courtyard. Jaida stood expressionless, her hands hanging by her side. The vibrant, carefree girl he remembered was gone, replaced by this cold stranger who seemed to not know him.

Jasce walked to the dungeon in a daze. Everything had deteriorated before his eyes, and now they were in a worse situation than before. And he had done nothing. He'd stood frozen, useless.

The cell door screeched open. Caston, after placing a new collar around Kenz's neck, nodded for her and Emile to enter. Kord stumbled into the one next to them, and Sabine pushed Jasce into the cell he had occupied weeks before.

He turned and held the bars. "Did you know?"

"That he had your sister?"

Jasce's knuckles whitened, the cold metal bit into his palms.

"Not until recently," Sabine said. "He surprised us all when he made her his Right Hand."

Jasce felt the blood rush from his face and slowly shook his head. "He's a liar and a traitor, and I blindly served him, bled for him."

Sabine straightened, her eyes darting to Caston. "For what it's worth, I'm sorry," she whispered, then she left the dungeon. Caston's jaw muscle pulsed as he held Jasce's stare before following Sabine down the corridor, the flickering torch distorting their shadows.

"Jasce?" Kord's voice broke through the silence. "Are you all right?"

Jasce squeezed the bars, his teeth grinding. No, he was not all right. Drexus had kept Jaida from him all these years, and the monster was still alive because of the people in the cells across from him, people he tried to save—tried and failed. Unfathomable rage erupted inside him and he screamed into the darkness, sounding like a wounded animal. He swore, smashing his fist into the wall again and again, wanting the pain to replace his despair, to snuff out his failure.

"Jasce, stop!" Kenz yelled, her voice breaking through the tempest of emotions.

Jasce panted, lowering his bloody knuckles to his side. He slid to the floor and dropped his head into his hands, at a loss of what to do. He felt like he was drowning.

Silence pressed down on Jasce, and finally his pulse returned to normal.

"So, was this your plan?" Kenz asked, her voice making him wince.

"Kenz, don't," Kord said, leaning against his cell door.

"No, really. I'd like to know. What were you thinking?" Kenz stood, gripping the bars.

"Why couldn't you have just returned to Carhurst?" Jasce's voice sounded strangled. "Why were you in Dunstead? I wanted you both to be safe."

"Did you actually think I'd believe what you told Vale?" Kord said, staring at Jasce. "We couldn't let you sacrifice yourself like this."

Kenz crossed her arms and anger flashed in her eyes. He looked away, unable to grapple with the disgust on her face.

After what felt like hours, Emile woke with a cry.

"Shh, it's okay," Kenz whispered.

"What happened?" Emile said.

Kenz stroked Emile's back as the girl stared at her shaking hands. "My magic feels weird, like it's boiling out of control."

Kord waved her near and reached through the bars, touching her forehead. He closed his eyes and jerked back. "It worked," he whispered.

Jasce stood and walked to the front of his cell, staring at Emile. "What do you mean?"

"I mean, she has your magic. Her Earth powers have combined with the Amplifier and Vaulter."

Kenz bit her lip.

Jasce swallowed. "Will she survive it? Having three powers?"

Kord's hand remained on Emile, who stared at him with wide eyes. "We need Amycus."

"Drexus can't know," Jasce said. "He can never find out. We need to get her out of here."

Steps echoed along the corridor. Kord took his hand from Emile and Kenz grabbed the girl, pulling her to the back of their cell. Jasce peered down the hall, at the long, golden hair illuminated by the flickering torch.

Jaida emerged with two Watch Guard soldiers shadowing her. She held up her hand, halting the guards at the entrance, and stopped in front of Jasce's cell. Her gaze traveled down his body, frowning at his bloody knuckles, then settled on his face, her expression blank.

Jasce's breath hitched, still unable to believe she was alive. "Jaida, are you all right?"

Even though she was shorter than Jasce by almost a foot, she looked down her long nose at him. "So now you care?" Her voice cut like daggers.

"I thought you were dead. I didn't know Drexus took you after he murdered our mother. That he was keeping you prisoner."

"I'm not his prisoner." Her voice snapped through the shadows.

Jasce held on to the bars, the familiar anger writhing through him. "Drexus killed her. How can you be with him?"

"And you killed our father. Which monster should I choose, Jasce? Mother was a traitor, and now, it seems, so are you."

Jasce stepped back, his eyes wide.

Kenz huffed. Jasce hadn't seen her stand, putting herself between the bars and Emile. "You don't know what you're talking about," she said.

Kord's eyes flickered between Jaida and his sister.

Jaida glanced over her shoulder, then turned back to Jasce. "Drexus rescued me. He's teaching me how to use my magic instead of hiding it like our mother did."

Jasce shook his head. It would do no good to argue with her. Drexus had poisoned her for thirteen years, making her believe the worst of his mother and him.

"I heard about you, you know. The Angel of Death. I didn't know until recently that the mighty Azrael was my brother, the same man who killed our father." She gripped the bars and hurt flashed in her stormy grey eyes. "Why?"

Jasce sighed. "Drexus ordered me to kill him as part of the Hunter's initiation." Jasce ran his hands through his hair. "But in all honesty, I wanted to. I blamed him for betraying our mother. That's when I became the Angel of Death." He peered into Jaida's eyes, his mother's eyes. "I'm glad Drexus has been kind to you."

"Was he not to you?"

Jasce's laugh sounded harsh, even to him. "No, and I have the scars to prove it." Jasce slowly reached out to touch her hand. He remembered them playing in the forest, laughing as they ran. She stared down at their clasped fingers and Jasce let out a breath, comforted by the warmth. To have his sister by him gave him a glimmer of hope.

"Jaida, get us out of here, and then we can start a new life somewhere safe—start over."

She jerked her hand away as if she'd been burned. "Why would I go with you?" She twirled with her arms wide. "I'm revered here, as Drexus's Right Hand. Spectrals will rule Pandaren instead of kneeling before Naturals. Surely you can understand that."

Jasce's hands fell to his side.

Jaida lowered her arms and pursed her lips. "You are weak and broken. I've heard stories of the Angel of Death, and I must say, what a disappointment." With a final glance at Kord and Kenz, she disappeared down the corridor.

Jasce sat on the bed of straw, his legs splayed out before him, shoulders slumped.

"I'm sorry, Jasce," Kord said.

"She's been alive all this time. How could I not have known?" He leaned his head against the cold stone. "I don't blame her for hating me."

"She doesn't hate you," Kord said.

"Yeah, wait 'til she gets to know you at least," Kenz said, a smile tugging at her lips.

"Kenz!" Kord stared at his sister with wide eyes.

Jasce scowled at her, and then his lips twitched. "She has a point."

Kord laughed and shook his head.

"What's so funny?" Emile said, getting to her feet. "In case you haven't noticed, we're stuck in a dungeon."

"We've been in worse places before, kid. Besides, I have an inside man." Jasce rose and paced his cell.

"What are you talking about?" Kenz asked.

Jasce stared at Emile. "Your brother is here."

Her eyes widened. "Lander is here?"

Jasce nodded and continued pacing. "Look, I need you three to get to safety."

Kenz raised a brow. "And what are you planning to do?"

"I'm getting my sister out of here."

"Yeah, I don't think she wants to come with us." Kenz said.

Kord stared through the bars. "Jasce, that's not a good idea."

"If it was your sister, what would you do?"

Kord sighed and nodded. "What's your plan?"

❧ ❧ ❧

"Let's go."

Jasce slowly opened his eyes. He had just drifted off to sleep when Caston's voice woke him. He held a set of cuffs and motioned Jasce forward.

"What's going on?"

Caston looked over his shoulder at two other Hunters, Elliot and Warin, who secured Kord, Kenz, and Emile. "Drexus got word that a group of Spectrals are preparing for battle. He wants to be in a more secure place, so he's taking everyone back to Orilyon."

Jasce went over his options as Caston secured the cuffs. The Hunter opened the cell door, grabbed Jasce's wrists, and yanked him closer.

"Drexus is expecting you to try something during the transport."

Jasce kept his eyes forward, barely moving his lips. "Why are you telling me this?"

"A story for another time," Caston said, leading Jasce and the others to the stable yard. Two carriages waited for them; the same type that had first taken Jasce from Delmar to the Bastion thirteen years ago. His life was coming full circle.

Kenz and Emile were shoved into one carriage while Kord and Jasce went in the other. Jasce scanned the yard for the recruits. Standard procedure was for them to help the other Watch Guard soldiers escort the wagons. His eyes found Emile's brother, Lander, who positioned himself close to his sister's carriage.

After hours of riding toward Orilyon, the hard benches pummeling their bodies, they arrived at the Bastion. Towering stone walls loomed over them.

"Is this where you grew up?" Kord asked, peering out the slats.

"Yes." Jasce looked out the other side, trying to glimpse his sister. He hadn't seen her since last night. He hadn't seen Drexus either. They rode through the entrance, the imposing metal gates clanging shut with a note of inevitability. "Kord, no matter what happens, get Kenz and Emile out. I will buy you as much time as possible, but you need to get free."

Kord shook his head. "I can't leave you here, Jasce. Kenz would kill me."

Jasce had no doubt Kenz would be livid knowing he had ordered Kord to leave him, but there was no other way. "You're too valuable, and Drexus can't get a hold of Emile, no matter what. Knowing you are safe, that Kenz will live—that's all I need."

The muscle in Kord's jaw twitched. He grabbed Jasce's forearm, his eyes watery, and nodded. Jasce held his stare, forcing a smile.

The door wrenched open, and Jasce and Kord stepped into the brisk dawn air. Dew covered the grass near the stables as the sky lightened to a purplish-gray. Jasce turned to the east, inhaling the new day, admiring the wisps of clouds that glowed as if on fire.

"The light chasing away the darkness," Jasce mumbled. His neck tingled, and he pulled his gaze from the smoldering sky. Jaida stared at him, her arms folded across her body in a tight embrace. She looked at the sky and back at Jasce, her brow furrowed. Drexus appeared beside her and placed a hand on her shoulder to steer her away.

Bronn's bruised face appeared before Jasce's. "You never told me how attractive your sister is."

Jasce rolled his eyes. Bronn didn't have any imagination, using the same tactics over and over to get under his skin. "How does it feel to be second best? First to me, and now to her?" He nodded at Jaida and Drexus, who were in a deep conversation on the other side of the yard.

Fury twisted Bronn's face, his nostrils flaring.

Kenz and Emile got out of their wagon. Sabine cuffed Kenz's wrists behind her but let Emile remain unbound. Emile hugged herself, her eyes wide with fear. Dark circles smudged Kenz's eyes, and strands of hair had fallen loose from her braid.

Bronn sneered, looking over his shoulder. "Might have a little playtime with that one before I end her."

Kord growled and Jasce stepped forward. "You touch her and I will slice you open. I will savor the hours I will take torturing you, like I did Distria."

Bronn raised his hand, but stopped when Drexus summoned him. He stormed off, Vale at his heels.

Caston led Jasce and Kord into the training yard, empty due to the hour, with the majority of the soldiers in their bunks or the dining hall. The familiarity set Jasce at ease for reasons he couldn't name. Kenz and Emile walked next to them, Sabine following, gripping her sword. The recruits marched in, exhaustion lining their faces, and Jasce caught sight of Lander at the back of the line. He quickly disappeared into the shadows behind a pillar.

Jasce cleared his throat and nodded at Emile, then said, "I'm curious, Sabine, how did it feel watching Distria fire arrow after arrow into me? Watching the village mob drag me away?"

Sabine slowly turned and stepped closer. Jasce edged back, away from Kord, Kenz, and Emile. Caston studied Sabine and Jasce, his finger tapping the hilt on his dagger.

"I had no choice," Sabine said. "You know that. Orders are orders."

"Sure—loyalty, honor, obedience," Jasce said through clenched teeth. "There was no loyalty or honor in what you three did. There's no honor in obeying him either." He nodded toward Drexus.

Sabine looked at Drexus, her lips downturned.

Jasce forced his gaze to remain locked onto Sabine's while Emile used her new strength to silently break the chains binding Kord and Kenz. They kept their hands behind them, their faces expressionless. Emile reached up and broke the collar from Kenz's neck.

Jasce sidestepped, turning his back toward Emile. Caston frowned but remained still.

Sabine looked at Jasce and shook her head. "There's no breaking free of him. Only death." She stared at the ground, her hands hanging loosely by her sides. Her head snapped up with the sound of a click. Sabine swore as Lander shot out from behind the pillar. He tossed a dagger to Jasce, who pivoted, elbowed Sabine in the face, and snatched the blade from the air.

Kenz's shield exploded sideways, knocking Caston off his feet. Jasce wrapped his arm around Sabine's neck, blood from her nose dripping onto his arm.

"Kord, now!"

Lander handed knives to Kenz, grabbed Emile, and ran for the exit. Kord yanked Kenz away from the courtyard and sprinted after them, but Kenz twisted out of his grasp, causing Kord to stumble.

Drexus, Jaida, and Bronn turned toward the commotion, and Drexus sent a wall of flame to block the exit. Lander and Emile barely escaped, but the fire trapped Kord and Kenz.

"Drexus!" Jasce used Sabine as a shield, wincing as her nails dug into his forearms. "Let them go or she dies."

"Go ahead," Drexus said, shrugging. "I can always train another."

"What?" Sabine lowered her hands. Bronn's eyes widened, glancing between Sabine and Drexus.

Drexus strode across the yard, Jaida and Bronn following. Vale hovered near the edge.

"Stop! I will kill her."

Drexus chuckled. "No, Jasce. I don't think you will. And like I said, there are more where she came from." Elliot, Warin, and the remaining Hunters entered the courtyard.

"Drexus?" Sabine's voice wavered.

Drexus's fire inched closer, pushing Kord and Kenz to the center of the yard. "I need the Healer alive." The Hunters aimed their crossbows at Kenz. She thrust her hands out and her shield erupted, forming a wall of her own. The arrows bounced harmlessly off the magical light.

Jaida waved her hand and Sabine shot out of Jasce's grip. His dagger wrenched from his hand and his feet lifted into the air. His arms and legs stretched wide as intense pain burned throughout his body. He bit down to keep from crying out, coppery warmth filling his mouth. His back arched and a rib cracked.

"Jaida, please," Jasce whispered and gasped as another rib broke.

Drexus laughed. "She's as vicious as you, but ten times smarter."

The sun glinted off a piece of metal sailing through the air.

"Look out!" Jasce yelled.

Jaida's eyes widened. Kenz's throwing knife stopped inches from piercing her heart—the blade vibrating in Drexus's hand. Jasce fell in a heap, groaning.

Kenz used her magic to push Kord through the flames and out of the courtyard. He yelled, pounding against the shield as he disappeared behind the wall.

"Do not let the Healer escape!" Drexus ordered, lowering his wall of fire. Three of the Hunters chased after Kord.

Kenz gripped her other knife, raising her free hand to create a shield between her and Jasce and the remaining Hunters. Caston helped Sabine to her feet, glaring at Drexus and Jaida. Vale sent a cyclone of dirt and rocks into Kenz's shield.

Kenz bared her teeth and aimed the knife.

"Kenz, no." Jasce tried to get to his feet as Kenz flicked her wrist. Two fireballs flew, one hitting the blade, the other sliding past Kenz's shield, knocking her to the ground and disintegrating her shield.

Jaida glared at Kenz. "How dare you attack me!" Jaida raised her arms and ropes flew from the nearby wall. They wrapped themselves around Kenz's body and tightened around her neck. Kenz grasped the ropes, her face turning red.

A barrage of rocks and dirt circled Jasce. A figure emerged through the dust and grabbed Jasce's hair, pulling his head back. Bronn pressed his dagger against Jasce's neck, just above the power-suppressing collar. The rocks fell to the ground as Vale stepped forward.

Kenz gasped, dropping to her knees.

"Jaida, please, don't." Jasce forced out, straining against Bronn.

"Why?" Jaida's face remained expressionless as the ropes tightened. Jasce knew she would kill Kenz and start down a familiar path of blood and death.

Jasce swallowed, Bronn's knife piercing skin, warmth trickling down his neck.

"Because I love her."

Kenz's eyes widened. Jaida frowned, looking from Jasce to Kenz, the ropes loosening slightly. Kenz sucked in a large breath of air, her gaze fixed on Jasce.

Drexus laughed and strode forward. "You fool. What have I told you about weak emotions?" Drexus spit on the ground. "Bronn, tie him to the post."

Jasce stiffened. The whipping post loomed in front of him, a bloodstained reminder of pain, of the disfiguring scars lining his back. He struggled against Bronn as blood oozed from his mouth, his breath labored from the cracked ribs.

"You finally get what's coming to you." Bronn thrust his knife into Jasce's side and Jasce stumbled, gritting his teeth against the pain, blood running down his hip. Ropes bound his wrists and he groaned as his arms were lifted above his head. Bronn sliced through his tunic, ripping the fabric free, exposing his ravaged back.

Jaida gasped. "Drexus, did you do that to him?"

Drexus ignored her and walked to the wall where the whips hung. He chose one embedded with bits of glass and metal. "You will learn, as my Right Hand, that some require more punishment than others."

Jasce looked over his shoulder, his eyes finding Kenz. Tears streaked down her face and onto the ropes that bound her. Jaida stared in horror at Jasce's back. The three Hunters returned to the courtyard, fear etched on their faces.

"Well?" Drexus said.

"We couldn't find him."

Drexus's face twisted in rage and black fire danced along his fingers. With a yell, he shot a fireball at one of the Hunters and threw his knife at another, piercing his chest. He drew his sword and stalked toward the remaining Hunter, who reached for his weapon but wasn't quick enough. Jaida covered her mouth as she stared at the third Hunter's headless body. Drexus retrieved his dagger and stabbed the first Hunter through the heart.

"Failures," he growled. Bronn swore, his eyes darting between Drexus and the bodies. Drexus turned to a group of soldiers and yelled, "Find the Healer, and do not come back without him!" The soldiers saluted and ran out of the courtyard.

Jasce had never seen Drexus like this, and this time he knew he wouldn't survive the whipping. He had seen it in Drexus's eyes. He had no patience for love, or weak emotions, as he called them. Jasce didn't regret telling Kenz he loved her. But he didn't want her to watch.

"Kenz," Jasce whispered. "Look away."

Kenz shook her head, looking from Jaida to Sabine. "Help him, please."

Drexus strode forward, snapping the whip. The splintered wood, stained and smelling like rusted metal, dug into Jasce's forehead as he focused on Kenz and the last night they spent together—the touch of her lips, her smile, the way her body moved under his.

Searing pain sliced through his back.

"Obviously, my previous attempts at ridding you of these useless emotions didn't work," Drexus said.

The whip cracked. Jasce bared his teeth, gripping the ropes.

"Lessons you refused to learn."

Crack. Jasce groaned, feeling his skin rip open.

"You're a traitor, just like Lisia."

Crack.

"Like Amycus."

Crack.

Jasce couldn't hold back the cry as blood poured down his back and legs. The whip snapped through the air.

Crack.

Again.

Crack.

And again.

"Drexus, stop. He's had enough," Jaida said, her voice trembling.

"I'll say when he's had enough."

Kenz sobbed. Jasce's legs collapsed, his arms taut above his head, straining the exposed muscles in his back. He moaned as the whip sliced his side, ripping flesh and revealing bone.

He heard the whip cut through the air, but never felt the impact.

"Jaida, what are you doing?"

"I said, stop. You're killing him."

Through an ebbing flow of consciousness, the sounds of bodies flailing in the dirt and the clash of blades rang through Jasce's ears.

A slash of ropes.

The stomp of boots bounded up the steps.

Jasce's head hung to his chest and blood poured down his legs, pooling around his knees. A sob sounded in his ear as gentle hands untied the cords around his wrists. He fell forward, sliding down the blood-soaked pole.

"Jasce, stay with me. Please, hold on, help is coming."

Kenz's voice was like a soothing balm. She brushed the hair off his face, her breath cool against his ear. "I love you too." Tears dropped onto his cheek. "Please, don't leave me."

He reached out, grimacing against the movement, and squeezed her hand. He felt his life bleeding out of him. He never cared about dying before—besides revenge, he never had anything worth living for. That was the miserable part of this whole thing. He finally found love. He found someone who loved him despite his scars and his ugly past.

He couldn't feel her hand as the life he longed to share with her bled into the darkness.

CHAPTER 31

"Come on, Jasce. Open your eyes." Jasce was blinded by an indigo glow as his eyes fluttered open. Warmth flowed through his back and side. At first, he thought he was dead, but the sounds of battle pierced the silence. Surely the afterlife wasn't an eternity of war.

"Is he healed yet?" Kenz asked.

"Give me a break, will you? He lost a lot of blood." Kord's large hand pressed against Jasce's back. The pain faded; only a stinging remained around the healing gashes. His magic strengthened, renewing his body and mind.

"I can't hold this shield much longer. Get him up."

"She's so impatient," Jasce mumbled, bracing his hands underneath him. Kord chuckled and helped him to his feet. Kord smiled, silver lining his eyes. "How are you here?" Jasce asked.

"Boys, save the story for later." Kenz glanced over her shoulder and Jasce's chest tightened. They were alive for the moment, and he would not waste it. He pulled her to him and kissed her, a quick and passionate kiss that promised more. Her shield sparked brighter, and as he pulled away, she beamed.

Kord huffed. "Please don't do that in front of me."

Jasce's magic surged through him. The magic that had altered his life for the better, the magic that helped him become the man he wanted to be. His eyes widened as he scanned the courtyard. At least fifty Spectrals—Elementals, Shields, Amps—fought side by side against the Watch Guard. Flynt saluted Jasce and launched a stream of fire toward oncoming soldiers; one by one, soldiers fell to their knees clutching their throats in front of Aura; Delmira used her shield to protect the recruits Jasce had shared breakfast with. They smiled at him, and Jasce remembered Sabine's words: *You captivated those young recruits. It seems they would follow you anywhere.*

Amycus, donning armor similar to Jasce's, battled Drexus with flaming whips and cyclones of dirt and stone. Drexus's black fire burned through everything Amycus threw his way.

Bronn and Caston squared off using their Amplifier magic while Sabine fought Warin, their swords a blur.

"Whose side are they on?" Jasce nodded to Sabine and Caston.

"It seems yours. Caston tackled Drexus while Sabine incapacitated Jaida," Kenz said.

Jasce couldn't believe Sabine and Caston had risked their lives for him, betraying Drexus and the Watch Guard. He couldn't see the other two Hunters, but he found Jaida pressed against the far wall, a silver collar around her neck. Her eyes landed on Jasce and fear and sorrow flashed across her face. His muscles tensed, needing to get her free from Drexus.

"Are you two ready?" Kenz asked, her arms quivering. Kord handed Jasce a sword and they both walked off the platform as the indigo shield lowered. They joined the fray, Jasce vaulting into the middle of the storm, cutting a path between him and Jaida. Everything in him wanted to fight Drexus and Bronn, to get his revenge, but protecting his own came first. His lips curved into a smile.

His own. Finally.

A flash of indigo light sparked in the corner of Jasce's vision, blocking a sword from an incoming guard.

"Still saving your life, it seems," Kenz said, ramming her shield into the soldier, sending him into the wall.

"You do have an excellent teacher." They fought back-to-back as more guards rushed into the courtyard. Jasce cut down the soldiers while keeping one eye on the Spectrals fighting alongside him.

Amycus wielded all the elements to protect the others from Drexus. Aura harnessed her Air magic to repel Vale's flying rocks, and Flynt hurled fireballs into a group of soldiers, blocking their entrance into the courtyard. A large stone slipped through Aura's defenses, striking her in the head. Flynt ran to her as she fell to the ground, her blood stark against her white hair. Vale raised his hands and the earth trembled. He yelled, and a mighty crack echoed off the stone walls before a fissure severed its way through the center of the courtyard, causing Watch Guard soldiers and Spectrals alike to jump back from the widening crevice. Vale panted and dropped to his knees.

Amycus cried out as a spear of black fire hit his shoulder, knocking him off balance. He teetered on the ridge of the fissure.

"Amycus!" Kenz yelled.

Jasce didn't have time to think. His magic tugged and he embraced the darkness. His fingertips grasped the edge of Amycus's armor.

"Got you." Jasce pulled Amycus back.

"Thank you." Amycus's voice shook. He smiled at Jasce and glanced around the courtyard. His face went ashen. Jasce followed his gaze.

"Is that Jaida? She's alive?" Amycus's eyes widened.

"Yes. Drexus has had her all this time."

Amycus took a step toward her but stopped, his legs shaking. Kenz ran over, using her shield to block arrows, fire, and rocks.

"Get Amycus to Kord and find a way to cross. I'll handle Vale." Jasce vaulted over the chasm and appeared in front of the Earth Spectral. "Vale, why?"

Vale's eyes hardened. "The same reason as you. Power. Respect. To be on the winning side."

"Look around you," Jasce said, waving his arm. "Drexus is using you. Just like he used me."

Vale shook his head and yanked his sword from his scabbard while cobblestones wrenched from the ground, circling his feet.

"I don't want to kill you," Jasce said.

"The feeling isn't mutual." Vale launched the stones and swung his sword. Jasce easily dodged and blocked the attack. He squinted against the dust and slashed his sword, glancing off Vale's armor—the same armor Jasce and Amycus had created. The dirt settled and the stones orbiting Vale slowed as his magic weakened.

"Surrender. Your magic is gone."

"Never." Vale gripped his sword with both hands, teeth bared. Sweat ran down his pale face.

The reflection of the sun on a discarded arrow caught Jasce's attention. He vaulted, then materialized behind Vale, shoving the arrow between the protected plates and into his shoulder. Vale cried out, blindly groping for the shaft. Jasce slammed the hilt of his sword onto his head. Vale and the circling stones fell to the ground.

A yell sounded behind Jasce. Bronn smiled and twirled his sword over Caston, who struggled to his feet, clutching his side, blood oozing between his fingers. Jasce vaulted again, blocking Bronn's killing blow. Bronn lurched back, swearing.

Caston groaned as Jasce yanked him to his feet. He remembered Amycus saying that once he mastered his magic, he could take someone with him. "Hang on." He dug deep into his well of magic, feeling the tug. They disappeared as Bronn's sword came down and materialized before Kord. Caston dropped to his knees and retched.

Kord jumped back from the splatter. "What the . . . ?"

Jasce patted Caston's shoulder and smiled. "Wasn't sure that would work."

Caston's eyes widened, his face a sickly green. "Please, don't do that again."

Jasce chuckled. He scanned the area looking for Jaida, but he was unable to locate her through the smoke and dirt. Delmira lay on the ground, blood dripping down her face. A recruit stood above her, sword drawn, protecting the Spectral as two Hunters approached, their skull masks grinning. The other recruits backed into the wall, their eyes wide.

Jasce recognized the girl as the one he helped months ago, right after he received the serum. Her stance and the way she held her sword were perfect.

He vaulted, appearing between the young soldier and the assassins. "Go. Report to the steward. I'll handle these two," Jasce said to the girl. "Oh, and nice form."

The girl smiled and ran with the other recruits through the gate, glancing back with looks of awe and appreciation.

"Elliot, Rafe." Jasce nodded to the Hunters, twirling his sword. "Drexus isn't worth dying for."

"You're the one who's going to die, Azrael," Elliot said.

"I don't think so." Jasce tapped into his magic and attacked, combining his vaulting with his speed. Swords clashed and fists flew. The lethal Hunters were no match for Jasce, and within seconds, they both fell.

Jasce heaved a breath and wiped his blade clean. His powers were weakening. He needed to get Jaida out of here while he still had the strength.

Jasce helped Delmira to her feet. "I need you to protect Kord and the others."

She wiped the blood off her face and nodded, jogging to where Kord fought alongside Caston. More soldiers filed into the courtyard, hemming in the Spectrals from behind. Jasce found Amycus using his scimitar against Drexus's fire, having used too much of the elemental magic at once. Jasce tried to vault, but his magic refused.

"Kenz! Help Amycus."

Kenz's head jerked, then she sprinted across the yard, using her shield as a battering ram to knock soldiers off their feet. Her shield enveloped Amycus, blocking a spear of black fire headed for his heart. She stumbled, a drop of blood falling from her nose. Her arms shook as another wave of fire hit. Drexus laughed, thrusting his hands forward, fireballs erupting, relentlessly pummeling her shield.

Jasce frantically looked around. He couldn't get there in time to protect Kenz or Amycus. Kord was too far away, engaged with other soldiers, and Flynt was dragging Aura back behind Delmira's shield, shooting green fire at any approaching soldier.

"Think," Jasce said, spinning in a circle. A crossbow lay feet away. He ran toward the weapon, yanking an arrow out of a fallen Spectral along the way. He lifted the bow and aimed.

Bronn leaped through the air, tackling Jasce as he let the arrow fly. Jasce swore as he hit the ground, Bronn's interference knocking the bolt off course. The arrow hit Drexus in the shoulder, twisting him around.

A cry cut through the smoke and dirt. Jaida stumbled toward Drexus, her hands covering her mouth.

Jasce lurched to his feet, grabbing his sword, but Bronn stepped into his path, teeth bared. "Just you and me," he said, "steel against steel."

Jasce gripped his sword and settled into his fighting stance. Bronn narrowed his eyes and attacked, his sword cutting through the air at an unnatural speed. Clashing metal clanged, the vibration twinging up Jasce's arm. He pushed Bronn back, his feet moving along the uneven cobblestones. He dug into the reserves of his strength, relying on instinct and years of training as he blocked and lunged, spinning on one knee and flipping through the air—a savage dance of muscles and steel.

Bronn snarled. "You're a useless traitor. When I'm through with you I'll kill that Shield of yours—slowly, intimately."

Jasce roared and swung his sword, aiming for Bronn's neck. Bronn ducked and spun, the tip of his blade glancing off Jasce's thigh. Jasce retreated, hiding his grimace, and Bronn laughed. He paced around Jasce like a lion stalking its prey.

Jasce ignored the jeers from the surrounding soldiers. Sabine spared a glance at him, then kicked Warin in the chest, knocking him off his feet.

Bronn yelled and raised his arm.

Silver flashed.

Swords crossed, sending a shock wave through the air. Jasce stumbled, his muscles quivering, and stepped back, regrouping. His magic was almost gone, and brute force wouldn't beat Bronn. He needed a different tactic.

Jasce's lip curled.

Bronn glowered. "What are you smiling about?"

"No matter what, you're still second best."

Bronn's face turned red. He charged, holding his sword above his head, his muscles bulging as he brought the weapon down.

Jasce dodged, smacking Bronn with the flat of his blade as he rushed past. Bronn turned, his eyes bulging, knuckles white on the hilt of his weapon.

"Drexus will never think of you as anything more than his loyal dog," Jasce taunted.

"Shut up!" Bronn growled, lunging forward, his technique getting sloppy.

Jasce laughed and blocked his strike, elbowing Bronn in the face. His nose broke with a satisfying crunch. "That's gotta hurt."

"I said, shut up!" He ran for Jasce, his eyes full of hatred, blood pouring down his face. He raised his sword.

Jasce spun around the attack and thrust his sword into Bronn's back. Bronn cried out, his knees slamming against the ground. Blood bubbled from his mouth, his eyes wide.

Jasce grabbed Bronn by the neck and whispered in his ear, "Never let your emotions take over." With a final gurgle, Bronn fell.

Jasce stared at the fallen soldier, expecting to feel satisfaction.

He felt nothing.

He scanned the courtyard for his sister. She knelt next to Drexus, tears streaming down her face. Vale stumbled toward them, pressing his hand against the open wound in his shoulder.

"Jaida, no!" Jasce shouted.

Drexus yelled as she yanked the arrow free. He struggled to his feet and glared at Jasce, sending toward him a bolt of fire that Jasce easily dodged. Drexus flexed his hands and inhaled. Vale helped Jaida stand, shielding her behind him.

Jasce's magic flickered. He grabbed Bronn's sword and stalked across the courtyard, twirling both weapons. Drexus stared over Jasce's shoulder, a vein throbbing in his neck, and he threw his hands forward. Black fire shot past Jasce.

He tracked the fireball as it hit Sabine from behind, launching her forward onto the end of Warin's sword.

"Sabine!" Jasce ran to her, swinging his blades so quickly Warin didn't have time to yell as his head separated from his body.

Blood poured between Sabine's fingers, staining the cobblestones. Jasce pressed against her stomach, trying to staunch the flow, feeling the sticky warmth. He looked for Kord.

She squeezed his hand. His eyes found hers as she ran a bloody finger down the tattoos along his left arm. "Make mine the prettiest, will you?"

Jasce swallowed and nodded. He laid her head gently on the ground, her vacant eyes staring at nothing.

His lips pulled back in a snarl as Drexus's laughter rang in his ears.

Drexus was smiling, lobbing a black fireball from one hand to the other. "Her compassion made her weak. I've put her out of her misery."

"Compassion isn't a weakness. It's a gift—something you'll never understand."

Drexus laughed. "You're a fool." He launched a volley of fireballs at Jasce—

—or where Jasce had been. He dug into his reserves of power, using his anger and grief to vault. He reappeared a heartbeat later, bringing down his sword.

Golden hair and gray eyes emerged suddenly, forcing Jasce to alter the blade's trajectory.

Drexus roared as his hand fell to the ground, black fire twirling through the twitching fingers.

"Jaida, move!" Jasce said, his knuckles whitening on the hilt. Drexus hunched over, clutching his arm. Blood poured from the severed wrist.

Tears filled Jaida's eyes. "I can't let you kill him." Vale put a protective arm in front of her, the ground quivering as his magic slowly returned.

White hot fury ignited inside Jasce. He would not allow Vale or his sister to get in his way. Drexus needed to pay for the crimes against his family and the Spectrals. He could not allow this monster to live.

"No," Jasce growled. He used his speed and spun, shoving Vale into his sister and out of his path. With a roar, he pivoted and plunged his sword.

Jaida screamed, wrenching free from Vale to catch Drexus as he dropped to his knees, his wide eyes focused on the hilt of the sword stuck in his chest.

Blood coated Drexus's teeth as he smiled. "Where's your compassion?" He asked as he fell into Jaida's arms.

"How could you?" Jaida said, glaring at Jasce, tears carving a path down her crimson face.

Jasce tore his eyes from Drexus and stared at his sister, lowering his other sword. "He's a murderer."

"So are you!" Jaida stood and fisted her hands. "You'll pay for this, Jasce. I swear it." Her hair floated in the air and she looked toward the sky, closing her eyes. Jasce noticed her bare neck and lurched back. Vale smirked, dropping the discarded collar. Rocks rose from the ground, circling his feet, gathering speed.

With a cry, Jaida raised her hands. Every fallen sword and forgotten arrow lifted off the ground and careened toward Jasce and the Spectrals behind him. Sand and rocks followed in a storm of metal and dirt. Jasce turned, kneeling to protect his body, and caught Kenz and Delmira out of the corner of his eye as they thrust their shields forward, blocking the incoming projectiles.

The ground trembled; not from Vale, but from the entrance to the compound. Soldiers on horses galloped through the gate, donning the colors of the royal family. The weapons and rocks fell with a resounding clang that echoed off the walls, drowning out the sound of hooves. Jasce wiped the dirt from his eyes and looked over his shoulder.

A silver collar lay in a puddle of blood next to Drexus's severed hand.

Jasce moved toward the side entrance, but the queen's guard blocked his pursuit. His sister and Vale had fled, taking Drexus's body with them. "Blast it, Jaida."

Someone called Jasce's name, the voice sounding far away. Amycus limped toward him with Kenz by his side.

Amycus forced a smile, resting his hand on Jasce's shoulder. "It's over."

Jasce glanced at the older man and then stared in the direction Jaida had gone. "No, it's not."

CHAPTER 32

The royal flag waved in the air, purple and gold threads glinting in the sun as soldiers fanned around the edge of the courtyard and surrounded the Spectrals. Jasce sheathed his weapon, willing his magic to replenish itself. Amycus also returned his sword to its scabbard and tied back his hair. Kenz glanced between Amycus and Jasce, but she kept her sword free, her gauntlets shimmering a light blue. A thin man, his gray hair falling to his shoulders, scanned the courtyard. His eyes widened when they landed on Jasce and Amycus.

Steward Kenneth Brenet reached for his sword. "Guards, seize them."

"Belay that," a soft voice said from behind him.

Jasce immediately dropped to a knee and bowed his head, followed by Amycus. Kenz gasped, lowering behind him with Kord by her side. Rustling and metal scraping on the cobblestones sounded behind Jasce as the other Spectrals knelt as well.

Queen Valeri slid gracefully from her horse, her crown sparkling on shiny chestnut hair that was twisted into an elaborate design. She moved past the steward and touched his arm. "Lower your sword, Kenneth." Her gown swept across the cobblestones, gathering dust along the gold edges.

Jasce quickly counted the guards. They outnumbered the Spectrals, their magic depleted and many of them injured despite Kord's healing. His muscles tensed as he tried to find a way out, but when he began to stand Amycus rested a hand on his shoulder.

"Amycus Reins," the queen said, "it is good to see you."

"And you, Your Majesty."

Jasce jerked his head to the side. Amycus knelt with his head bowed, the corner of his lip quirking. Amycus was more of a wanted man than Jasce. How could he be so calm?

"You may rise." The queen glanced across the courtyard at the kneeling Spectrals. Her gaze hardened and she summoned one of her guards, whispering a command. The soldier nodded and signaled to more soldiers, who ran out the opposite exit.

Queen Valeri tilted her head, her chocolate-colored eyes staring at Jasce. "Azrael, I believe you're wanted for treason."

A murmur rustled through the queen's guards. The four soldiers surrounding the queen drew their swords, stepping closer to Jasce.

"It's Jasce, Your Majesty, Jasce Farone." Jasce bowed his head, keeping his eyes fixed on the soldiers. The dregs of his magic stirred.

The queen's perfectly sculpted brows shot up. "It seems we have much to discuss. Where is Commander Zoldac?"

The steward sputtered and hopped from his horse. "Your Majesty, both these men are wanted criminals. He killed your husband." Kenneth pointed to Amycus with his spindly finger and licked his lips. The man reminded Jasce of a weasel with shifty eyes.

"Kenneth, I am aware of the accusations made against Mr. Reins."

"They have an army of Spectrals. We cannot let them go free."

Jasce reached for his dagger, but Amycus again placed a hand on his arm and quickly shook his head.

"This is hardly an army, and they will go free," the queen said, still focused on Jasce and Amycus. "You two will come with me." She turned on her heel and glided back to her horse. Kenneth huffed, glared at the Spectrals, and mounted his horse, riding out of the compound. The surrounding soldiers filed out of the courtyard, leaving five to escort Jasce and Amycus to the palace.

Jasce found Kenz's hand and squeezed it tightly. "It'll be fine."

Kenz nodded and returned the pressure. "Be careful." She brushed her lips against his. Jasce wrapped his hand around her waist and pulled her closer, deepening the kiss until Kord cleared his throat. Jasce stepped away, memorizing the freckles scattered across Kenz's nose.

They exited the Bastion and the Orilyon Palace loomed before them, the white stone reflecting the sunlight, giving the structure an ethereal glow. The cacophony of boots echoed down the corridor, the marble floors shimmering. Portraits of the royal family lined the wall with colorful tapestries that surrounded enormous windows overlooking the Merrigan Sea.

Jasce glanced at Amycus. The man was covered in dirt and ash, dried blood on his face from a newly healed cut. Grime and blood coated Jasce's clothes, his tunic in tatters from the whipping. He was exhausted and filthy, craving a bath and a drink. He would have to wait for both as they entered the throne room.

Gold chandeliers dripping with crystals hung from the gilded ceiling, illuminating the adorned drapes embracing the windows. Soldiers fortified the room like imposing columns, stone-faced and immovable. The queen swept up the stairs of the dais and sat in the smaller of two thrones, leaving her deceased husband's vacant. The steward took his place next to the empty throne, his eyes shifting between the queen and Amycus.

Jasce balled his fists at the presence of the guards behind him; even more stood in front and to the side of the queen and steward. Jasce peered over his shoulder and his eyes widened as another set of boots echoed in the cavernous room. Caston marched in, nodding to the guards, and knelt before the queen.

"What is the Hunter doing here?" Kenneth asked, his eyes wary.

"He's one of mine," Queen Valeri answered.

Jasce felt his jaw drop. He glanced quickly at Amycus, who shrugged his shoulders.

"Rise."

Caston stood and retreated to stand next to Jasce. He looked at Jasce out of the corner of his eye, but his face remained expressionless. The steward paled as he stared at Caston.

The queen leaned forward. "Well?"

Caston shook his head.

She sighed and tapped her fingers on the arm of her throne. "First, let it be known that Amycus Reins is cleared of all charges regarding the death of King Valeri." The queen's voice trembled slightly.

Kenneth's head shot up. "Your Majesty, I have to object."

She raised her hand and the steward's mouth snapped shut. "Kenneth, you and I were led astray the night my husband died. By the time I learned the truth, you already had your claws sunk into the council with the nobles on your side. I have worked all these years to gather the evidence to prove that

Commander Zoldac is the one who murdered the king. He then manipulated the council into promoting you to steward, claiming I was too grief-stricken to rule." Her eyes flashed with restrained fury.

Kenneth's eyes widened, his mouth opening and closing like a dying fish. Jasce pressed his lips together and stared at his filthy boots.

"Commander Zoldac has orchestrated this war against the Spectrals. And you," her expression hardened as she glared at the steward, "were his willing puppet."

Kenneth swallowed. "Your Majesty, I—"

"You are henceforth removed of your title."

Kenneth's face turned red and his eyes bulged. "You can't do that."

The queen raised a brow and nodded to her guards. "Yes, I believe I can. Remove this man from my sight."

The former steward struggled and yelled curses as the guards dragged him from the throne room. The door slammed shut, silencing him.

Queen Valeri stared at Jasce, her face expressionless. "Now, what to do with the Angel of Death?"

Jasce lifted his chin, having expected this. Second in command to the murderer of the king was certain death, not to mention his other crimes against Spectrals and Naturals.

Amycus stepped forward. "Your Majesty—if I may? Jasce Farone has proven himself a worthy ally, helping to destroy the medical sites and defeat Drexus. We wouldn't be in this position if it weren't for him."

Jasce glanced at Amycus.

Caston stepped forward, bowing his head. "It's true, my queen. Azrael—I mean Jasce—fought against Drexus and saved my life." Caston sighed. "Twice."

Jasce's lip twitched.

Amycus cleared his throat and Jasce's shoulders stiffened as he focused on the queen.

"Well, well, Mr. Farone. It seems you have two of my most trusted men vouching for you."

Jasce lowered his head. "Yes, Your Majesty."

Her fingers tapped again on her throne. Jasce counted silently to twenty before the queen spoke again.

"So, Amycus, whatever took you so long? I've been slipping you information for months."

Jasce jerked his head, feeling his mouth drop. "The queen is your source?"

Amycus smiled and nodded. "I'm sorry, Your Highness. I had some convincing and training to do first." His eyes slid to Jasce.

"I see." Her humorous tone shifted. "What happened to Drexus? Is he dead? My men didn't find his body."

Jasce stepped forward. "My sister and an Earth Spectral took him."

The queen's eyes darted to Amycus. "Jaida Farone is alive?"

Amycus closed his eyes briefly and nodded. Jasce frowned.

"Either way, that doesn't answer my question. Is Drexus dead?"

Jasce gritted his teeth. "Unless his heart is located somewhere else."

"Jasce," Amycus said, his tone reproachful.

Jasce cleared his throat and added, "Your Majesty."

The queen's eyes narrowed. Amycus explained Drexus's experiments, with Caston providing missing information. Jasce tried to focus on their words but only saw Jaida's arms lifted, rage hardening her eyes, her hatred crashing over him.

The throne room grew silent and everyone stared at Jasce.

"I'm sorry. What?"

Queen Valeri drummed her fingers on the arm of her throne. "I asked about the facility in the Arcane Garrison. Were all the vials destroyed?"

"It was a blazing inferno when I escaped. I don't believe any made it."

"You don't believe?" The queen looked at Caston. "Take a contingent of soldiers to Arcane. I want a thorough search of the entire complex."

"If I may?" Jasce interjected. The queen peered at Jasce and Amycus slowly shook his head, sighing. "Caston, there's a recruit named Rowan. His mother, Maera, was forced to help Drexus. I don't know if she survived, but can you check?"

Caston nodded, bowed his head, and strode from the throne room.

Queen Valeri stared at the two men and signaled to a guard on the far side of the room. He opened the door and a man emerged carrying something wrapped in cloth. He placed it on a table and stepped back. The wrapping fell away, revealing a leathery black claw.

Both Jasce and Amycus moved closer. "What is that?" Jasce asked, his eyes narrowing.

"That, Mr. Farone, is part of your mission. It was found on the outskirts of Wilholm, near the Desert of Souls."

Jasce tore his gaze from the severed claw. "Part of my mission?"

"I want Drexus's head. He isn't dead until I have proof, and I want Jaida and the Earth Spectral found." The queen stood and walked down the steps, her guards trailing behind her. "Those are your orders. You now work for me."

ॐ ॐ ॐ

A week later, Jasce and Amycus arrived back in Carhurst, the cottage and forge a welcome sight. During the long ride home, Jasce had thought about the missing vials. Caston and his team had searched the Bastion and Arcane and had come up empty-handed. Thankfully, Caston had found Maera. One of the soldiers had pulled her free of the flames and kept her alive until help came.

Jasce still bristled at the queen's words. *You now work for me.* His hopes for a normal life in the forge had disappeared with that one command. He thought about Jaida and Vale taking Drexus's body. Was he still alive? Jasce didn't see how. And now he had to find Jaida. He didn't need the queen's orders for that—his plan all along was to search for her. He just didn't have a clue where to start, and the creature's severed claw created another mystery for Jasce to solve. At least he had the backing of the Watch Guard behind him, renamed the Paladin Guard.

A hand rested on Jasce's shoulder. He looked and saw Amycus smiling, his blue eyes sparkling. "It's good to be home," the man said.

Jasce nodded and peered longingly at the forge. The need to hammer metal and create something, to lose himself in the fire and steam, stirred inside him. But he had to do something first. He rubbed his hands down his face, stifling a yawn. His mind hadn't relaxed in a week.

"Jasce, the sooner you talk to her, the sooner you can rest." Amycus squeezed Jasce's shoulder and disappeared inside his cottage. Jasce shook his head, dumbfounded at Amycus's uncanny way of reading his emotions.

Jasce walked down the street toward Kord's house, passing through the busy marketplace and among the people who were unaware of the battle that had taken place across the desert. Colorful booths and enticing aromas filled the air. Vendors haggled with shoppers and children darted between the stalls, their laughter creating a soothing melody. Jasce glanced at Kord and Kenz's booth, hoping to glimpse midnight hair, but their assistant leaned behind the counter selling an ornate chair to an older man.

Jasce paused in front of the Iron Glass Tavern. Garin's booming voice barking orders at Linnette drifted out the door, accompanied by the clinking of glasses. Azrael would have gone in and immersed himself in the bottom of a glass, but Jasce was no longer Azrael. The Angel of Death had lost its grip, the skeletal fingers loosening their hold on his heart. The revenge that had dominated every thought and action had disappeared, replaced with a fierce need to protect those he loved, especially the woman who had turned his life upside down.

Jasce focused on the cottage down the road, the smoke rising from the chimney and the smell of fresh pastries making his mouth water. Before Jasce could knock on the door, Maleous yanked it open and smiled, wrapping his arms around Jasce's waist.

"Hey, kid." Jasce ruffled the boy's head as he entered the homey living room. Emile and Lander stood by the fireplace, Lander's arm draped protectively around his sister's shoulders.

Jasce lowered to one knee and stared into Emile's warm eyes. She reminded him so much of Jaida it hurt to look at her. "How are you feeling?"

"Good," she said. "Kord and Kenz are helping me control the magic and silence all the emotions."

Jasce chuckled. "It's annoying, isn't it?"

Emile smiled. Jasce shifted his focus to Lander. "We need to talk when you're ready."

Lander frowned, then his eyes widened when he saw the royal symbol and commander emblem on Jasce's cloak. "Okay."

Jasce nodded and stood, laying the cloak on the couch. The hairs on his neck tingled and he turned to find Kord leaning against the wall, his arms crossed, a slanted smile on his face.

"Glad you're back. Maleous drove me nuts asking when you'd be home." Kord handed Jasce a steaming mug of coffee. The bitter, chocolatey aroma was as welcoming as the sugary concoction Tillie was baking. The three children rushed out of the room toward the kitchen.

Jasce nodded his thanks and plopped onto the couch, letting his head fall back.

"You look dreadful," Kord said, sitting in the chair opposite him.

Jasce gave a suppressed laugh, remembering a similar conversation before in this same room months ago. "I've heard that one doesn't learn if one doesn't suffer through the pain."

Kord chuckled, then took a sip of coffee. "Are you all right?"

"Just tired."

Kord scanned Jasce's face with his penetrating stare. "Uh-huh. Want to tell me what's really going on?"

What Jasce wanted was to sleep for a week, but Amycus was right. He wouldn't be able to rest until he said what he needed to say.

"Where's Kenz?"

Kord raised a brow.

"Right here."

Jasce's head jerked to the side. He stood, quickly scanning her from head to toe. The green tunic made her eyes glow, and she wore the form-fitting pants that made him wish they were alone. He didn't know what to do with all the emotions rushing through him: desire, fear, gratitude. Kenz's mouth twitched as Jasce stared at her like an idiot.

Kenz sat in the chair next to Kord. "When did you get back?"

Jasce returned to the couch. "Just a little while ago." He scrubbed his hands over his face, wishing for something stronger than coffee.

"What's going on?" Kord asked, worry filling his eyes.

Jasce rehashed the meetings with Queen Valeri, about the steward's removal from his position, and Caston's involvement.

"We're forming an army, with both Spectrals and Naturals, and the queen wants proof Drexus is dead." Jasce described the claw that was found in the desert. Kord's face paled and Kenz's knuckles whitened on the arm of the chair. Jasce let out a breath and leaned back, staring at the ceiling.

"You said, 'we,'" Kenz said after a minute.

Jasce held her gaze. "You are now looking at the Commander of the Paladin Guard, servant to the queen." Jasce couldn't hide the bitterness in his voice. He hadn't lied when he told Drexus he wanted command of the Guard, but he'd wanted it on his terms. "She also requested Amycus return as a blacksmith and a liaison between the crown and the Spectrals."

Kord looked from his sister to Jasce and rose from the chair. "I'll give you two some privacy."

Kenz's eyes followed Kord. She turned back to Jasce and stared at her entwined fingers, biting her bottom lip.

Jasce's pulse throbbed in his neck. He didn't know how he wanted her to respond, but he knew he couldn't leave without telling her exactly how he felt. He leaned forward and grabbed her hands.

"Kenz, I meant what I said back in Opax. I've fallen in love with you—something I didn't think possible for someone like me. But I did."

Kenz raised her head and smiled.

Jasce swallowed and stood to pace in front of the fireplace, his thrumming nerves making it impossible to sit still. He felt her stare as he walked back and forth. Better to just say it and be done with it.

"I wanted to start fresh, try a different way of living, not one defined by battles and death. But that can't happen now." He raised his hands and then lowered them. "I don't know if or when I'll be back. Plus, I have to find Jaida. What if Drexus is still alive?" He rested his hands on the mantle, squeezing the stone until it dug into his palms. So many unknowns, so many what-ifs.

"What are you talking about?" The chair creaked. She grabbed his shoulder, turning him around. Her cheeks flushed and her eyes sparked. "I'm going with you."

"What?" Jasce's eyes rested on her mouth, wanting to get lost in the feel of her against him. He shook his head. "No, I won't ask that of you."

"If I want to join your army, do you think you can stop me?" Kenz rested her hands on her hips and glared at him. "I'm a Shield. I protect those I love. It's what I do."

"Kenz, I—"

Kenz placed her fingers against his mouth, her touch igniting a fire deep inside him. "Jasce, get it through your thick head—I love you."

Jasce felt a tightness behind his eyes and something flutter in his stomach. He had never felt this emotion—couldn't even name it. He smiled and wrapped his arms around her, pulling her against him. Everything about her felt right, felt like home. Maybe he could have a semblance of a normal life, after all.

"Marry me," he said, the words muffled against her neck, out of his mouth before he could overthink them.

Kenz pulled back, her eyes wide.

"I love you, Kenz Haring. I know the timing is wrong but—"

She kissed him, silencing whatever he was about to say. "Yes."

Jasce grinned and crushed his mouth against hers, wishing they were alone so he could show her how much he adored her. But Kord cleared his throat, his arms crossed against his massive chest. Jasce gently untangled himself from Kenz's embrace and gave Kord a guilty smile.

Kord strode over to Jasce, his frown turning into a smile. "I've always wanted a brother." Kenz laughed as Kord pulled Jasce into a hug.

Jasce gazed at the woman he loved and the friend that would one day be family. Whatever darkness the future held, Jasce would face it.

But this time, he wouldn't be alone.

ACKNOWLEDGMENTS

Who would've thought? If you asked me years ago what I wanted to be when I grew up, an author would not have appeared on the top of that list. After retiring as a stay-at-home mom and facing the empty nest, the thought of writing a book bubbled to the surface, and I'm honored and humbled to have that idea turn into a reality.

First and foremost, I want to thank God for giving me the purpose and creativity to write this novel. It was a challenge to write a fantasy about an assassin while still trying to honor the Perfect Storyteller, but with the help of friends and family, I hope I got it done.

I want to thank my early readers who walked me through the story, characters, and finding all those dreadful repeated words. You have helped and supported me more than you could ever know. Your encouragement and feedback where invaluable, and I loved having people to talk to about my book.

Thank you to Beth Tannaz, who first planted the idea in my brain to write a book. Who would've known sharing a cup of coffee would lead to all of this? Thanks for sticking with me. Thank you, Tracey McClain, for the miles and miles of walking through the mesa and hashing out the story. Your wisdom in all things has kept me sane. To my golfing buddies—Karla DeGroft, Elaine DeLand, and Sue Hancock—your enthusiasm spurred me on when editing became as challenging as putting. A big thanks to Darin Rasberry for giving me a guy's perspective, especially with the ending. Thank you, Meg Greve, for doing the first round of edits. I appreciate all the time you spent going over the manuscript. It couldn't have been easy being between your sister and me.

Karen Holmes, I absolutely adored our "story time," but do not call me Mother Goose. Reading *Chasing the Darkness* to you and hearing your gasps and "oh nos" made it so worthwhile. You are my Kord but without the right hook.

And to Janine Goff—what can I say? You spent hours and hours helping me through all aspects of this story from start to finish, and you pushed me through, especially during crunch time. Thank you for the visuals of Azrael/Jasce and bringing him to life.

Thank you to all the wonderful people at Morgan James Publishing and for taking a chance on an unknown. To Terry Whalin, who first believed in *Chasing the Darkness*. To Bonnie Rauch, for being my go-to gal and helping me every step of the way. To Cortney Donelson and your help cleaning the book up, especially Chapter 26 (wink wink), and all the people who made it beautiful. And lastly, a huge thanks to Jim Howard and David Hancock for taking this project on. I'm blessed beyond measure.

To my awesome editor, Rachel Oestreich at The Wallflower Editing. Finding you was a gift, and it feels like we've been friends for a long time. Working with you was wonderful and easy, and I still want to have that cup of coffee one of these days. I appreciate all your hard work, finding those "ing" sentences, answering my grammar questions, and being available whenever panic set in. Your encouragement and support helped me press on.

To Mom and Dad, thank you for instilling in me my faith, perseverance, and love for family. Because of you, my moral compass points north (most of the time).

Chase, you inspired me to start writing, to step out of my comfort zone, and go for it. *Chasing the Darkness* wouldn't be here if it weren't for you. To Tyler, my go-to expert on all things magical. I loved bouncing ideas off you and working through some of those crazy plot points. I'm so proud of both of you and am lucky to be your mom.

To my husband and best friend. Without your love and support, none of this would have been possible. Thank you for your strong shoulder through the tears and frustration and your encouraging smile and faith when I struggled to keep moving forward. Here's to another twenty-five years.

And lastly, if you've read this far, I want to thank my readers. Your excitement for *Chasing the Darkness* has been contagious. Thank you for picking up this book or buying it online, and for trusting me enough to take you from the beginning of Jasce's story to the end. Here's to not having to go through tough times alone.

ABOUT THE AUTHOR

Growing up, Cassie Sanchez always wanted superpowers and to be a warrior princess fighting alongside unlikely heroes. Suffice it to say, she lost herself in books, from fantasy to sci-fi to a suspenseful romance here and there. Currently, Cassie lives in the Southwest with her husband, Louie, while pestering her two adult men-children. She can usually be found drinking too much coffee while working in her office with her dog, Gunner, warming her feet. When she isn't writing about magic and sword fights, she enjoys golfing, spending time with friends, or partaking in a satisfying nap. You can visit her online at cassiesanchez.com.

A free ebook edition is available with the purchase of this book.

To claim your free ebook edition:

1. Visit MorganJamesBOGO.com
2. Sign your name CLEARLY in the space
3. Complete the form and submit a photo of the entire copyright page
4. You or your friend can download the ebook to your preferred device

Morgan James BOGO™

A **FREE** ebook edition is available for you or a friend with the purchase of this print book.

_____

CLEARLY SIGN YOUR NAME ABOVE

Instructions to claim your free ebook edition:
1. Visit MorganJamesBOGO.com
2. Sign your name CLEARLY in the space above
3. Complete the form and submit a photo of this entire page
4. You or your friend can download the ebook to your preferred device

Print & Digital Together Forever.

Snap a photo   Free ebook   Read anywhere